Well Met in
Cyprus

Well Met in
Cyprus

Javaid Qazi

NIYOGI
BOOKS

Published by
NIYOGI BOOKS
D-78, Okhla Industrial Area, Phase-I
New Delhi-110 020, INDIA
Tel: 91-11-26816301, 26813350, 51, 52
Fax: 91-11-26810483, 26813830
email: niyogibooks@gmail.com
website: www.niyogibooks.com

Text © Javaid Qazi

Cover Painting: Sheila Davis
Author Photograph: Carol Ferdinandsen
Design: Nihar Ranjan Das
Editor: Gita Rajan

ISBN: 978-81-89738-74-7

Publication: 2011

This is a work of fiction. The names, characters and incidents
portrayed in it are the work of the author's imagination. Any
resemblance to actual persons, living or dead, events or localities,
is entirely coincidental.

Printed at: Niyogi Offset Pvt. Ltd., New Delhi, India.

This book is dedicated to Carol, whose love
and support never wavered.

ACKNOWLEDGEMENTS

I would like to thank the following people for giving me untold amounts of advice, assistance and support while I was working on this book. Most of all I want to thank my good friend and advisor, Ed Teja, who kept reading fragments and kept helping, advising, editing when all seemed hopeless. I thank my neighbor, Nancy Sorsa, who read an early draft and encouraged me to keep going. Thanks also to my dear cousin and counselor, Naureen Amjad, who pushed me when I needed to be pushed. I also want to thank Gita Rajan, my editor, who helped me refine the work and prepare it for publication. Last but not least, I want to thank Ainura Siddikova who provided the inspiration for the story.

I would like to add a special thank you here for Sheila Davis, who graciously permitted the use of her lovely watercolor "Karaman" for the cover.

"That time is past,
And all its aching joys are now no more,
And all its dizzy raptures."

William Wordsworth (*Tintern Abbey*)

CHAPTER ONE

Section **1**

I met her in Almaty in the season of turning when the birches had begun to squander their golden coinage with a shocking prodigality and the rains of autumn started coming down the Tien Shan Mountains that loomed behind the city and washed away the fallen leaves and made the streets gleam like black steel mirrors. I met her at a time when I had reached the middle years of my life, that grim and sere autumnal phase so crowded with regrets and memories. I had come to this place to teach some ill-conceived courses on American laws and society at a university. But beyond hitting the high notes of Abraham Lincoln and Huckleberry Finn, I doubt that I even managed to carry a tune.

It took me a while to learn the rhythms of the city because I had never been here before and everyone spoke Russian. Since I had no Russian at my command, my circle was limited to those who spoke English at the university and I tended to stay within the orbit of their social activities. Thus it came about that I happened to be at a party given by an instructor who taught in the English department. It was at this gathering that I met Anara.

Aa – naa – raa. Three syllables. Three lyrical sounds that pour out as you open your mouth and the throat resonates. The tongue taps N on the upper palate and then produces the trill of the final R against the alveolar ridge. Her name sounded like a song to my ears. Aa – naa – raa. Pomegranate blossom in the Kazakh language.

At this time I was enduring a type of unwanted celibacy that divorced men of a certain age get to know very intimately. So when a colleague pointed her out and said she was the Dean's secretary, I meandered over to where she stood drinking orange juice and managed to get introduced.

"This is Robert, the teacher from Chicago."

"Hello," she said shyly, giving me a small-boned hand, "my English not good."

"My Russian zero," I said, making a circle with my thumb and forefinger.

I gazed at her with open admiration. She was small and slender and young – too young, I thought, probably half my age. Her glossy raven black hair fell straight down her back and her bangs got tangled in her eyelashes. Every once in a while she would toss her head to shake them out of her eyes so she could see more clearly. She had high cheekbones and oblique oriental eyes that seemed half awake. For a while we just stood there looking at each other. Making small talk in such circumstances can be murder.

"You like my country?" she said, finally.

"Very much. Very beautiful."

"I like America. Hollywood. Fantastic!"

"Yes, yes, certainly. Fantastic!"

Everybody likes Hollywood and I was only too glad to tell her that I was the direct, lineal descendent of Mickey Mouse and knew all about the latest movies, hottest stars and best directors.

This amused her and she started to laugh. She had a low, warm voice and the way English purred past the filter of her Russian accent was pleasant to the ears. An aura of simple elegance surrounded her.

She wore tight-fitting black pants flared slightly at the ankles and a snug white top. She was pale – pale as can be – pale as magnolia petals or peeled almonds and her pallor contrasted vividly with her dark hair. At first it didn't look as though we had any kind of future together simply because we had so little in common. But slowly we did manage to bridge the canyons of culture and language.

"How long are you here?" she asked, using that odd contracted syntax that Russian speakers use when they switch to English.

"For a year," I said.

"That is good, no?" She smiled, revealing pearl-perfect teeth.

She reminded me of actresses I had seen in old black and white films with her jet black crescent eyebrows, satiny skin and full mouth emphasized by black cherry lipstick. All evening our glances kept clashing. I seemed to have aroused her curiosity. When someone pulled me away to talk to some other people, I noticed her firing coy looks my way. But I did not speak to her again that evening. Nor did she approach me, out of shyness perhaps or because she felt limited by her lack of fluency in English. Then on a cold but sunny day in late November, I met her in the Green Bazaar where I shopped every Saturday for groceries. We were in a milling crowd of babushkas pinching and prodding the produce and harassing the vendors. She remembered me.

"Where have you been?" I asked, "I haven't seen you in quite a while."

She said she had quit the job at the university and now worked at the *Astana Palace Hotel* as a receptionist. She looked a little older, more mature, in the bright sunlight and underneath her V-neck sweater I noticed the superb swell of full, round breasts.

"We must get together," I said, getting bolder.

"Yes," she said. "I give mobile number. Call me."

Then, one Saturday afternoon, she did come to my apartment. It was an awkward, rather tense meeting. She seemed nervous, distant,

as if she was wondering, calculating the odds of the game. I offered
her some wine. No, she said. Beer? No. vodka? No. She didn't drink
alcohol. Nor did she smoke. So I did the drinking and the smoking
for the two of us while we talked about inconsequential matters. But
I was desperate for something more than chitchat and tried to make
her understand my needs. I explained that I had no desire to repeat the
lengthy courtship rituals of my teen years. I understood and appreciated
her cautiousness, of course, but an urgent, predatory passion gripped
me and I was eager to fast-forward our relationship. We spoke to each
other in polite, roundabout terms. We were like boxers in a ring, going
round in wary circles, watching, throwing out the odd exploratory jab,
feinting, bobbing, ducking. It was an odd verbal match – she struggling
to put her thoughts into imperfect English while I countered with
arguments that had to strike a delicate balance between frankness and
courtesy. Ultimately, I suppose it all came down to the cards we held.
She had a strong hand. Youth and beauty. I could not match those cards.
But I had others. My strong cards were my status as a foreign visitor –
an educated foreign visitor – and my Americanness. This combination
endowed me with a powerful, perhaps even aphrodisiac, appeal.

She whispered something about a boyfriend in Moscow whom
she hadn't seen in two years. Had they been close? I asked. Yes, very
close. This was good news because it meant that she had enjoyed the
pleasures of the bed and probably missed them. She mentioned her
mother with whom she lived and who kept watch over her activities.
But as the afternoon faded into evening and tangerine colored rays
of the setting sun streamed into the room, I could see her defenses
crumbling. Slowly, ever so carefully, she lowered her left and then
her right. I could almost see the machinery inside her head working.
Breaking an old link is difficult. On the other hand, establishing a new
one has its own attractions. I represented something alien, someone
from another world, another planet almost. I may not have been a

dream vision out of a Hollywood fantasy but what I offered was real, tangible, enticing.

A few days later I went to see her at the *Astana Palace*, a five-star establishment that sat across from a park and had rows of wrought-iron balconies fronting every room. She was not at the reception desk and when I asked about her I was told to wait. When she came, a harried moroseness seemed to have dimmed her glow.

"They have given me another job," she said.

"What job?"

"Housekeeping," she said in dejected tones.

Now I understood why her spirits were low.

"I just stopped by to say Hello," I said.

"I can't talk now," she said. "I have to work."

"I understand. I'll call you later."

As I left, I could feel the hostile dagger gaze of the hotel staff piercing my shoulder blades. Later that evening, I called her. Could she come? How about the weekend? No, she said. She worked on Saturdays and Sundays. But Thursdays were free. I said Thursday evening was fine. We can go to a restaurant. She agreed.

That evening I took her to a place called *Baltika* where they served Russian food. The small dining room paneled with honey-colored wood exuded a cedary aroma and candle-lit tables covered with crimson tablecloths and glittering china and silverware created a perfect setting. But Anara seemed overwhelmed by a consuming melancholy and neither the ambience nor the food raised her spirits. In the amber gloom of the restaurant she looked more desirable than ever. Her smooth forearms, round and bare, had the sheen of antique ivory and her dark dreaming eyes glittered liquid and hot like black pearls behind her glossy bangs. And that silken head that I so wanted to stroke the way one would stroke the sleek mane of a racehorse, was bent in utter humility.

"How is your job?" I asked, trying to make conversation.

She made a face.

"Not good," she said. "They said I work in reception. But now they make me clean rooms."

"That's terrible." I said.

I sensed that she needed cheering up but I didn't know what to say to ease her distress. I had my own needs and urges that demanded attention. I wanted her with a keen intensity the way a starved man wants food. I made up my mind to be frank, plead my case. If I failed to play the game with skill and daring all would be lost. I ordered a vodka martini and downed it quickly to stiffen my nerves.

"I want you, Anara. You understand? I need you."

She lowered her gaze, her dark hair tumbling down on either side of her face like a black waterfall, the tips almost touching the tabletop. I took her left hand in mine and squeezed it hard as if to punctuate my words with a physical gesture. Her fingers were long and thin and soft. She didn't say much. Nor did she eat with any relish.

After dinner, we walked back to my apartment and I curved my right arm around her waist tightly. The night sky was clear and stars glittered like ice crystals in an endless black sky. Our hips bumped together as we walked along a dark road lit by street lamps that threw down yellow cones of light. An occasional car went by. Yielding to a sudden impulse, I stopped in the shadowed lee of a building, pulled her close and kissed her. She responded with eagerness, her tongue seeking mine as if she wanted to communicate something to me directly, tongue to tongue, bypassing words and sound. I figured she had made up her mind. And, sure enough, that night the dance began. At first, I sensed an awkwardness that turned her limbs into hindrances. Her shyness and timidity made her seem hesitant. But gradually she opened herself the way a flower opens, helplessly vulnerable, ready for the aggressive burrowing of a bee. And soon we were caught up in the same rhythm, the heavy drumbeat of blood. Not too long after this encounter she quit her job and was spending most of her time with me. In another week she brought over her toothbrush, pajamas, make-up kit and a few clothes. And then over the next nine months we were a pair, seen together everywhere. A couple. Anara became my guide, my guest, my companion.

All I've said so far is clear enough and comprehensible but the question I am trying to answer is: when did Anara and I create that special bond, that invisible link that transformed our relationship into something deep and deeply significant? Did it happen suddenly? Or slowly? What were the signs that convinced us that our *affair* wasn't something casual, something transitory? These are difficult questions. As the seasons changed, as fall turned to winter and winter turned to spring, we got closer and closer. No public ceremonies or rituals marked the stages as we moved towards each other. There were no exchanges of symbolic tokens. No rings or bracelets. If there were any signs, they were all barely visible, small gestures, words spoken almost casually, acts of courtesy and tenderness that gradually formed the links of the chain that connected us, that stretched from her to me. There were moments when I literally felt my heart skip a beat or two, keenly aware that something magical, something important had just happened.

　　Consider, for example, how something so simple as holding hands acquired significance. It sounds silly now to even mention this, except that it symbolized something special. Anara always held my hand when we were out walking. Whether we were going to the supermarket or just to the corner kiosk for cigarettes and beer or walking in the park, she would take my hand and hang on to it like a trusting child. But the gesture also had a possessive aspect. It was as though she wanted everyone to know that I belonged to her. Unused to this, I felt a bit uncomfortable at first. No one had held my hand since I had been a little boy in short pants. In fact, this holding of hands did bring back memories of childhood, of the sense of security that you felt when a grown-up held your hand. This gesture made a deep impression on me. I began to enjoy the sensation and I would reach out and grasp her hand as soon as we were outside the apartment.

As the seasons changed our intimacy acquired a deep maturity. We were comfortable with each other, enjoyed each other and were satisfied with each other. When the snow came down in soft, feathery flakes outside the window, covering the city in a white coverlet, we spent the long winter nights nestled naked and snug against each other.

In early spring, the snow finally melted and we went walking in Panfilov Park. The silver birches had started to put out tiny, pale yellow-green leaves once again. It had rained all through the night but now the storm had rolled away and the firs and pines and oaks were dripping and streaming and steaming as we walked along the paved paths. Whole armies of tiny snails were out creeping along on the sidewalks and you had to be careful to not step on them. I said something to Anara about the snails being hermaphrodites and I explained how that worked.

"I wonder what they say to each other," I said.

"They don't say anything," she responded. "They prefer silence."

The way she said that in her overly formal English made me chuckle.

Dozens of reddish-brown squirrels with fluffy tails were hopping about on the branches of the big oak trees. They looked like the ones you see in children's books with their bushy tails, big, shiny eyes and small paws.

"They are beautiful, aren't they," I said.

She laughed. "I have walked through this park many times before, but I never realized until this moment how beautiful it was."

And she put her arm through mine and held me close and we walked hip touching hip – almost clinging to each other like two old people. She always clung to me like this, when we rode in the mini-buses and the tram-trolleys. She would hook her arm through mine, not to steady herself, but to protect me and to make sure no one came between us. Perhaps she had been deprived of affection as a child. Conversely, she may have been taught how to be affectionate and this was her way of showing how she felt. Whatever the case, it became clear to me gradually that our personalities were compatible. It also became clear that leaving Almaty would be painful. It would hurt like hell, in fact.

Anara never talked much about her family, or her past. And when I questioned her, she became evasive, unwilling to go into details.

"Tell me about your father," I asked her one day as we were sitting down to dinner in my apartment. I lowered the volume on the TV, hoping to draw her out.

"He left my mother when I was ten or eleven," she said.

"Did you like him? Did you miss him?"

She nodded, her face blank, totally empty of any emotion.

"Do you see him now?"

"Not very often. He lives in another city, quite far away."

"Where?"

"Astana. He has another wife now and children."

I stopped my questioning. It seemed indecent to probe further. Nor would she tell me much about her mother.

"Does your mom work?" I asked her.

"Yes."

"Where?"

"In a factory."

"What kind of factory?"

"I don't know."

I did not really believe her. But I sensed that she did not want to reveal too much about the sort of work her mother did. I decided to stop asking questions. I didn't want to embarrass her.

But then quite by accident, many months later, I discovered that she had a child. Early one morning, not long after she had moved in with me, her mobile phone rang. She was sitting right next to me on the couch and I could easily hear the voice of the person on the line. The speaker sounded like a small girl. I heard her say "mama" several times. The two spoke in Russian but the frequent repetition of "mama" made it plain that the voice belonged to her daughter.

When she hung up, I asked, "Who was that?"

"Oh my sister," she said and turned her face away.

Rather stunned, I did not challenge her or call her a liar to her face. I figured she did not want me to know that she had a daughter, at least not just yet. Several days later, her mobile rang again and she spoke for a while. Then she said, "My sister not feeling well. I go home for a few hours."

"Fine," I said. "That's okay. You should go and see her."

She left quickly and did not come back for two days but she did call me.

"My sister not feeling good. But getting better. I will come back tomorrow."

"Fine," I said. "We'll go to *Faiza*, that Uzbeg restaurant that you like."

I knew for certain that she had gone home to see her child. She had her own reasons, no doubt, to hide this side of her life and I, for my part, did not feel that I had any right to pry into her past life or her private concerns. I hadn't told her much about my past, partly because she had been gracious enough not to probe and partly because I didn't think it had any bearing on how we related to each other. When she came back, I took her to *Faiza*. I knew she liked the place.

They served simple, inexpensive food and the restaurant had a friendly, informal atmosphere. People brought their own bottles of beer and vodka because the restaurant did not have a liquor license. I carried in a tall bottle of Kazakh beer.

"How is your sister?" I asked her. "Is she feeling better? What was it? Flu or a cold?"

She stared down at her plate intently and then she looked at me with her luminous, candid eyes from across the table. "I didn't go to see my sister. I went to see my daughter."

"Your daughter?" I feigned surprise. "I didn't know you had a daughter. Why didn't you tell me?"

She stared down at the table, unable to come up with a response.

"But you said you weren't married," I said.

"I'm not," she said, shaking her head from side to side.

"Where is the father, then?"

"He went to Vladivostok, to the diamond mines. He may still be there. I'm not sure."

"Does he know he has a child?"

Anara, shook her head.

"I haven't heard from him in five years."

I reached across the table and took her hand in mine. I had thought a great deal about how I would respond when she finally volunteered this information. I had rehearsed every word I would say many times over.

"Look, this won't have any effect on our relationship," I said. "I'm delighted to hear that you have a child. Do you realize how lucky you are? I bet she is as sweet and lovely as you are. But someday she will ask you about her father. Who was he? Where is he? Or he might show up. And if he does, you will have to tell him that the child is his. It is only fair. As far as we are concerned, I would love to meet her. Will you bring her?"

Anara looked away, deep in thought. She did not know what to say. My response was a total surprise.

"I didn't think you would like this news," she said.

"Come, sweetie. I'm not a teenager. That's the one advantage of having lived for nearly half a century. You learn a thing or two. Whether you want to or not. Life isn't a fairy tale or a Hollywood movie. It's much more complicated. In my opinion motherhood has been good for you. It's made you more feminine, more tender, more caring. I felt this as soon as I met you. That is why I liked you so much. It's this generous gentleness that drew me to you."

When we got back from the restaurant, we sat up late into the night talking. I poured a jigger of vodka for myself and decided to open the musty volumes of my dreary past: the two marriages, the two divorces, the two kids (a boy and a girl whom I hadn't seen in nearly a decade) the overly-possessive mother, the domiciles established and disestablished, the suburbs that got obscured in the car exhaust as I pulled away. Anara may have found this sorry saga interesting, but to anyone familiar with the pattern of middle-class American lives as they unraveled in the seventies and eighties, it would be trite, predictable. This is why I have no desire to present the dull details in this narrative. Let us assume that all concerned learned a few lessons. On the other hand, I may have learned nothing. The illusions one clings to when young are replaced by illusions of middle age. Perhaps it is these illusions that sustain us. Many of us would gladly accept a handful of sleeping pills, the bullet in the brain-pan, the noose around the neck or the leap off a tall building were it not for the illusions that keep us going.

My son – from my first marriage – now in college, rarely communicated with me. His mother, who raised him, drilled into him the fixed belief that I epitomized selfishness. The girl, (from my second wife) still in High School, appeared to be making the same mistakes that many girls of her generation were making. Fifteen, she had started dating, started hanging out at the Convenience Mart. Very soon I expected to hear that a pregnancy had made her leave school, that she had left home, that she had gotten a job at a Beauty Parlor. I will not have been able to influence her destiny or alter it in any way. Even if I were living in the same house with her and her mother, I don't think I could prevent her from going down the path that her social environment will push her along.

Anara wanted to know why my marriages had ended.

"Divorces are common in the United States, aren't they?" she said.

I had to agree.

"Why? Why is that?"

"Well, I'm no social scientist, but there is something about our society, some sort of force that destroys marriages. Of course, the husbands blame the wives and the wives blame the husbands. The problem is much deeper. I think it is rooted in our system – the way we live, the way we work. It is hard to explain."

"That's okay," she said. "Don't worry. I don't understand why my relationship failed either."

"People used to swear 'Till Death do us part,'" I said. "People still say the words, but no one really believes that. Not anymore. We seem to lack tolerance. I got married the first time because that's what everyone did. There was all this sexual pressure and this confused us, blinded us. Debbie and I never realized that we were not right for each other. And the second marriage ended because Rachel came to the conclusion that I would never be the man she wanted me to be, the rich and famous lawyer of her dreams. 'You're a failure,' she told me bluntly. 'I don't want to be married to a failure.'"

Anara nodded sympathetically. She never probed, or second-guessed or contradicted what I told her. I don't know where she had acquired such large-minded tolerance, this vast, patient acceptance of the way-things-are. Nor did she pronounce judgment, or assign blame or guilt. And I refrained from launching into a full-scale analysis of my marriages. What good would it have done? At best I would have managed to establish the time and cause of death. Nothing more.

We talked quietly, lying side by side in the dark. A warm spring breeze heavy with the scent of lilacs stirred the nylon curtains, catching and releasing them in languid embraces. Every once in a while, I got up and poured a little vodka into a glass and sat and sipped and smoked a cigarette. She listened with her eyes closed and may even have fallen into short phases of sleep. But occasionally, I heard a murmured "Yes, honey. I understand." Finally, I too became sleepy and lay down beside her, kissed her soft breasts one last time and closed my eyes.

Now summer was upon us and the date of my departure loomed – a sentence that could not be lifted, a judgment that could not be repealed. And the closer that day came the more we clung to each other. And as if to cancel the pain of impending separation we decided to distract ourselves by playing the role of tourists. We started going on little excursions to places I'd never seen. A trip to Bishkek, the capital of Kyrgyzstan and to a resort near Lake Issyk Kul. But beneath the gaiety of sightseeing lurked the keen awareness that our days together were few, and getting fewer. The last hot, dusty month arrived, then the last few days and then the last hours. I packed my suitcase grimly, trying my best to remain calm and unemotional. I remember clearly the agony of the long, wordless ride to the airport late at night. The headlamps of the taxi pushed back the blackness that surged around us. The lights of lonely farmhouses glimmered in the distance. We didn't dare look at each other. Words had become deadly scorpions, ready to sting the tongue. She didn't even reach out to hold my hand.

In the vast departure hall of Almaty airport amidst garbled echoes, I promised her we would be together again. I have a good chance of getting a teaching job in north Cyprus, the Turkish enclave, I told her. I had been corresponding and negotiating with a university. The Head of the Law department had looked at my resume and written encouraging emails, assuring me they needed me. I felt confident they would be hiring me but there was still the matter of the contract. Until I had the contract in hand, signed and sealed, I hovered in a region of uncertainty. I did my best to reassure Anara. The moment they hired me, I would fly to Cyprus and send for her. She wept silently, the bright tears clogging her long eyelashes. I am sure she had doubts. I certainly had mine. The future was obscure, a question mark, and there was no certainty that we would ever meet again. I left her standing by the candy vending machine, a frail figure, her head bowed in grief, the very image of despair. That was certainly the most horrible day of my life.

∼

Section 2

But then, amazingly, my luck held. It was as if we were fated to be together again. The stars and planets aligned themselves in the most propitious orbits, trans-oceanic winds held their breaths, tides took turns fashioning favorable currents. Dame Fortune nodded and I got the job. Call it Kismet, call it Destiny, call it what you will, for once in my life I felt as though Lady Luck was smiling on me, holding the door open, leading me by the hand, protecting and guiding me.

Then on a cool September morning, I was walking down Ecevit street towards the old harbor of Kyrenia in north Cyprus. The sky was a deep delphinium blue misted over lightly like frosted glass but the keen, direct sunlight held promise of more heat later in the afternoon. I could smell pungent aromas riding the air currents, possibly those of eucalyptus and crushed fennel. I felt giddy, light, buoyant and floated along filled to bursting with the helium of happiness. I had accomplished what I had promised. I had made it to north Cyprus not as a tourist or a visitor but for a long-term stay with a teaching contract in hand. At the end of each month a paycheck would slide silently into my bank account. I grinned inwardly like a smug Cheshire cat and felt like celebrating but there was much to do, many tasks required my attention. I had to contact Anara and tell her that I had reached Cyprus and make arrangements for her plane ticket. I had to contact my chief at the university and check in with the personnel office to complete necessary paperwork. I had to get some sort of transportation. I had to find a suitable house or apartment to rent, a process I dreaded since one can rarely afford the type of place one wants. But luckily I met Cardiff and his help and advice eased my difficulties.

Cardiff was a transplanted Englishman and had been in north Cyprus for several years, teaching Law in the same department I was in. With thinning, light brown hair, big, nicotine-blotched Stonehenge teeth, neckties imprinted with soup-maps and an ever-wrinkled white linen suit, he could be recognized from afar as he strode across the campus. Cardiff loved to drink almost as much as I did. He used alcohol the way other people use vitamins – to improve the quality of life. This may have been one reason why we started spending a lot of time together. When he had finished teaching his classes, he could be found in some local bar. He never cooked. Nor did I ever see him eat. And he smoked nonstop. I think he even smoked as he slept. It was Cardiff who introduced me to *Pegasus* – the bar/restaurant where Brit expats spent long hours drinking. Cardiff spent most of his leisure hours here. It was located on the coast road very near the campus and had a vine-shaded terrace outside where one could sit on hot days under dappled green shadows and drink beer. The men wore sandals, shorts and open collar, half-sleeve shirts. They looked like mummies: dry brown skin stretched over bones. Inside, around a D shaped bar, half a dozen or so could be found at all hours, clinging to life and leisure. They sat there and wrangled over old soccer matches, cricket scores and the Royal brats, in accents that varied from Ox-Bridge to cockney, talking about topics I had no interest in. Later, when the cold weather set in, everyone gathered around a huge, circular fire-pit filled with fragrant olive wood embers glowing red-hot.

On many an afternoon, I'd see Cardiff's lean, concave shape perched on a barstool as he peered through thick lenses at a TV screen tuned to a British channel. I don't think he could see anything very clearly. I don't think he cared. He had given up caring for things that happened in England. Once or twice he mentioned a wife he'd left back there – divorced, of course. And a son, who visited him once in a while. The family happened to Cardiff the way accidents happen to people. He made a quick recovery and a fast getaway. He left behind the Barrister-at-Law life of London town. The striped black suits and sober neckties. He left the daily commute on the Tube to legal routines and judicial boredom. He left the wife, the decade old marriage and the small son. And came to Cyprus to start a different sort of life. He bought an apartment and got a teaching job to pay for the booze and cigarettes. Beyond that, he needed little else. All he wanted was freedom – a sunny beach, some cold beer and an occasional sexual encounter. Most expats – male and female – came to Cyprus in pursuit of the same dream.

I liked Cardiff. He drank steadily but carefully and he said less and less as he got more and more drunk. The legal training kicked in, I suppose. Because anything you say can be held against you in a Court-of-Law. When sober, Cardiff spoke fluently in a mildly impeccable, uppity Brit-twit accent. He had a deep, burly voice that seemed to have been strained through lashings of liquor and smoke. When he spoke he sounded very calm and convincing. It didn't matter what he said. You believed him instantly. He could say: "The moon is made of mashed potatoes," and you would believe him. As a snake-oil salesman, he would have made millions. With a little training, he could have sung opera. But on the Island-of-love, he used his dark-brown, treacle tones to hypnotize nervous young English dames. That resonant rumbling voice of his and a few drinks soothed their ruffled feathers and they became quite docile. The fact is, every female tourist on the island, if she happened to be young, wanted to find a man. And there were plenty of strapping young Turks working in the restaurants, casinos and nightclubs who were only too happy to be of service. Even with minimal English skills they easily managed to get these girls to a dark beach or a rented room. All very harmless and innocent. Each party got what it wanted and both went away satisfied. To function as a successful stud in North Cyprus, being under twenty and illiterate gave you an edge. Being middle-aged and educated was a handicap. But Cardiff made up for his shortcomings with his smooth, sly ways. When he played his instrument with proper attention to pitch, tone and volume, the object of his desire fell into his lap, somewhat drunk and well past the point of caring who did what to whom. I couldn't tell whether the tourists were corrupting the locals or whether the locals were corrupting the tourists but it all went on with light-hearted casualness. Occasionally, I suppose cash did change hands but, on the whole, no one appeared to suffer any permanent physical or psychological harm.

The mini-buses used by tourists and locals to get around were rolling disasters. Ancient wrecks kept on the road with wire coat hangers and prayers. No shocks, no air-conditioning, no brakes. Every instrument on the dashboard appeared to be permanently dead. Under the blazing summer sun, they turned into super-heated ovens, ripe with odors of diesel fuel and sweat. On my second day in Cyprus, I realized I had to get a car, and I had to get it fast. The mini-buses served as mobile homes for vast armies of fleas. After every trip my ankles would be covered with small, hard red nodules that itched like crazy. I scratched and scratched till I made them bleed. Like tiny, vicious vampires, the fleas lived on tourist blood, simply loved it. The locals, on the other hand, seemed immune to their attacks.

As soon as I could, I hurried over to a used-car lot not far from the center of the town. The dealer, a handsome, young Turk with a bandito-style mustache spoke English quite fluently. I told him I needed something inexpensive, not a status symbol. He nodded and led me to a dented old Renault covered with a leprosy of rust. He said it had belonged to a saintly old Turk who drove it only once a week to go to the mosque on Fridays.

"Does it run?" I asked him.

"Certainly it run," he said with a trust-inspiring grin. "If not run, bring back."

"Fine," I said. "I'll take it."

The vehicle had once been clean and new but that was long, long ago and I doubted seriously that it was road worthy, but the price was one I could afford. I figured I'd use it till it died and then get another one. Cautiously, I drove my choking and chugging purchase out of the lot, ready to take on the next challenge: finding a place to stay. At first I considered getting an apartment near the old harbor, a busy place, full of tourist hustle and bustle. The yellow ochre bastions of the medieval castle guarded its eastern flank and a broad sea wall protected the entrance. Shaped like a perfect horseshoe, with its flotilla of colorful pleasure boats and yachts and a curving esplanade lined with bars, restaurants and nightclubs, it seemed like the epicenter of the "Good Life." Blaring music and bright lights and tourist trinket shops gave the place an air of non-stop gaiety and festive excitement. But I realized very quickly that living in this neighborhood would not be a good idea. I didn't think I could deal with the constant to-and-fro-ing of tourists, the discos pounding away late into the night and the drunks quarrelling and throwing up in the parking lots.

"Let's do Plan B," I said to Cardiff. "I want a place as far as possible from the squealing tires of hormone-powered cars and the debaucheries of commerce."

Cardiff nodded sagely.

"I know a place," he said, as we stood chatting in the university quadrangle. "It's an old Greek village, high up on that mountain yonder. In fact, you can see it from here." He turned and pointed at the Beshparmak range covered with greenery that rose up behind us. "See, up there, those white houses. That's Karmi. It's an old Greek village. I'll take you there. It's not my cup of tea – too many bloody Brits, but you're an American. They won't bother you."

Way up the slope of the mountain, I could see a small cluster of white houses, clinging to a steep crag, shaggy with greenery, shimmering behind a scrim of sunlight and sea mist. That afternoon, with me at the wheel of my relic of a Renault and Cardiff in the passenger seat, we started for Karmi. From the slope on which the university sat, one could see the stone houses gleaming like sugar-cubes amidst the emerald and viridian growths of trees and bushes. Getting up the mountain presented severe problems for the Renault. The engine wheezed and chuffed like an asthmatic donkey and almost died several times. Laboriously, we climbed for about ten kilometers, going round hairpin bends, past deep drop-offs, down steep gradients and up nearly vertical slopes. As we climbed higher and higher, it got cooler and the foliage kept getting more and more dense. Wild flowers by the side of the road nodded cheerily to us in jolly profusion. My spirits rose with every foot of altitude gained. The landscape held the promise of dreams and adventures.

Cardiff recited relevant details. Karmi had been a Greek village when the island was under British control. Then in the mid-Fifties the village became a nest of violently anti-British guerillas. They launched a campaign of systematic terror: bombings, shootings, assassinations in an effort to kick the Brits off the island. But in 1974, when the Turkish army landed on the north shore, the Greeks all moved to the southern part of the island and Karmi went to weeds and ruination. Eventually, the North Cyprus government decided to revive and rebuild the village. The houses were sold or leased to Europeans (who had the money) and they renovated them and turned them into summer homes.

After negotiating some serious S-bends and a couple of nearly vertical slopes, I brought the Renault to a halt in a small, cobblestone plaza ringed with cypresses, pines and mulberry trees. A whitewashed church with a tall bell-tower and a red-tiled roof stood on one side. I parked the car under the damp shadow of a Carob and switched off the engine. The sudden emptiness of silence pooled up around us and I could hear the mooing and cooing of pigeons sitting in the alcoves of the tower. Sunlight streamed down on the scene with a sharp intensity that made the shadows more black than black and the aroma of crushed rosemary and wild fennel filled the air.

About a hundred or so stone houses scattered in a haphazard manner athwart the steep slopes could be seen drowning beneath wild growths of bougainvillea, honeysuckle and jasmine. A few streets shaded by grape vines and cypresses radiated out of the plaza and went twisting past beds of nasturtiums and irises. Almond trees, lemon trees and olive trees sighed and shivered as the sea breeze touched them tenderly. A profound, sun-soaked silence held the village in a trance. No traffic, no smoke, no noise. On the stone walls half a dozen cats dozed undisturbed. At first glance the place seemed to be devoid of humans. But then I noticed a few elderly Europeans taking the sun on rooftops and terraces.

Cardiff located the estate agent, an English lady named Fiona. A friendly, maternal sort of person, Fiona had a ready giggle and a large haunch and paunch. Nevertheless, she managed to move with considerable grace and agility. She gave me a skeptical once-over and seemed to form a negative opinion. But Cardiff erased her doubts with a glib speech on my noble qualities and unimpeachable integrity. As an American, I earned bonus points.

Fiona agreed to show us a couple of houses that were available and we set forth to see them. The one I liked and the one that suited my budget sat off the main path. It had two levels and stood on a broad shelf of the mountain and faced a narrow, cobblestone lane. Through a stone archway you entered a terrace shaded by an almond tree and paved with flagstones. A luxuriant jasmine bush on one side and a lemon tree on the other protected this space from prying eyes. From the terrace, marble steps led up to a cobalt blue front door that opened into a living area that included the living room, the dining nook and the kitchen. Several windows and a couple of French doors brought in light and air and provided a view of the topmost branches of the almond tree and nearby cypresses. The two bedrooms on the ground floor that you reached via a wooden staircase were cool and dark as wine cellars.

"I'll take it," I said to Fiona and we went to her tiny office located behind the church to formalize the agreement. I signed a document containing more clauses than the Magna Carta and handed over a sheaf of pretty English money with the queen's face on every note. Fiona gave me the keys to the house, plus sage counsel on how to cope with the plumbing. I breathed a sigh of relief. Now Anara could come.

～

Section 3

A constant worry tainted my tranquility during the days, weeks and months of separation from Anara. I feared she might lose interest in me. This possibility loomed large in my imagination. She could find someone closer to her own age, someone who spoke her language, shared her culture and traditions. I had done my best to keep in touch through emails, text messages and occasional phone calls. But this anxiety made for worry-wracked, restless nights and days as though I were running a low fever. I could never get rid of this feeling of apprehension even though I tried to keep myself busy with stints at a gym, yard-work and handyman tasks. Only with booze was I able to calm my thrumming nerves, only booze could stop the scenarios of betrayal that my imagination staged for me. But when the liquor wore off, the haunting worries returned.

Anara's weak command over English limited her ability to communicate and the short messages she managed to send did not reveal much about how she spent her time. Here is one: "Darling I miss you. Miss your hugs and kisses. Mama cooked good food yesterday. Went to Green bazaar with Mama. Got some spices that you like. I am okay. Luv U. It is hot now in Almaty. Okay, bye-bye. Many kisses."

Most of her emails were like this one – brief and ungrammatical. She never provided very many details about what she did or did not do, nor did she give long descriptions of her activities or family-related events.

What could I do? Very little. I made up my mind to simply accept whatever she said, be satisfied with the information she supplied. If I had doubts about anything she wrote, I never expressed them in front of her, nor did I try to cross-examine her. Instead, to amuse her or, perhaps, to retain her attention and interest, I sent her erotic messages. I would describe in detail what I would do when we got together again. I became very creative, invented sexual games and made up clever-cute names for our sex organs, developed scenarios of prolonged and contortionist lovemaking. What else can you do when the girl you want to be with is far away? But eventually all this proved to be less enjoyable than you might imagine. Composing these pornographic letters turned into a form of self-flagellation, an exercise in frustration. Occasionally, if she happened to be at a well-equipped Internet café, we even managed to see each other via web-cams and chat in real time. I would compliment her on the clothes she wore and she would send flying kisses at me. Occasionally, the chat would get racy, with hot sexual banter. She would promise to arouse me till I screamed for mercy. And I threatened her with the same fate. Once, I was going to expose myself before the web-cam but she begged me not to. "Too many people all round," she warned. All this cyber-sex got me excited but I could find no satisfactory outlet, no release. Finally, even terms of endearment sound hollow and meaningless. Mere clichés. "My dear: My darling: My precious heart."

We somehow got through the months of separation. Anara never wavered in her determination to be with me and expressed her eagerness (in fractured prose): "You send ticket I come. Miss my squirrel. Dying to see you."

The University had assigned me a small office complete with a steel desk, a chair, a telephone and a computer. The room also had a window that faced north, towards the sea. The window was a privilege, a special favor and a sign of consideration since I was a foreigner. The administrators wanted expat teachers to be happy, to enjoy their stay on the island. From my office window I could see the Mediterranean, glimmering far away. It looked like a strip of teal blue fabric stretched horizontally between a cloudless, Cobalt blue sky and the buff and beige and brown plain that dipped and crumbled down to the coast. Rows of newly built off-white tourist villas formed a sort of windbreak between the university buildings and the seashore. Occasionally I would see a pleasure boat ease into view from the right side of my window and move dreamily westwards or emerge from the left and proceed eastward. The boats were far away and looked like two-dimensional paper cutouts. For a while, I stood there looking out, until my eyes ached from the dazzle.

I shared my office with Farhat Bey, my chief. He was a stocky, middle-aged man with an efficient crew cut and a diffident manner. He spoke English haltingly, choosing his words with care, afraid of making grammatical errors or letting slip something that he did not wish to say. Not an effusive or over friendly person, he reminded me of a tightly wound up watch spring: a lot of coiled up energy. But this energy could not be released suddenly. It had to unwind, slowly, gradually, tick-by-tick. Farhat Bey spoke with me briefly about my duties, about the students, about my classes. He wanted me to create several syllabi that set forth the requirements of my courses, describe in some detail what I would be teaching, the texts I would use and the various deadlines that students would have to meet.

The main quad of the university consisted of three buildings arranged in U. A large green space made up the middle, and had been planted with all kinds of flowering bushes and trees: roses, hibiscus, irises, palms and olives. A shallow reflecting pool of an irregular shape in the center of this space captured and held the blueness of the sky. A lot of young men and girls were standing in the shade of the formal porch of the admin building smoking cigarettes and chattering and kibitzing with each other. The girls were tender darlings, all in tight low-cut hip-hugging jeans that exposed sweet tummies and innocent looking belly buttons. All of them followed fashion trends in the United States and Europe. But I found those exposed bellies rather comical and anti-erotic. Moreover, my mind was elsewhere. I wanted to find a travel agent and purchase Anara's ticket.

Later that afternoon, I drove to the center of Kyrenia and ended up quite by chance in Osman Bey's travel agency, directly across the street from the Dome hotel. I suppose I must have seen a sign and just walked in. I felt giddy with joy and excitement as I paid cash for Anara's ticket and then hurried to find a pay phone to tell her to go and pick up her ticket at the Turkish Airline's office in Almaty. In one of the streets that connected the harbor to the main bazaar, I found the "Orange" pay phone center. It sat on the sidewalk, a kind of kiosk made out of two halves of a huge plastic orange, the sort of gimmicky vending stall you might see in Los Angeles. The upper part served as a canopy and the lower part formed a circular counter. Once upon a time it must have been an orange juice stand but now it looked more like an architectural pimple on the fair cheek of Kyrenia, the very streets where Crusaders, Venetians and Moors had once marched.

Even through the long-distance wires I could sense Anara's excitement. She had never been on an airplane, never left her homeland. This journey from Almaty to Istanbul and then from there to Cyprus would be a test of nerves for her. I did my best to give her some idea of what she could expect, how to handle the passport formalities and where she could find some food. But I didn't think she'd be able to retain much of what I said. Images and ideas must have been whirling about in her head. I did not keep her long on the line. There would be time later on for all that we had to say to each other.

Elation and relief flooded through me. I felt I had kept my promise. I had designed and deployed the plan. Now I just had to sit and wait. It had been a long, tense summer. Much could have gone awry. But my luck held. Now I felt like celebrating. I headed for the harbor to have a drink and let my nerves unwind.

I chose a table by the water's edge and ordered a beer. "Bring me a local brew … made here. You understand?" I said to the waiter. He nodded and turned on his heels. Someone had left a local newspaper on my table, written in English – *Cyprus Daily* – I think. I picked it up and started scanning the stories. Rather skimpy and scanty, it had the look and feel of a community paper back in the States. The top of the front page carried a huge color photo of a new multi-story gambling casino that had just opened. The text described the details of a party held to celebrate the opening and gave the names of the dignitaries and socialites that had attended the ceremony. The lower half of the paper offered something more interesting. "Shepherd Killed by Mine" a headline screamed. Intrigued, I read on. Attila Dengdash, a 35 year-old shepherd from Guzelyurt, had entered a minefield by mistake and stepped on a mine in the zone that separated North Cyprus from South Cyprus. The mine exploded, killing the man instantly. Attila Dengdash left behind a widow and four children. Government officials were planning on some sort of compensation for the widow. Apparently, Mr. Dengdash had gone after a goat that had wandered away. He may not have realized that he had entered a zone seeded with mines left over from the 1974 war between the Greeks and the Turks, or he may have been so eager to get his goat back that he ignored the posted warnings. The tragedy had shaken the community and local leaders were calling on the government to accelerate the mine-clearing operations.

I had no idea that Cyprus still had mines left over from the 1974 conflict. The image of the island as a war-zone littered with unexploded mines seemed at odds with the vision that the tourist bureau tried to project for European tourists, that of an idyllic vacation destination. The Island of Love, dedicated to the rites of Aphrodite. The land of sun and fun on pristine beaches! But the island did have a violent history going as far back as the Middle Ages and the wars of the crusaders. In fact, King Richard the Lion Heart took over the island for a time, spent his honeymoon here with his bride Berengaria and ultimately sold it to the Templar Knights. After the Christian onslaught came other invasions. Bloodshed begets more bloodshed. This is the First Law of History.

The waiter brought a foaming, sweating mug of ice-cold *Efes*, a beer they made in Turkey. Very much like the more popular American brands, it had a bright effervescence that chilled and refreshed the palate.

"Look," I said to him pointing to the story about the dead shepherd. "Does this sort of thing happen often?"

He stared down, read the headline and shook his head.

"No, not often," he said. "More shepherds get killed by lightning than anything else."

"By lightning?"

"Yes ... every year," he said nodding his head. "Many die."

I had no idea. But now the old Greek myths about Zeus and his thunderbolt all made sense to me and I understood how relevant they were in the Cypriot context. Slowly the sun had begun to go down behind the Beshparmak range and cool shadows were collecting in the horseshoe-shaped esplanade. But the lemon-colored sky above the harbor still glowed with the held heat of the afternoon. A saline breeze left a film of salt on my lips. The Prussian blue water in the harbor had the look of shiny silk as it rippled and rustled. Pleasure boats and sailing craft moored side-by-side bobbed and dipped gently. A bronze Byzantine light fell on the walls and parapets of the castle transmuting the yellow ochre stones to tarnished gold.

The evening devolved from royal blue to mauve to deep magenta. Gradually all the lights came on. Garlands of bulbs, neon signs and the bright interiors of the restaurants all spilled into the harbor and were liquefied as though a kaleidoscope had spilled open. Now the promenade of tourists began and the tables started to fill up. Waiters ran back and forth with trays of drinks and food. Loud rock and roll poured out of the open doorways of the restaurants along with odorous exhalations of the kitchens. I was starting to feel hungry but I wanted to find a less touristy, more tranquil restaurant, perhaps a place patronized by locals. The restaurants on the esplanade were expensive. They were meant for Europeans with money. I had no desire to be a part of this scene.

CHAPTER TWO

Section 1

Quite unexpectedly a hot wind blew over northern Cyprus, whipping up dust and torn wrappers on the side of the roads into small tornadoes. The sun scorched the flank of the Beshparmak and dried out the grasses turning them into yellow strands of glass that shimmered in the strong sunlight. A stunned stillness settled over the coastal shelf and the curved dagger-shaped leaves of eucalyptus trees hung motionless. The weather imprisoned me in a kind of mental and physical paralysis, as I waited for Anara, waited for classes to start, waited for my life to begin.

I often wondered what Anara saw in me, why she had attached herself to me so easily, naturally, speedily. It is difficult – if not impossible to understand another person, to get a glimpse of the gears and levers, all the mental machinery that generates beliefs, attitudes, desires. My physical deficiencies lay heavy on my head and she surely saw them all. Then there were the cultural and linguistic barriers between us that were not easy to jump over. Nor could I point out to her a future in which we might build something, plan a life together. The future for us was a gray and misty landscape where I could see no roads or paths that might lead us somewhere. So what could it have been that made her cling to me? Perhaps it was my "differentness."

That can be and, in fact, *is* a powerful magnetic force and it can bring men and women together. Vive la difference! As they say. Perhaps it was the fact that I had experience on my side. The failed marriages, the long list of employers and the places where I had lived are impressive credentials for any man. For my part, I knew perfectly well what I saw in her. I saw a gracious disposition and eyes like black diamonds. I saw someone who said very little, someone who expressed herself through touch, and someone I needed with the knife-sharp need of a teenager.

Driving up the mountain road in the Renault, I noticed kestrels spiraling down to their roosts on the topmost branches of the pines. On the green flank of the crag, Karmi shimmered in the sunlight, a white assemblage of sugar cubes set amidst the pointillism of boulders and pines. When I got to the central plaza, I parked the car under the shadow of a mulberry tree. In the drowsing afternoon even the cantankerous magpies had left off their quarrels and settled down for a snooze in the dark depths of the cypresses.

When I got to the house, I stripped to my underwear, grabbed a beer from the fridge and lay down on the floor to savor the coolness of the tiles. Presently I heard the sound of human voices float up from the alley. The syllables did not express any meaning for me nor did I recognize English or Turkish, nor any other language that I knew. Moved by curiosity, I pulled on a pair of shorts, opened the shutters and stepped onto the balcony. My downward gaze collided with the startled upward stare of two women and an elderly gentleman with short, white hair. Foreshortened by my angle of vision their faces loomed large and rather dazed and amazed. I must have surprised them materializing suddenly on the balcony, like a bare-chested satyr lurking among the purple flames of the bougainvillea.

By way of greeting, I raised my beer can in a kind of toast and said, "Hello."

At first, I got no response, just silent looks. But then the man said, "Hello."

"Is it hot enough for you?" I said, cheerily.

I had never seen them before. They were tourists, no doubt, like many others one saw rambling and scrambling around in excited groups, clicking cameras and chattering amongst themselves. Karmi attracted many travelers, especially people who wanted to see the old, historic Cyprus, not the Cyprus of gambling dens and discos.

"Too hot," said the younger of the two women.

"Would you like some water," I said. "I have some cold bottles in the fridge."

This invitation violated a kind of unwritten and unspoken rule that most Karmi residents lived by. Beyond shy eye contact, politely murmured verbal greetings and cheerily expressive hand gestures, one did nothing to establish links with tourists. Tourists came and went, washing over Karmi like a tide that hardly ever touched the lives of the residents. The world of the tourists and the world of the residents swung past each other like planets rolling through space, each in a different orbit, adrift on a different trajectory. Tourists saw us; we saw them. Some waved at us in friendly fashion, others pretended we weren't there. They walked around, admired the views, took a few pictures and then got into their cars and drove away. That's how most of the residents interacted with tourists and that may have been the reason why I did not get any response initially. They must have been taken aback and it took them a few seconds to decide what to do: accept or decline my invitation. Finally, the man spoke. "Thank you," he said. "Some water, please."

"Come around," I said, "through the wrought iron gate and up the stairs."

While they were finding their way up, I threw on a shirt and straightened out the chairs.

One by one, they filed into my living room, and I introduced myself and shook hands with them and they gave me their names. The elderly man called himself Gustavus, or Gus for short. He introduced the older lady, as his wife, Zenia and the young girl, as their daughter, Yulie. Gus had a squarish head, a short and stocky build and he was deeply tanned, with lots of wrinkles around weary-looking eyes. He had a bushy, droopy mustache that made him look like Albert Einstein. Zenia displayed the heaviness of haunch that older ladies of the Levant often display. She wore a shapeless, pale blue cotton dress that came below her knees and a floppy cloth hat made of denim. Yulie, who looked as though she may have been in her early thirties, had curly honey-gold hair streaked with blonde highlights. Her eyes, like those of a harrier hawk, had tawny irises with tiny bronze flecks in them. She looked very nautical and fresh in a white cotton shorts and a T-shirt with blue and white stripes.

I urged them to sit down and got busy fetching the water and setting glasses on the coffee table. They arranged themselves on my not-very-elegant plastic chairs and gazed around with curiosity filled eyes. I started up the pedestal fan and soon its gentle oscillations filled the room with cool air currents.

"Where are you folks from?" I asked, placing the water bottles before them.

A natural question, I suppose, and a way of starting a conversation. They remained silent as if trying to figure out what to say.

Finally, Yulie spoke up.

"From the Greek side, south Cyprus."

"Oh," I said, genuinely surprised. "Your English is so good, I thought you were from England.

"We lived in England," Gus said, "for many years. I worked there. In a hotel."

"Really? Which one?"

"*Dorchester.*"

"Oh, that one is super-expensive. Only oil millionaires can afford to stay there."

Gus nodded.

"I know," he said with a wry smile. "I worked in the kitchen as a chef."

"You're from America. Right?" Yulie asked.

"How did you guess? Is it that obvious?"

"Your accent," Yulie said. "And you have a certain way. No shyness. Americans are like that. Bold and friendly."

"You have a British accent." I said. "Were you born in England?"

"No. I was born right here."

A little smile flitted across her lips. Her mother said something to Gus in Greek. I had a feeling the old lady understood everything we said but preferred using Greek.

"What do you mean right here?" I said.

"I mean, *right here*. In this very house."

"You're kidding me."

Gus shook his head and chuckled, a mischievous gleam lighting up his eyes.

"She's telling the truth," he said. "This was my father's house. I grew up in this house. Yulie was born here. This whole village used to be Greek."

"That's amazing," I said, a bit shaken by this revelation. "You must have left when the war broke out."

I didn't want to say "the Turkish invasion in 1974." The topic stirred painful memories and neither Cypriot-Greeks nor Cypriot-Turks relished bringing it up.

Gus nodded.

"We left just hours before the first soldiers of the Turkish army landed on the beaches. Yulie was just a child, about six years old."

"Is this the first time you've been back since then?" I asked.

"No. No. We've been here several times, over the years," Gus said. "We have British passports, you see. It is easy for us to come and go."

I felt a bit more at ease. They did not seem to mind talking about their experiences. The passage of years had tempered the sense of loss and grief and the anger they must have felt at being uprooted by the hand of history. "Has it changed much? I mean, from the way it was back in 1974."

"Completely," said Yulie. "Many of the houses are still the same, of course, and the streets are the same, but it feels different."

"You were so small when you left," I said. "Do you remember the way it used to be?"

Yulie laughed.

"In a strange way. But my memories are also mixed up with memories of similar villages in south Cyprus."

Gus spoke up. "It's so different now – so clean. Like a model village in a glass-case. Every time I come here, I only hear silence. It is so quiet. And I hardly see any people."

"I love the silence," I said. "It is such a relief to get up here, far from the noise and crazy traffic of Kyrenia."

Gus sighed.

"I understand what you say," he said. "But for me this silence … it is like a cemetery. It feels like a village of ghosts. When we lived here it was a loud, busy place with children laughing and shouting, goats bleating, dogs barking, women gossiping in the lanes, men – old and young – busy with their daily tasks. All the chaos and well-ordered muddle of Greek village life. And the smells – Ouff – strong! All the normal odors you have around farms. You see, donkeys were everywhere and also cows and sheep and chicken. We lived like that. Every house had a donkey room on the ground floor. Farm animals were always nearby. But for us that wasn't a foul smell. It was okay. It was natural."

"I still remember the crowing of roosters early in the morning," Yulie said. "They always woke me up. And the smell of smoke rising from cooking fires at dawn."

Their point of view, the picture they painted of the village fascinated me. The Karmi they remembered had been a different sort of place.

"I've never heard the crowing of cocks," I said. "I've seen a few dogs around but I haven't really heard any barking. Nor have I seen any children."

"And no fleas, I bet," Gus said with a chuckle. "Fleas were our constant companions. We got so used to them, hardly noticed them. And huge, furry, black spiders."

"Oh, yes. I've seen them. Tarantulas, right?"

Gus nodded.

"This is not the village I grew up in," Gus shook his head sadly. "Cyprus has changed a lot. And not all the changes are good. But that is a discussion for another day. We should be going."

"No, no, stay," I said. "Finish your water. This is your house, really. I am just a visitor."

Gus rose and the others rose with him.

"We are all visitors, my friend," he said, gently. "This is something you learn as you get old. And, sooner or later, we must leave."

"Please come again," I said. "I want to hear more about Karmi, I mean the old Karmi."

I didn't want them to leave. My curiosity had been roused and I wanted to learn more about the house, about their experiences as refugees, about life before 1974 when the Greek and Turkish communities lived side by side.

"Where are you living now," I asked Yulie. "England?"

"No. We are in Lefkosa," she said. "The Greek side, naturally. We call it Nicosia."

"That's not far," I said. "You must come again."

Yulie smiled and nodded. Her eyes radiated friendliness.

"Can I have your phone number?" I asked. "I want to stay in touch. There are so many questions I want to ask."

Her parents had already gone down the stairs and stood waiting in the courtyard. Yulie dug into her handbag and produced a pen. I grabbed a notebook and she wrote down her number.

"My mobile number."

"Thanks."

I walked with them to the wrought iron gate and we shook hands. As they walked down the stone steps that led to the plaza, I waited under the shade of the jasmine bush. At the bottom of the stairs, they looked back and waved once and then turned onto the street.

Transforming strangers into friends is always a good idea, I suppose. But just then I wasn't really sure I would call Yulie. I didn't want to mislead her in any way or give her the impression that I was interested in establishing a romantic link with her. She certainly did seem like an intelligent and clear-headed young woman — an impression that was underscored by her fluency in English. And I was glad she had given me her phone number.

Section 2

A few days later, on a Friday afternoon, I called Cardiff. I was on my way to Erjan airport to pick up Anara and I thought he'd be good company on the long trip to the airport.

"Are you free?"

"Why?"

"A friend is arriving at Erjan. I am going there to pick her up. Can you come along?"

"I was just on my way to *Pegasus*."

"No problem. We can stop there and have a drink before we start."

That pleased him.

On the way to the airport, I told him about Anara, who she was and how we had met in Almaty. The whole story. The trip to the airport took an hour. I had plenty of time to give him the big picture, explain what she meant to me. Long car trips impose a kind of compulsory togetherness, an enforced intimacy that in turn creates the proper ambience for confessions and revelations. Somehow it is easier to admit your most secret desires when you are driving, your eyes hypnotized by the unreeling ribbon of road ahead of you. You talk as though you were alone in the car, as though you were talking to yourself. Cardiff was a good listener. And he kept saying "humm, humm" to encourage me, I suppose, and to indicate that he had not fallen asleep.

"She's young, you said?" he asked eventually.

"Very. No more than twenty-five, I think."

"Not married, but has a child? A girl. Six years old."

"Those are the facts."

"Hummm," he said. "And you claim that she likes you. That, in fact, she is in love with you?"

"I do make this claim," I said, grinning.

"Upon what evidence do you make this claim?"

"She moved in with me, lived with me for nearly a year …"

"She may have done that to get away from dear old Mama."

"Not true. They get along very well."

"Hummm," Cardiff said and then added, "When she lived with you, did she have a job?"

"No."

"Ha, so you supported her?"

"I suppose. But listen, we had a wonderful time together. We cooked together, ate together, slept together. Isn't that evidence enough?"

"And she said she loved you?"

"Yes. She said that quite often, as a matter of fact."

"And she's a normal girl – not blind in one eye or lame or deficient in mental powers?"

"Wait till you see her. She has the style and grace of a fashion model – real elegance."

"This is strange. Very strange."

I had to laugh over this gentle teasing. "That it is, mon ami," I said. "On this point I have to agree with you. But there are more things in heaven and earth than are dreamed of in your texts on Jurisprudence."

Cardiff did not say anything for a while. We were speeding through a flat, featureless plain now, the "Mesaoria," fuzzy with bleached buff grass, ochreous stubble and raw sienna passages of bare land here and there. As we got closer to the airport, I could see the flash and glimmer of corrugated metal roofs and glass towers in the distance.

"She might have a problem getting a visa," Cardiff said in a low voice, almost as though he were talking to himself.

"They issue them at the airport, don't they? North Cyprus has no embassies in many countries to give visas."

"Yes, but they don't like young girls from Russia."

"She's not from Russia."

"I meant Russian-speaking countries – former members of the former Soviet Union."

"Oh, really. And why is that?"

"They don't want them working here. It's this thing about these girls working in the gambling casinos and night-clubs … creating problems."

"But that's absurd," I said. "She'll be a tourist like any other tourist from England or Germany. They get six-month visas, don't they? Renewable six month visas."

He nodded and then added. "That's a different category. Those are old folks with money, mostly retired Europeans."

"Why should that make a difference?"

"It shouldn't, but it does. These people don't take away jobs from the locals. And they bring in lots of money."

"Anara has no plans to work. She'll be my guest." I said.

He made no response but I could sense his unease. His mind seemed to be processing a thought or two. His unease made me uneasy, but I kept quiet.

In the Arrivals concourse I paced restlessly, my palms wet with sweat in spite of the chilly air-conditioning. Eventually, the Turkish Airlines flight from Istanbul landed. I watched the passengers get off, collect their luggage, come out and greet their friends. Ten minutes went by, then twenty. No Anara. Perhaps she had missed the flight somehow. But that did not seem possible. She had called me just before boarding the plane at Istanbul. Then, suddenly, as a door opened and closed, I caught a glimpse of her bending to pick up her bag from the luggage carousel. Relief flooded my chest. Our eyes met and we waved to each other. She mouthed some words I could not understand and then walked down a corridor accompanied by a Customs official.

I looked at Cardiff. He looked at me. We both knew this meant trouble. A kind of helpless anxiety made my knees weak.

"They could make her go back, you know," Cardiff muttered gloomily, adding to my tension.

"Damn them. Cardiff, we've got to rescue her somehow."

As we were debating the best course of action, a guy in uniform came out with Anara at his side. She pointed a finger at me and the official made a gesture to indicate that I was to follow him. I grabbed Cardiff's arm.

"Come," I hissed into his ear. "You've got to help me."

Soon we were in a small office lit by pale fluorescence, located somewhere in the middle of the airport's maze of offices and cold corridors. The only decoration, Attaturk's portrait, directed a stern look at us from a wall. Men in dull green uniforms stood around, with guns at their belts. Anara looked at me, her eyes wide with worry. I flashed her an encouraging smile as we walked in.

"So what's the problem, officer?" I asked. The man in charge, a middle-aged fellow, spoke just enough English to understand basic syntax. Cardiff knew a little Turkish. Now began a confusing three-way conversation. The questions were simple enough. Who are you? Why are you here? How do you know each other? Etc. Etc.

It took an hour of garbled dialogue in English and Turkish, before we were able to establish that I taught at the university and that Anara would be staying with me.. No, she was not going to work during her stay in North Cyprus. Yes, she had enough money of her own. Some of the remarks they made and concerns they displayed hid rather ugly questions that they could not ask directly – Was she a drug-mule? Did she intend to corrupt the morals of the Turkish Republic of North Cyprus by prostituting her body? So on and so forth. The discussion went round and round like a snake trying to swallow its tail. Cardiff argued brilliantly with British clarity and precision. Finally, they gave in, stamped a visa on Anara's passport and handed it back to her. Relieved to be out of their clutches, I did not stop to check how much time they had given her. Later, when I looked at her passport, I realized that they had only given her 60 days! All my anxiety came flooding back, but I said nothing to Anara. I did not want her to worry. Surely there would be a way to extend her stay. For the moment, just the thought that I would have her with me, in my house, in my arms, in my bed, pushed all other thoughts out of my mind.

"I can't believe it." I said to her when we were finally back in Karmi. "We did it. We actually did it."

A secret, smug pride filled me with self-satisfaction.

"Were you worried?" I asked her teasingly. "Tell me. Did you think we'd never see each other again?"

"Of course," she said.

"I was also worried. Though I tried to hide this from you."

"I thought you would forgot me. And find another girlfriend."

Her bad grammar made me chuckle.

"Shame on you! How could you think that?"

She giggled uncontrollably. Then she turned a serious face to me and said: "Honey, how about your visa?"

"The university takes care of that," I said. "They do it for all the expat teachers as a group. Simplifies the whole process. Thank god, I don't have to worry about it."

"O, that's wonderful," she said.

On that first evening we were like two puppies, giddy with joy, tumbling over each other, terribly relieved to be together finally. For the time being, at least, nothing else mattered. All worries, all problems seemed to recede, fade away. Now that I had her with me – a physical presence, a real, living, breathing person – I realized suddenly how much I had missed her. Through the weeks and months of separation, I had kept my emotions in check. I had kept a tight control over all thoughts and feelings connected with her. I wouldn't permit longing, despair or any regrets to shadow my mind. I had not permitted myself to entertain any other thought beyond a firm belief that we would be together again. But now all kinds of suppressed emotions welled up along with memories of our time together. Everything we had said and done came flooding back into my mind.

Anara loved the house. She laughed with uncontrollable delight when she saw the climbing yellow rose bushes, the bougainvillea and the jasmine that shaded the wrought iron gate and our little courtyard. Everything about the village pleased her. She loved the narrow cobblestone lane that led from our house to the main street and the marvelous quietness of the place. She loved the blue wooden shutters. She loved the crimson floor tiles. "I'm so happy," she said, as I kissed her eagerly under the dappled shade of the almond tree surrounded by an immense and ancient silence. And as I held her close to me, I could hear her throbbing heart above the rustle of sea breezes stirring the cypresses and the soft crooning of pigeons. In the evening, after the sun went down behind the dark fingers of the Beshparmak range, we went up to the flat roof. From here, at an altitude of a thousand feet, you had a fabulous vantage point. You could see the entire coast sinking northwards in gradual undulations, the muted green and raw umber terraces tumbling down to the sea where the harbor and chalk-white buildings of Kyrenia melted and re-assembled themselves in a trembling haze. To the south, high on its crag, sat St. Hilarion, its gold and sulphur stones glowing against a sky now turning a deep heliotrope. Then as a violet dusk settled over the island, the valley filled up with purple and mauve shadows and the walls of the ancient castle caught and held the bronze beams of the setting sun and throbbed like an amber casket lit up from within.

On that first night, after months of enforced separation, months of longing, we romped around the house like children, made love greedily, as though we were sitting down to a feast of nothing but cakes and candies. All the desires pent up for weeks and months rose high and spilled over as we came together in the jasmine-scented darkness. Not saying much, just letting kisses and caresses speak, just letting shattering, shuddering spasms of the flesh sweep us away. For a little while at least the worries of the world went away and only the taintless joy of being in each other's arms remained. Later, when I woke up in the wee hours, the pleasure of finding Anara asleep with her beautiful back towards me engulfed every nerve of my body with desire. As I squeezed myself up close seeking her warmth, she drew up her knees sleepily so that we fitted into each other, her long spine snug against my chest. She seemed to stir slowly into a semi-wakeful state and reached back. I felt her hand seeking me and I responded to her touch.

I heard the phone ring as though in a dream. Struggling up out of a deep sleep, I glanced at the digital clock on the desk. The glowing, orange numerals announced 3:05. No dream, this. The landline phone was ringing, loudly, relentlessly. At this hour of dawn, it had to be mother. She had this number, not the one for the mobile. I hadn't given her the mobile number because I feared she'd call me at inconvenient times: when I was in class, teaching or in a faculty meeting or in bed. She had little notion of time zones, especially when it came to regions that were many time zones away from Chicago.

I stumbled out of bed groggily, tangled in bedsheets, placed bare feet on cold tiles and picked up the receiver.

"Hello."

"Robbie, is that you?"

"Yes, Ma. What is it? It is three in the morning here, for god's sake."

"Come back," she said, in a high-pitched whine. "I want you back. Come back!"

"Why? What's the matter?"

"I'm sick," she said. "I don't feel well."

"Have you seen the doctor?"

"I've seen him," she shouted.

"What did he say? What's the problem?"

"You know – diabetes, weak heart, weight."

"Yes, I know. Did he prescribe something?"

"Some new pills. But they don't do any good."

"Well, go see him again."

"I want you here. Can't you come back right away?"

"Look, Ma, be rational. I've got a contract. I can't just up and leave in the middle of the semester."

"Break the contract. You don't have to work. I'll …"

"But I want to work. And if I break the contract with this university, no one will hire me. I'll …"

"It doesn't matter. I want you back."

I detected a note of hysteria in her voice.

"Just go see the doctor. He'll fix you up."

"If you do not come back, I'm cutting you out of my will."

By now she had started to scream.

"You won't get a penny from me. I won't leave you the house – nothing. I'll … I'll …"

"Stop it, Ma. Go see the doctor. Don't threaten me."

She always fell back on such tactics, made drastic statements, whenever I wouldn't do what she wanted me to do, whenever her frustration overwhelmed her self-control. With a kind of bravado, I always ignored her ill humor and tried to cajole her back to some form of rationality, but she worried me. In her crazy moods, she could do anything. She could – the possibility existed – leave everything to her pet poodle, Frodo.

I heard her sobbing, her voice choking on her words.

"Now listen, Ma. Go see your doctor. I'll talk to you tomorrow. Okay?"

I hung up.

The phone call had woken up Anara. I snapped on the stair-hall light and in the obliquely, yellowish glow, I saw her looking at me with questioning eyes.

"Mother," I said.

"Is she okay?"

"It's the same old thing. She just wants me back."

"What did she say?

"What she always says. "Come back. I need you. Come back."

"What will you do?"

"Nothing. Go back to sleep."

But for me returning to sleep was now impossible.

I reached for the bottle of Cypriot brandy that sat on the dining table and poured myself a couple of double-shots. Cardiff had introduced me to this stuff. It goes down smoothly, he had said to me, gets to work quickly on your system, and later when you are in the sobering up phase, it doesn't inflict the nasty after effects that other drinks inflict. Cardiff could be trusted on such matters. Soon a pleasing warmth started to spread over my limbs. I turned off the light, sat down on the edge of the bed in the brooding darkness and sipped the brandy slowly. Mother's impetuous, imperative calls were (and always had been) a normal part of my life. And whenever she called, I heard the same refrain, the same commands and threats. I had learned to deal with them over the years. Politely but firmly, I would tell her to calm herself. At times this approach worked, at other times she continued her harangues and accusations until I hung up. I had pretty much stopped taking her tantrums seriously.

Within days it seemed our life in Karmi fell into a comfortable pattern. We established our daily routines and also adopted some rituals of the natives. As a rule, we got up early to enjoy the sight of the rising sun and the cool morning air that tasted like a chilled glass of white wine. After lunch we would lie down for a siesta and at sundown we were always on the roof – either our own or that of a neighbor – having drinks and watching the stones of St. Hilarion turn to glowing embers in the fading light.

On Friday evenings Cardiff would hire a taxi and come up to Karmi and we'd ask Fiona to join us. She had a fund of amusing stories about the village and the people who had lived there and she did not mind sharing them with us. We also got to know the Bralestones, an elegant, elderly couple from Ireland, who were year round residents of Karmi. They lived right next door and were as dedicated to the cocktail hour as we were. They would come over bringing along bottles of Gin and Tonic water. And we'd hail Barbara Preston, the retired schoolteacher, who lived in the house near ours and invite her to come over. She also enjoyed spending every evening on her roof with a ready supply of scotch and soda at hand. She'd been coming to Karmi since her teens and loved the island. A few yards further up the steep road lived Marsden, an elderly English chap who rode a powerful Japanese motorbike. But he didn't like it very much and often waxed nostalgic for English makes. He would say to me that he'd give his left arm to own an old *Ariel,* a *BSA,* a

Norton or a *Royal Enfield.* Many an afternoon I whiled away with him, drinking beer on his spacious terrace under the speckled shadow of an olive tree, discussing the historic and economic factors that led to the decline of British industry. Marsden was witty and under the influence of gin he became even more amusing and rather sarcastic and his rapier-sharp comments on the deeds and misdeeds of his fellow countrymen were always hilarious.

To me it looked as though these expats had mastered the art of living in Karmi. They focused on each day, each moment, keenly aware of the vibrant and vital Present. The Past and the Future did not matter much. But it would be a mistake to think that they were all idlers who spent their days toasting themselves in the sun. I found, to my surprise, that nearly all the people I got to know were engaged in some art, or craft or hobby. Some painted in oils or watercolors, some sculpted and everyone got involved in gardening and home-improvement projects. Often I would see frail, elderly chaps up on rickety ladders plastering, painting, and pruning. Some worked in the restaurants and bars in Karmi; some even had jobs outside of Karmi. They were Zen masters, these expats. They knew how to suck the marrow out of the moment gifted to them by life.

~

Section 3

Anara had never seen the sea, never been on a real beach because the Kazakh Republic is land-locked. All her swimming had been done in the municipal pools of Almaty.

"This is absurd," I said to her. "We've got to go swimming."

"Let's go," she said, her eyes bright with excitement.

She had brought a bikini with her and wanted to show it off.

"Let's take Cardiff along," I suggested. "The fresh air will do him good."

But Cardiff had planned to spend his Saturday afternoon in *Pegasus* and it took a bit of prodding and cajoling to make him change his mind.

"Look, there is a good seafood place nearby." I told him. "We can eat there and watch the sunset. My treat. You'll love it."

He tried to resist but I pressed him.

"We're coming to pick you up. Be ready."

We got to the beach in the late afternoon, paid a small fee to the gatekeepers and walked onto the esplanade. By now the sun was beaming down bright and hot and everything seemed to tremble and melt in the shimmering heat waves. Three rows of beach chairs and umbrellas with red and blue stripes curved along the water's edge. A crowd of men and women of all ages plus lots of children frolicked in the water or lay on the chairs. Most of the people looked European but there were many locals too. The sand scalded the soles of my feet and glittered like flakes of mica and the sunlight chipped the water into jade shards that stabbed one's eyes. We stripped down to bathing trunks and headed for the water quickly.

It felt chilly at first, but then it turned nice and warm and cradled one's body in a snug embrace. The beach faced a tranquil cove, protected from big waves by a natural breakwater created by a barrier of jutting rocks. From the line where the waves expired in dry sand, the ground sloped gently down towards deep water. The sea moved lazily in this zone and low waves made indecent advances with liquid, probing fingers. Cardiff walked carefully into the water because he did not want to get his hair wet. He went in until the water came to his shoulders. Then he walked back out and lay down on a chair, lit a cigarette and ordered a beer.

Anara and I flung ourselves into the water, splashing and thrashing wildly. Almost delirious with joy, she could not stop laughing and giggling as she dove in and popped up like dolphin, her wet hair slicked back, her undulant body riding the waves. I pursued her in mock attacks and every time I tried to grab her arms or legs, she squealed with delight like a little girl. She would dive under water and grab my ankles trying to throw me over. I would let her come near, then wrap an arm around her waist and wrestle her down. She'd wriggle free and come up sputtering and laughing. We fooled around like this until the cold began to pinch.

I came out of the water, got a beer and lay down on a beach chair next to Cardiff to dry off and warm up. Anara continued to swim by herself. After a while I saw her walk up out of the water. A rain of diamond-bright drops of water fell from her limbs, as she came towards us, her spread fingers combing the blue-green sea. Her body glistened in the strong sunlight. A creamy froth clung to her thighs and it looked as though she were being carried ashore on a raft of foam.

"Here comes Aphrodite," said Cardiff.

And indeed, she looked lovely as the goddess and all the men and women nearby stared at her. The taut muscles along her thighs flexed as she walked up onto the dry sand and her hips had the flared elegance of Grecian amphorae.

"Brrrr," she said. "I'm cold now."

She lay down on a chair next to me. We soaked up the heat until it became unbearable and then went back into the water to cool off. We did this several times.

As we lay there, the sun sank lower and lower gradually and people began to leave. Presently, we decided to leave also and find food. We washed the sand and salt off under a shower and got into dry clothes. I was parched and hungry and felt ready for some refreshment.

"Ooooh God!" Anara said. "I had so much fun today."

"Who's hungry?" I said. "Let's get something to eat."

By now the sun had vanished below the horizon and the sky took on the tint of diluted lemonade and a throbbing mauve quietness settled on the coast. It was that mysterious hour between day and night when Nature seems to halt its operations for a few minutes and takes a deep breath. We walked along a paved path that ran adjacent to the beach towards a seafood place. The restaurant had a wide terrace set with tables and chairs. From the edge of the terrace one could see the waves crashing and frothing on the rocks below. A young Turkish girl took us to a table covered with a white cloth and gleaming cutlery. A fresh, salt-scented breeze came up from the sea and made the tablecloths flap and flutter. A waiter came and lit a small oil-lamp that sat in the middle of the table and took our drink orders. Cardiff wanted scotch and soda. "I'll have the same," I told the waiter. Anara opted for cherry juice, this being her most favorite drink.

The sun had darkened Anara several shades and her skin glowed now with rosy-golden warmth. The sea in front of us, infused with the day's heat, smoldered in its crucible going from Prussian blue to the deep mottled purple of ripe plums. On the horizon towards the north, towering cumulus clouds could be seen bubbling up above the mountains of Anatolia.

As we were studying the menu, the drinks arrived.

While we were in the midst of a discussion about what we should order, Cardiff spotted someone he knew.

"My god! That's Janet. I haven't seen her in ages," he said. "Excuse me a sec. I'll go over and say hello."

He walked over to a table where an elderly man sporting a blue blazer and trim white mustache sat next to a deeply tanned woman who could have been his wife. With them was a young girl with straw-yellow hair, their daughter possibly. Cardiff greeted them, said a few words, and came back.

"They are from Guildford," he said. "I got to know Janet briefly during a phase of my life. Then she got married. That's her husband, James Morton and their daughter, Freya. They are here for a few days."

He didn't say anything more and I didn't probe.

When the waiter came around again and stood by our table, his pen poised over his note-pad, I said, "How about a bottle of wine? A white, I suppose?"

But Cardiff shook his head.

"The whites are often terrible, especially the imports. They let them sit through the hot months on the dock at Adana and ruin them."

"A red?"

"But we are ordering fish, right?"

"Right. Then what do you suggest?"

"Beer is best." Cardiff said. "Efes, isn't half bad and they serve it ice-cold, exactly the way you Americans like it."

"But you? You don't like it ice-cold."

"Oh, I'll let it sit till it loses its chill and fizz."

Cardiff ate very little as a norm but what he ate he chose carefully and knew a lot about local food and drink. I let him guide us, help us make the right choices. We all ordered farm-raised trout, pan fried in butter with steamed vegetables and pilaf on the side, though it seemed odd to order farm-raised fish on an island.

"The ocean's all around us for god's sakes!" I said. "Can't anyone catch fish?"

"They do, but not in great numbers," Cardiff said. "The Mediterranean around here is fished out. There isn't much left. The restaurants get it from Turkey or the North Sea – frozen."

As we were eating, lights twinkled on one-by-one in the houses on the hills and the lower slopes of the Beshparmak range began to glitter like the star-cancelled sky above. Sitting there on the jutting terrace I felt as though we were on an ocean liner, heading out to sea. Anara reached out and grabbed my hand.

"Are you enjoying yourself?" I asked her.

She nodded her head vigorously but then made a face.

"My visa will expire soon. I don't want to go back to Almaty."

Her words brought me down to earth quickly. Like the serpent in Eden, this problem still lurked in the background poisoning our happiness.

"We've got to get her a visa extension," I said to Cardiff. "I don't want her to stay here illegally."

"You can try," he said. "You'll have to go to the police."

That sounded odd to my American ears. But I figured there must be some logic to this. Cyprus did things in its own Cypriot way. We would just have to play along, follow the rules.

"In Kyrenia?" I asked.

"No. To the main police station in Lefkosa. They handle immigration-related matters over there." Cardiff said.

"Fine," I said, squeezing Anara's hand to reassure her. "We'll go to Lefkosa."

I felt sure that getting an extension would not be difficult. We would just show up in front of the proper functionary and it would all be handled smoothly. I had been impressed by the casual attitude of the immigration chaps when I had landed at Erjan. I had no doubt that the business would be taken care of in a logical, rational manner.

The terrace strung with fairy lights, the luminous evening and the scotch and sodas in my belly conspired to chase away all anxieties. Surely we would be able to overcome minor bureaucratic problems? Hadn't we leaped over the hurdles of time and distance to be with each other? I was not going to let some low-level minion in the immigration office wreck our dreams.

The Renault lurched and bounced violently as it raced towards Lefkosa. Leaving Kyrenia behind, we cut through the bare, brown hills that make up the eastern edge of the Beshparmak range. Tall cliffs, the color of raw liver, rose up on either side of the road. This part of the island does not get much rain so the terrain looked dry and sandy, dotted with huge burnt umber boulders in odd shapes and sizes. Soon we were sliding down a long, straight slope that led towards the central plain or "Mesaoria." The sun directed a flame-thrower at us and the heat sat on my head like a skullcap made of hot sheet metal. The further away we got from the coast, the hotter it became. By now a thrombosis of pain had begun to swell and throb at my left temple. Anara also seemed to be wilting and her misery seeped into me and increased the sum of my misery.

"We have to do this," I said grimly. "We have got to get your visa extended."

She nodded and squeezed my hand.

Eventually, Lefkosa appeared on the horizon, a putty-gray collage of three and four story concrete buildings. I did not see much greenery.

Nor did I notice any Moorish motifs one sees in Turkish cities. No domes or minarets or stone filigree. The city loomed before us like a cinderblock nightmare, a collection of featureless cement boxes in pastel hues.

"I'm glad we don't live here," I muttered.

"I did not think it would be like this," Anara added.

I parked the Renault at the bus terminal where many unshaven men were lurking about in the shadows of buildings. When they spotted Anara, they gazed at her with hungry appreciation. We went into a little café and greeted the proprietor with polite "Merhabas."

"Could you tell us how to get to the Police Station?" I asked him.

He assessed us with weary eyes for a full minute, unhappy that we had not purchased anything. Then he waved a hand in a generally northeasterly direction.

"Teshekkur ederim, Teshekkur ederim," I said, thanking him profusely. And we set forth to find the place.

We left the car parked where it was and set off on foot to find the police station. The blazing sun brought my brain to a brisk boil. I cursed the litter of airport officials whose bureaucratic myopia was putting us through this torment. Then I cursed myself for dressing up in a blazer and necktie thinking that formal garb would make an impression on clerical foot-draggers and they would expedite everything. But now the necktie seemed to be strangling me and the blazer felt like woolen blanket.

"I'd like to murder that mothersucking bastard who gave you a two month visa," I muttered.

Anara simply shook her head silently, her mouth clamped in a grimace of agony. Speaking required too much effort and she obviously needed every ounce of energy to simply stay conscious. Beads of sweat stood out on her forehead and her blouse had turned a darker color in areas of dampness. After a hot hike through some dusty streets we finally reached the Police Station – another charmless, concrete bunker. Several young men were loitering in the lobby waiting as though they were expecting some outcome of terrific importance. I asked them about the visa office.

"Kapitan," one said and pointed down a long corridor. "Muhajerat office. Go right there."

"Muhajerat" was Turkish for immigration.

We walked down the corridor and found the room. The Kapitan sat behind a small desk and several men with heavy mustaches sat in rows of chairs arrayed against the walls on either side leaving a clear area in the middle. He was an obese, fair-haired young man, and he had trussed himself up in a tight fitting uniform. His belt cut his belly deeply, rather cruelly, I thought. He had pink cheeks, a pink mouth and pink eyes with up-curled eyelashes.

The mustachioed audience with three-day growths of beard on blue jowls sat staring adoringly at the Kapitan, giving him their fullest attention so as to not miss a syllable of what he uttered. Obviously clients, they had come to fawn on him and bask in the bureaucratic glow of his ineffable presence. By standing in the doorway and staring, I finally got the Kapitan to notice me.

"Hello," I said, "This young lady would like her visa extended."

It took a few seconds for the English to filter through his sluggish brain cells and get translated into Turkish. Then his eyes narrowed to slits to indicate, I suppose, that he had understood me.

"Passaport," he said.

Anara gave me her passport and I handed it to the Kapitan.

He examined it carefully for a few moments and then flung it across the desk.

"Cannot do," he said.

"But they told us to come here."

"Who said?"

"The police in Kyrenia."

"No, no. Go to airport."

"We did go to airport. They said go to Lefkosa, to head office."

"No," said the sweet-faced Kapitan, "go to Erjan."

"Look, I teach Law at the University. This lady is my guest. She would like to stay for six months."

"Do you know her?" he said suddenly.

This question took me by surprise. But I volleyed back deftly, I thought.

"Yes, of course. I know her," I said. "We met in Almaty – the Kazakh Republic. I was teaching there."

"What is her mother's name?"

"Excuse me?"

"What is her mother's name?"

The question came as a total surprise. I tried to remember Anara's mother's name but my memory couldn't dredge up anything. My cheeks burned with frustration.

"I don't know her mother's name," I said, feeling flustered and rather stupid.

He directed a quick, knowing glance at his friends and the corners of his lips curled upwards in a little smile. His buddies smiled back at him and they said something in Turkish. He had clearly made some sort of point. Then he leaned back in his chair and started to swell and expand as though he were being pumped full of air. He clearly relished the power that his position invested him with. His mustachioed fan club also seemed to enjoy seeing their friend exercise his authority.

"Only airport police give visa," he said, a distinct finality in his tone. "Go to Erjan."

He wanted to be rid of us. Any lie would do. My mouth shut itself tight over my tongue. I had nothing more to say to him. My nerves twanged like breaking banjo wires and a helpless exasperation overwhelmed me. I wanted to kill the man. Had I a pistol in my hand, I would have emptied it into his stupid, arrogant skull. I picked up Anara's passport from the desk, said "Thank you, thank you" and bowing with exaggerated formality, backed out of the office. I thought I would puncture his officious smugness and pomposity with politeness. Whether I accomplished this goal or not, I cannot say.

We tramped back by scalding sunlight to the car, speechless with frustration and repressed anger. Anara said not a word on the return journey from Lefkosa to Karmi, but her mouth, set in a thin, grim line revealed her state of mind. My personal disgust found expression in mouth-deep abuse as I cursed visa officials born and yet to be born in their generations and wished them consigned to the hottest lodgments of Hell. Only after we had reached the cool air of high Karmi did we make an effort to speak. Later, after refreshing showers and drinks we went up to the roof to watch the coming on of lights in the valley below and ponder the lessons of the day.

"What will we do, honey?" Anara asked me, as I studied the lengthening shadows in the valley far below.

"I don't know," I said glumly. "I'll talk to Cardiff. Let's see what he says."

"If I got a job, I could get a work visa," Anara murmured.

"I suppose, but jobs are hard to get," I said. "And you'll need some sort of transportation."

We left the matter there, unresolved.

Anara's visa problem certainly held our attention in the days that followed but there were other matters that we had to think about.

"I wish I had a scooter," Anara said, one day. "I could go and get groceries by myself."

"Do you know how to ride one?"

"No," she said and admitted that she had never even been on one.

"They can be very dangerous, honey," I said. "You could get yourself killed on this twisty mountain road."

"I'll be careful," she countered. "I just get bored sitting in the house all by myself."

"Then come with me to the university."

"I do come with you … but if I had a scooter, I would be more independent … do more. I could get over to Kyrenia. I might even get a job and a work-visa."

She had a point. She came with me to the university quite often and while I did my work, she kept herself busy at the library or did English lessons on the computer. Around lunchtime we usually went over to the cafeteria and ate excellent Turkish food for very little money. Then in the late afternoon, we would head home, stopping on the way at the grocery store to pick up any items we needed. This had become a routine.

On other days, she opted to stay home because she wanted to wash her hair, deal with the laundry or clean the house. But it soon became apparent that without any mode of transportation at her disposal, she felt a bit stranded and isolated in Karmi. She had no way of going to Kyrenia. Mini-buses only plied along the coast road and did not come up to Karmi. To catch one she'd have to walk ten miles down the mountain. If she got a scooter, I would also feel freer, and I could come and go as I pleased. I wouldn't feel guilty that I had left her stranded in Karmi if on a whim I decided to stop at *Pegasus* and have a beer with Cardiff. Eventually, after much discussion and analysis, it was decided that she should have her scooter. The climate of Cyprus certainly seemed ideal for scootering.

The shop that sold motorbikes and scooters sat on Ecevit Street, one of the busiest thoroughfares in Kyrenia. Cleverly named "The Motorbike Shop" and rather tiny, it was cluttered with different models of motorcycles and scooters, both new and old. John, a jovial young

Englishman who had as round and as full a face as Henry VIII, owned and managed the place. He had a most trustworthy smile and a friendly manner and the selling skills of a seasoned Levantine businessman. Soon he had me well in hand, malleable as silly-putty and ready to pay any price he chose to demand. He had spent much of his life in Cyprus. He knew the laws and regulations that went with owning a vehicle and he promised to handle all matters relating to insurance and registration.

Anara's eyes alighted on a shiny, new cherry-red scooter and she fell in love with it instantly. I tried to haggle with John over the price, knowing that in the end he would win and I would lose. But I bargained anyway, thinking that he expected me to and at one point I even got up and pretended to leave. Clever John was just waiting for me to make this gesture. He countered my move with his trump card ... He threw in a carryall box for small items and a matching ruby-red helmet. That did it. I knew when to admit defeat. I gave in and handed over fresh green American dollars and he handed over the keys. We signed more papers to complete the transaction and I pushed the scooter out of the showroom. Anara jumped up behind me and I eased it into the flow of traffic on Ecevit Street as a new sense of freedom made my heart race.

The air felt fresh as it skimmed over me and the sunlight lost its sting. I saw and sensed a different Cyprus. Everything seemed more vivid, more immediate. The sky looked like a polished sapphire and the colors of the Beshparmak range seemed richer. To avoid the traffic on the coast road, I took a back way to the university where we had left the Renault. This road had a rural, deserted feel as it meandered through olive groves and frothing fields of yellow flowers that wild mustard puts out. We putt-putted through the Zeytinlik, a tiny village that always seemed to be snoozing in a welter of shadows where a few old men could always be seen sipping tea and smoking. We waved to them as we scootered past and they waved back pleased, I'm sure, by the sight of a pretty girl riding pillion. We got to the university late in the afternoon and the parking lot had emptied out. I told Anara to sit astride the scooter and I started going through some preliminaries. I showed her the brake levers on the handlebar, got her to start the engine and get accustomed to the sound and showed her how the accelerator grip worked to rev up. A bit scared and nervous at first, she, nevertheless, did not hesitate to get astride the machine and take over the controls. In her eagerness to become a rider she hardened her nerves and overcame her fears.

She revved the engine and just as the scooter started to move forward she let out a little scream. I grabbed the handlebar and started jogging alongside her. We circled the parking lot like this a few times. She seemed to be feeling more and more secure and started using the brakes and the accelerator with greater skill and confidence. Pretty soon, I decided to let her be on her own and as she picked up speed, I took my hands off the scooter. Away she went, completely on her own, controlling the machine with considerable skill. She seemed to know what to do instinctively.

"Slow down!" I yelled as I loped after her, thinking she had gone far enough down the road. "Put your feet down and brake to a stop."

I heard the putt-putt of the engine change to a soft purr as she let up on the accelerator and started to slow down. She flung out a leg on either side to balance the machine, applied both brakes at once and brought the scooter to a smooth halt.

"That's pretty good," I said, genuinely amazed by her fearlessness and the speed with which she could learn a difficult task.

I had thought it would take her a couple of days before she managed to learn the basics. But within an hour she started to go round in perfect circles all on her own and within two hours she declared that she felt confident enough to ride all the way back to

Karmi. So we set off, with me following her in the Renault just in case she faced any problems. As we slowed down to make the left turn at Karaoglanoglu, the gaggle of toothless old fellows who were always sitting outside the cafes and shops smoking and gossiping, stopped their chatter and stared at Anara. A girl on a scooter was a rare sight, a rare treat in fact. Anara swept past serenely, head held high like a queen. She made it to Karmi without any difficulty, negotiating the sharp S-bends and steep rises and falls of the road with skill. As I watched her bend into the curves, in the yellow-gold late afternoon light, she looked cute, perched pertly on the scooter with the cherry-red helmet on her head and her ponytail, a skein of sable smoke, fluttering cheerily behind.

Around about this time Yulie called. She wanted to know if we could meet and have lunch somewhere. I was surprised but pleased by her call since people you meet casually seldom keep you in mind. Then it occurred to me that she might have some ideas about Anara's visa problem.

"I've a bit of a problem on my hands," I said to her.

"What sort of problem?" she asked.

"Well, it's a long story."

"Perhaps I can be of some help."

"Perhaps you can."

In a few words, I sketched out my relationship with Anara and all the snags and hurdles we'd been trying to jump over in our struggle to get her a long-term visa.

"I understand," she said. "Finding a solution to this riddle is going to be difficult. But in any case, I would like to meet your friend."

"That's wonderful. She's been wanting to meet you since I told her how we met and the history of your house."

"Have you been to Bellapaix? Have you seen the Abbey?"

"No," I said. "Haven't really had the time. Been too busy with all this other stuff."

"Why don't we meet in Bellapaix on Saturday? I can play the role of tour guide and show you the Abbey and we can also talk about the visa issue."

This sounded like a good idea. I had been meaning to go and see the Abbey.

"There is a restaurant there, *The Tree of Idleness*. I can meet you there at noon."

"Fine," I said. "We'll be there."

I'd heard and read a lot about the medieval abbey of Bellapaix. An impressive ruin, it was reported to be.

On Saturday in late October we left Karmi at about 11:00 in the morning and rattled down the mountain in the Renault with fennel-scented breezes drifting through the open window. Anara was excited and happy. She had been intrigued by the account I had given her of Yulie and her family. Now she looked forward to meeting her. Both of us made an effort to set aside the ever-present anxiety that she might have to return to Almaty and put on a cheerful face. A kind of fatalism had settled on us. Que sera, sera. Whatever will be, will be. The morning was cool and a brisk breeze coming from the north had cleansed the sky. The road to Bellapaix cut through Kyrenia, going past a zone on the edge of town with small shops, offices and business. Beyond this exurb, we climbed over low hills dotted with cinder-block villas, each with its drum-shaped water tank on the roof. The houses were in various stages of completion and lacked any architectural flourish that might have relieved their essential drabness. The rooftop water tanks did not help, nor the fact that the landscape around the villas had been shaved clean of all vegetation by the blade of a bulldozer. Nothing remained of olive groves, orchards of oranges and vineyards.

Once past the hills, the road took sharp turns as it entered a region of steep canyons and gullies, much rutted and eroded by rain and runoff. From here I could see the towering rampart of the Beshparmak range on the far horizon. There was more greenery here. Stunted pine, carob and arbutus as well as native shrubs and grasses. Then, as I approached Bellapaix, the road swooped downwards suddenly and then rose like a roller coaster. On either side there were many old houses that had been repaired and renovated carefully. It looked as though the village had managed to modernize without losing its character. I drove the Renault into a parking area where gleaming motor coaches dropped off tourists. The Abbey stood before me, its sulphur-gold stones glowing softly in the bright sunlight. People speaking different languages scrambled about excitedly, admiring the views and posing for photographs. The little kiosks that sold souvenirs were doing a good trade and the jingle of euros, British pounds and Danish kroner must have sounded sweet to the ears of the vendors. The monastery may have been a money-losing operation in its hey-day, but as a ruin it was certainly bringing in cash.

I looked around to see if I could locate Yulie and "*The Tree of Idleness.*" It had become quite warm by now and I looked forward to having something cold to drink. I found the restaurant easily with its breezy verandah facing the abbey and the infamous tree. And there sat Yulie at a table set in a zone of dappled light and shadows made by the leaves of a spreading Robenia. She wore a floppy straw hat with a wide brim and huge sunglasses.

"Hello," I said to get her attention and then introduced Anara. She got up, shook hands with me and gave Anara a warm hug.

"Welcome to Cyprus," she said.

Anara shot her a brief, surprised smile but didn't say anything. I rather doubt that she was feeling very welcome.

"What's all this?" I said to Yulie, waving a hand at her hat. "Are you hiding from someone?"

"Sort of," she said and smiled. "I know several ladies who live here. If they saw me, they'd come right over and never leave. They would talk and talk and you wouldn't be able to say a word. I am hoping no one will recognize me. Do I look like a tourist?"

"You do but the hat and the sunglasses didn't fool me."

"I hope the disguise works," she said. "There are so many things I want to talk to you about. I just don't want any interruptions."

"Have you been inside the Abbey? Have you seen it before?"

"Many times. I come here often with guests, usually friends and relatives."

"Good. You can show us around, give us a history lesson," I said.

"Certainly. "But let's eat first. I haven't eaten anything all day."

A glass of pale wine sat foaming in front of her. Small bubbles formed in its depths and rose up in long lines and burst on the surface. On the outside of the glass, beads of condensation slid slowly down.

"This looks delicious," I said. "What is it?"

"Vouvray petillant," she said. "It's on the wine list,"

"Is it good?" I asked her.

"I like it," she said. "In fact, I was surprised to see they had it. Most Turkish restaurants don't have extensive wine lists."

I called a waiter over who had been watching us. He was a stocky, middle-aged Turk with a shock of gray hair and a gray mustache.

"Effendim," I said, "the same for me and for the lady, a cola."

"You will be impressed by the Abbey," Yulie said. "It has a certain tragic grandeur."

I asked her about her parents.

"Papa is busy as usual with his bees. They require constant attention, you see. Mama helps him with the bottling but she stays away from the hives. She is terrified of being stung."

Presently the waiter brought our drinks and I took a timid, tentative sip. The wine proved surprisingly well structured with a floral bouquet that blended on the back palate with a muskier note, like the odor that escapes when you cut a melon in half.

"Good choice," I said to Yulie, raising the glass in a toast.

From where we sat I had a good view of the Abbey ruins and the valley beyond. Flanked by fronds of date palms its weathered walls made of massive honey-colored stones stood out against a blue sky and its roofless gothic arches with their graceful trefoils had a disturbing eloquence. An air of melancholy grandeur clung to the ruin. Beyond the monastery, the ground dropped suddenly and the valley beyond stretched to a blurred buff-colored horizon. By now the crowd of tourists in front of the Abbey had grown larger. More and more coaches were pulling up and disgorging streams of visitors. Suddenly, Yulie's question brought me back to my private problems.

"How long would you like to stay?" she asked Anara.

Anara shrugged and punted the question to me.

"For as long as I am here," I said. "Till the start of June at least. That's when my contract with the university will end."

"You've been to the police and the officials at the airport?"

"That's the story in a nutshell."

Yulie patted Anara's hand.

"Don't worry, my dear. We will find a way to keep you here."

"This is good wine," I said, swallowing a tart mouthful. "Let's get a bottle. It should go well with lunch."

I made a sign to the waiter and he came over. "A bottle of this, Effendim and could you put the bottle in a bucket of ice?" I asked him. "I know this is not champagne but I like my white wine really cold."

He smiled and nodded vigorously to show that he understood me. No doubt he had long experience with the idiosyncrasies of foreigners and was happy to oblige.

"Look at the menu," Yulie said. "See what you would like to order."

As we were absorbed in examining the menu, the waiter brought our wine bottle in a bucket of ice and set it on our table. He took out the bottle, wrapped it in a snow-white napkin and pulled out the cork. Then he poured it for us very slowly and carefully.

"Teshekkur ederim, Effendim," I said and he smiled again. For some reason, I seemed to have made him very happy.

"This is a nice place," Anara said, looking around. "But I think Karmi is nicer. It is greener. Don't you think?"

Yulie nodded in agreement.

"This was also a Greek village," Yulie said, "before the division took place."

The shadow-dappled veranda where we sat was pleasant. Cool sea air drifted up from the coast and stirred the leaves of the large robenia. As we sat and chatted, the throb and rumble of passing cars and the excited cries of the tourists seemed to fade away. But in spite of the wine, I couldn't shake off the heavy mood that afflicted me. The worry that Anara might have to return to Almaty hung over us like the sword of Damocles. This fear, this anxiety poisoned every moment of our lives. But at the same time we had to continue to live as normally as we could. Each day we spent together was like a gift we unwrapped with keen anticipation, trying to savor it, enjoy it to the fullest. But as each day ended there was always the tormenting awareness that now we had one day less to look forward to.

"Let's order," I said to Yulie and called the waiter over. "Let's enjoy the moment. This is one unforgettable lesson my father taught me. For who knows what tomorrow will bring."

Yulie and Anara ordered the same item – smoked salmon salad. I opted for a chicken sandwich. We also ordered sigara boreks, small rolls made of flaky pastry, shaped like blimps and stuffed with cheese and parsley. By now the gusts of wind were quite strong and I was enjoying the way the palm fronds swayed like dancers moving their arms. As we sat there, eating and talking, the sun went around and started its descent in the western sky.

"I'll talk to my father," Yulie said. "He knows a lot of people, on the Greek side as well as the Turkish side. Moreover, there are many relatives in all sorts of important positions. Some are with the police; others work in government offices, hotels, banks and travel agencies. The Greeks can always find someone with connections. They've learned how to manipulate the administrative machinery of the island. They see and hear things most tourists or expats have no inkling of."

I was glad to hear her say this. The thought that there was hope, cheered me up. Even Anara, whose face seldom registered an emotion, began to smile. By now we had finished most of the wine. I wanted to order another bottle but Yulie stopped me.

"Let's go and look at the Abbey," she said. "Remember we are sitting under the Tree of Idleness. If we stay here we will become so lazy, so lazy that ... come, you need a spiritual boost, not more wine."

"But I want more wine," I said.

"Up, up," she said, pulling my arm. "You'll see what I mean."

When the bill came, Yulie would not let me pay.

"I invited you," she said. "Please. I'll take care of this."

I tried to argue but she pulled the elderly waiter aside and gave him the money.

"Come," she said, "Let's go. You need the atmosphere of a monastery for your nerves."

Yulie put an arm through Anara's arm and started chattering with her about feminine topics that held no interest for me. I marched on rapidly to secure entry tickets before Yulie could get there and make a fuss. She did wag an accusatory finger at me.

"You should not have done that," she said. "You are my guests."

We entered the Abbey and just as we passed the barbican, it absorbed us into its stillness the way sand absorbs water. The somber, ash-gray ambience of the portico with its groined vaulting demanded a respectful silence. The cloister was a simple rectangle of grass. Four dark green cypresses stood at formal attention on the four corners and four gothic arches framed the western boundary like hands folded in prayer. Slowly, I understood why monastic life had proved attractive for some men. It offered peace and tranquility and security at a time when those commodities were hard to come by. Yulie never unhooked her arm from Anara's elbow even for one second as she led us through the chambers and courtyards of the Abbey, talking non-stop. She seemed to have bonded with Anara easily and naturally, as though she sensed some innate qualities in her that she could value and admire. Women, it seemed to me, established relationships with women quickly perhaps because they trusted their instincts. They didn't go through the tense, stand-offish phase that men go through before forming friendships. Over the course of the afternoon, I witnessed the flowering of a genuine and cordial friendship between Anara and Yulie.

Inside the church, the gloom resonated with faint odors of incense, melting candle wax and the damp exhalations of invisible multitudes that had shuffled in over the centuries. As we entered from the outside brilliance, darkness blinded me at first and I closed my eyes. This, as it turned out, was the proper reaction. You were expected to shut the outer eye and open the inner one when you came into the church. Icons loomed up out of the black shadows like figures seen in a trance and their gold leaf inlays took the glow of the candle flames and gave it back.

The large refectory, a spacious and well-lit room, was the final, most pleasant surprise of the Abbey. It had four large windows that looked northwards toward Turkey. A circular rose window formed a perfect annulus on the eastern wall to let in the light of the rising sun. The chamber was infused with a soft, indirect brightness and breezes drenched in the aroma of fennel and thyme came drifting into the room. The refectory had served as an all-purpose workroom for the monks. They ate their meals here, read, wrote and practiced liturgical music.

"This is the best room in the Abbey," Yulie said, shaking me out of my reverie. "Now they have music concerts here."

I had to agree with her.

"Who built this place?" I asked her.

"Augustinian monks," she said. "They left Jerusalem after Saladin captured it in 1187 and came here. But most of the buildings were completed in the last half of the 13ᵗʰ century."

"How did it become a ruin? This is hard to understand. Look, Christianity survived on this island, in fact, thrived … generally."

"But the Turks, you see took over the island in the middle of the 16ᵗʰ century."

"They attacked the monks?"

"No, no. They generally left them alone, out of a kind of respect. But to be honest, by then the place was already rotting."

"Really?"

"Yes, from the inside. Monastic discipline broke down completely. Poverty, chastity – the simple life – all that just vanished. The monks got rich and fat. They took wives, kept mistresses, produced bastards and gave them high positions."

"That is pretty nasty."

"The Muslim invasion was the last nail," Yulie said. "Islam does not approve of the monkish way of life. Men are expected to marry, participate fully in worldly activities: business, politics, even warfare. Living a life of isolation, without wives, without children, is not considered an ideal life."

"So it was a combination of factors – the rot within and the political changes outside that wrecked this place," I said.

"Something like that," Yulie agreed.

Leaving the Abbey was like swimming up out of a dream. The world of tourists and traffic assaulted our senses, bringing us rudely back to reality. It was time to say goodbye. Yulie promised to contact me after she had spoken with her father and figured out an appropriate course of action.

I could see that Anara was considerably reassured by Yulie's optimistic attitude and I also made a resolve to try and be positive. All we could do was try various avenues and hope that one would lead us to the elusive visa. I suppose, the fine art of living lies mainly in holding despair at bay and keeping alive the flame of hope.

"Don't worry," she said to Anara, taking up her hand. "We will find a way."

~

CHAPTER THREE

Section 1

For me, Karmi quickly became a refuge, a haven. I walked around the place like a smitten mooncalf admiring the views, appreciating the thickness of the stone walls, the flower-festooned lanes and cobblestone walkways. And our house, though not very large, had everything we needed. Our living area on the second floor was filled with light and air. The wrought iron balcony was smothered in the blossoms of bougainvillea. It had climbed all the way up here from the alley below and then pushed itself to the roof. But the very best feature of the house was the flat roof. From here you got a fantastic eagle's eye view of the coast and the blue Mediterranean stretching north all the way to Turkey. One could also see all of Kyrenia and the old harbor and in the foreground St. Hilarion perched on its peak like an eagle poised for takeoff. I loved coming up to the roof at sundown. The air became cooler and the light of the setting sun transmuted the stones of St. Hilarion into ingots of gold. And then as the blue shadows became longer in the valley below, the lights of Kyrenia twitched on one by one like sparkling sequins.

The terrace in front of the house shaded by a single almond tree was another bower of bliss. Hidden from the eyes of neighbors, by thick growths of Oleander on one side and a rambling Jasmine bush on the other, it became our secret sanctuary. We could perform the most outrageous acts in this secluded spot, act out all kinds of fantasies. And we did. I was Adam in this Garden of Eden and each conjugation, each consummation with my Eve became a voyage of discovery, a journey into undiscovered territories. But every Eden must have its mundane problems. And one fine day our kitchen sink got plugged up and would not drain at all!

I called Fiona.

"Our pipes are all plugged," I lamented into her British ear. "We can't even wash dishes."

"Did you flush something big down the toilet?" She responded in an accusatory tone.

"I did not."

"A pillow? A sheep?"

"I swear upon the King James version."

She giggled.

"Don't worry," she said. "We have a man who knows the location of every underground pipe in the village. His name is Erkan. Call him."

She gave me the phone number.

Erkan Bey spoke an English I had never heard in my life before. He had a gruff, gravelly voice and his words sounded like a series of unfriendly growls uttered with much gasping and wheezing as though he were out of breath. Somehow, I managed to convey the fact that the pipes in my house were clogged and I needed a plumber.

"Okay, next week, I come," he said.

"No, no," I shouted in panic. "Come now. Can't cook. No bathroom. Everything kaput. Please, please, please."

Anara stood behind me trying to keep from laughing.

Erkan Bey did understand the word "please." He heaved and wheezed, gurgled and chuckled and I heard him say, "Okay, okay, I come."

The next morning I heard a tremendous screeching and slipping of tires on the steeper segment of the road that led to the house, followed by such a clattering and rattling that I thought an entire junkyard was being dragged up. Eventually an ancient Renault, once yellow but now covered with grievous dents and entire archipelagos of rust, came into view and stopped. A door creaked open and a squat, bare-chested, old gnome stepped out. He could not have been more than four feet tall. His thin, severely bowed legs stuck out of oil-stained and tattered Bermuda shorts and his hairy dugs sagged towards his belly and his wrinkled and crumpled belly flopped over his belt. When he opened his trunk and started taking out tools, I knew he had to be Erkan Bey.

He walked on his short legs with a rocking motion swinging from side to side as though he were crossing the deck of a storm-tossed ship. We exchanged "Merhabas" as he came up to the house and took my right hand in an enormous paw and flashed a gap-tooth grin at me. So wide and sincere was his smile that for a second it looked as though the man had vanished and only his dentures remained suspended in air.

"Come," he commanded. "I give you."

He led me to his car and opened the trunk. Among diverse piles of tools and plumbing parts, sat a cardboard box filled with grapes. He picked it up and handed it to me.

"Take. From my orchard," he said.

"Teshekkur ederim, Erkan Bey, thank you," I said and carried the box back into the house.

"Look what Erkan Bey has brought for us," I said to Anara. "Grapes from his own orchard."

Anara loved grapes, in fact, she loved every kind of fruit, apples being her most favorite.

In a few words, I acquainted Erkan Bey with the problem. He meditated upon the soapy water standing in the kitchen sink for a while and shook his head and made a terrible face. Then he got to work. He tried the easy remedies first – plungers and pokers and the pouring of acid down various pipes – but nothing helped. The problem turned out to be more serious. The clog seemed to be somewhere further down, perhaps beneath the house. Then he got the pick and the shovel and started to excavate the courtyard.

"Roots," he said, between grunts, as he dug away. "The roots get into pipes."

I nodded.

"Thank you for coming" I said. "Now I must go to the university. Anara will be here if you need anything."

Erkan Bey looked like an ogre out of a children's book. Wider than he was tall, he had bulging biceps and an enormous barrel of a chest hooped round with a massive rib cage. All his strength lay bulked up in his torso. His legs were short, bowed and spindly. But he could have moved a mountain with his arms given enough leverage. Anara seemed a bit afraid of him but I told her not to worry.

"Let him come into the house if he wants to," I told her. "He may need to get at the pipes that lead out of the bathroom."

I spent the day at the university hoping and praying that Erkan Bey would solve our plumbing problems. When I got back I saw a big hole in the courtyard and another big hole in one of the downstairs bedrooms. Erkan Bey had been busy all day.

"He is digging his way to China," Anara moaned. "We can't cook. We can't wash. What will we do?"

"And we don't have much in the way of groceries," I said. "Let's just go to a restaurant."

"Where should we go?"

"I just found out about a place in Lapta," I said. "A teacher in our department said they served excellent Cypriot food."

"Where is Lapta?" she asked.

"About fifteen kilometers west, along the coast road. It's a small village."

She clapped her hands.

"Let's go," she said.

Then with the sun dropping behind the western escarpments, we rattled down the mountain in the Renault. I took a left turn in Karaoglanoglu and headed westward. Here the road from Karmi hits the coast road at a right angle and passes between some dusty, flyblown shops. The sky had taken on a deep, scarlet hue with feathery cirrus clouds pink as flamingoes flying across the sky. I drove past Escape Beach, Alsanjak and Lapta. Finally, I saw a small sign that said *Asmali Restaurant* hanging from a power pole and turned left onto an unpaved road that cut through a grove of orange trees. By now a violet darkness was everywhere and I could only see a rutted, dusty track before me in the beam of the headlamps. Then a cluster of bright lights and stone structures loomed up silhouetted against a backdrop of inky-black trees. In front of the buildings there was a spacious courtyard covered with a trellis of grapevines and strung with electric bulbs. A few roughly made picnic tables and benches had been set up underneath the latticework of leaves and lights. The place looked like a farm. I parked the car and we went and sat down. I did not see any other customers. Only the clucking of chickens and the nervous giggle of a goat broke the silence that enveloped the place.

Soon the proprietor appeared and welcomed us with effusive "Merhabas." He introduced himself as Talat. He said he worked as a bus-driver for the university and recognized me, having seen me on the campus. Apparently, his whole family lived on the premises. His wife and daughters did all the cooking for customers who happened to drop by.

We ordered the slow-baked lamb cooked with red onions, potatoes and tomatoes in olive oil. They prepared it in the traditional domed oven that you often saw sitting outside most village houses. For starters, we ordered dolmades and tabouleh salad. When I asked for some red wine, Talat said he had some excellent stuff that he purchased directly from a Turkish wine-maker.

I wanted to mark the moment as special but Anara didn't need anything stronger than fruit juice to make her any happier than she was. She looked lovely in a flouncy white blouse. Her dark hair floated freely about her bare shoulders and glimmered in the light that got strained through the vine leaves.

"You smell nice," I said to her. "What is that perfume?"

She held her wrist under my nose. I got a whiff of gardenias and vanilla mixing with some musky undertones.

"I got this at the duty-free shop in Istanbul airport," she said. "Do you like it?"

"I love it," I told her squeezed her hand. "I feel so happy tonight. Let's try to forget all our problems and just enjoy ourselves."

"I'm glad we are together, honey," she said.

"Do you miss your little girl?" I asked her. "Do you miss Sara?"

She shook her head and smiled.

"Not as much as I thought I would," she said. "I know she is happy with my mother. They get along so well together. I think she likes her babushka better than she likes me."

"Kids can be funny that way," I said. "They live in their own world. Back in Almaty, did you ever think you'd end up on this island with me?"

"Never," she said. "This is like a dream."

She took up my hand impulsively and kissed it. Of all her gestures, this one always made my heart skip a beat. The sky hung over us like a canopy of purple velvet covered with silver stars. The Turkish wine Talat served turned out to be excellent and presently he brought out the food and his family also gathered around at a table nearby for their evening meal. As we ate, we could hear them talking in Turkish and the words floated over to us not as a language but as a kind of music.

Anara and I were in our own little world by now, a universe made up of two people.

"Do you like the food?" I asked her.

She nodded.

"The best," she said.

I thanked Talat and his wife and paid the bill and Anara and I walked back to the car, hand-in-hand. As I turned east to head back home, I could see the lights of Lapta glimmering on the hills. I drove for a while and then pulled over along a lonely stretch of coastline. I turned off the engine and we sat there for bit, just savoring this dense quietness, not saying a word. There were no lights here, no hotels, no villas, no beachfront restaurants, nothing at all but an expanse of sandy, scalloped beach where one could hear the thunder of the surf nearby. We got out of the car and lay down on the warm sand and turned towards each other greedily. My kisses melted into her hot mouth and she took my firmness into her hands and guided it into herself. Alongside the systolic rhythm of the sea we found ours and as the final spasm ripped through me I ceased to exist as a separate entity. And for a brief moment Anara and I vanished into each other and became one body, one soul, one world, one universe, exploding and expanding forever and ever.

Ertan Bey took three days to fix our plumbing problem. When he finally packed up all his tools and gear and squeaked and rattled out of Karmi, we decided to lay in some groceries and start doing some serious cooking. Cardiff had told me about a supermarket called *Leman*. Following his directions, we went looking for it and found it on the coast road, not far from the campus. Brightly lit and air-conditioned, it had been laid out just like a supermarket in the U.S.

but on a smaller scale. Way too computerized and clean for my taste, it left me cold.

Europeans, I noticed, loved the place and patronized it in droves. They would come straight from the beaches dressed in beach clothing – bikinis, bathing trunks, straw hats and sandals. I tried not to look at their feet or their fried, freckled and sun-blistered hides oily with sweat and tanning lotion. The supermarket should have forbidden anyone from coming in without proper attire but I suppose the dollars and euros they spent here were too desirable. Oblivious to the looks of disgust on the faces of the locals, the tourists busied themselves picking up products from their home countries. The Irish went mining for Kerry Gold Irish butter even though it cost five times more than the Turkish variety. The Germans grabbed German beer and were quite willing to pay triple what they would for a Turkish brand. The French dove into expensive French wines and cheese and the Italians snapped up packages of over-priced cured Italian meats, packets of pasta and cans of spaghetti sauce.

I made it my mission to discover the shops where the locals shopped and over the next few weeks we drove around and discovered several nearby villages that had small bazaars. Edremit, Alsanjak, and Lapta, all had little shops that sold the kinds of goods that an average household might need. They weren't shiny with chrome and glass or lit up with fluorescent lights. Nor were they very clean. But I liked the dim, odorous interiors of these shops. They were relics of old Cyprus, the Cyprus that existed before it got invaded by supermarkets and superhighways. A quieter, slower Cyprus. These shops were family owned and operated. As you entered the premises, you exchanged greetings with the patriarch or the matriarch of the clan who sat by the cash register, always enveloped in a dense cloud of cigarette smoke. While this respected elder rang up the purchases, the young ones scurried about, hauling in heavy boxes and crates and baskets.

I could not spend like a tourist and made an effort to interact with the local economy, and live like a Cypriot. But, in all honesty, being thrifty did not inflict any hardship on us. Cyprus produced an abundance of good things to eat and drink. There were the fat olives and grapes and oranges, of course. And there was the justly famous Cypriot brandy. Besides the fact that Cardiff approved of it heartily, it came well recommended by guidebooks and went down smoothly and easily. I also discovered a passable local red wine called "Aphrodite." It was relatively inexpensive and when you sipped it sitting on the roof at sunset it proved quite satisfying, even inspirational.

Anara, I discovered to my amusement and surprise, did not know much about cookery. The awkwardness with which she handled a Chef's knife scared me. I knew she would lop off a finger or two one day. So I did most of the cooking. She helped, of course, and it became a game for us to discover new recipes on the Internet and then try them out, with me playing the part of a pompous instructor and demonstrator.

"Watch and learn," I would say. "Lesson Number One. Hold the tomato on the cutting board like this with the fingers of your left hand on top. Move the knife downwards, down toward the cutting board. Don't hold the tomato in the palm of your hand. That way if the knife goes through the tomato, it will slice your flesh. And this is German steel – very sharp."

Then I demonstrated the art of baking a chicken. You take a thawed pullet, remove most of the skin and massage it with olive oil and lemon juice. Then you insert slivers of garlic into random incisions made in the breast and thighs. Next you sprinkle it with salt and pepper and fresh rosemary. For a good measure you stuff the inner cavity with more rosemary and diced up lemons. Then you put it in an oven pre-heated to 375 F. and let it cook for an hour. Voila! Specialité de la maison. Rosemary-Lemon Chicken a la Americain. The rosemary grew in aromatic profusion all around our house and there was a lemon tree in our courtyard. All I had to do was simply reach out of a downstairs window and pluck what I needed.

Dinner done, I would grab a bottle of wine and we would head for the roof to savor the violet hour. In the west, the sun would be below the western range by now and the sky would take on a wash of warm pink. And above the church tower swallows would start to stitch the sky with sudden flights, diving into clouds of gnats that rose up like smoke.

Section 2

But behind the normal façade of our lives, lurked the ever-present time bomb of the visa problem that went on ticking away steadily. And even as the expiration date came closer my anxiety increased. I had not heard back from Yulie. And I was starting to lose hope that I would be able to find a way to keep Anara with me. I decided to call Cardiff.

"Why don't you come up on Sunday," I said to him, "have lunch with us."

"Okay," he said. "But I'm bringing Freya along," he said. "You are forewarned."

"Who's this now?" I asked.

"Remember the people we met at that restaurant? That English couple from Guildford – The Mortons."

"Yes, yes."

"Well, I ran into them again at the *Windmill* a few days ago."

"And?"

"They went back yesterday. But their daughter – Freya – well, she refused to return with them. She wanted to stay on. They are frequent visitors and she has lots of friends here. But she couldn't afford a hotel room. So I told her she could stay with me."

"I see. Okay." I said. "Bring her along. "It's your funeral.""

I also invited Fiona, her husband, and our neighbor Barbara Preston. By the time Cardiff showed up, it was well past noon and I had started to barbecue the meat.

Freya was a bone-thin, pallid, hyper-energetic stalk of a girl, obviously much younger than Cardiff. She had rinsed-out, gray eyes, the color of a rainy English seascape, a small, upturned nose, thin lips and sun-dried, yellow hair that hung down her back, straight and limp. She wore jeans torn at the knees and a blue T-shirt with the logo of some beer company across the chest. She held a can of coke in her left hand and a cigarette in her right. Her breasts were barely noticeable underneath her T-shirt and she had the narrow hips of a boy.

The introductions done, I turned my attention towards the grill.

"I can't stay long," Freya said. "I have to see some people later."

I looked at Cardiff. He turned his eyes skywards.

Freya placed the can of coke on the dining table and took out her mobile phone.

"I need to make a call," she said.

"She's always on that bloody phone," Cardiff growled. "She seems to know everyone on the island."

"That's good, isn't it?" I said. "Here, have a beer. Calm down."

"I need something stronger," Cardiff said, handing me a bottle of gin. "Pour this out for me with some tonic, will you?"

Cardiff's nerves obviously needed bolstering and Freya also seemed, on edge and kept making calls on her mobile. Apparently some arrangements were being made, important decisions taken, urgent matters discussed. Nothing could be left to chance. She had to give directions, express her opinions.

A fragrant blue smoke rose from the grill and the aroma of cooking hot-dogs, sausages and ground beef patties started to spread everywhere. Barbara Preston had brought a potato-salad and Anara prepared a large bowl of tabouleh. Fiona took charge of setting up the portable table and brought out the cutlery and plates. Freya kept her distance from the culinary operations. I don't think she had any notion of how groceries got transformed into lunch so this was just as well.

Everyone appeared to enjoy the food, that is, everyone except Freya. She had no appetite, it seemed. She placed a hotdog in a puddle of ketchup on her plate, cut it into small pieces and pushed them around.

"I'm not much of a meat person," she said.

"Have some potato salad," I said.

"I don't like potato salad," she said. "And what is this?"

"Tabouleh," I said. "It's a Middle-Eastern dish. Contains couscous and parsley."

"Oh, yes," she said. "I've seen it before. I'll have some."

Freya did not talk very much, at least not to the guests gathered on the roof. She preferred talking to people who called her on the mobile.

I tried to start a conversation with her but before she could say a word, her mobile rang and she moved to a corner of the roof to take the call.

"Yes, no, yes, no, maybe, no, yes-yes, okay, later, maybe, okay, no-no, okay yes-yes." This is what I heard. It was painful to sit there and listen to this one-sided conversation.

We had barely finished eating, when her mobile chirruped again.

"Yes, okay," she mumbled and jumped up.

"You didn't eat much," I said.

"She only eats French fries," Cardiff said.

Freya made a face.

"I gotta run," she said. "The taxi's waiting near the church. Thanks for everything. Bye."

Cardiff nodded and raised his glass in a farewell gesture and Freya went down the stairs.

"Where is she going?" I asked Cardiff.

"Oh, she has a job now. Responsibilities etcetera." Cardiff said with a little smirk.

"A job? Really. Where?"

I was intrigued and amazed that she had been able to find a job so quickly and easily.

"At this disco called *Triton*."

"What does she do there?"

"Not much, from what I saw."

"Waitress?"

"No. More like a hostess. She receives the customers and seats them."

"That's nice."

Freya was a child of the 21st century, addicted to junk food and her mobile phone. Cardiff couldn't possibly understand her. Nor could I. Compared to Freya, Cardiff and I were cave men, Neanderthals. We read books. We belonged to the past. We were cynical and jaded and intensely romantic by turns, burdened by private histories, personal failures and unsure of the future. Freya, on the other hand, had no awareness of the past, nor any worries about the future. She lived in an eternal, on-going, continuous present – the moment – like a primitive, a pagan dancing to the accelerated drumbeat of her own pulse.

After she left, everyone appeared to exhale a collective sigh of relief. The balloon of tension her presence had inflated, slowly started to lose air. Her hyper-alert manner and nervous energy seemed out of place in the sleepy atmosphere of Karmi. After she left, everyone relaxed. There was more laughter, more joking, more teasing. We turned our attention to the food and it began to disappear rapidly. Barbara's potato salad proved particularly popular.

As we savored post-lunch cigarettes, Fiona talked about how life in Cyprus used to be.

"There used to be a man in Kyrenia who gave day-long tours on donkeys," she said. "His name was Orhan, but everyone called him 'The Donkey-Man.' I loved going on those trips. We would start at about ten in the morning and follow a mountain trail for a couple of hours. Around noon we'd stop near a waterfall in Lapta and were served a fabulous lunch of kebabs and salad. Then, after a short rest, we'd start back, reaching Kyrenia just in time for tea."

"Is he still doing these tours?" I asked.

"No," said Fiona. "He retired or gave up the business and no one seems to have picked it up again."

"I would love to ride on a donkey," Anara said suddenly.

Laughter greeted this statement but she was perfectly serious.

"Sure," agreed Barbara, "we all would."

"Don't romanticize donkeys too much," I said. "They can be stubborn, cantankerous beasts."

"And they bite and kick," added Cardiff.

"Oh, but Orhan Bey's donkeys were gentle creatures. Very docile. No one got bitten or kicked," said Fiona.

"He must have drugged them," said Cardiff.

By now the sun had disappeared behind the western peaks and one could feel heavy dew coming down. It was time to call it a day. Fiona and her husband had to go into Kyrenia to do some shopping and they offered to give Cardiff a lift into town. But just before he left, I pulled him aside.

"Do you think Freya could help Anara get a job at that disco?"

He thought for a while and then said, "She does seem to know a lot of people."

"Could you talk to her? We are running out of time."

"Of course," he said. "I'll bring it up."

"Thanks," I said. "If she got a job, her employer would have to arrange for a visa. Right?"

"Right."

"Give it a try, will you?" I said to him. "It just might work."

After the guests left, Anara and I took care of the dishes and then went for a walk around the village. Once it got dark, Karmi assumed a more mysterious personality. The clamorous perfume of the night-blooming Jasmine filled our alley and overflowed into the upper road. There were very few street-lamps in our section of the village and the ones we did have shed a very feeble light. But once your eyes adjusted to the penumbral gloom, the milky luminescence that fell from the sky sufficed to show you the way.

"That Freya is a strange girl," Anara said.

"You didn't like her?" I said.

"Not really," said Anara. "She seemed sort of cold to me."

"Oh, well," I said. "Cardiff likes her. That's all that really matters."

Anara's reaction to Freya certainly had a lot to do with the resentment she felt over the ease with which Freya had found a job.

"If I had a job," she said to me, "my visa problems would be solved."

True, but it would also mean that she would be away from me for several hours. Did I really want that? But these concerns quickly lost relevance as events now started to proceed at their own pace, take their own shape and form.

On Friday evening, I got a call from Cardiff.

"I say, I'm at the *Triton*. Why don't you and Anara come down? You could meet Tony. He owns the place. Maybe he can help Anara get a job."

I turned and asked Anara.

"Cardiff wants us to come to the *Triton*. Do you want to go?"

I thought she might say no. But her eyes lit up and she nodded vigorously.

"I *love* to dance," she said, clapping her hands. "Let's go. Let's go. It will be fun."

For me disco dancing had a limited attraction. I could never step onto a dance floor stone sober. It took several drinks before I could shed my inhibitions and succumb to the lure of the music. But for Anara the prospect of the bright lights and disco dancing had a strong appeal.

"Okay," I said, realizing that an evening out would make her very happy. "Let's go."

We started from Karmi late, around nine or nine-thirty and rattled down the mountain in the Renault wearing our best clothes. Anara had taken pains with her make-up and wore heels and a short frock that ended mid-thigh revealing the sleek sexiness of her legs. It wasn't hard to find *Triton*. Kyrenia is a small town and I had an idea of where it was located. When we got near the place the loud thumping of disco music pouring out of the place and the blinking lights led us right to its door.

Freya stood at the entrance surrounded by a glowing nimbus of neon. I hardly recognized her. She looked very different. She was wearing a black ankle-length evening gown and heavy eye make-up and her mouth was a garish crimson scar. The *Triton* charged an entry fee and Freya had been given the responsibility of collecting the money. Also, she was to make sure that only the "right sort" of people got in. She could keep out anyone, lacking style or who seemed the wrong type. In practice, this meant that only the young and the beautiful and the fashionably dressed got in.

The disco was basically a bare concrete hangar with a bar on one side and the disc jockey's booth on the other. Some rickety tables and chairs were scattered around a clearing in the middle where the dancers were jumping and gyrating. Not much had been done to create an ambience beyond the mirrored ball dangling from the ceiling and the strobe lights that throbbed in time with the drumbeat.

We found Cardiff sitting in one corner together with a middle-aged Turkish man whom he introduced as Tony.

"Tony owns the *Triton*," Cardiff said. "As well as several other properties in North Cyprus."

Tony smiled in a self-deprecating manner.

"I just businessman," he said.

I introduced Anara and myself.

The music was ear-splittingly loud with a powerful, driving bass that made the furniture vibrate. Talking under these circumstances was all but impossible.

Tony made a sign to a waitress in a skimpy miniskirt and ordered us a round of drinks. I opted for a double scotch and soda and Anara requested pineapple juice.

When Tony learned that Anara was from Kazakhstan, he smiled approvingly.

"Many girls from Kazakhstan here in Kuzey Kibris," he said.

"Many Russian and English girls too," Cardiff said directing a level but meaningful glance at me over the rim of his glass. "Especially blondes. Turkish men really go for blondes."

I could see he had a point. Most of the waitresses in the *Triton* were blondes.

Tony nodded vigorously in agreement and shrugged as if to say that he had no control over the attitudes of his countrymen.

Anara tapped her foot restlessly to the beat of the music, obviously itching to get onto the dance floor. I nudged Cardiff.

He got up and held out his hand to her. She flashed a happy grin and jumped up.

I enjoyed watching her move to the music. Her slenderness and flexibility gave her dancing a natural liquidity and grace and she seemed to have an ear for rhythm. Cardiff on the other hand could barely make himself move in time to the beat. Stiff and awkward, he bobbed up and down like a barely broken in puppet, flailing his arms and legs as if these appendages were obstacles that had to be pushed aside.

Dancing was certainly not something he did well, but he did his duty gamely and kept going through the motions as long as Anara wanted stay on the dance floor. They danced for a couple of songs and then returned to the table to cool off. At some point an obese man, with a chalk-white, expressionless face joined us. Tony introduced him as Vitaly. He had pale blue eyes with black centers. It occurred to me that I had seen eyes like that in a photograph of a Siberian wolf in *National Geographic* magazine. Vitaly held out his hand so that all of us could take it one by one and shake it. The second I touched it a shiver went through me. His hand was cold and damp and felt soft as kneaded dough, a blubbery lump of cold flesh without any bones.

"Vitaly own *Starlight Casino*," Tony said.

Vitaly's face did not register any emotion but he placed his bulk in a small chair carefully and folded his arms over his whale of a belly.

Gradually the scotch warmed my blood and strengthened my nerves. I started to enjoy the jackhammer strokes and the systolic bass beat made my bones bounce. Most of the dancers were young and alarmingly agile and had the kind of kinetic energy that only the under-30 crowd can display but sprinkled in between there were a few elderly European tourists. I took Anara's hand and led her out on the dance floor. She grinned impishly at me and began to dance, moving with a natural and spontaneous sensuality, coaxing me, enticing me to mimic her fluid moves. Soon I too entered the groove and mimicked her movements. The driving, insistent drums took over my limbs and I lost my self-consciousness. We moved in harmony facing each other like reflections in a mirror, printing the air with signs and gestures for each other and for a while the world stood still.

When we got off the dance floor, Tony and Vitaly had left and Cardiff was sitting alone. Then Freya took a break from her Hostess responsibilities and came and joined us for a while. Cardiff bought a round of drinks. Freya didn't like the taste of alcohol, it turned out.

"It doesn't agree with my chemistry," she said. "Makes me all tense and nervous."

She took it occasionally and then only if it had been mixed with some fruit juice or some sort of sugary soda to disguise the taste and flavor.

Not much was said because not much could be said or heard in the din. Nor had we managed to talk to Tony about a job for Anara. We simply let the music and the pulsing lights take our minds into a euphoric state. Eventually, Freya returned to her duties at the front door and Cardiff and I decided it was time to leave. He wanted us to go with him to *Pegasus* but we begged off and drove home to Karmi.

"Did you enjoy yourself?" I asked Anara.

She nodded her head vigorously and yawned. She had enjoyed the dancing and the music and the ambience but she wasn't used to staying up late. Neither was I. Imperceptibly, our life together had taken on the rhythm that the lives of old married couples have. We lived quietly, frugally. I could neither afford nor had any stomach or energy for the lifestyle of teenagers still playing the dating game. Nor did Anara have any interest in being out on the town every night. At least she never indicated as much to me. For us disco nights would be rare.

What should we do? What should we do? This was the constant refrain on our lips as the end of November loomed closer and closer. A kind of tense, inexpressible panic tainted all the hours of our nights and days. One evening, Anara started crying. It turned out she was profoundly depressed over the thought of returning to Almaty. I did my best to comfort her.

"Please don't cry," I told her. "I'll go talk to Tony. We never really had a chance to discuss your visa problem with him. Perhaps he can do something."

"Please do," she said. "Please. Please. I'll do anything, any sort of work. I just can't bear the thought of having to leave you."

"And I don't want to lose you, sweetie."

To save on gasoline, I decided to take the scooter to Kyrenia. In the heavy late afternoon traffic, one made better progress on the scooter anyway.

Luckily, Tony was at the *Triton* though it was still too early for the music and dancing to begin and shook hands with me warmly.

"Sit down. Sit down. What will you have?"

"Nothing stronger than orange juice," I said. "I'm on the scooter, you see."

"Ah, yes. I haven't ridden one of those in years. They are fun, right?"

We chatted for a while about scooters and then I brought up the matter of a job for Anara. Suddenly he was less effusive.

"Right now I have all the girls I need," he said. "If I need, I will call you."

I didn't like what I heard. I thought he was being evasive. I couldn't help feeling that if Anara had been a Nordic blonde, he would have created a job for her. He was a clever man of business, indeed a prominent figure on the commercial scene, but I found him to be rather slippery and unreliable.

"Have you tried to get an extension?" He asked. "It is a simple matter usually."

"We tried," I told him. "We went to the main office in Lefkosa. They refused to do anything."

He must have seen the look of disappointment on my face because he suddenly put a hand on my shoulder and said: "Don't worry, my friend. I will try to find something for her. I will talk to Vitaly. He is always hiring girls for his casino. Perhaps he can find a place for her."

This was encouraging news.

"Really?" I said.

"Of course," Tony replied. "There is always a chance."

A ray of hope streamed through the dark clouds that hovered above us.

While we were talking, Freya arrived to take up her duties. I spoke with her for a few minutes but then I begged leave of Tony.

"Don't give up hope," he said as we parted.

Outside, the wind had picked up and a storm seemed to be headed our way. I wanted to kick myself for having come on the scooter. Heavy black thunderheads were rolling in from the north. By the time I got to Zeytinlik, rain started to come down in sheets. I couldn't see anything through the visor of my helmet. The whole world turned into a streaming, melting grayness. Within minutes I was totally drenched. I decided it would be best to keep going. It made little sense to try and wait out the storm under a tree. It could go on raining for a long time. When I got to Karmi, the temperature had dropped quite a bit and a cold breeze had come up as if from nowhere, scented with the odor of rain-soaked vegetation. As I rode into our narrow lane, I saw Anara leaning out of a window looking down.

"Did you get wet?" She called down cheerily.

"I sure did."

"Tch, tch. Poor baby." She clucked sympathetically. "Come up quickly. I'll help you change."

I took off my wet things and got into some dry clothes. She carried all the wet items downstairs to hang them on the clothesline we had stretched in one of the bedrooms.

For a while the rain and wind seemed to slack off and a single shaft of light poked through a break in the piled up thunderheads. But then the wind picked up again and bent back the cypresses till they looked like dark green crescents. Thunder shattered the jagged edges of the Beshparmak crags and lightning skittered across the bare shoulders of rocks. And a heavy, steady rain made the gutters gurgle through the night.

Anara had never lived away from her mother, never traveled outside her country, never lived on an island. Naturally, she took delight in everything and enjoyed every sight and sound and sensation.

Even going down the mountain on the scooter to get groceries became an exhilarating adventure. While I drove, she rode behind me and I let the scooter gain speed from the steep angle of the slope and the sheer momentum. We got to the coast road and then turned east to reach the grocery store. On Sunday mornings there was very little traffic usually. We had our little list – Meat, potatoes, vegetables, eggs, milk, cheese, bread, pasta and rice. Normally, I also got some beer and wine for myself and cartons of cherry juice for Anara. We focused on the essentials and never bought more than we needed. But as we approached the ice-cream display the temptation became too strong. Oh, what the hell! Succumbing, I picked up a couple of chocolate bars sprinkled with almonds. Those things were deadly delicious. Who could resist them?

Then loaded down with bags of groceries we headed back up the mountain. All went well until we reached the half way mark. Then the scooter started to slow down. The road was too steep and the weight of two persons plus that of the groceries proved too much for the little machine. It slowed to a walking pace and then started to stutter and choke and stagger. It became clear that one of us would have to get off to lighten the load. Anara volunteered.

"I'll walk," she said. "Once we get past that turn, it will be okay."

I took the scooter up the gradient to the turn, about fifty yards or so, and then stopped and waited for her to catch up. She trudged up bravely in the bright sunlight. I saw her pink slacks standing out in bright contrast against the gray gravel of the road. Then she got back up behind me and we started again. But just before we reached Karmi, the road became almost vertical. I stopped the scooter before it started to die. Now it was my turn to walk.

"You take it up to the house." I said, grabbing a bag of groceries. "I need the walk. It will help me lose some weight."

Anara took control of the machine and continued up the steep road and I followed slowly, huffing and puffing, feeling the pain of the drastic gradient along the muscles of my calves. Unfortunately, we had to go through this little dance every time we came down the mountain on the scooter together. But I didn't mind this inconvenience in the least and neither did she.

The almond tree that dominated our courtyard shed its leaves but many ripe almonds remained attached to its branches. At first I didn't pay much attention to the brown-black husks that looked quite unappetizing. When they fell to the ground, I simply swept them up along with the dead leaves. It was Anara who discovered that each ugly-looking husk contained an almond and each almond contained a sweet and fragrant kernel.

"Let's get them," she said. "Otherwise the tree rats will steal them."

"But how?" I asked.

We did not possess a ladder or any other means of reaching the branches.

"Well we need a long stick or something to knock them off the branches."

"We don't have a long stick," I said.

"Let's make one," she said.

Suiting action to words, she promptly attached two broomsticks with duct tape and began whacking the tree. This contraption proved effective and in a short while she had collected a nice big pile. I took over the task of cracking them to extract the kernels and within half an hour I had amassed almost a kilo.

We also went often to observe the marine life that made a home in inter-tidal pools. Worn by centuries of wave action, the pocked surface served as a hospitable ecosystem for many kinds of sea creatures. Anara trudged meditatively across this moonscape, leaning over craters for minutes on end, looking for marine life. These pools existed only for a few hours each day. Once the sun heated up the rocks, the pools evaporated, everything died or disappeared only to return when the tide came in again. Among moss-bearded rocks we found many small crabs and every pool had its population of tiny fish. In shallow waters protected from the pounding surf, we also found whole communities of sea urchins waving their prickly spines like so many rust-colored pincushions. Once a large moray eel darted out from beneath the ledge I was leaning over. It looked at me with a glaucous eye and vanished as quickly as it had appeared. I never saw it again, though I looked for it every time we visited that part of the seashore. Another time I saw a large cuttle-fish moving with an undulant elegance, waving its frills and flounces like a flamenco dancer. But it was our encounter with the sea cucumber that proved most memorable. About the size of a fat sausage, it had a wrinkled pinkish-orange exterior. It lay outside the tidal pool and looked quite dead. I had no idea what it was. I watched and waited but it did not seem to want to move even when I nudged it with a stick. I rolled it gently towards the water and pushed it in. Suddenly it spewed a milky liquid from one end (mouth? anus?) spreading sticky, membranous, strands. Anara made a sound to signify disgust but I had to laugh. We had obviously chanced upon the "Penis-of-the-Sea" or "Zub-al-Bahar" in Arabic. I had read about this creature but never imagined that it actually existed or that I would ever see it.

～

Section 3

We did our best to live our lives as normally as we could, but underneath the outward pretence of normality lurked the ever-present fear that Anara might have to go back to Almaty. I did my best to contain my anxiety and appear calm in front of her but it wasn't easy. Every moment now acquired a peculiar urgency. The visa problem poisoned our daily lives. It loomed on the horizon like a toxic mushroom cloud, constantly growing in size, a constant threat.

There was a feeling of fall now in the apricot-colored afternoon light, in the cool air, in the bronze and gold and copper tints of the almond leaves as they broke off the branches and fell on to the ground below. Anara and I stepped over the teal-blue shadows that fled steeply down the cobbled stone street and made our way towards Karmi Shop.

Anara's silence and the firm set of her jaw, revealed her mental state.

"I'm worried, honey. What will we do?" she said at last.

"We'll find a way," I said. "Don't worry. There is always a way out of these jams."

"I don't want to go back to Almaty," she said. "My mind is made up. I'll stay here illegally, but I won't go back."

I disagreed with that approach.

"No, no, you have to be legal," I said. "We'll find a way. Let me talk to Derek. Let's see what he says."

Derek and Karen, the English couple who owned and operated the Karmi Shop, had moved to Cyprus in search of an easygoing way of life. They were not young anymore and showed signs of considerable wear and tear. Karen looked older than Derek and had a deeply furrowed forehead and faded, wrinkled cheeks. Derek, with his shock of red hair and glowing red visage looked youthful. He fancied himself to be a poet-in-the-making. I'd often see him sitting outside the store under a big sun umbrella with a glass of red wine in front of him, scribbling away in a notebook. Back in England he had done journalism for auto-racing magazines to earn a living. Now he made it known to all that he was merely engaged in shopkeeping while he composed works that would win him a reputation. For Derek running the store was more like a hobby. Much of the burden of managing the shop fell on Karen's weary shoulders. The shop took up two tiny rooms on the ground floor of a house located on the street behind the church. Derek and Karen lived above.

They were always running out of items and rarely opened and closed according to the advertised hours. This rather cavalier attitude towards storekeeping proved to be a bit of an irritant.

Derek knew a great deal about Cypriot laws and regulations and the ways and vagaries of petty government officials and local bureaucrats. The shop was a clearinghouse for all sorts of useful and useless information, insider tips, gossip and folklore that the locals exchanged over their inter-personal grapevine.

Derek greeted us by raising his glass and taking a sip and then followed us into the store. By the time we had picked up the beer, milk and bread, he had positioned himself behind the counter, ready to play the role of the shopkeeper. His eyes were bloodshot and his right hand shook slightly as he took a drag on his cigarette. He placed it carefully in an ashtray and started adding up our purchases on a hand-held calculator. Being a mom-and-pop operation, the Karmi Shop lacked a proper cash register.

"That's ten lira," he said.

"We need your advice, Derek," I said. "Anara's visa is going to expire in a few days. What should we do? How can she get an extension? Can you suggest something?"

He looked at Anara with genuine interest.

"Well," he said. "You know what most people do? They just go over to Turkey and come back. It's simple. They get a new visa stamp, good for another six months."

"Istanbul?" I asked.

"No, just get over to Adana or Tosuncu. Those places are much closer. You can fly to Adana or take a ferry. The ferry is cheaper."

"Sounds like a good idea," I said. "We'll take the ferry. I love ferryboats. It will be fun."

"Sure," he said.

"How's the writing coming along?" I asked.

"It's okay, I suppose," he said with a chuckle. "I'm just getting some ideas down on paper."

"Good," I said. "Keep at it. See ya later."

As we left the Karmi Shop, I put an arm around Anara's waist.

"See," I said. "There is a way to skin this cat. Let's go tomorrow. I'll cancel classes and go with you."

That made her happy.

So the next day, we went to a travel agent in Kyrenia to buy two round-trip tickets for the ferry. The Turkish lady who sold us the tickets was well groomed, friendly and polite. She told us that the ferryboat left the Yeni Liman (New Harbor) for Tosuncu at midnight and returned next day at noon. That would suit us just fine, I told her. I hadn't really relished the thought of Anara going to Adana alone.

I didn't think the ferryboat would have much of a restaurant on board so we decided to prepare a travel bag and get some food. Since Anara loved fruit, we got apples and oranges and bananas plus bags of taco chips and cookies for me. Then on the way to the ferry terminal we stopped at *Ezic* restaurant. *Ezic* was known for doing the best rotisserie chicken in Kyrenia. I got a couple of take-away dinners, some cans of soft drinks and a couple of beers.

We got to the ferry terminal around nine, well ahead of the time of departure. With nothing else to do, we went and sat on the steps outside the building and watched an endless stream of taxis disgorge passengers and then leave trailing clouds of acrid smoke. Most of the arrivals were men, rugged-looking fellows with heavy mustaches and unshaven jowls, working-class chaps dressed in ill-fitting suits that hung awkwardly on their muscular bodies. They had come from all over Turkey to do all the rough, tough work, make money and send it to their families. Decent chaps all. Salt of the earth. Waiters, dishwashers, taxi-drivers, bricklayers, plasterers, plumbers, electricians, welders. They had gnarled hands, faces seamed with furrows and the powerful limbs of men who labor long and hard in all kinds of weather. We found out that they were all returning to the Turkish mainland to celebrate *Kurban Bayram*, an important Muslim festival. Most families sacrificed a sheep or a goat to remember the moment when Abraham nearly sacrificed his son to please God. The men were returning with all manner of gifts and goods, bulging bundles and huge suitcases crammed with purchases and secured with cords and straps.

The scene inside the departure hall was pure chaos. An incoherent babble of voices greeted our ears as we entered and the place was packed with bodies. People were pushing and shoving and the atmosphere crackled with a palpable anxiety. I saw very few women in the crowd and hardly any children. And to make matters worse, all the men stared at Anara the way hungry Israelites must have looked upon manna.

As we watched, the crowd became larger and larger until the vast hall was a sea of bobbing black heads and flailing arms. Everyone seemed excited and agitated and a miasma of nervous anxiety filled the hall. Obeying some invisible signal, the sea of tightly packed bodies would surge towards the door that led to the ferryboat ramp and then fall back and then surge forward again. The vast interior echoed with an incomprehensible roar and Anara and I found ourselves getting pushed further and further away from the entry gate till we were on the extreme periphery of the tightly packed throng. It dawned on me that we didn't have much of a chance of getting on the ferryboat.

I pulled Anara outside the departure hall to debate our next move. What should we do? Finally, I said, "This is ridiculous. We'll never get on that boat. Why don't we just go home and you can take the airplane over to Adana by yourself?"

Exactly the same idea had occurred to her.

"I hate this," she said. "I'm exhausted. I can't breathe. I feel as though I am being crushed."

"Come," I said. "Let's get out of here."

We found a taxi and headed for Karmi.

What a relief it was to inhale the cool and fragrant midnight odors of our quiet little mountain village again. Scented dew seemed to be coming down around us almost like a fine rain and the fragrance of night-blooming jasmine was everywhere. But underneath my sense of relief, a worry still lurked – we had lost yet another skirmish in the visa war.

Derek clucked sympathetically when he heard about our misadventure at the Yeni Liman.

"Yes. It can get crazy. Better to go by air. Bit more civilized, I should think. The ferry boat is always crowded but I think the *Kurban Bayram* business made the situation much worse."

So back we went to the travel agent, the pretty Turkish matron who had displayed such a friendly attitude earlier.

"We never went," I said. "Couldn't even get near the ferry boat. The crowd made it impossible. There were thousands of men and mountains of luggage. We'd like to return these tickets. We never used them."

The friendly smile dropped from her face with a stunning suddenness. She consulted another lady at the desk next to her in rapid Turkish.

"I'm sorry," she said. "Those tickets cannot be returned after the departure time."

"But we couldn't use them. The ferryboat was too crowded. That is not our fault."

Another consultation followed in machine-gun Turkish.

"I'm sorry. But that is our policy. You can use them next week."

"We've decided to go by air to Adana."

"We have a policy ..."

"Look," I said. "We never stepped onto the ferry boat. Why should we have to pay for a trip we never took? Do you understand my logic?"

Much annoyed and irritated, she got up, smoothed her tight skirt and high-heeled into a back office to consult with some "higher authority."

Anara looked at me morosely and I looked at her. Then the lady returned and punched up some numbers on her calculator.

"We can give you half your money," she said. "As a special concession. My boss says."

"Fine," I said. "Thank you very much. We'll take half."

I swore under my breath never to even go near the ferryboat.

We hurried to another travel agent, the one near the Dome hotel from whom I had purchased Anara's ticket to get a round-trip air ticket for Adana. The plane left at six in the morning and she would have to be at the airport at four, two hours ahead of the time of departure. This in turn meant that she would have to leave Karmi at three, and that I would have to call ahead of time and make the arrangements for a taxi to pick her up and take her to the airport.

Luckily, Derek had the phone number of a taxi service that he had used. "You can rely on this chap," he told us. "He's never late."

On the night of her departure, I could not sleep and neither could she. I made her a couple of chicken sandwiches, wrapped them in waxed paper and packed an apple and a coke for her in a day-bag. We watched TV morosely, too depressed and tense to do anything else and waited for the taxi to arrive. I hated to see her go, but we had no other way of dealing with the problem.

At three sharp, I heard the rumble of a car encroach upon the silence as it labored up the switchbacks of the mountain. I knew this had to be the taxi, so I picked up her day-bag and we made our way through dark streets to the plaza. By the time we got there, the taxi had arrived and stood in rumbling, its lights throwing a glow over the gravel. I gave Anara a quick peck on the cheek and handed her in.

"Keep the knapsack near you," I said. "Do call when you get to Adana and also when you get back to Erjan."

She nodded, tight-lipped, obviously nervous but keeping up a brave front. The taxi made a wide u-turn and then slowly drove off, the taillights glowing hotly in the darkness. I trudged back to the house, feeling empty and listless and filled with a sense of foreboding. By now I knew that one could never depend on things going right in Cyprus.

Somehow, I managed to get through the day. Wracked with tension and worry, I staggered from class to class, barely aware of students addressing questions to me or of the answers I gave them.

Finally, towards noon, Anara called from a pay phone. She seemed quite calm and self-confident.

"It's a really small airport," she said. "It has only a tiny restaurant and a tiny duty-free shop. I'm so bored, honey."

"You'll be home soon. Just relax. Did you eat the sandwiches?"

"I still have those. But I ate the apple."

"Eat them later," I said to her. "And call me when you land at Erjan."

"Okay," she said and hung up.

Her return flight was scheduled to land at 7:00 p.m. I figured she'd call me by about 7:30, get a taxi and get home around 8:30. So around 6:00 I started to cook up a lamb stew and boiled some rice to have food ready when she got home. But the 7:30 call never came. I waited and waited, getting more anxious by the minute. I wondered if she'd run into some problem.

Finally, at 8:30, the phone rang.

"Honey," I heard her say, her voice slightly higher than its normal pitch, "they won't let me enter. They are telling me I have to go back to Adana."

My heart jumped into my throat and for a second I couldn't breathe. I had expected something like this.

"Why?" I asked.

"I don't know. They say I must go back. They wouldn't even let me make a phone call. But I told them about you. Please come. Do something."

"Okay," I said. "Don't worry. I'm coming. We'll sort this thing out."

I didn't want to increase her fear by letting her see my terror. But panic gripped me as I hung up. I had not anticipated anything like this. What to do? Who could I call? Who could I turn to for help?

I threw some clothes on in a hurry and sprinted over to Barbara's house. She had just settled down to eat her dinner in front of the TV. In a few words I explained the situation. She got up immediately.

"This is abominable. Bloody high-handed, I say. Let's take my car."

"I thought it would all be normal," I said. "They'd stamp a three month visa and that would be the end of it. I don't understand this attitude."

"You expected rational behavior from low-level robots in uniforms," she said as we hopped into her car.

"Let's pick up Derek," I said. "It was his idea. He told me there wouldn't be any problem."

"Fine," she said and swung by Derek's house. He must have heard the sound of the car pulling up and came to the door, a bewildered look on his ruddy face.

"Come," I said. We've got to go to the airport. They won't let Anara enter. We've got to rescue her."

He looked back and said a few terse words to his wife and jumped into the back seat.

"Let's go," he said.

The streets of Kyrenia were free of traffic at this hour, so we made good time. Everything seemed to be happening very fast, like a film passing before one's eyes at high speed. Within minutes, it seemed, we were negotiating the blind curves of the pass that separates the Mesaoria from the northern coast. A grim silence filled the car, broken only by the occasional oaths and curses that Derek uttered.

"These fuckers make up rules as they go along," he muttered. "That's what irritates me."

I dreaded the worst and did not allow myself to even think about the various scenarios that could play out, what the airport goons might make us do. Derek tried to cheer me up.

"Buck up, old chap. We'll get her out."

"I've been coming to this island since I was sixteen," Barbara said. "It keeps changing. You never feel you know the place. Just as you start feeling secure, everything changes and you say to yourself: is this really Cyprus?"

Finally, we were at Erjan, a small army come to rescue a damsel in distress. One middle-aged American, one brave, dinnerless English lady and a would-be poet. The long drive to the airport had made Barbara irritable and neither was Derek in any mood to tolerate the high Pooh-Bah tactics of the visa Gestapo.

We accosted an airport security guard and told him why we were there. He nodded and led us to a small, bare office with Attaturk on the wall where a uniformed "Kapitan" sat behind a desk. It wasn't the same office where Cardiff and I had been earlier but similar in size and décor. He listened to Derek's unholy mixture of bad Turkish and English. The lady is fine, we were told, but she must return to Adana. But why? Derek argued. She did the right thing. She wanted to stay legally. That is why she had gone to Adana. Wasn't this the normal way of getting a visa extension? All the English did that.

Ah, but she wasn't English.

Why should that matter?

But it matters you see. We have a big problem here with young women.

This young lady will not cause any problems. She is a guest of this gentleman (I was pointed out) – An American. A professor.

Then Barbara intervened, "Look here. It's rather unfair. Don't you see? She should be treated like any other tourist. How can you treat her like this? What crime has she committed?"

I simply sat and listened as the argument went on – back and forth – like a tennis ball being volleyed back and forth by players. I would turn my head every time one of them spoke. The Kapitan looked vaguely familiar but I was quite certain that he wasn't the same one from whose clutches we had saved Anara the last time. By now my head had begun to throb with a vicious migraine and my vision became distorted. The faces of the people in the room began to melt and flow into each other like superimposed images. Meaningless voices echoed and bounced off bare, beige walls. Men in uniform floated in and out of the room and I found it difficult to understand why they had come and why they were going. Hours, it seemed, went by.

Finally, after endless wrangling back and forth, Derek managed to win a point and the Kapitan reached into a drawer and pulled out Anara's passport and handed it to a guard. The guard went out of the office while we waited held in a straightjacket of wordless tension. Then the guard returned and handed the passport back to the Kapitan, who in turn handed it to Derek and nodded to the guard. They had decided to release Anara. We got up, shook hands all around and muttered Merhabas several times and followed the guard outside to a building that stood separate and apart from the main airport – the detention cells, obviously. I followed the guard inside the building. Barbara and Derek hurried towards the parking lot to get the car. They made me wait in a sort of lobby, while the guard went and brought Anara. She burst into sobs as soon as she saw me and almost collapsed. I put an arm around her and steadied her.

"Come, come, honey," I said. "It's okay. It's all okay now."

I could see she was very distraught and needed comforting. I got into the back seat with her, Derek took the front seat and Barbara was in the driver's seat. She released the clutch, the vehicle jerked forward with a shriek of protest from the tires and soon we were speeding back to Karmi.

It wasn't until we were safe back home that I looked at Anara's passport. The bastards had given her just 30 more days. I knew we were in serious trouble.

～

CHAPTER FOUR

Section 1

It is amazing how a place that is almost like paradise can start to lose its glow when you are worried about rock-hard, ugly realities of life. I found I was paying less attention to Karmi's charms as the steel mesh of regulations invented by the bureaucratic mind started to tighten around us. Anara's visa problem had become a constant worry, a barbed hook in my flesh that I just couldn't pull out. We were running out of time and we had to do something quickly. One solution that presented itself was enrolling her at a university. In fact, Farhat Bey suggested this option but warned that it should be "some other university – not ours – because that would not look good." I understood what he was implying. The administration would not look kindly upon a teacher living with a student. With this caveat ringing in my mind, I contacted a university near Nicosia. They would admit her, they said, but wanted four thousand dollars per semester. This was a damned expensive way to get a long-term visa; moreover, I just didn't have that much cash on hand. Nor would Anara let me do this.

"There has to be another way, honey," she kept saying.

"Look, I'll borrow from my mother," I said. "I'm sure she can spare four thousand."

"What will we do next semester?"

"We'll manage somehow. We'll worry about that bridge when we get to it."

"No, honey. Don't."

"Let me try at least. Let's see what she says."

Anara hung her head, confused and exhausted.

I called mother, as soon as I got the chance.

"When are you coming back?" was her very first question.

"You know, Mom. Not till the end of the Spring semester."

"You are so stubborn," she said. "Just like your father. He was the most stubborn man I ever knew. Stubborn as a mule."

This was her favorite mode of whipping me. Any trait or habit she did not like in me, got compared to a similar quality in my father. And as I got older, this list got longer and longer, until I wondered why she had married the man if he had been such a bastard. In her book, I was lazy and so was my father. I drank too much and so did my father. If women could manipulate me easily, I had inherited this weakness from my father. If I could not save money, my father had the same problem. He wasted more money than ten normal men. And so it went.

"Mom, I need some money," I said.

I got the words out but I felt as though I was tearing out my gall bladder with bare hands.

"Why?"

She needed a plausible reason, something that would make sense to her.

"I've got to buy a car." I began. "The old wreck I have keeps breaking down. I'm spending a fortune on getting it repaired. I'd like to get a better one."

"You're always wasting money."

"I was being thrifty. I didn't want to spend too much on a car."

"How much do you want?"

"Can you spare four thousand? Four thousand should do the trick."

"That's a lot. I don't have that kind of money lying around."

"Of course, you do."

"No, I don't. Moreover, I don't want to support your overseas junkets. You lose more money than you make. You just wrap up everything and come back."

"I can't, mother. Just tell me. Will you give me the money or not? You know I will pay you back."

"You won't. You never do. I paid off your credit card bill back in spring. You still owe me that. You never did pay me back for that."

"I will Mom. I promise I will. When I get back."

"I'm not giving you one single dollar. And that's that!"

She hung up abruptly.

My cheeks burned as though I had been slapped hard. That was, indeed, that. I knew she wouldn't change her mind. There was no sense pleading or arguing further.

Suddenly, our situation became much clearer. When Anara saw my face, she knew what I already knew.

"I tried," I said.

"I know you did, sweetie," she said in soothing tones. "But don't worry. Everything will be fine."

"I hope so," I said. "I certainly hope so."

Late on a sunlit afternoon Anara and I walked down the stone steps that curved sinuously between houses and led to the central plaza. If you were on foot, the steps provided a quick way down and you avoided the long, looping switchback of the main road. A fig tree loaded with ripe figs provided shade and attracted armies of bees. Fallen fruit got squished into a sticky jam on the stone steps and attracted ants. Sheltered as it was on either side by the white walls of houses, it was odorous as a wine cellar.

The fear that Anara might have to go back to Almaty lingered in the back of my mind night and day but I did my best to hide my concern and appear calm in front of her. Now, every moment spent with her acquired a new urgency. Near the lily pond we ran into Fiona. Usually Fiona spent a couple of hours in her office every afternoon, taking phone calls, directing the gardeners, solving tenant problems. Afterwards, she walked around the village along a fixed route with a big plastic bag full of dry cat food filling bowls at several locations for the cats that led independent lives around the church.

"The cat population exploded a few years ago," Fiona told us once. "There were a hundred or so roaming around here, fighting with each other, sick, starving, injured. The residents complained. We had to do something. Then we began a program of getting the males neutered and the females spayed and sent many to the Animal Shelter for adoption. Now we just have a few – thank god!"

We found her alone in her office, a strictly functional room with a desk, a phone, a computer and three easy chairs for visitors on which several cats sat thinking deep thoughts. Fiona sat in a swivel chair – a large, earth mother presence.

"What should we do?" I asked her, after I had explained our dilemma. "The days are slipping by and I really don't want her to stay here illegally."

"So the police just made you run from one place to another?"

"Right. No one would lift a finger," I told her. "We even went to the Immigration office – that ugly building near the bus-terminal in Nicosia. They shunted us back to the airport. We've been to Erjan twice. We've been to the Kyrenia police station. No one can do a thing, it seems."

"Well, I suppose you know about the student option, right?"

"Yes. My chief, Farhat Bey mentioned that."

"Why not get her admitted into the university where you teach?"

"There would be a scandal," I told her. "They'd say I was living with a student. I might even get fired."

"Well, there's that university near Nicosia."

"Too expensive," I said. "We looked into that. I Just don't have the funds."

"Ahh," sighed Fiona and started to caress the all-black office cat she called "Inky-Binky."

"The only other way is getting a job and applying for a work visa. The employer is actually responsible for getting her one."

"We thought about that," I said. "The problem is she doesn't speak Turkish and her English isn't too strong. She went looking once and talked to some store managers. All of them said they wanted her to be able to talk in Turkish to the Turkish-speaking customers. Knowing Russian does not carry any weight."

Fiona listened in silence. Perhaps she had run out of ideas.

"Keep trying" she said, finally. "I've seen many Russian-speaking girls working here. Try hotels, restaurants, nightclubs, casinos. They are always hiring. I'm sure she'll find something."

Anara and I stared at each other gloomily.

"Know anyone who works in a bar or disco?" Fiona asked.

Anara and I almost simultaneously said, "Freya."

"Good," said Fiona. "Talk to her. Maybe she can help."

"Thanks," I said. "We'll do that. We've got to do something."

The thought of getting Freya and the disco involved in our affairs did not appeal to me. I didn't much care for the Freya lifestyle. But Anara said she wanted to try this option.

"I thought you didn't like Freya," I said.

"I don't," she responded. "I just want to see if she can help me get a job."

"What job?" I said, rather harshly. "Waitress? And you'll have to work nights. Our life will be turned upside down."

"Honeeee, I'll just do it for a while," Anara said, soothingly. "Once I get the visa, I can quit. What's the alternative? Going back to Almaty? Do you want that? I don't!"

This shut me up. What alternative option did I have? The game, as it was being played in Cyprus, restricted my moves.

"Okay," I said. "You talk to Freya. Let's see what she says. I'll have a chat with Cardiff."

It must have been a Friday because on Fridays I usually stopped by the fish seller on the way home from the university to pick up something for our evening meal. The fish seller was an elderly Turk with very few teeth left in his mouth and sunken melancholy eyes. He seemed to have very little do and on most days I would see him sitting outside his shop with a friend or two puffing away on a cigarette. I had found his place quite by chance as I was driving by one day. It wasn't very large and there were no external visual cues that it was a fish shop. But one day I noticed a hand-written signboard sitting on the sidewalk with the names of several types of fish that I had learned to recognize – Levrek, Cipura, Barboun. These were the Turkish names for Sea bass, Gilt-head Bream and Red Mullet.

Much of the fish he sold was frozen solid, kept in large, glass-fronted chillers. Through the misted glass I could see rust-colored blocks of shrimp stuck together and hard, frost-furred filets of cod and sole that did not look very appetizing. Being a fish vendor for the Turk was mainly a matter of keeping the freezers stocked and waiting for customers to drop by. I had a feeling he saw very few customers like myself. But I enjoyed exchanging greetings with the old guy even though he had almost no English and my knowledge of ten Turkish words meant that beyond cordial "Merhabas" and some eloquent sign language, we said little to each other. I pointed at the fish I wanted and held up two fingers. He weighed the fish, cut off the heads and tails and wrapped them in clean white butcher paper for me. Then he would enter the amount I owed him into a hand-held calculator and hold it up for me to see.

I got a couple of healthy-looking Levrek with clear eyes and firm flesh, each a foot long. One Levrek made a good meal for one person easily, supplemented with rice, mashed potatoes, salad and bread. Then I stopped at the supermarket and picked up two bottles of Sancerre – a special treat, something to cheer the inner man. I figured the chilled Sancerre would go well with the pan-fried Sea Bass. By the time I had made the long, twisting climb up to the village in the Renault, the sun had declined behind the western ridges of the Beshparmak range and long blue shadows stretched from the cypresses. Anara, I figured, must have started boiling the potatoes by now and would be preparing the salad, the way she normally did, anticipating my arrival. But when I entered the house, it felt strangely quiet. I set down my purchases on the kitchen counter and called her name. No response. Then I saw the note on the dining table.

"Honey, going to *Starlight* on scooter. Freya get me job. May be late home. Don't worry. Kisses, A."

I didn't know what to make of this. Was she interviewing for a job? ? Had she started working? Did this mean she would get a work visa? Questions jumped around like popping corn inside my head. She had her mobile but I decided not to call. Instead, I put the wine in the fridge to cool and started to cook dinner. It made little sense to freeze one fish, so I decided to cook them both. I thought I'd make her food and set it aside in case she came home late and hadn't eaten. I put a cupful of rice on the boil, started the potatoes in another pan of water and sliced and diced tomatoes, cucumbers and scallions for the salad. Then I filleted the fish carefully, dredged the filets in flour and pan-fried them till they were golden brown on the outside.

I ate sitting in front of the TV and watched the news. But I couldn't focus. I just stared at the screen and moved my jaws automatically as though I were chewing cud. Death and destruction everywhere. Explosions. Murders. Mayhem. The Sancerre had a vaguely metallic taste. Perhaps I should have left it in the fridge a bit longer. Nor did it lift my spirits as I had hoped it would. I ate quickly without thinking about taste or flavor, then washed the dishes and the greasy pans and put them away. Then I took the last of the Sancerre and went up to the roof. As I sat there drinking and smoking, the sky went from pale orange to deep blue. In the tangential light, swallows appeared suddenly and did aerobatic loops and dives as they went for the rising clouds of flying insects. Then as the light dimmed, squadrons of bats rose up to attack the insects. Gradually, the lights of Kyrenia began to twinkle and I could see the headlights of cars creeping along the coastal road.

I thought Anara might call, but she didn't. They had probably put her to work right away. I missed her, but I also felt a sense of relief. The job could lead to a visa and that would be a blessing. I would just have to put up with long evenings and nights without her. This was a price I would have to pay. Nothing came easy. It would have been better, of course, if she could have gotten a student visa. She could have studied English or even Turkish. That would have been so convenient. But … things were as they were.

Telling mother about Anara did not seem the thing to do. I knew exactly how she would react, what she would say. I raised a fool, she'd scream, a woolly-headed, gullible fool. Squandering his money on foreign women … Who is she, anyway? Some tramp out of that … That … Jerkistan … Or whatever. And why do you have to put her through college? You always end up with these teen-queens who never have a dime of their own. She's using you … I can see that. Can't you?

Getting mother's approval for any of the women I had dated or had relationships with over the years had been difficult, if not impossible. She had high standards – super high standards. No one I brought home met with her approval. Too well-mannered to wage open war or mount an explicit campaign of hostility against someone whom I brought home as a "special friend," mother chose subtler ways of undermining these relationships. She would focus on a person's weakness or deficiency and mention it as something I should keep an eye on, in case it became more pronounced with the passage of time. Thus, if my "date" had a slightly fuller figure, she made it point to warn me that this meant gross, morbid obesity in coming years. If the woman displayed signs of intelligence, some strongly held opinions, mother felt sure she would become a domineering Harpie, a nagging shrew. If the lady in question, happened to be quiet and shy, mother assured me that this indicated a deep anxiety about mixing with people, in fact, could be the early signs of paranoia!

So on and so forth. Need I say more?

My years in the Law school at the University of Chicago were the worst as far as female companionship went. Only the brightest ones got admitted into the Law department and only the toughest ones survived. The bias of the university in favor of male students meant that girls felt unwelcome. They sensed this, of course, and reacted by turning into cold, hard-boiled man-haters. Going out with these driven careerists took nerves of steel if not testicles of tungsten. I never had much luck with them, no matter how many hours I wasted in the *Medici* coffeehouse hoping to pick up one of these brainy types. Weekends usually found me wrapped in my own Existential gloom, drinking scotch and soda in *Jimmy's Bar* on 55th street where they played Classical music non-stop to calm the nerves of depressed grad students. Later, when I entered the world of Chicago law firms, it became even harder to find someone you could take to bed or home to mother.

When I came down from the roof, I couldn't sleep. So I went out and took a turn around the steep streets of the village, going as far as the lily pond and then turning back. A serene darkness had spread everywhere except for occasional rectangles of chrome yellow light spilling from some open window or where the diffuse glow of street lamps penetrated the branches of trees to make lacy leaf patterns on the ground. Everyone seemed to have gone inside by now. I felt like a solitary, inquisitive spy as I peered into windows. I had become so accustomed to having Anara with me every evening that her absence made me nervous, ill at ease. I couldn't help thinking what she might be doing, who she might be talking with? Bars and discos can be rough places for waitresses, what with the drunken men and the pressure to sell drinks and earn tips utilizing just the right degree of flirtatiousness. I wondered how she would fare in this world of sex, booze and music. When I got home, I poured a little brandy into a glass and sat sipping it as I watched some silly show. At some point, I dozed off.

The scooter's familiar putt-putt-putting came drifting over the still night air. I woke up with a start and glanced at the desk clock. The green digits were set at 2:20 a.m. I must have dozed off in front of the TV sitting in the easy chair.

"Well, well," I said, as Anara came in. "They let you come home finally."

Anara flashed an unhappy smirk at me and kicked off her high-heels in one smooth motion.

"How did it go, dear?" I asked.

"I'm so tired and my feet hurt. I must have a dozen blisters."

"Are you hungry? I made some food. It is on the dining table. Must be cold by now but I could heat it up for you."

"No. Too tired to be hungry," she said. "I couldn't eat a thing. I'll just have a glass of milk."

"Suit yourself," I said, giving her a quick hug. "I better get some sleep if I am going to have any strength to teach tomorrow."

Now that she had come home a sudden fatigued relaxation came over me. I didn't think she had any desire to talk or give me details about her evening. Nor did I feel like listening. The de-briefing could wait. I fell on the bed and closed my eyes.

∾

Section 2

One evening I ran into Fiona by the lily pond. I had just stepped out to smoke a cigar and she was on her usual cat-feeding jaunt about the village. Seeing me alone, she said: "Where is Anara?"

"She started working," I said. "At this casino. *Starlight.*"

Fiona raised her eyebrows. She could express a wide range of feelings by simply raising her eyebrows – mild interest, surprise, alarm, even shock. The higher they went, the more intense her reaction. Now they seemed to be at the "alarm" level.

"She'll get a work visa," I said, hoping this information would make her lower her eyebrows.

But Fiona simply nodded, her mouth locked firmly.

"They need a lot of people," I said, genially. "Waiters, waitresses, bartenders, card dealers, croupiers."

Again Fiona nodded without saying a word.

For some reason, I felt a compulsion to explain the hiring practices of gambling casinos and the advantages of working for one.

"She could learn to be a card dealer," I said. "She'll make good money."

I don't think I was telling Fiona anything she didn't already know. Everyone in north Cyprus knew how gambling casinos operated.

"Does she like the work?" Fiona asked.

"I don't think she has much choice," I said. "She has to work to get the visa."

"I understand," she said, with a tight smile. "I'm sure it will all work out."

She started to walk away but then she stopped, her head inclined as if in thought. In the demi-darkness I could barely see her face.

"It's funny," she said in a muted voice. "These Turks, they have a strange love-hate relationship with casinos. They don't like gambling, but are excellent business people and they realize they need the casinos … for the revenue."

"They have other sources of revenue," I said. "Oranges, olives, grapes bring in revenue, no?"

"No," she said. "All that is going fast, if it isn't gone already. The groves are being ripped up to build all those villas. The fact is, casinos attract tourists and tourists bring in money. Q. E. D. You see, they look at Monte Carlo and become glassy-eyed. North Cyprus could also become a moneymaking machine. Dollars, Pounds, Euros would rain down! How wonderful would that be? No need for factories or products. That approach takes too long, anyway, requires too much effort … But casinos? All you need is a roulette table and a few slot-machines and you are in business."

"Sounds like a win-win deal all around," I murmured.

"Yes, but the casino culture brings problems also," Fiona said. "All the other ancillary *stuff* that comes with them. The same way an incoming tide brings a lot of garbage."

"You mean drugs? Gangsters?"

"And prostitution … ."

"Naturally … ."

"The fellows who run these places do everything they can to attract gamblers: free food, free drinks, pretty girls …"

"That's where the Russian girls fit in."

"Exactly," Fiona said. "They are not just workers. The girls are the lure, you see, the bait. They clean the rooms, serve drinks and deal cards, but their real job, the most important job, is to be nice to the customers."

"How nice?" I said curling my lips into a sly, sardonic smile.

Cardiff and I had discussed the seamy side of casinos many times. But I let Fiona go on talking. I think she was telling me all this in a spirit of helpfulness, not malice.

"These men come and spend a lot of money and all they are looking for is entertainment, excitement."

"Naturally."

"And the girls are there to make them happy."

I didn't like the implications of what she was driving at, but I decided to keep it all light and casual.

"Everybody is happy."

"No. Not everybody." Fiona said.

She seemed determined to make a point she really didn't have to make, at least not in front of me.

"For immigration officials these *female guest-workers* can be a headache," she went on. "They come by the hundreds, hoping for good jobs, good money, the good life. A few know what is expected of them. They co-operate, earn some cash and return home safe and sound. But some are not so lucky. They get themselves into ugly situations; they get exploited, abused, even murdered."

"But these guys at the airport – how do they figure out that a certain young woman is a troublesome *guest worker* and another is just a legitimate tourist?"

"That's not so difficult," Fiona said. "With a bit of training and experience and keen powers of observation anyone could do the job easily. Girls from Russian-speaking countries are prime suspects, and if they are young and pretty they set off alarm bells right away. Your genuine tourist is old and rich and usually from Europe. They come to spend money not to make money."

"Seems to me these guys at the airport have turned the whole thing into a racket."

"Of course," Fiona said. "They have a kind of partnership with the casino owners. They permit a few girls to come, the ones who are being sponsored by a casino, and in return the casino owners treat the officials well, make them happy."

"What a system," I said. "Works well, I suppose."

"Most of the time. But when someone says *no* ... well, that's when the fireworks start."

These were her final words and she hurried off down the lane, leaving me to ponder the full implications of what she had said. Surely, she was trying to be helpful but she had made me uneasy.

On Monday afternoon, Anara's day off, we were walking to the Karmi Shop to get some beer and milk. She skipped along beside me, giddy with glee. Both of us were buoyant with hope.

"I want to meet this Vitaly fellow," I said. "Talk to him. See if he means what he says."

He really wasn't the sort of person I usually enjoyed meeting. I had little in common with business types, no shared interests. I saw nothing in their values or worldview that would prove attractive to me. But I decided I had to do this.

Anara, nodded.

"Okay, come," she said. "But remember, Vitaly speak bad English."

"I understand," I said. "Maybe someone can do the translating."

"You can gamble, if you like."

"No. I won't gamble. I just want to see our Mr. Vitaly."

I had met him only once, very briefly, at the *Triton*. I had a certain curiosity about him. Moreover, I just I didn't want him pushing or pulling Anara into some caper she didn't need to be in. This was my only reason for going to the *Starlight Casino*. I had no interest in gambling nor did I get any pleasure out of games of chance. Sitting at a slot machine, pulling levers and pushing buttons did nothing for me. Nor did I like playing cards games. All that bored me.

When we got to the Karmi Shop, Derek was sitting under his umbrella. His eyes looked pink and watery and his cheeks flamed red. His fingers trembled as he brought the cigarette to his lips.

"Hi, Derek, how are you?" I called out.

"Fine," he said, without looking at me.

His eyes were fixed on Anara as he examined her with frank, masculine interest. Then he rose and followed us into the store. Men looked at Anara in this manner all the time and she simply loathed being stared at. I urged her to accept this scrutiny as a compliment but she could not bring herself to do it. I knew that Derek thought of himself as a "player," a bit of a ladies man and I had warned Anara to be careful when she was around him. There was no telling what he might do or say, especially if he'd been drinking. In England he had followed the auto-racing circuit and still loved to talk about fast cars and even faster women. He had done some reporting for papers that followed the personalities, the products and promoters in auto racing. At times, I think he missed the danger and excitement of that world. Being the proprietor of a small grocery store in a small village on a small island must not have been much fun for him. As Anara and I picked up milk and beer and bread, we almost bumped into a pair of English women who were milling around, trying to decide what to buy. Derek paid no attention to them. Instead, he pulled me by the elbow and handed me a newspaper clipping.

"Read this," he said, with a note of pride in his voice.

His speech was a bit slurred and his face glowed red and his carrot-colored hair positively bristled with a kind of liquored-up good cheer.

I took the clipping from him, positioned myself in a corner and started to read. It was an article he had written for a Cyprus paper, describing a vintage car rally he had participated in some months earlier. The two English ladies poked about for a while and then one of them picked up a kerosene lantern.

"How much for this?"

Her accent sounded distinctly upper class to my ears.

Derek stared hard at the lantern, wondering what to say. It had no price tag.

Finally, he said, "How much would you pay for it in England?"

There was a mischievous glint in his ruby-red eyes.

The lady, thought for a second and then said: "Five or six pounds."

"Okay," said Derek. "I'll take six pounds."

I think he meant this as a joke, as a way of starting a conversation. But the lady didn't get the humor, apparently.

"We aren't in England," she snapped. "This is Cyprus."

The tone of this remark appeared to flick a switch in Derek's brain. He went from "Nice" to "Nasty" in a flash.

"I don't give a damn," he said, sharply. "Take it or leave it."

The woman backed away in alarm and put the lantern back on the shelf.

"Come on, Annie," she said to her friend, "let's go."

And the two walked out, haughty noses tilted skyward. As she left, I heard her say in an overly loud, indignant tone of voice, "We've been coming here for ten years and I've never been treated ..."

I acted as though I hadn't seen or heard a thing.

"This is a nice piece," I said, handing the newspaper clipping back to Derek.

"We had a grand time," Derek said, as he added up our purchases. "I'm going to try and organize another one soon. It's a great way to attract tourists to Karmi."

Just as we were leaving the shop, we ran into Karen. She looked at me and then at Anara with a certain envious wistfulness.

"Great weather," I said. "I was getting tired of the heat."

"Yes," she said in a melancholy tone. "I hope we have a few nice days before the rainfall begins."

"That's okay," I said. "I don't mind the rain. It's the hot weather that I can't stand."

"Well, you better wait and see," Karen said. "It gets pretty damp and foggy up here."

"Great. I'll love it."

"Haven't seen your lady friend much lately," Karen said. "Where have you been keeping her?"

Karen addressed her question to me because she knew Anara's English wasn't very strong.

"You tell her," I said to Anara.

I wanted her to speak, to use her English and build up her confidence.

"I work now," she said. "I have job at *Starlight Casino*."

"That must be fun," Karen said, in joyless tones.

"Is it fun?" I asked, turning towards Anara.

She sensed I was mocking her, so she just started walking away.

"Thanks, Karen," I said. "See ya later."

Anara may have been ambivalent about her job but she loved her scooter and the freedom of movement it allowed her. It amused me vastly to see how much affection she lavished on her scooter and how hard she tried to keep it shiny clean at all times. Washing the scooter became her favorite activity, a religious rite on Sundays. And for me, watching her at this task was a perpetual delight. She prepared for the job by stripping down to skimpy shorts, a T-shirt stretched over bra-free breasts and rubber sandals. I was told to station myself near the garden tap. This I did, beer in one hand, a lit cigar in the other, ready to call out free advice and turn the hose on or off as required.

First came a general, overall dousing with fulsome amounts of water. This went on for quite a while. Then I was given the order to open the tap ALL the way as she directed a powerful stream at the wheels and tires to break loose the larger chunks of dirt and road grime. Then I'd hear her shout, "Turn it off! Off! Off!"

Now began the soaping phase as she dipped the sponge in thick, rich suds and passed it slowly and lovingly over the plastic faring, the mudguards and the engine covers. She performed this part of the ritual in a kind of meditative silence. I think she drifted off to another, more exalted state of mind as she slid her hand over the slippery surfaces. Once the soap had been applied thoroughly and generously it was time for the rinse cycle. After the soap and foam had been removed from all the surfaces, the drying phase commenced. This had to be done quickly. Any delay meant that the hot sun would quickly make water spots and those were hard to rub off. When all this been done, she moved the machine to a dry spot away from overhanging tree branches to avoid bird droppings and stood back satisfied and happy to admire her handiwork – the clean, shiny, bright red scooter sitting on its stand in the sunlight.

～

Section 3

I went to the roof soon after sundown with a glass of wine. A pale, lavender light still lingered in the sky but a blue-gray darkness had begun to settle over Karmi. Then, slowly, the sky got darker and filled up with a violet glow and down and away on the coast, the lights of Kyrenia started to glitter and glow like the wreckage of many galaxies scattered across the black emptiness of space. I wondered what the future had in store for me and for Anara, what the coming years would bring, or, indeed, if we had a future together. Looking straight ahead into the vista of time, everything seemed misty, undefined, and vague. Where might I get a chance to teach, I had no idea? And if I returned to the States, would Anara be able to follow me there? I rather doubted that. Getting a long-term U.S. visa for her would be difficult if not altogether impossible. Marriage could provide a way, but it seemed a terribly selfish act on my part and filled me with forebodings and fears and doubts. The age difference between us always lingered like a ghost at the banquet, but there were other factors too. Being a bachelor had become a habit, a way of life. How matrimony would suit my temperament, how it would affect me at some deeper level, remained an unresolved issue. Not that I equated being a bachelor with the career of a stud or a sexual athlete. I had felt no driving urge to go from woman to woman in an endless and repetitive series of relationships. That seemed a fruitless and circular endeavor. I had never been a "Casanova," not even in my younger days. And that I would turn into one, after having passed the half-century mark, did not seem very likely. Then there was my mother, whose attitude I could easily predict.

As I sat there, mulling over these issues, heavy dew seeped into the night air and I felt the dampness settling over my clothes. I gulped down what remained of the wine and headed down. By 10 o'clock when TV news came on everyone in Karmi had retired for the night. I put on a freshly laundered white shirt, a blue blazer, and dark trousers and headed for the *Starlight Casino*. There wasn't much traffic on the road from Karmi to Karaolagnoglu and the November night was chilly enough to make me raise the window of the Renault. But on the coastal road, there were plenty of cars, moving east and west, some going insanely fast.

I found *Starlight* easily, ablaze in splendiferous neon Las Vegas style. Flashing signs in bright colored lights throbbed and pulsed across its facade. A parking attendant took my car from me as soon as I pulled up at the front door and it dawned on me that I had entered the domain of high prices and costly glamour. The hectic, mechanical drumbeat of techno-rock assaulted my ears as soon as I stepped into the casino. Every molecule in the place seemed to be charged with an electrical energy. Lights flickered and blinked all around, bells bonged and clanged and I heard the typical ka-chung, ka-chung and ka-chung of slot machines arranged in glimmering, sparking rows. The green baize surface of gaming tables gave off an eerie, radioactive glow. People gathered around them in small clusters, followed the action – the throw of dice, the clattering circuit of the roulette ball and the slap and shuffle of cards. Loud laughter and hoots of joy were undercut by moans and groans and beneath all this noise, I heard the brooding hum of subterranean machinery.

Not knowing what else to do, I headed for the bar and ordered a scotch and soda. I asked the bartender if he knew where I could find Mr. Vitaly (I didn't know his last name). The bartender said he would check and went around behind the bar and talked to someone. Then as a waitress swung by, teetering on high heels, I stopped and asked if she could let Anara know that I was sitting at the bar. The girl nodded and rushed off. I had just finished my drink, when I saw Anara approaching. I hardly recognized her in the dim light. She was wearing her working "kit" – a short, red skirt that flared out like a tutu, a pink blouse made of some shiny material and a black-bow tie. And she had piled up her hair on top of her head in a sort of dark domed heap. She walked up to me, her legs encased in black fishnet stockings, and gave me a quick, superficial, perfunctory peck on the cheek.

"I'm busy, honey," she said, breathlessly.

"I understand. Is Vitaly here?" I asked.

"Yes," she said. "I'll go and get him. But you must excuse me. I have to work."

"No problem, sweetie," I said. "You go ahead. Do what you have to do. I'll wait for him here."

Presently, I saw Vitaly coming towards me. He looked paler and even more obese than he had looked when I saw him the first time at the *Triton*. He was wearing a brown, ill-fitting business suit and he lumbered towards me slowly, placing his feet wide apart to keep his thighs from rubbing together. His face was covered by a thin greasy sheen of perspiration and he had carefully plastered his thin strands of blond hair across the top of his bald head. He was quite short in stature but he made up in width what he lacked in height and he had the girth of three normal men.

"Hello" he said, sticking out his small, pudgy hand. "I remember you. You friend of Anara?"

I nodded.

"Ah, yes, yes, she told me. You teach at university, no?"

"Yes, I do," I said.

"Come," he said, tacking sideways, "we go my office. Less noise."

He led the way around and behind the bar and we walked into a small, brightly lit room with a gray steel desk, a couple of standard office chairs and an old couch that did not look too sanitary, having obviously seen much hard usage. A beige telephone and a brass vase containing some plastic flowers in garish primary colors took up one side of the desk. The "office" seemed strangely lacking in the usual items that clutter up offices. I saw no papers, or files, or pens and pencils, not even a computer. Vitaly closed the door behind him, cutting off the sounds of the casino. I noticed a calendar and a bulletin board on a wall, but there was nothing else to relieve the bareness of the room. Vitaly maneuvered his bulk behind the desk with some difficulty. The springs of the chair clanged and creaked as he lowered his weight.

"What will you drink?" he asked, picking up a phone. "Coffee? Tea? Juice? Myself don't drink much now. Just water. Stomach finish."

He patted his front and smiled sadly.

The harsh, incandescent light falling from the ceiling threw a gray-green tint over his skin and there were half-moons of darkness under each eye. His eyes looked almost white, with intense centers of blackness that seemed to be sucking all the light out of the room.

"I just had a drink at the bar," I said. "I'm fine."

"You are guest. Have something."

"Oh, okay. I'll have some water too. I have to drive home."

He raised a hand.

"I understand," he said and spoke into the phone in terse Russian.

"You like Cyprus?" he said.

"Yes," I said. "But not during the summer months. I don't like the hot weather here."

"Yes, hot weather no good. I never go out. Stay in all the time."

He looked at me intently for a while. Then he said, "American, yes," his eyes still fixed on me.

"Yes."

"You like university?"

"Yes," I said. "I enjoy teaching."

"You are smart man," he said, his pale blue eyes boring into me. "For me, no education. Just business. Business, business, business all the time. No time for education."

"I understand," I said. "In business you make money."

He shook his head sadly.

"No money," he said. "I pay everybody. Government, taxes, this man, that woman. Pay. Pay. Pay. Vitaly always pay. Everybody come to Vitaly."

I nodded in sympathy.

There was a gentle rap on the door and a waiter walked in with two glasses and a bottle of water on a salver. He set them down and walked out without saying a word.

Vitaly poured some into each glass.

"Wish this vodka," he said, looking at his glass of water. "No vodka for Vitaly now. Bad kidneys, bad heart, bad liver. Everything finito, kaputski."

He thumped his chest.

"Thank you," I said. "Thank you also for giving Anara the job."

"She hard worker," he said. "I like that."

"She really wants to stay in Cyprus," I said, "with me."

I paused for split second, to make sure he understood the full import of my words. Then I said, "That is why she needs the work visa. I want her to stay here as long as I am here. When I leave, she will return to Kazakhstan."

"No problem," Vitaly said, sipping his water meditatively. "She will get visa. Don't worry."

As we were talking, there was a little commotion at the door and then someone knocked.

"Enter, enter," Vitaly said.

Anara stuck her head in at the door and said something in Russian.

"Okay, okay," said Vitaly

And two middle-aged men in dark business suits entered and greeted Vitaly in Russian.

Anara spoke to them in Russian and then she made as if to leave.

"Sit, sit," Vitaly said, waving his arm in an inclusive manner. "We are all friends."

I nodded briefly at the visitors. They nodded back, their faces expressionless.

The two men said some words in Russian and then sat down on the couch. Anara took a chair beside me.

"These my friends from Ukraine," Vitaly said. He pronounced it the Russian way – ooo-kra-eeena. "We do business."

A common language provides an instant link even between strangers. The visitors and Vitaly were totally at ease and I sensed that they all wanted to speak in Russian. Since I really didn't have much more to say to Vitaly, I decided to beg leave. He looked like a harried businessman, with a million matters to attend to, many masters to please, many daggers to pull out of his spacious back. Anara also looked uncomfortable, perched uneasily on the edge of her chair, holding on to a tight smile as though she had something in her mouth that she couldn't swallow or spit out.

"I'd better be going," I said, standing up abruptly.

I put out my hand at Vitaly. "But I am glad I met you. I'm sure I'll see you again. What's the Russian? … Dosvidania."

Every one said "Dosvidania" almost in unison and I left the room. I did not say anything to Anara as I left, nor did she anything to me.

I did not want to indicate to the two Ukrainians, by gesture or words that Anara and I were linked in anyway.

To say that I was jealous of Anara's new Russian-speaking friends would be overstating the matter somewhat. But I must admit to a certain degree of apprehensiveness, a slight anxiety that stabbed my brain at odd moments. I felt, quite unjustifiably, that she was closer to them than to me and I did not relish this very much. Nor was I too happy about the fact that she was spending more and more time at the casino and when she was home, she was often tired and irritable and sleepy and interested in little except eating and sleeping. In some ways I felt sorry for her. Her work drained most of her energy, sapped her strength both physical and mental, but in general she seemed happy that she was making a little money and would soon be getting the much-coveted and necessary work-visa.

So far I have not said much about Vitaly. Mainly, because it took me a while to understand his personality. It took a while to see the person whose arc of life intersected ours at many points and around whom we orbited like satellites going round a massive planet. Moreover word portraits of people are difficult to paint in our time. "Characters" in the old fashioned sense have, more or less, vanished. People don't have stable personalities and what they do reveal are seldom their true natures. They hide behind false claims, public statements, self-serving lies. They also keep changing, mutating, morphing. They take on new names, new identities. Even the portraits of Anara, Cardiff and Freya that I have attempted seem incomplete and inadequate to me. They exist on the page as pen and ink sketches. They can only truly come alive, if the reader shines the light of his own imagination on them.

I never did get to know Vitaly very well. Most of the time, I saw him from a distance or through the eyes of Anara. Vitaly only had one interest: the *Starlight*. Mine was the university. We had little in common. He (no doubt) saw me as a (head-in-the clouds) academic, removed from what he considered the "real world." My being an American may have been another reason why he kept me at a distance. No, that is not quite correct. Actually, I kept myself at a distance from him and rarely visited the casino. The garish décor, the loud, brain-numbing music and the fake gaiety did nothing for me.

I hated shaking hands with Vitaly, touching his cold, pudgy fingers. It was like touching a boneless slug. I am ashamed to even mention all this. Focusing on a person's physical handicaps is neither helpful nor very kind. But many people admired him, especially his generosity and friendliness. Anara noticed qualities that I never saw. She said he worked hard to make the casino a success because that was the only thing that mattered to him. He had no family, no hobbies and no interests outside the casino. He spent all his waking hours on the premises overseeing every detail, making sure the entire operation was functioning smoothly and efficiently. Not only did he obsess over the gambling machines (they generated a large portion of the revenue and had to be monitored and maintained round the clock) but even the humbler, less glamorous sides of the casino were the objects of his unremitting scrutiny. He inspected the bathrooms to make sure they glistened; he monitored the health of the decorative plants; he examined the doorman closely to make sure he looked smart in his uniform. He paid surprise visits to the kitchen several times a day to taste-test the food, kept a vigilant eye on the restaurant and poked his head into the guest-rooms to keep the housekeeping staff on its toes. And yet, he never seemed to get tired or appear out of sorts or upset or angry. Thorough training and many years of experience plus a natural aptitude for management had prepared him well for his job. And he performed his duties effortlessly without showing any signs of strain or stress.

I must admit that I felt a real sense of relief, now that I felt sure that Vitaly would arrange a work visa for Anara. He knew a lot of people, all types of people, ranging from government officials, to politicians to construction magnates. Running a casino with an attached hotel, brought him into contact with the wealthy and the poor, those with influence and those who had none.

Anara always referred to Vitaly as "sweet." "O, he's so sweet." I heard this refrain often. But I found it hard to warm up to him and felt ill at ease in his presence. And whenever he invited us to one of his "gatherings" (which he did quite often) I invented some "prior commitment" to avoid going. Of course, Anara felt a certain obligation to attend these affairs and if she didn't go as an invited guest, she had to go and help serve the food and drinks. In a very real sense, Vitaly treated everyone who worked for him as a member of his team, as a member of his large, extended family. And he expected his "team members" to put in extra hours without getting paid for them. He had pretty much erased the line between his own private life and working at the casino. He expected similar dedication from everyone and, by and large, he got what he wanted. Most of the workers were young, like Anara, and they needed the work. They did their best to please Vitaly, transform themselves into selfless, self-sacrificing "team" members; and if they couldn't do this, they left.

"We are like one big happy family," Anara often said. "Vitaly is so sweet. He treats all the workers as though they were his relatives."

I filed away this information with an inward smile and said nothing to contradict her or make her see the exploitative aspect of Vitaly's management strategy. We needed his help in getting the visa for her. I didn't want to spoil his image, pull down the statue of the "great and good" Vitaly from off his pedestal. Once she got her visa, she could quit. I really didn't want her working in that atmosphere.

So when she told me that Vitaly had invited me to join some of his friends for drinks on Saturday night, I did not feel very elated. I had turned down three invitations from him already, pleading "prior commitments." If I kept making excuses he would surely feel slighted. I knew I would have to go.

"I will be working, honey," Anara told me. "He expects me to help with the drinks. These are rich Russians – gamblers – important people. He said if there were more people at the party who spoke Russian it would make his guests feel more at ease."

"By all means. We must make sure that his rich Russian friends are at ease," I said.

Gambling casinos had taken the place that temples, churches and abbeys used to have. The labor of the best architects, the most qualified masons and the finest artisans went into their construction. Who could deny their importance?

"Well, if you really don't want to go, I can tell him you are busy."

"No, no," I said. "I'll go. He doesn't invite the male friends of all the cocktail waitresses, does he?"

"No, sweetie. You are special. You are teacher."

"Oh, in that case …" I began. I don't think she quite noticed the sarcasm in my voice. On the other hand, she may have. She could be quite inscrutable at times.

A wet darkness engulfed the mountain. Strong gusts rocked the little Renault as I slid and skidded down the switchbacks. In the light of the headlamps I could see the rain coming sideways in long, gleaming streaks and the leafless branches of almond trees tossing and twisting in a frenzied manner. Normally I relished this sort of weather, but just then I wished I were home sitting in front of a fire, a glass of brandy in my hand and the TV blathering away. A sign of age, no doubt.

I stopped at *Pegasus* for a quick one. The usual crowd of expats sat at the bar, drinking and watching a soccer match on TV, but I didn't see Cardiff. By the time I entered the large, brightly lit main hall of the *Starlight*, where the wet bar and buffet table had been set up, many of the guests had arrived and were milling around, drinks in hand, eating canapés. Waitresses clad in their standard-issue uniforms were circulating among the guests with trays. I saw a lot of men in dark business suits, most of them middle aged or older, and very few women. Vitaly, as usual, formed the nucleus of a cluster of Russian speakers. I managed to penetrate the perimeter of bodies and said "Hello."

"Ah, Robert, I am very glad you came," he said. "Let me introduce you to some of my friends."

He recited some Russian names – Vassili, Ivan, Piotr, and so on – that I knew I would never remember. I shook their hands and said what one usually says but none of them knew English. They smiled politely and nodded. I didn't quite understand my role in this gathering. Perhaps I symbolized the inclusive and catholic nature of Vitaly's social circle. Turning away from this group, I spotted some faces that looked vaguely familiar. I may have seen these people in the local supermarkets or in the crowded lobby of a bank. North Cyprus is small place and you tend to see the same people in the same places over and over again. I bobbed my head and waved and dropped a few civil words here and there.

The fact is you can only enjoy yourself at a cocktail party if you refrain from saying anything truly meaningful or important. Getting drunk also helps, making it easier to tolerate the witless chatter that assails you from all sides. I looked around for Anara and saw her in another part of the room, trotting around on wobbly spikes carrying a tray loaded with drinks, looking quite sexy in her cocktail waitress garb. She saw me and waved but did not come over.

I wandered around for an hour or so, going from group to group, "mingling" dutifully. I consumed two glasses of mediocre white wine and nibbled on slices of a gristly sausage placed on dry-as-sawdust crackers. Obviously, the cook who had made those canapés knew for a certainty that he would not have to eat them. At some point, I noticed that Vitaly had vanished and the Russians were nowhere to be seen. I took this as a sign that I that I could leave too. I looked around to locate Anara. I wanted to say goodbye to her and make some plans about retrieving her later because of the storm. I didn't think she could make it back on the scooter. But I didn't see her. I asked one of her co-workers if she had seen Anara, but the girl just shrugged and was about to rush off on her stiletto heels when I stopped her.

"If you see her, could you please give her a message?" I said. The girl nodded as though she understood me.

"Please tell her I went back home. But I will come and pick her up in the car when she is ready to come home. Tell her to call me. The weather is awful. She won't be able to ride the scooter."

The girl nodded again and hurried away.

I figured the party had reached the high water mark and now the ebb phase had begun. People were leaving. When I stepped out, I saw that the wind had become pretty wild and the rain had turned into a heavy downpour. I knew for sure I would have to come back to pick up Anara when she got off work.

I made my way back up the mountain with difficulty, straining to see the road through the heavy rain and mist. I got home near midnight feeling drowsy and tired. But instead of going to bed I got a beer and turned on the TV. I sat there for the longest time quite unable to focus on the pictures on the screen or the words I heard. Confused bits of music and quick-flashing scenes flickered across the borders of my awareness and at times I think I even faded into some kind of coma. Outside, the storm raged on and the wind whimpered to be let in.

When I woke up I realized that I had been sitting there for several hours. A sudden stillness and silence surrounded the house. The storm had drifted away but the TV still rumbled on. Bright tangential rays of the rising sun streamed in through the windowpanes and made egg-yellow rectangles on the wall. The beer can had slipped from my hands and had fallen onto the floor; it lay in a small puddle of liquid. Surprised, I looked around.

"Anara" I called, thinking that she might be in the bathroom but I heard no response.

Then I went downstairs, thinking she may have gone to bed. But the bed had not been slept in. She hadn't returned. Obviously. Puzzled and somewhat alarmed, I called her mobile phone. It rang and rang but no one picked up.

I made some coffee, splashed some water on my face and waited. It didn't make any sense for me to head to the casino.

Finally, around eleven, she called.

"Where are you?" I said, with some exasperation in my voice.

"At the casino," she said. "It got late and the storm was bad. I couldn't come home on the scooter. Vitaly was very sweet. He told me and another girl who lives in Lapta, to take a room and stay."

"Why didn't you call me," I said. "I was waiting to hear from you. I could have come and picked you up."

"I thought you would be asleep," she said. "I didn't want to disturb you."

"Well, I am disturbed now," I said. "Do you want me to come and pick you up?"

"No, I can come up on the scooter. It's a nice day outside."

"Yes," I said somewhat testily. "It's a lovely day."

When she got home, we had our first real fight or argument. Well, it wasn't a fight in the ordinary sense of the word. Anara and I never fought the way couples trapped in hopeless marriages fight. We never got into one of those venomous screaming matches that end up with objects getting thrown and vicious name-calling. Anara didn't have that sort of fight in her. No matter how angry she became, her anger never overpowered her natural docility and gentleness. She simply listened while I grumbled and muttered and complained and marched around the living room in my underwear. But I did notice a sullen, set look on her face and that bothered me. Her job at the casino meant a lot to her and she didn't want me belittling it or jeopardizing it in any way.

"So Vitaly let you girls take a room," I sneered, trying to inject as much nastiness into my voice as I could. "How nice of him. And have a party. Who else was there? Those waiters who are always hovering around you girls with their tongues hanging down?"

She fired an angry "Are you out of your mind?" look at me.

I'd hit a nerve, or so it seemed to me, so I bored in.

"Who else? Who was this other girl? Does she have a name?"

"It was Zeynip, if you must know."

"Frankly, I don't want you staying there."

"Look, Vitaly did us a favor. Otherwise, I have to wait in the lobby till morning."

"I would have come to fetch you," I said. "You should have called me."

"Okay, next time if I can't come home on the scooter, I'll call you," she said. "But don't get angry, okay? If I wake you up."

"I won't," I said. "Why should I? I don't need to sleep."

"I'm tired," she said with a sudden finality. "I'm going to bed."

She went downstairs and got into bed. I made some coffee and went and sat outside for a long time, thinking of Vitaly and his casino and all that went on there.

~

CHAPTER FIVE

Section 1

I could see – in fact, anyone who looked closely at Cardiff could see – that all the smoking and drinking and not eating any sort of normal food had begun to affect his health. One day, he drifted into my office to discuss some departmental matter and he happened to open his briefcase to take out some papers. I caught a glimpse of a bottle of scotch inside. Noticing that my eyes had widened with surprise, he said, "Just got it at the store, old boy."

But even as he said this, watery eyes and the pungent sour mash smell on his breath made it plain that he'd been drinking. Of course, everyone in the Law department knew that he liked his booze. And, in general, nobody objected to his drinking, even though we knew that on occasion he abused the bottle. But tippling on campus during working hours took the issue into another dimension altogether. A student laughingly mentioned to me that he'd given a rambling lecture in not entirely a state of sobriety. I suppose I should have warned him. I was thinking about talking to him about this but I didn't get the chance. Some of our colleagues also noticed this trend and expressed concern. They conferred in whispers with me, wondering how to tackle the matter, without insulting him or making him resentful. But no one seemed to know quite how to accomplish this delicate task.

In addition, he was having problems with Freya, someone told me, someone who had witnessed their quarrels. Cardiff complained that she took all kinds of pills – uppers, downers and in-betweeners. She, in turn, accused him of drinking too much. He feared she was consorting with rather rough and ruthless characters who hovered around the periphery of discos and nightclubs ready to buy and sell anything and anybody they could to earn a quick profit. There are bad guys, crooks, pimps and hustlers in all societies, but the Levantine bad guy is a breed apart. He is a product of several thousand years and the collapse of several civilizations. He has survived amidst the wreckage of cultures and communities. His type was hardly the proper sort for an English girl from a middle-class background. But Freya insisted that she had the right to see her *friends* whenever and wherever she desired.

Actually, this new, possessive Cardiff surprised me. I never thought he would try to control Freya or attempt to change her wayward ways.

Perhaps his nerves finally melted, got liquified by the quantities of brandy and scotch he consumed everyday. Perhaps he thought he could save Freya from herself. In effect, he broke his own rules, the very principles he had preached to me. As could be expected, she threw a fit and told him to go to hell. He called her parents and requested that they come and retrieve her. She marched out of his apartment. He didn't know where she went. Nor did she call.

I did not witness much of this drama. I only knew what Cardiff chose to reveal, in bits and pieces, over drinks at *Pegasus*. But then one evening he called.

"They are here," he said.

"Who?" I asked.

"Freya's parents," he said. We're going out for dinner. Meet us at *Valentino's* around eight."

"Are you sure you want me on hand?"

"I need you," he said. "You must come."

"Fine. I'll be there."

I had been to *Valentino's* several times and knew it well. It sat on a rocky outcrop overlooking a small cove where the waves kept up their ceaseless slap and rustle. On clear days you could see the coast of Turkey from this spot, a ribbon of purple haze on the horizon. On one side of the restaurant's terrace, a swimming pool glowed like a bowl filled with blue fire. An English woman ran the place. She had come to Cyprus in search of sun and sea and sex and found herself a sturdy Syrian – younger than her by a decade or two – who could perform in the kitchen and the bedroom with equal expertise. She put him in charge of all the culinary matters and took bartending into her own capable hands, dispensing drinks, pouring gossip, myths and fantasies into tourist ears in an endless flow. She understood the needs of Brit expats. She knew what they wanted and quickly turned *Valentino's* into a popular destination. Customers came by the carload to loll by the pool or to sit for hours around the circular cabana-style bar outside in the brindled shade of a roof made of reeds, drinking British beer.

By the time I got to *Valentino's*, Cardiff and the Mortons were well into their pre-dinner drinks. Cardiff introduced me and I sat down feeling as though I had interrupted nothing but an uncomfortable silence. The Mortons were typical middle-aged, middle-class types, the sort who had led blameless, boring lives guided by the standard illusions of their time, place and class. Whatever hopes they might have had for their only child were pretty much dashed and I could see their disappointment engraved on their seamed, tired faces.

Unable to stand the deadly silence, I said, "Cardiff tells me you come to Cyprus often."

Before they could answer, Cardiff leaned forward and said in very clear, precise tones. "The question we are wrestling with is how to get Freya to return to England with her mum and dad."

"I know the question," I said. "But I don't know the answer."

In the grim silence that followed, the waiter came and everyone ordered something. I don't think food held any interest for the Mortons or for Cardiff. They were in Cyprus on a mission. Their minds were obviously preoccupied.

"I wonder how she supports herself?" Janet Morton wondered aloud. "Does she have a job? Is she working somewhere?"

"Yes, yes," said Cardiff quickly. "She works at the *Triton*."

"What sort of work?" Mr. Morton asked.

"Some sort of hostess, I suppose," Cardiff said. "She greets and seats the customers as they come. Not a bad deal, really. Light work. Good pay."

"I wish she'd come back and finish college," Mrs. Morton murmured, staring at the shrimp salad. The note of uncertainty in her voice revealed that she did not have much hope of this dream coming true.

When the food arrived, the talk shifted to other matters. The Mortons were thinking of buying a vacation house on Crete and wanted Cardiff's opinion on the relative merits of owning property in Greece and Turkey. I think they were eager to avoid talking about Freya.

Moreover, nobody really had any idea how Freya could be convinced to return to England.

"Well," I said, thinking of a via media out of the dilemma, "what if she could join a university right here. There are several good ones. She obviously likes being in North Cyprus, has lots of friends here."

"If she actually studied I would like that," Mr. Morton said. "But I don't know if she can be a good student now."

I nodded. I had the same doubts.

On this note, we all fell into a ruminative silence the consequence partly of the oily pasta and the wine and partly an all-encompassing despair. The waiter came again but nobody expressed any interest in the gritty Turkish coffee or in the familiar dessert menu that featured typical, overly sticky-sweet items. So Cardiff called for the bill, paid and we left the place.

In the parking lot, Cardiff made a sensible suggestion.

"Let's go to my apartment," he said. "I'm sure I can produce some decent coffee."

Cardiff, to his credit, had made an effort to clean up his place. Gone were the empty booze bottles, old newspapers and magazines and grease-stained cartons of Chinese food. The couch had also been cleared of blankets and pillows and no longer looked like a bed. Even the kitchen nook had been sanitized and seemed somewhat orderly.

I directed an approving smirk in his direction and he chuckled smugly. The Mortons and I sat down in the living room while Cardiff betook himself to the kitchen to address the business of coffee making. The Mortons were not ones for sparkling small talk or cheery chitchat but for the sake of cordiality we exchanged the usual banal remarks about the weather, the economy, the world political scene and agreed that things were going down the proverbial hill at a rapid rate. Presently, Cardiff emerged with a pot of steaming coffee and the blessed aroma of a Java blend spread like a benediction in the room. I have to say, Cardiff did know how to make pretty good coffee and he did this quickly and almost without effort.

We had barely taken the first few sips when, without any warning, the front door of Cardiff's apartment burst open and Freya stood on the threshold, garbed in her favorite torn-at-the-knees jeans and beer logo T-shirt. For long tremulous seconds she stared at us even as we stared back. I don't think Cardiff expected her and she certainly had not expected her parents. She bit down on her lower lip. She looked pale and sickly. Her gray eyes peered out of purplish hollows and her skin had the yellowish cast of a patient suffering from liver failure. She stood near the door, hesitant, assessing the situation in the room with nervous, keen, darting glances.

"Hi Mum, hi Dad," she finally said, in a dead, robotic voice.

"Hell – o, darling. Glad you are here, because …" Cardiff started a sentence but never completed it.

Freya took no notice of Cardiff, slammed the door behind her and stalked into the kitchen.

Cardiff looked at the Mortons. The Mortons looked at each other. I looked at the three of them. All of us seemed to be waiting for a cue from Freya. The cue finally arrived, after a dramatic pause, in the form of sentences shouted from the kitchen in a ragged voice.

"I'm not going back. If that's what you want, it is not going to happen. I am not going back."

"Will you at least come here and talk to us like a civilized human being," Mr. Morton said directing his words at the wall that separated the kitchen from the living room.

"There is nothing to talk about," Freya's disembodied voice floated towards us as though it were coming out of a radio.

"Will you listen to your father, dear," Mrs. Morton said in weary, patient tones. She had the tense air of a woman who has been able to hold on to her sanity only by consuming generous quantities of gin every day.

"I really should be going," I said, making an effort to rise up from a sofa.

That's when the first plate came zinging across the room. Everyone ducked instinctively, remembering reactions learned during the London Blitz.

"Leave me alone. Just leave me alone," Freya shouted and then she started kicking the cabinets with the zeal of a soccer player.

"Go back to England," she yelled. "Stop interfering in my life. Who asked you to come, anyway?"

As she spoke, she kept throwing whatever she could lay her hands on as if to emphasize the points she made: – Glass salt and pepper shakers, a teapot, a soup ladle, a fork. Then a saucepan inscribed a silvery stainless-steel arc across the room and thudded onto the coffee table shattering several cups. A toaster, trailing a black power cord, tumbling end-on-end followed, crash-landed on the TV. She had a good arm, or so it seemed. The Mortons crouched behind the couch. Cardiff held a tray as though it were a Roman shield. I had flattened myself on the carpet, hands over head. The barrage continued, methodical and deadly. As did the screams. On a rough estimate, I figured she had a substantial supply of missiles made of various materials – steel, tin, ceramic, and glass. Even if she kept launching them at the current rate, she could keep up her assault for a couple of hours. Cardiff made no effort to move towards the kitchen. Nor did I. Nor did her parents. The fear of being skewered by a flying Chef's knife kept me glued flat to the ground.

Suddenly Cardiff had an idea.

"I'm calling the emergency number," he said to me in a theatrical whisper, even as he pulled his mobile phone out and dragged himself into the bathroom on his elbows.

How long we waited for the Medics to arrive, I cannot recall. It seemed like an age. But it must have been just a few minutes. Kyrenia is a small town and they are trained to respond quickly. In the meantime, all of us stayed hunkered down, protecting ourselves as best has we could. Crying and sobbing, Freya kept up her assault nonstop, mainly with plates and saucers at this stage. I suppose she appreciated the way they sailed through the air in graceful, Frisbee trajectories and the way they exploded into a glittering shower of ceramic shards when they made contact with the walls. I felt the fragments strike my back and legs as they rained down on me.

Eventually, the front door did open and a couple of burly Turkish chaps in white coats burst in with a pair of policemen in dark blue uniforms right behind them. They sized up the situation quickly and laid firm hands on Freya. She screamed and squealed and squirmed and resisted with all her might. But she could not resist the collective strength of the attendants. They had very little trouble half walking, half dragging her into the ambulance. After this drama was over, Mr. and Mrs. Morton, signed some forms, thanked the attendants and promised to follow them to the hospital in their own car. Then the ambulance skidded away from the curb, sirens wailing, lights flashing.

Soon after all this commotion, the Mortons left and a calm descended on the apartment. Cardiff opened a fresh bottle of brandy and we consumed it slowly and steadily, not saying much, just thinking and blinking into the middle distance. Finally, he roused himself.

"I better clean up this place. What a bloody mess!"

"You better," I said.

I said goodbye and as I was closing the front door, I saw him pulling out a broom and dustpan from a closet.

After this fiasco, I lost track of Cardiff and Freya for a while. In fact, I made it a point to maintain a distance. If I saw him on campus, I would do an about turn and go another way. If he called, I would talk briefly, make an excuse and end the conversation quickly. I don't know why. I think I was afraid that if we got together for drinks, I would invariably start criticizing Freya. He would get annoyed and this would spoil our relationship. I did not want to say anything negative about Freya but in my heart I thought she represented everything that was wrong with that whole class of women.

Not too long after Freya's spectacular breakdown, I stopped at the *Pegasus* for a quick beer. I was hoping Cardiff wouldn't be there, but he was. And as soon as I entered the place he grabbed my arm.

"Come," he said, in a tone that indicated that his wish could not be denied.

"Where are we going?" I asked.

"You'll see," he said. "Just drive, towards Kyrenia."

I took the wheel and as we headed towards town with the setting sun behind us, I wondered what Cardiff had in mind. He probably wants me to see a new bar he's discovered, I thought, or meet one of his English friends. What else could it be? Usually, nothing short of a tidal wave or a cataclysm could pry him lose from the *Pegasus* in the afternoons.

The traffic was light, mercifully and the Renault wheezed along in the marmalade glaze of the afternoon's siesta hour when everyone slowed down and those with good sense chose snoozing over strenuous activity. We were almost within sight of the last roundabout, where you turn left to go to Kyrenia harbor, when Cardiff started signaling with his left hand.

"Pull over, pull over," he said suddenly. "Stop here. We can cross the road on foot."

I did as instructed still not sure what he planned on doing.

"Follow me," he said, getting out of the car.

We crossed the road and found ourselves in front of a small wrought iron gate let into a low wall. Beyond the wall my eyes focused on the green-black drooping foliage of some trees that could have been cedars or yews. On either side of this acre of greenery stood modern buildings of breathtakingly dull design. A small sign on one side of the gate read "British Cemetery" in black letters chiseled into a marble slab.

"What are we doing here?" I asked, not very eager to enter a space where I didn't belong for more than one reason.

Cardiff gave no response, instead he nudged the gate and it swung open with a plaintive squeal.

"Come," he said. "I want to show you something."

A couple of large carob trees cast oblique shadows over uneven ground. Cardiff swung along swiftly, sidestepping here, leaping over a moldering mound there and hopscotching over stone slabs. He moved with purposive strides like someone going towards a familiar destination.

Presently he stopped and pointed.

"Look," he said. "My father."

We were standing in front of a simple white cross and on it I read the following inscription: "Thomas Dodson Cardiff 1930-1958."

So this is what he wanted me to see. This was his link with Cyprus, the mysterious magnetic force that had pulled him hither.

"There he lies in all his dusty glory," Cardiff said. "A little bit of England."

"He died here? In Cyprus?" I asked, stupidly.

"Yes. Right here in Kyrenia."

"Really?" I said. "Why … I mean, how did he die?"

"Actually a meaningless death."

"Was he in the army?"

"No, no," Cardiff chuckled. "He was a salesman – worked for a company that made electrical components – meters, motors, switches – items like that. He came here to meet some customers. Someone shot him at close range."

"Hey, that's horrible," I said. "Who was it? Who did the deed?"

"They never found out," Cardiff said. "This was the start of the Greek guerilla insurgency and nobody claimed the hit. Later they were less bashful."

"That is bizarre."

"Definitely a case of mistaken identity. The gunman must have thought he was someone else – a government official."

"What a tragedy," I said.

"No," said, Cardiff. "Not a tragedy, just a bloody mishap."

"Well, you lost a father. Your mother lost a husband and for no good reason."

Cardiff shrugged and kicked a tuft of dried grass sending clouds of pollen and dust into the air.

"I'll probably lie here one day. Not a bad place as last resting places go."

"So you never really knew him," I said. "You were just a child when he was killed."

"Quite right," he said, "Never knew him but I knew that chap over there."

He pointed to a grave.

"A dedicated toper and funny. A real Yorick. I knew him well."

Then as we turned to leave, he pointed at another stone sarcophagus.

"Sergeant Samuel McGaw. He was with the 42 Highlanders. The Black Watch regiment. Won the Victoria Cross for bravery in Africa. Helped suppress the Indian mutiny. Survived bullets and bayonets only to die here of heat stroke. There's irony for you."

"Look: 1878. He's been here a while."

"Quite a while. Another piece of old England."

"The island is full of surprises, isn't it? A mosquito could kill you here," I said.

We got back in the car and as we drove back to *Pegasus*, Cardiff talked about his father.

"I guess you could call him an innocent victim," he said. "But as I was growing up he became a figure of mystery and romance in my imagination. I heard the story of his journey to Cyprus and it fascinated me. I wanted to see the place some day. Funny how these things work out. I wanted to see the exact spot where he had been shot and where he died."

"Did you?"

"No," Cardiff said. "All I know is that it happened outside some restaurant in Kyrenia. He had just finished lunch and stepped out and lit a cigarette and *Bang*! The End."

"Did your mother ever visit Cyprus?"

"No, never. I think she developed a hatred for the place. This was the awful place where her husband had been killed. She never wanted to set foot here."

He spoke with empathetic warmth about his mother.

"Being a single mother is a fate I wouldn't wish on Beelzebub. Poor woman! How she struggled. Raising me must not have been easy. I was a sickly, skinny, runty little fellow always coming down with fevers and infections. But with heavy doses of *Bovril, Seven Seas Cod Liver Oil, Waterbury's Compound and Ovaltine* she managed to keep me alive."

"She never married again?" I asked.

"No. In fact, I think she should never have married the first time. She was a type who never got any pleasure out of owning a body. Nor did she like being a mother."

"I know what you mean," I said. "I don't think my mom enjoyed motherhood either. Some women should never procreate. Would you include Freya in that category?"

Cardiff nodded. By now we were back at the *Pegasus*. Cardiff got out and I drove back to Karmi, wondering where my last resting place would be.

Section 2

Anara was at her daily ritual, getting ready for work, selecting clothes, brushing her hair, putting on make-up. With a preoccupied look on her face, she positioned herself at a north-facing window and held up a round mirror. In profile her regal nose revealed its inherent nobility and the late afternoon sun flung a scarf of apricot-colored shadows along her throat. She did not speak as she concentrated on getting ready. I suppose she wanted to look her best, like a warrior going into battle. Plumes and face paint and shiny armor. The *Starlight* became a battlefield for her every night. She waged war on other waitresses for good tables; she quarreled with bartenders to get her orders filled quickly; she hustled for the brusque, casual attention of customers who would never remember her name or her face the next day. No wonder she became tense.

She seemed to be creating a distance between herself and me as she transformed herself into this new persona – the "Warrior-Waitress." I could feel her becoming remote, moving away from me. No man who has an emotional connection with a woman can deny feeling twinges of anxiety when he senses that his woman is distancing herself, becoming less accessible. You start examining the relationship. Its strength, substance. How long will it last? Will someone steal what you have? Disturbing questions, odd doubts invade your mind.

The age difference between us was like a barbed hook that remained stuck in my brain. Not that she ever brought it up. In fact, she insisted that it didn't matter, had no significance whatsoever. She chided me if I called myself "an old man."

"You are not old, honey," she would say in gentle, mildly-critical tones, her Russian accent adding an extra softness to her words, "don't say that."

In bed, I never faced any problems. I firmed up and stayed firm until I sensed that she had reached her moment. Only then did I move towards my own release. As a matter of fact, the agility and enthusiasm I brought to our conjugations even tested her stamina. "Enough, honey," she would murmur finally. "Enough." Of course, her lithe, youthful body and her kisses and caresses were a powerful aphrodisiac, but I also had the help of something my doctor had prescribed to maintain optimum hormonal levels.

The best times were, of course, when we showered together, a ritual we had established when we were back in Almaty. I loved the wet vulnerability of her naked body in the shower. When she submitted to being soaped and rinsed, I read her silken skin in a leisurely fashion, the way the blind read Braille letters, touched her curves, the rise and swell of her breasts and buttocks, and reached down into mysterious sopping wet valleys, discovering her, exploring the exquisite geography of her limbs.

We planned this ritual carefully, making sure that we would have plenty of time and no interruptions. So usually on a Saturday or a Sunday morning, I took the kerosene heater into the bathroom to heat it up to a comfortable temperature, kill the chill of the white ceramic floor tiles and warm up the icy-cold surfaces of the sink and the toilet. Gradually, the little bathroom got as hot as a sauna or a Turkish "hammam," and filled up with dense, billowing clouds of steam that obscured the mirror and made it hard to see anything.

Then we gathered towels and clean underwear and entered the bathroom together and shut the door to keep the heat inside. I helped her take off her bra and her skimpy nylon panties and we would step into the shower stall and draw the plastic curtain all around.

"Are you cold?"

"Just a little."

"You'll be fine once you feel the hot water on your skin," I told her.

I turned on the shower, adjusting the mixture until it felt just right. Then both of us got good and wet and the soaping began. We took turns. First I would soap her, eager to feel the slippery smoothness of her skin underneath my fingers. I lathered every part, every limb in a gentle, meditative manner, with a certain objective detachment almost, taking particular care to go in between her thighs, rubbing her delta till it frothed up into a mountain of foam. Her arms were disturbingly fragile and her ribcage had the fretted elegance of a musical instrument. At such moments, she got transformed into a little girl, a child almost, extremely vulnerable and trusting.

Then she soaped me, rubbing my chest and legs briskly the way I remembered my mother doing it, ordering me to raise my arms or spread my legs with sharp, terse commands.

Soaping done, we rinsed each other off giggling and laughing like daffy fools, spraying water into each others' faces, splashing about just for fun. The final step was the toweling. I loved blotting her dripping slopes and declivities, planting kisses as I went up and down the marvelous terrain of her body. The two of us – Adam and Eve. Naked and clean in our Paradise.

Nevertheless, our lives were changing and this worried me. No longer were we spending our evenings and our nights the way we used to. She got home very late, (often at 2:00 or 3:00 a.m.) too tired and nerve-wracked to be interested in much except downing a quick a glass of milk, flinging off her clothes and throwing herself into bed.

I opened my eyes just long enough to make sure she looked okay (no bruises or any signs of physical abuse) and then turned over and fell asleep. In the morning when I left for work, she'd still be fast asleep. I couldn't bring myself to disturb her. And when I returned from the university late in the afternoon, she would be busy getting dressed to repeat the cycle all over again and in no mood for genial chitchat.

O my prophetic soul! I knew this would happen. And now I wondered where we were headed.

I had no doubt she met many healthy, hot-blooded young Romeos at the casino every night. And I'm sure they made every effort to get her to join them in after-hour romps in their hotel rooms or on the beaches. Hell, I would do exactly that if I were in their place. How long would it be, I wondered, before one of these fellows charmed her right off her high heels and into bed? Shallow, ugly thoughts like these crowded into my head unbidden during the solitary, starlit hours that I spent walking around Karmi alone.

We never fought or quarreled. Aah, no, this is surely an exaggeration. Perhaps I should qualify this statement and say that we hardly ever quarreled. Like most couples, we did argue on occasion. But our arguments never turned into fights or the sort of insult-hurling contests or verbal and physical assaults that could be termed "battle royales" in the real sense. Rarely did we find ourselves on opposite sides of an issue, but when we did, we sought a compromise quickly, unwilling to let differences of opinion fester and foul up the atmosphere in the house. There seemed to be no point in letting sour notes disturb our generally harmonious daily interactions.

Most of our arguments were about minor matters, trivialities. I accused her of eating too much ice cream and she stoutly (stoutly?)

denied the charge. She claimed I drank too much and I claimed I did not. Or my desire to watch TV, clashed with her need for sleep. I don't think we ever quarreled over any truly contentious topics, the kind of issues that tear marriages and relationships apart such as money, sex and work, the three nodes that triangulate and strangulate most lives. Since there were only two of us in the house and there was no one to referee our bickering or serve as umpire or arbiter, we had to settle our differences ourselves. I let the air out of the balloon of tension by laughing or walking away or simply giving in. I never felt any sense of disgrace or defeat in conceding to her demands and seeing a smile of victory light up her face. Her happiness was my reward and with it came other tender and affectionate dividends.

But there were times when Anara simply refused to give in. Yes, on occasion she could be extremely obstinate and got us stuck in the logjam of her inflexibility. This happened when she was convinced that her position was logical and rational. I discovered this stubborn streak when we got into a row over her desire to cut her hair. She had just started working at the casino and began to complain that washing her hair and drying it and brushing it took up too much time. She wanted it cut short so it would settle into a nice shape with a minimum amount of fuss and effort as soon as she stepped out of the shower. I was against this move. I thought a "boy" cut would detract from her feminine grace. Moreover, there was an erotic aspect to long hair that held me in thrall. Touching it, playing with it, running my fingers through the dense, dark, rippling, silky waterfall aroused me at the deepest levels of my psyche. I was against any violation of the very source of such sensuous loveliness. So we argued and the argument went on and on and ruined our evening and then poisoned our night and the next morning. Then all day long we kept crossing swords, neither fighter willing to give in, admit defeat. I felt a woman's hair is her glory, a part of her sexuality and womanliness. I couldn't bear to see it trimmed or shortened. On the other hand, a working woman has different priorities. She has to consider different needs and requirements. She must get ready quickly. An hour spent on fussing with hair is an hour wasted. Naturally, Anara refused to give in on this matter. So we kept arguing, debating, discussing the topic for three whole days and nights. Finally, I gave in. You are right, I told her. I would just have to accept the new Anara with bobbed hair.

But I think our bitterest, most painful argument took place when I suggested that she quit her job at the casino. I really wasn't sure that Vitaly had been able to get her a work visa and there seemed to be no way of finding out how matters stood. He had her passport and apparently mysterious wheels were turning, levers were being pulled, Cypriot bureaucracy was being manipulated.

"These things take time," he kept telling her. "This is Cyprus."

When she started working at the casino she left the house at 5:30 in the evening and returned around 12:30. This was bad enough. But I had to accept this routine because there was no alternative. Casinos don't keep normal business hours. Then, for reasons that were never very clear to me, never very satisfactory, she started coming home later and later. Soon 12:30 became 1:00 and that turned into 2:00 and on certain nights she didn't come back till 3:00 or 4:00 in the morning. This routine began to wear my nerves away. I became resentful. And when I questioned her about these long hours, the answer was always the same, "They need me."

"Well, I need you too," was my sullen response.

"But honey, I have to work. When my supervisor asks me to stay and help, I can't ignore her. Please understand, honey. The casino really starts getting busy around midnight and then if we get a big group of tourists it gets crazy. Extra servers have to come and help."

But I was in no mood for rational arguments. All the frustration and irritation and anger that had been building and bubbling up inside me like molten lava inside a volcano now exploded. I raged and raved and cursed the casino and those who managed its affairs.

Anara was taken aback by this display of temper but not intimidated and calmly informed that she was not going to quit her job and that I should show some maturity and farsightedness. We should remember (she said) why she had taken the job – what the goal was – and I should keep an eye on the ultimate objective. But I had (by now) lost sight of the ultimate objective. I was more concerned about my immediate needs. So I kept on grumbling and growling and venting my spleen in the sort of language men employ at such times. This went on for several days, as I recall. But Anara stood firm, unfazed, unyielding and I just had to shut up and accept the inevitable.

I wondered how Cardiff tolerated Freya's *lifestyle*. One afternoon, I met him in the hallway of the building in which both of us taught our classes.

"I'll see you in *Pegasus* later," I told him. "Wait for me."

Cardiff nodded and I hurried off to my office to meet with some students: a Cypriot boy and a couple of Turkish girls. The boy had some questions about a research paper he had started to write. He read a lot and really did want to become a competent lawyer. The girls just wanted to flirt and flaunt their navels. They had grown up in England and spoke fluent Cockney and considered themselves more European than Turkish. I shook them off as tactfully as I could by telling them that I had to leave to attend a meeting with the Rector.

"I'll see you ladies in class tomorrow," I said, as I picked up my briefcase.

They made faces to show their disappointment. But I left the office with determined strides. When I got to *Pegasus*, I spotted Cardiff right away, in the cool darkness of the main room. His frame drooped over the bar and he had a tall beer in front of him.

"How are the classes?" he asked, with mild curiosity.

"Pretty good. I've got a couple of bright bulbs. They make it worth the effort of getting out of bed."

"I know what you mean," he said. "What'll you drink?"

"A beer," I said. "I'm parched."

Cardiff signaled the barkeep, Ahmet, a middle-aged Turk with gray hair and the heavy-lidded eyes of a weary hawk. Ahmet owned the place and functioned as a kind of oracle for the local Brits. They consulted him on all sorts of issues, particularly about buying and selling cars, houses, or any other hurdle that the island threw up.

"Thanks," I said. "I can only stay a while. I want to get home before Anara leaves for work. I hardly see her anymore, it seems."

"You'll get used to it," Cardiff said.

I shook my head side to side.

"Where's Freya?" I asked him.

He shrugged. His way of indicating that he did not want to talk about her. Cardiff and I had set up a system that worked well. You were permitted to ask any question, but if the other refused to answer, you were expected to drop the matter.

I did not ask him about Freya again. Moreover, my own problems were on my mind.

"I don't like this *Starlight* business one bit."

"Why?" said Cardiff.

"I just don't like that scene ... the discoing, the gambling."

"What do you mean?" Cardiff said. "It's a younger set to be sure, but are they any different from you or me?"

"No," I said. "That's what worries me."

Cardiff chuckled.

"My advice – don't worry too much," Cardiff said. "You can't control what goes on at the *Starlight*. You can't control people. I gave up trying to do that a long time ago. Relax. Look, when Freya feels the urge, she is good to me. I am grateful and appreciative. When she is away from me, she may feel the urge to be good to someone else. I can't chase after her, monitoring and supervising her liaisons. Nor bully or browbeat her into some sort of fake fidelity. It makes no sense."

"I just don't want any bloody tourist with an erection stealing my girl," I said.

"So what's your plan? Put a chastity belt on her?"

"Where can I buy one?"

"The crusaders tried that," Cardiff said. "They even built castles and locked up their wives inside. In spite of all these efforts, many a crusader – when he got back – discovered he had a child or several children. The ladies, you see, discovered ingenious ways of by-passing all these measures."

"Really? What did they do? Thrash the wives, punish them for having been unfaithful?"

"Not at all. Being deeply religious men – believers in divine miracles – they didn't ask too many questions. They accepted their paternal responsibilities with good grace."

"A sensible approach," I said, "but I am not a crusader. Nor religious. I don't relish the idea of sharing her with some traveling troubadour."

"Come on," Cardiff said. "You are jumping to conclusions. And get off your moral high horse before it throws you. What if the troubadour is interesting and exciting? Here's what I think – putting women in cages built out of some arcane morality is barbaric. Moreover, if you take this approach you seldom get the results you want. They always escape and you earn their undying hatred."

"I suppose you are right," I said morosely.

Perhaps I should get off my moral high horse, I thought, as I drove home, and gave myself a little lecture. Instead of smothering her in a stifling possessiveness, I should help and support her. I should encourage her as she makes an effort to solve the visa problem. Instead of creating imaginary scenarios of betrayal, why not fix her favorite dish so she'll have something to eat when she gets back from work.

I admired her spirit, the calm courage she displayed in a crisis. The *Starlight* presented her with new challenges every day because she knew very little about the business of bars and restaurants. But bravely and without complaining, she did what she had to. Her adaptability and initiative impressed everyone she dealt with.

Once I asked her how she managed to distinguish between different types of cocktails.

"I remember color," she said, giggling happily, "and the way they smell."

"Clever girl."

"But I don't like the cigarette smoke," she said, squinting. "My eyes burn, get itchy."

I nodded in sympathy. Her eyes did indeed look red and irritated when she got back after her shift.

"But really the worst – the very worst part of working at the *Starlight* is having to wear high heels," she said.

"Really?" I asked. "Are they that uncomfortable?"

She gave me one of those looks that seemed to say – you men just don't understand. I suppose I didn't, never having worn high heels.

"Imagine," she said, standing up and raising her left arm, the flat of the palm facing upward, pretending she held a tray loaded with drinks. "I run like so, from table to table. People bouncing and jumping all around. Drunk. After a few hours heels feel like spikes stabbing my brain."

I didn't say anything. But her words scalded me. I wished there had been some other way of getting the goddamned visa. A surge of anger washed over me. Silently, I cursed the entire race of governmental factotums, born and yet-to-be-born.

It is very late, nearly 3:00 AM. Anara should have been home by now, snuggling up beside me under the blanket, twining her legs around mine. Where was she? What could be the problem? In the heavy darkness that echoes with the damp odors, I lie awake waiting to hear the first, faint purr of her scooter from almost a mile away down the mountain. There was an S-bend at this point and from the house a clear line of sight to the curving road visible far below. Sound came up easily, cutting between trees and houses. Now anxiety started to eat my insides. Realizing that sleep had fled on, I get up, turn on a few lights and open a beer. The minutes of waiting seem to turn into hours. I step out of the house and pace up and down the road in front of the house, blowing furious clouds of cigarette smoke that rises as though some sort of combustion were going on inside me.

Unfamiliar constellations drift by overhead, serene and unconcerned. Finally, around 4:00 AM, I hear the scooter take the final turn and put-put into our into our lane.

"Why aren't you in bed?" she says, seeing me standing there.

"Why are you late?" I ask, somewhat testily. I want her to know that I am upset, even angry.

"Oh, two of the girls decided to go get some food before heading home," she says airily. "I went along."

"I was worried. You should have called."

"I thought you would be asleep."

"You know I don't really sleep till you get home. Anything can happen. You could have had an accident."

"I would call if I make accident. Certainly," she said blithely.

"Okay, forget it. Let's go in."

I don't think she had any idea of how worried I had been. She was getting comfortable with the girls she worked with, the busboys, the waiters and the cleaning ladies. They were a part of her new world where she spent many hours.

I was also concerned that once the rains of winter began and the nights got colder and colder, she would no longer be able to use the scooter. Either I would have to drop her and pick her up in the Renault or teach her to drive and then help her get a driver's license. I didn't know anything about getting a driver's license. I hadn't bothered to get one and I feared they might ask her for identification papers she did not have. She could, of course, drive without a license. But then she ran the risk of being confronted by ugly complications in case she got pulled over. None of the options were pleasant to contemplate. But the season of mists and cold winds would soon be upon us and it would force us to change our routines.

On the following weekend I decided – she decided – (almost simultaneously) we decided that driving lessons could not be postponed. They had to begin right away. I wanted her to learn how to drive so that when it became necessary for her to use the car she would be ready and I wouldn't have to crawl out of bed in the wee hours of the night to go and pick her up. But I was apprehensive. Learning to drive a car would not be as easy as learning to ride the scooter had been. The reluctant stick shift and perverse gearbox of the venerable Renault would prove tricky. Even I, with months of experience behind me, could crunch the gears and did so often. If I tried to change gears too hastily or at mismatched speed, the nasty grinding of steel cog against steel cog was my well-merited reward. Letting up on the clutch while pressing down on the accelerator was an exquisite art. Naturally I was tense, when on a cloudy Saturday afternoon, we betook ourselves down the mountain to a parking lot at the university. I put her in the driver's seat and showed her where to place her feet. The interior of the Renault was awkward, with badly designed and poorly placed controls. I always felt I was handling a tractor when I wrestled with the clumsy steering wheel and the arthritic pedals. But Anara surprised me once again. She took to driving a car instinctively. Of course, she did stall the engine several times and, yes, she did go through several, obligatory herky-jerky starts. And she did make the gearbox groan and grind as though river rocks were tumbling around inside it. At one point she also knocked down several plastic garbage cans, because she looked down to check the position of the gearshift lever. Another time we headed straight for a wall but she managed to get the car into neutral and brake us to a halt within an inch of a disastrous collision. But in spite of these problems she managed to master the essentials within half an hour and was soon out of the parking lot and on a secluded road, shifting gears quite handily, her eyes luminous with sheer joy and excitement.

Section 3

Rather suddenly I detected a change in the weather. We were seeing more and more rainy days. Sunlight felt pleasant as a kiss against one's skin. The direction of the prevailing winds had also changed. They were coming out of the west now, out of Europe, swooping across the icy palisades of the Swiss Alps and the foam-fettered Mediterranean. They carried intimations of winter, the smell of snow. It felt good to crawl under a blanket at night. The rains of winter started in earnest now. Monumental thunderheads crashed into the Beshparmak range and lightning stabbed the slopes. Rain came down in blinding downpours turning the streets of Karmi into bubbling streams. The island burst into bloom. Wild flowers sprang up everywhere, waving colored flags along the roadsides, between the clefts of rocks and the crevices of stonewalls. Fields that had been bare, that had looked like raw sienna scars on the landscape, became verdant pastures, green with tender herbs and grasses.

We rejoiced, naturally. And so did the frogs. They convened in large numbers around the lily pond and serenaded us all night long with their mating calls and arias of amour. The drought had finally ended. But our joy did not last long because now an old problem reappeared. The kitchen sink got plugged up again.

In a panic, I called Erkan Bey. He listened politely to my tale of trouble and then said he could not come for another two or three days.

"I am in Guzelyurt," he said. "I have orchard here. I am working on vines."

Being a landowner, Erkan Bey had to handle a wide range of responsibilities. Keeping the drains of Karmi open was just one more item on his list of tasks and duties.

"I'll come on Monday," he said.

"Okay," I said, meekly. "Thanks." What else could I say?

But the prospect of spending an entire weekend with a plugged up sink, unable to wash dishes or cook, was not appealing. I decided to try and fix the problem myself. I figured I couldn't make the situation any worse and I might even be able to clear the blockage. I decided to dig where Ertan Bey had gone in and see what I could see. The obstruction had to be there, somewhere near the base of the almond tree, where the pipe from the kitchen entered the septic tank. So, early on Saturday morning, I went to see Fiona.

Fiona was in her front yard with a steaming mug of tea in her hand, watching her cats playing around.

"I need some tools," I said.

She shot a dubious look at me.

"What kind of tools?" she asked. "What are you planning on doing?"

"Gardening," I said. "Bit of gardening. That's all."

"You need a trowel, I suppose. A rake?"

"No, no," I said. "I have those. I'd like to borrow a spade and a shovel and, possibly, a pick."

"My, my, we are ambitious," Fiona said. "What brought on this sudden urge?"

"The weather," I said. "It's pleasant now, after the rain. Feels good to be outside – you know – puttering around."

Being English, she understood the impulse.

"Patrick," she called out to her husband. "Robert's here and he wants some gardening tools."

I didn't want to alarm her. The sewage system in Karmi was old and temperamental and prone to sudden failures and Fiona had often urged me to be careful. She was always afraid that I might damage the pipes somehow and I knew she wouldn't want me mucking around with the plumbing. Fortunately, the tall, pink and white oleanders on one side of our courtyard and the over-grown jasmine that rose above the low stonewall on the other, would keep prying eyes from observing what I did. Even if she walked by on the upper road, she would not be able to see anything.

The morning was pleasant. The sky held a rinsed-out brilliance and an after-the-storm freshness infused the light breezes that came up from the sea. I got busy right away. I pried up the flagstones carefully with the pick and set them to one side in a neat pile. I tried to be as quiet as I could be. Anara still lay sleeping having come home quite late and I did not want to wake her up. In a short while, I had managed to expose an area approximately two feet by two. Then I went in with the spade, digging slowly and carefully. I was afraid of breaking pipes. They were the plastic ones, not cast-iron. One careless blow and they'd shatter like eggshells and I'd be in big trouble.

I began to enjoy the sensation of physical labor. Pushing the spade down with my foot into the damp earth, breaking off clumps and hauling them out felt good. I kept going for quite a while with a single-minded focus on the task at hand. Soon my palms were red and raw and the muscles of my arms began to hurt.

By noon I had made quite a large cavity, large enough for a person to sit in but I hadn't come across any pipes. What if I had miscalculated? I wondered. Had I missed the spot where Ertan Bey had gone in? But I was determined to get at the clogged pipe and kept on digging. By now I could stand knee-deep in the pit and it had started to look like a small grave. Occasionally, my blade stuck buried stones and I would have to pry them out before I could continue. Most of them were small, about the size of oranges but some were as big as melons. The walls of the hole I was making kept crumbling inward, forcing me to make it wider as I went deeper. Gradually, it became quite clear that I had been digging in the wrong place. By now I had become weary and disgusted, I thought of giving up. But just as I was about to, my spade struck something. I heard a dull, hollow thud. Could it be the pipe? With a renewed sense of mission, I started scraping away the dirt. In a few minutes, it became apparent that I had struck a wooden surface, much rotted and softened by dampness. I dropped the spade and picked up a small trowel and began to clear away more dirt. Then I saw the edges of the object and got an idea of its dimensions.

It appeared to be a box or chest of sorts, about a foot wide and two feet long. I scraped away more dirt from the sides to see how much further I had to go to free it from the clutches of the earth. An energetic excitement gripped me now and I panted and gasped as I worked, eager to get the thing out of the ground. Another hour went by. Finally, it looked as though I had freed it from the surrounding dirt.

Having done this much, I decided to get a beer and catch my breath. By now Anara had woken up. I heard her in the bathroom.

"Come see what I found," I shouted.

She came down the stairs still a bit groggy from sleep and stared aghast.

"What is that?" she said in a scared whisper, peering wide-eyed into the hole.

"I don't know," I said. "But I am going to find out."

"Maybe you should leave it alone," she said, restraining my arm.

"It's just a box," I said. "Not a coffin for god's sake."

When I tried to lift the chest out by sheer force, it refused to budge. I decided to wrap a rope around it a couple of turns and then drag it out.

"Come, help me," I said to Anara and together we dragged the box out slowly, inch by inch.

The outer surface of the chest looked soft and decayed. But just beneath this layer, the wood had survived and still retained its solidity. The chest seemed old but not ancient. I had seen similar chests at several furniture stores in Kyrenia. The locals used them to store bed linen and other household items. The traditional bas-relief carving on the lid and the sides were hard to see. A rusted padlock hung from a hasp. A few blows of the spade and the hasp broke free and fell, with the lock still attached. Anara uttered a little cry and stepped back a few paces.

"Be careful, dear," she said in a breathless whisper.

I could feel the nervous tremors of my heart beneath my ribs. I wondered what I would find. I placed the edge of the spade in the seam between the lid and the base and threw it open.

Crumpled up newspapers printed with Greek writing formed a layer on the top. Yellow with age and brittle, the paper disintegrated as soon as I tried to pick it up. Using a trowel, I scooped up this desiccated debris as carefully as I could. Underneath this layer I found a couple of small, black and white photographs in glass-covered wooden frames – very formal – as though they had been taken at a photographer's studio. One showed a handsome, young man with a mustache and the other showed a young girl with big, dark eyes in a flouncy white frock looking squarely and seriously into the camera lens. I brushed aside more of the crumbling paper and I saw a transparent plastic bag with a white garment inside. It turned out to be a wedding dress. Beneath this there were more items: several embroidered tablecloths, pillowcases, bed-sheets, even towels. I brought out the things one by one and handed them to Anara. She took everything into the house.

Beneath this layer of household linen, I found china plates of various sizes, some silver knives and forks and a porcelain coffee set. I got all these items out and handed them to Anara who carried them upstairs. At the very bottom of the chest I found another odd-shaped object, wrapped in brown paper and tied with a string. Dark oil-stains made random continents all over the package. It had a strange weight and heft to it when I picked it up as though it were some sort of iron tool.

"Honey, could you please get me the scissors," I asked Anara.

I wanted to open the package carefully instead of just ripping it open apart. I placed it on the ground, cut the string and pushed the paper wrapping aside gently. The sharp odor of machine oil spread everywhere and I saw a pistol and a cardboard box containing 12 bullets. Sunlight bounced off the shiny gunmetal blue surface of the weapon. It looked brand new and the grip bore the name of the manufacturer: Webley. It had an hexagonal barrel, just above the chamber, "Mark IV .38" had been stamped and on the opposite side: "Made in England." The .38 caliber bullets in the box matched the gun.

"Put it back, honey," Anara said in a quavering voice. "I don't like this. Let's put everything back and leave it."

"It's nothing, sweetie. Just a wooden box full of old junk," I said to Anara. "They must have buried all this stuff thinking they would return some day."

"What will we do with all these things?" Anara. "We don't need them."

"I know, but we can't just put them back in the ground," I said.

"Who do you think buried them?"

"Probably the folks who lived in this house," I said. "I'll call Yulie. I am sure she'll know something about this."

After we had emptied the chest and brought everything into the house, I closed the lid and dragged it into the donkey room downstairs. Then I filled up the hole with dirt. After Anara left for work, I placed the flagstones on the top just as I had found them. Then I called Erkan Bey. Fortunately, he came the very next day and managed to clear the blockage in a few hours.

"So you found the chest," Yulie said, with a little, nervous laugh when I got her on the phone. "We knew someone would find it some day."

"It was a bit of a shock," I said.

"I can imagine," she said. "Was everything okay, I mean, in good condition?"

"Yes, in general. The outside of the chest is quite rotted out but the inside is fine. Should I tell you what I found?"

"No, you don't have to," she said. "I already know. My mother's told me a thousand times. Those things were for my older sister, Eleni. Her 'Hope Chest.' They were planning her wedding, you see, when all the trouble began in 1974. When they ran from Karmi they couldn't take the chest, so they buried it."

"Well, you can tell your sister that all her things are safe," I said. "She can come and take them anytime."

"Eleni is dead," Yulie said quietly.

"I'm sorry to hear that," I said, a bit taken aback.

"She had been sick for a long time," Yulie went on. "My parents had no idea she was seriously ill. But then, when we moved to the Greek side in '74, my parents took her to a hospital in Limassol. They found out she had TB. They tried to save her but she died in 1980."

"That's terrible," I said. "What about her husband, the young man in the photograph?"

"They never got married," Yulie said. "The war started, you see. He got killed in the first few hours of the fighting, near Five Mile Point. You can see the spot from Karmi. He wasn't really a trained soldier, you see, just a village boy who got caught up in the dreams of Greek unity. Nearly all the young men got carried away by the

high-sounding slogans about 'heroism.' They thought they could resist
with rusty shotguns their grandfathers had used to chase crows from
the fields. But they didn't stand a chance. The death of Herakles had
a terrible effect on my sister. The disease killed her but I think grief
hastened her death. She never got over the loss of her fiancé."

We talked for a while. She said she would talk to her father, tell
him about the chest, see what he wanted to do and then call me back.
Before she hung up, I told her about Anara's job at the casino.

"That is fantastic!" she said. "My father also felt that getting a visa
through an employer was the best approach. But you know, he does
not have the sort of contacts on the Turkish side who could have been
approached."

"I understand," I said. "I think this Russian guy who owns
Starlight has the right connections. He's influential, well-known in
north Cyprus."

"That's the sort of person you want on your side," Yulie said.

We talked for a little while longer and set up a time for her to come
and pick up the things I had found in the hope chest. But for some
reason, I didn't mention the pistol. Nor did she bring it up. Perhaps she
didn't know anything about it. The gun fascinated me and I wanted to
keep it. I had never owned a firearm, but when I held the pistol in my
right hand the cold steel sent a shiver of excitement through me. The
weapon stirred something deep within me, something long suppressed
and never acknowledged. I wanted to use it.

Yulie called on Sunday morning and said: "We are on our way."

"Great," I said. "Fantastic. Please come. We are waiting for you."

Anara seemed a bit apprehensive. I think she may have had some
anxiety about Yulie and regarded me with keen, probing eyes.

I don't think she suspected that I had any sexual or romantic interest
in Yulie, but women always harbor an undercurrent of uncertainty

about their hold on their men. Even the possibility of a potential rival hovering about can make them nervous. Men are obtuse about such matters. But women have invisible antennae that they can tune into frequencies men cannot. Women can detect the slightest changes in the temperature of a relationship.

We had now moved into winter weather in earnest. Towering cumulus clouds, grand as galleons, sailed over the peaks of the Gothic range. In the afternoons, gauzy veils of mist fluttered between the pines, filtering the sunlight, giving it a cool, gray tint. Karmi had the look and feel of a canton in Switzerland, poised on some unimaginable height, floating in a cocoon of fog.

I was glad the real owners of the chest would finally get back what they had tried to save and, in fact, I looked forward to returning the items I had found, even the pistol. As we were laying out all the items on the dining table, I noticed Anara looking longingly at the wedding dress. She took it out of its plastic envelope and spread it out on the bed to admire it. The silk had yellowed with age and the fabric had acquired to a warm hue like that of butter or cream. Anara caressed the fabric lovingly and then held it against her body.

"It is exactly my size," she said, dreamily. "Look."

"You would look fantastic in it, angel," I said. "Unfortunately, we can't keep it."

"I know," she sighed, and put the dress back in its plastic covering. She put it on the dining table with the other items and we covered everything with a towel.

Yulie and her father arrived around noon. And as they came up the outer stairs, I introduced Anara to Gus.

He smiled and said, "I can see why you don't want this one getting away."

I urged them all to sit down and offered them Turkish coffee but they said they didn't want any.

"Later," Gus said, "later," a nervous tremor in his voice. "I want to see the things. It's been thirty years. I want to see the condition they are in."

I led them to the dining table and removed the towel.

Gus immediately picked up the photograph of Eleni and a kind of choked sigh escaped from his throat. He gazed at it for the longest time.

"My daughter," he said. "She was so beautiful. May her soul rest in peace."

Then he picked up the other photo, the one of the young man.

"Ah, Herakles. He was the son of a friend of mine. Herakles and Eleni were going to get married"

"I know," I said. "Yulie told me."

"He got killed in 1974 when the fighting started between the Turkish army and the Greek-Cypriot forces. On the very first day … July 20th."

I shook my head and made sympathetic noises. For me as an outsider, a neutral outsider, every death seemed a waste, a triumph of hate over good sense and reason. I did not feel comfortable taking sides because I knew very little about the roots of the conflict. And now, thirty years later, the tides of history had inundated and obscured the facts that could have helped explain what happened and why it happened. Now, at the dawn of the 21st century, new realities – economic, political, and social … confronted the Greeks and the Turks. As both sides tried hard to maintain a fragile peace on a divided island, many among the younger generation were beginning to wonder if more could not be gained by accommodation than antagonism.

Yulie examined the wedding dress and touched it lovingly.

"Nice, isn't it?" she said.

"Lovely," I responded.

"I am amazed at how small it is," Yulie said. "I didn't know my sister was so small. I would never be able to get into it."

"There is a pistol here," I told Gus. "Is this yours?"

I unwrapped the oiled paper packet and held it towards him.

He looked at it with a strange look of distaste and amazement on his face and made no effort to take it from my hand.

"My father," he said. "His."

"But why didn't he take it?" I asked.

"I don't know." Gus said, meditatively. "People were being searched. The British had roadblocks everywhere. They were trying to catch Greek guerilla fighters. If they had found the pistol on him, they would have arrested him."

"I see," I said.

"It was a strange time. A confusing time," Gus said. "We didn't know what to do, which way to turn, who to trust, who not to trust."

"Well, take it now. Nobody is going to search you now," I said.

"I don't want this … this weapon," he said suddenly. "You keep it … throw it away. Do what you wish. I have no use for it."

I didn't know what to say. Perhaps I should have said, I don't want it either. But I didn't. My tongue stiffened inside my mouth and I could not utter those words. Instead, I said what I longed to say, "Okay, I'll take care of it."

Anara brought in a large cardboard carton and we started to put everything in it for them to take home. Yulie helped with the packing, taking care to place the china plates in between layers of newspaper and fabric. She made sure the delicate coffee set was placed inside a soft hollow of towels and bed sheets. When Anara handed her the wedding dress, Yulie asked, "Do you think this will fit you?"

Anara turned very red and glanced at me.

So I spoke up.

"It's just the right size for her."

"Then please take it," Yulie said without a second's pause. "I am sure you will be wearing it soon."

"But this your sister's wedding dress ..." Anara murmured.

"We bought it for her but she never wore it," Yulie said. "Take it. It fits you. Get married in it."

"Yes, yes," said Gus. "Please take it. I hope to see you as a bride in this dress. It will make me very happy. I am sure my wife will also be pleased."

"Thank you," Anara said, her voice almost breaking. "Perhaps, some day ... I will wear it."

"I'm sure you will, I'm sure you will," Yulie added. And I really think she was being sincere. By now the sky had become a mass of blue-gray clouds and a strong wind whipped the branches of the almond tree. The clouds opened up and rain rattled against the windowpanes. The world outside appeared to be melting, dissolving, flowing away. Loud thunderclaps exploded like artillery and then would come the hot white flashes of lightning that seemed to sear the clouds, tear them apart.

"Good," said Gus. "Rain. We need this. Summers are so hot and dry here that you feel you are drying up. When the rainy season starts it is such a relief. Life flows back into your body."

"I love it," I said. "I could go out and dance in the rain."

"Oh, no, don't do that," Yulie said. "You could get hit by lightning. Every year we hear of cases."

While the ladies turned their attention to making coffee, I invited Gus to see the chest and took him downstairs.

"Would you like to take it back with you?" I asked, glad that I had dragged it inside because earlier in the day there had been no sign at all that we might get rain.

"Just throw it away," he said. "The wood is pretty rotten. It has served its purpose."

When we came back up Anara served coffee and we sat around sipping it.

"This has been a very strange experience," Gus said meditatively.

"Tell me, Gus," I asked him, "do you think this island can be united again?"

He shook his head.

"Not just yet. Not the way things are," he said. "There is too much anger, too many bad memories on both sides."

"Would you like to see it united?"

"Certainly," he said. "This split, this division, it is unnatural. But it will take time, when people feel safe and there is less fear and mistrust, then ... then."

"Look at Europe – an armed camp for centuries, nation against nation. But now they live in peace."

"Yes, we can too," Gus said. "If the French and the Germans can forget the mud of Flanders and the occupation of Paris, I think we can too. If there is a will ... right?"

"The Brits could have played a more constructive role," I said.

"They tried, believe me," Gus said. "I had many English friends who wanted Cyprus to be independent. And before the Greek guerillas began the attacks, most Greek-Cypriots wanted the English to stay – but not as rulers. We wanted them here as friends, helpers, advisors. But those at the top in London were determined to keep us under their thumbs. They had given up many pieces of the empire and they did not want to give up Cyprus."

I did not contradict him. As an American, I felt I had no right to judge those who had lived and suffered through that phase of Cypriot history. Decades of neglect, decades of shortsighted policies had planted dragon's teeth into fertile ground. This is why the events that led to the split seemed to me like a carefully choreographed dance, with the dancers locked in a death-spiral the way two eagles lock talons and hurtle earthwards. As they say, you had to be there.

The rain slacked off gradually, leaving Karmi a dripping, steaming world where tattered curtains of mist trailed between pines and cypresses like ghostly visitants from another world. Damp earth odors spread everywhere, rich, loamy smells of awakening fertility, germinating seeds. We finished our coffee and Gus and Yulie rose to leave.

"You must come again and eat with us," I said.

They said they would.

As they were getting ready to leave, Gus pulled me aside and said: "Yulie tells me that the visa problems have been solved."

"Almost," I said. "She is working at a casino and she should be getting a work visa pretty soon."

Gus directed a peculiar look at me as if he didn't quite believe what I had just told him.

"A casino?" he said, and a furrow appeared between his eyebrows. "Now that is a world I know little about. But some people enjoy them."

Then he flashed a sudden smile.

"I'm sure all will go well," he said and slapped my shoulder playfully, a silent, wordless message, hidden therein.

I helped Gus carry the cardboard box down the stone steps. Anara and Yulie followed. We went to the plaza where they had parked their car and stowed the carton in the trunk. We shook hands with them and they got into their vehicle and drove off. As we were walking back home, I put an arm around Anara.

"You lucky girl," I said. "You got yourself a wedding dress."

She smiled.

"Now all I need is a husband."

"That should be no problem for someone as pretty as you," I said.

"Will you marry me?" she said.

"Of course, sweetie pie," I said. "But you don't want and old goat like me. You want a handsome young fellow."

She laughed and punched my shoulder playfully.

By now the sky seemed to be clearing up.

"Let's go sit on the roof," I said. "It is clearing up."

The light falling across the littoral was golden that day and the far away the sea sparkled like a salver of chased silver.

Cyprus, long-suffering, long enduring, long-neglected Cyprus. Like the rocks that make up its stubborn heart, it has weathered the assaults of centuries. It has withstood invasions, attacks and conquests with patience and an enduring determination. Empires came and crumbled, rulers ruled and vanished, dynasties died out like fires flickering and failing in the dim, forever bifurcating labyrinths of history. On Cypriot shores landed the knights of Richard Lion Heart, the soldiery of Saladin, the janissaries of Sultans. Here came the argosies of Venice and the cannonading frigates of Britannia. Here they clashed in life-and-death struggles for domination. They built castles and forts and mosques and minarets. Here they bled and died. Cyprus is littered with ruins that point to departed grandeur. But the Cypriots remain – a hardy and hospitable people, always ready to share what they have.

～

$\mathscr{Section}$ 1

We went to the Wednesday bazaar late in the afternoon. Usually, Anara went alone but since I was done with my classes, I decided to go with her. When we got there, I discovered that all the parking slots near the bazaar had been taken. I had to park the Renault almost a block away. We jumped out of the car. I grabbed Anara's arm and we sprinted across the main road and through a little park where some acacias made a pleasant shade. It was a cool and sunny day in early spring and the bazaar was crowded with shoppers. People walked along like sleepwalkers, bumping into each other. Thrifty Cypriots on the hunt for good deals were out in droves, plus dozens of Europeans. Everybody was fingering the goods and looking for bargains. This open-air market was a remnant of a Cyprus that belonged to the past, a world that existed before air-conditioned malls and supermarkets with their chilly, anti-septic aisles arrived on the island.

Anara enjoyed shopping here and once she had discovered it, she went every week to buy fresh-from-the-farm vegetables. Here she could also get fruit, nuts, spices and even clothes at prices that were lower than those charged by fashionable boutiques. Every Wednesday farmers and traders came from surrounding villages and set up temporary stalls. They arrived early and erected canvas awnings and large market umbrellas on the stretch of street that connected the main road and the Police Station. And by the time the sun cleared the battlements of Kyrenia Castle, buyers were on the prowl to get the pick of the market. Here we could buy dark-as-molasses honey, big, white chunks of hard Hellim cheese that you could crumble on a salad or cut into slices and fry till it turned a crispy, golden brown and lime-green olive oil that they poured straight into your bottle from big, greasy demi-johns. You could get anything you wanted, actually.

Most of the vendors sold new goods but there were a few who dealt in second-hand merchandise, particularly tools and common household gadgets. All day the market hummed with the clamor of commerce. Then around sundown everything got dismantled and carted away and the road was clear for normal traffic.

We browsed among the stalls examining the goods that were on display, assessing what we needed. Eventually, Anara bought a kilo of shelled walnuts from her favorite nut-seller and a liter of olive oil, as well as several kilos of onions and potatoes. I bought a pair of pliers, an adjustable wrench and a screwdriver.

Suddenly, Anara spotted a girl she knew.

"Oh, there's Regina," she said, and called out to her.

Regina turned and waved at us.

When we were near her, Anara greeted her in Russian and then leaned over and kissed her on both cheeks. Regina had the style and looks of a fashion model.

"This is my friend, Robert," Anara said, pushing me forward.

"Glad to meet you," I said, putting out my hand.

Regina said something in Russian.

"Regina work at *Starlight*," Anara said. "She is from Moscow."

Regina had grayish-blue eyes, long, blonde hair and very white skin. From a distance she gave the illusion of being very young. But standing near her, I noticed a certain fullness of bosom and hips that pointed at ripe womanhood. She smiled a controlled, almost mocking smile that did not reveal her teeth. Only the corners of her mouth curved upwards, expressing a prim and coy reserve.

Anara and Regina started chattering away in Russian. So I moved towards a stall displaying some gardening implements. I didn't want them to think they couldn't talk in Russian because of my presence. I felt glad that Anara knew someone with whom she could have a woman-to-woman conversation in her native language. While the two talked, I amused myself by stopping at various stalls and chatting with the vendors who sold tools and automotive parts.

When Anara re-joined me, her eyes sparkled with excitement.

"Honey, Regina is organizing a picnic for a few friends. She wants us to come too," Anara said.

"A picnic? Where are they planning to go?"

"Hilarion castle."

"Hey, that's Wonderful!" I said. "I've been meaning to take you up there. Maybe this is our chance to see the place? When are they going?"

"Not on the coming Sunday, but the Sunday after that."

"But you have to work on Sundays."

"Vitaly will give me the day off. He's coming too with some of his friends."

This surprised me. I couldn't imagine Vitaly in an open-air environment. It would be odd to see him in an ambiance other than that of the casino. The casino was his natural habitat.

"Will you come? Should I tell her we'll both come?"

"Do you want to go?"

"Yes," she said. "I'd like to."

"Fine," I said. "Let's go."

In the out-of-doors atmosphere of a picnic, I figured, everyone would be more informal and Anara and I would be able to go off by ourselves and do some exploring.

She was bubbling over with energy as we drove back home.

"Regina told me so many things," she said. "She is a smart girl."

"She certainly has style," I added.

"Did you like her?" Anara quizzed me with a sudden intensity in her tone.

"Well, I don't really know her but she seemed nice."

"She very helpful. She lived in north Cyprus for three years – knows a lot of people."

"She must like it here."

"She makes lots of money."

"That's good, I suppose. Why don't you invite her up to Karmi? We could barbecue. I'm sure she'll enjoy that."

"You don't mind?"

"No, of course not. Does she speak any English at all?"

"A little. But she make mistakes and get embarrassed. So she doesn't use it much. She told me she get nervous when she is talking in English to Americans or English people."

"But that's when she needs to use it most," I said.

"I know, I know," said Anara. "I'll ask her to come. She can practice her English with us. We can barbecue on Monday evening, my day off?"

"Sure. That's a good day. And let's invite Cardiff and Freya. I bet they haven't eaten a decent meal in several days."

"Well, Cardiff hates to cook and Freya doesn't know how."

Section 2

Monday turned out to be a nice day. After several days of rain and drizzle the sky was clear again. I lit the charcoal early on in the evening since I wanted it grayed over with ash to lessen the heat and got the ground beef patties and hotdogs and sausage links ready to go on the grill when everyone arrived.

Cardiff and Freya came early via taxi, both looking a bit tense as though they'd been arguing. Cardiff's face was flushed. I figured he'd already had a drink or two. And Freya's eyes glittered with a bright, hard energy and she spoke in a vehement, overly loud tone of voice.

"I want a drink," was the first thing Cardiff said to me. "What have you got?"

I took him by the arm and steered him to the table where the bottles of scotch and gin and brandy stood. A bit later, Regina drove up in her own car bearing a bottle of vodka much to Cardiff's delight. After I had made the introductions, Cardiff relieved Regina of the vodka and got busy right away making some kind of punch. He squeezed a dozen or so lemons into a big bowl, poured in the vodka, added sugar and ice and stirred everything vigorously.

"This concoction is known as *Micawber's Downfall*," he said. "You'll love it."

Freya, it turned out, had seen Regina once or twice at the *Triton* in Vitaly's company. They also had several friends and acquaintances in common, people who frequented the disco as well as the casino. As the evening wore on, Regina lost some of her shyness about speaking English and managed to keep up a fairly decent conversation with Freya. Regina sipped a little white wine but I could see that she didn't relish it very much. And as usual, Freya clung to her can of coke and played with her food and took several phone calls on her mobile.

Cardiff did not look happy. Nor did Freya, for that matter. Both of them wore a look of sour misery on their faces, the sort of look that one can see on the faces of some married couples who really don't like each other anymore.

Soon after we were done eating, Freya announced that she had to go. A car was coming to take her. An urgent crisis had erupted somewhere and she alone could avert an impending disaster. After she had left, the rest of us decided to go for a walkabout around the village. I wanted to point out the beauties of Karmi to Regina. Regina nodded and smiled a lot but I don't think Karmi appealed to her as much as it did to me. Perhaps, she expected something grander, more sophisticated – Florentine palaces, Parisian boulevards or the long perspectives of St. Petersburg. Karmi's narrow lanes and small houses that had once belonged to sheepherders and olive-growers did not impress her very much.

I handed off Regina to Anara and sought out Cardiff's company.

"What's going on, old chap?" I quizzed Cardiff. "Looks as though you and Freya are not getting along very well."

Cardiff shook his head.

"She's always running off somewhere," he said. "Half the time, I don't know what she's doing or who she's doing it with."

"She's young," I said to him. "They all go through this phase."

"I hope she grows out of it soon," Cardiff said. "I don't think I can take much more of this."

As we walked, I did my best to cheer him up.

Anara, I could see, was really enjoying Regina's company and displayed a vivacious chattiness I had not seen before. She twittered nonstop in rapid Russian, laughing, giggling and playing the part of a perfect hostess. Between the two of them they firmed up the plans for the picnic and worked out all the details of food and drink and transportation down to the last bowl of potato salad and ham sandwich.

By now darkness had settled over Karmi. We went up to the roof to see the lights of Kyrenia in the valley below. Finally, as if to announce the end of the evening, the Scops owl called out once or twice and then withdrew into the dark heart of a grove of pine trees. While we were talking about calling a taxi for Cardiff, Regina volunteered to give him a lift to his apartment.

When our guests had finally departed, Anara threw herself on the couch. A little frown formed a crevice between her eyebrows.

"What is it?" I asked. "It went well, don't you think?"

She shook her head from side to side.

"I don't think Freya enjoyed herself. That's why she left early."

"She's got her own agenda," I said. "Who knows what she's doing? But what about Regina? Do you think she had a good time?"

The frown between Anara's eyebrows got deeper and she shrugged.

"Regina is happiest when she in the casino," Anara said. "Karmi is not the sort of place where she feel comfortable. She is a big city girl – discos, dancing, restaurants – she likes that sort of life."

On Sunday morning, all the people who were going on the picnic gathered in the parking lot in front of Astra supermarket. Regina had chosen this rendezvous point because everyone knew its location.

Moreover, the large apron of concrete in front of the store provided ample space for parking. There were eleven of us all together but it made no sense to take too many cars. Two vehicles would suffice. The ride to Hilarion would not be very comfortable but it would be short since it wasn't very far from Kyrenia. There was much giggling and laughter as people packed and folded themselves into the vehicles like contortionists. Limbs got tangled up with limbs. This created an atmosphere of intimacy that could only be relieved by embarrassed laughter. But no one complained. We were a mixed lot – there was the massive presence of Vitaly, of course, and two Turkish-Cypriot boys (waiters, probably), two English girls (waitresses, no doubt), Regina and the same two Ukrainian men I had met in Vitaly's office. They were wearing the same black business suits I had seen them in earlier. Rather an odd way to dress for a picnic, I thought. Vitaly, because of his enormous bulk and also because he represented authority, functioned as the magnetic center of the party. Always cordial, polite, soft-spoken and well mannered, the role of the host suited him to perfection.

We moved swiftly out of Kyrenia taking the highway that goes towards Lefkosa. Vitaly drove the car I was in and Regina sat up front by his side in the passenger seat. I was in the back seat with Anara on my lap. One of the English girls and a Turkish boy came with us. The other car carried the rest of the party. Everyone was jabbering at the same time. A kind of hysterical jocularity that tends to afflict picnickers had taken possession of us. Much squealing and mock complaints filled the car as bottoms squirmed and bounced on laps. Anara bounced more times per mile than could be accounted for by the number of bumps and potholes in the road. She did this gleefully even as I made faces to express my discomfort. Once off the main highway we started to weave up towards Hilarion on a series of switchbacks that swung us from side to side like rag dolls. As we climbed higher and higher, we left behind the layer of smog and dust that lay over the coastal plain. Rockroses and asphodel nodded cheerily by the roadside and the sky became an eternity of sapphire blue.

We parked just below the castle in an area set aside for cars and tour buses. From here the hampers of food and the coolers containing the iced drinks had to be carried up past the ticket booth and through the barbican. Several volunteers made this task easy and everything got hauled up to the middle enceinte and deposited on a shelf that hovered high above the valley floor. Looking north one could see Kyrenia and its suburbs spread out far below us, above it a band of slate-colored sea and above that the blurred purple line of the Turkish coast on the horizon. To the east stretched the Karpaz peninsula tapering to infinity and right in the middle, the granite silhouette of Kantara castle was visible poking up through a silver-gray haze.

Our gang split up into small parties and scattered in separate directions to explore the various overlooks and chambers of the castle. Vitaly, very short of breath because of the hike, chose to sit and rest in the shade of a stone wall.

"Come back when you want to eat and drink," he said. "I will guard everything for you."

Anara and I set forth together, clambering over battlements that seemed to hover in empty space. The air was soaked in the odor of wild fennel. Most of the chambers of the castle were roofless. But their generous dimensions and massive walls of sulfur yellow stones gave them an air of grandeur. Every room afforded a new vista, a new angle of vision, and a new perspective. I felt as though I had invaded the aerie of an eagle. The sky, a powdery Wedgwood blue, seemed near at hand. You felt you could take a pinch of this blue substance between thumb and forefinger. The ground fell steeply away from the castle, the way it does when you are taking off in an airplane. A monarch would naturally choose this peak as his abode. From here he could survey his kingdom and feel secure.

A large reservoir of water took up the middle part of the castle. Winter rains must have filled it every year. All the people who lived in the castle must have taken water from this source. But now it looked stagnant, full of dead leaves, algae and all sorts of debris.

We then made our way to the Queen's chamber with its two windows that looked west towards Karmi. From here the houses of Karmi looked like a collection of white origami boxes nesting in green vegetation. From our rooftop we had often seen the full moon loom past these windows. Anara and I sat down on the stone benches that faced each other, savoring the thyme-scented breezes that came up from the valley floor.

Towards noon, members of our party starting drifting back to where Vitaly sat guarding the cache of food and drinks. Sandwiches were handed around, wine bottles were opened and everyone sat down to eat. The fresh air and the exertion of tramping around the castle had whetted appetites. We began with caviar on crackers paired with a crisp champagne that went down your throat like a chilled steel sword. Anara's crabmeat sandwiches were much appreciated and we also had roasted chicken, baked ham cut in thin slices and fried sausages. And there were several bottles of red and white Aphrodite, Turkish and Danish and Dutch beer and fruit juices and colas of all kinds. It was quite a feast and everyone attacked the food with gusto.

Regina paid particular attention to the needs of Vitaly. She hovered near him most of the time, responding to his whispered requests, making sure he had whatever he wanted. He drank only water and ate very sparingly, holding his sandwich with both hands and taking small, meditative nibbles. Nor was he much of talker. He seemed to enjoy hearing other people talk, and listened attentively to all the chatter around him.

After lunch, I asked Anara if she wanted to see Prince John's Tower, one of the highest chambers of the castle. But she said she was worn out and wanted to stay behind to rest and chat with Regina.

I started up by myself along a stone staircase that climbed steeply and had no handrail to keep you from falling. In places the stones had come loose and shifted when you came down on them with your full weight. At certain points along the trail, you had to jump across deep ravines and scramble up walls using your hands.

After nearly thirty minutes of this, I finally reached the spot from where Prince John is said to have flung his Bulgarian guards because he suspected them of treachery. The view from up here was stupendous and well worth the strenuous hike. One could see the entire Mesaoria, a lion-colored expanse with patches of dull green vegetation here and there. And far to the south, on the blurred, misty horizon lay Limassol.

As I sat there, I felt a kind of calm descending over me. I was glad Anara had found a friend in Regina, someone nearer her age with whom she could share the sorts of secrets that girls like to share. They had a language in common and they shared common traditions and a common culture.

Of course, Anara and I also shared a great deal. A full, rich life filled with good and bad experiences. We shared the daily routines of domesticity, the rituals of the bedroom, the bathroom, the kitchen. She shared herself with me, shared her body – generously, unstintingly – without ever holding back. I felt grateful to her for these gifts, grateful and satisfied. But in spite of this intimacy, this closeness, there were times when I felt that she had certain secret rooms in her soul I would never enter, certain doors that she would never open for me. I didn't know where those doors led or what I would see once past the door. Frankly, I did not want to know. At times when I saw her sitting in the courtyard, her face innocent in repose, and that rational nose pointing down at a meditative angle, I wished I could read her mind. At such moments she seemed so far away from me, so remote and unreachable.

By the time I got back down from Prince John's Tower, the afternoon sun was hot and tourists were hurrying to find shade wherever they could. Obese, elderly northern Europeans were particularly uncomfortable. I could hear them wheezing and panting and mopping their brick-red, sun-blistered faces with handkerchiefs and fanning themselves with their straw hats to keep cool.

Vitaly lay in the shadowed lee of a wall, his eyes closed, breathing quietly. Regina sat near him with her back propped up against the stones, leafing through a fashion magazine. There was no one else around.

"Where is everyone?" I asked Regina.

She looked up, flashed a prim little smile and shrugged.

I was hot and thirsty. I got a can of beer from the ice-chest and took a long pull, wondering where Anara was. Presently, I saw some other members of our party coming back – the two English girls and the two Turkish boys, who had obviously formed a tight bond. They flopped down near me and helped themselves to beer and potato chips.

We made some remarks about the castle, but then a somnolent silence descended on everyone. Talk required effort and no one felt like making an effort of any sort.

After I had finished the beer, I didn't feel any better and my unease about Anara started to increase appreciably. She had said she was tired and I expected to find her exactly where I had left her. For a change of taste, I poured out some champagne into a plastic glass and drank it off too fast. This is why chilled champagne can be so deadly. No normal human being can drink it slowly on a warm day. The bubbles give you the sensation of having nothing but air in your mouth. Naturally, I kept gulping glass after glass until my brain became a bubble -- a big, golden, bubble floating on emptiness.

The sensation was rather pleasant and I kept reaching for the champagne. At some point I saw Anara coming up a long slope flanked by the two Ukrainians. This is odd, I thought. What is she doing with them? In the strong sunlight, the figures seemed to flicker and flutter as they came up.

"Where were you?" I asked Anara.

"We were looking for a cafeteria," she said.

"Why? I said. "There's enough food here."

"For cigarettes. They wanted cigarettes."

"Oh," I said. "Did you find it?"

"Yes," she said, "but it was closed."

I felt vaguely irritated and resentful and wondered if she was telling me the truth. Odd, unpleasant thoughts were jumping and bouncing around my champagne-soaked brain. I didn't want her to be chummy with those two guys. Then I thought, maybe she went with them because they don't speak Turkish or English. But who needs words to buy cigarettes? You just point and pay. The Ukrainians looked at me and smiled in a silly, superior way. I smiled back as if to show that I had no fear that they would succeed in stealing my girl. By and by, Vitaly woke up. All the wanderers were back now and everyone had something to eat and drink. The idea was to consume everything we'd brought so we'd only have empty bottles and cans and wrappers to carry back. When the food was all gone, we packed up everything carefully, got all the trash and litter into garbage bags and headed for the parking lot. I held Anara's hand to steady myself. The muscles in my legs were feeling weak and rubbery and I was having a hard time keeping my balance. I was glad I didn't have to drive us down the mountain.

∿

Section 3

I heard the phone ringing as if from very far away, as if in a dream almost, a sound heard in an intermediate state between sleep and wakefulness. It kept on and on nonstop and then suddenly I was awake feeling irritable, a sharp pain gonging my head.

I picked up the receiver and said, "Yes," in a gruff manner.

"Hello, hello," I heard a woman say. She sounded Turkish from her accent.

"Yes?"

"Mr. Robert?"

"Yes. I'm Robert."

"I'm calling from the hospital. Kyrenia Hospital – Akcicek Hastanasi. You know Mr. Cardiff?"

"Yes. What is it? Is he okay?"

"We have him here. He asked us to call you. He is not well. He cannot teach tomorrow."

"What happened?"

"The doctor can tell you … Many problems."

"Can I see him?"

"Yes, of course."

"Okay," I said. "I'm on my way."

I checked my wristwatch. It said 10:30. I must have dozed off on the couch after dinner. An empty bottle of Aphrodite sat among some defunct beer cans on the coffee table. I must have hit the booze quite hard earlier in the evening. My head throbbed like a thumb that's been hit with a hammer. It would be another couple of hours before Anara got back from *Starlight*. I glanced out the window to check the weather. The night looked murky. The wedge of a waning moon made of corroded brass slid behind some clouds that were being torn to shreds by a high-altitude wind. Far to the north in Antalya, lightning strobed inside the bellies of huge platinum-gray cumulous clouds, lighting them up with a sinister magnesium glow.

I threw some cold water on my face and sat down and wrote a brief note for Anara.

"Sweetie: Cardiff is in Kyrenia hospital. I am going down to check up on him. There is some baked chicken and rice in the fridge. I'll be back as soon as I can."

I stuck the note to the TV screen with a piece of scotch tape so she wouldn't miss it and hurried down to the car.

Akcicek hospital sat on a dimly lit road that went from the center of Kyrenia to the Yeni Liman. A rather plain structure that must have been built in the mid-70s as an inexpensive response to the city's needs, it had all the charm of a morgue. As soon as I pulled up in front of the building, a terrible depression came over me. I did not want to go in. It took an enormous effort of will to drag my feet forward one step at a time and force myself to enter.

In the bare lobby people huddled in silent groups and stared at me with empty eyes as if to say, "Abandon all hope, etc." A guard conducted me to the nurse's station. I explained my business to the nurse on duty, a stout matron with a downy mustache between nose and upper lip. She nodded and led me through several stark corridors that reeked of sinus-burning antiseptic odors. Eventually, we reached the Male Ward where she deposited me at the entrance to Cardiff's room, turned on her heels wordlessly and left. I eased open the door and peeked in.

Cardiff lay in the metallic embrace of the hospital bed, covered with a white sheet, his eyes closed. A chilly white luminescence filled the room. I thought he looked dead and the hair on my forearms and neck bristled up. But then I noticed his chest rising and falling gently. Across from his bed, a TV tuned to a Turkish channel blasted the fuss and fury of a soccer match. Three other beds in the remaining three corners of the large room were unoccupied.

He must have heard the door handle squeak as I came in, because he opened his eyes and regarded me with an air of uncertainty.

"What are you doing here?" I said, grinning broadly. "Another ploy to get out of teaching?"

He flashed a wan smile. His fair hair, usually combed firmly back on his scalp, now looked tousled and stuck out here and there.

"Did you bring any brandy?" he asked.

"No," I said. "And you are not getting bon-bon either. You better get well and get yourself out of here. This is no place for law-abiding citizens."

He chuckled.

"I'd rather be in Philadelphia," he said.

"So, what gives? What's all this nonsense?"

"I don't know," he said. "I was just sitting at the bar in *Pegasus* talking to Neil. You know Neil? He teaches English. When all of a sudden, everything went blank. I think I fell off the stool and landed on the floor. Someone must have called an ambulance and here I am."

As he spoke, he suddenly started to cough and tried to sit. I placed my hand between his shoulder blades and propped him up with a couple of pillows. The coughing fit lasted for a minute or so. In sign language he indicated that he wanted to get out of bed. I helped him out and he stood there swaying slightly to get his balance. Then he shuffled over to a sink attached to a wall of the room, leaned forward and brought up a mouthful of bright, red blood. Afterwards he rinsed his mouth, gargled and ran more water to clean the basin.

I went over, took him by the elbow and helped him back into bed.

"Could be pneumonia or something," I said. "A bad lung infection."

He nodded, his face totally without color, white as his pillow. He looked strangely gaunt with sunken cheeks and yellow eyes that protruded from the sockets in an odd way. He had never been sturdy but now his limbs looked thin and brittle as wooden sticks. He seemed much older suddenly, more wrinkled, frailer.

"Some Penicillin," he said, faintly, "and I'll be fine."

I nodded.

"Hey, does Freya know you are here?"

"Yes, she was by earlier. She's not keen on hospitals. Can't stand the smells."

I nodded again.

"You should rest," I said. "Take it easy for a while. I'll tell the chaps in the Department. We'll find someone to cover your classes. Don't worry."

"Thanks, he said. "And bring some cigarettes and brandy when you come."

"Sure," I said. "That's what you need. Hair of the dog."

"Look," he said. "If something should happen to me … ."

"What rot! Nothing's gonna happen to you."

"In that jacket over there, I've got something. I wrote it down."

"What is it?"

"An addendum to my will, a Codicil. I want you to take it and keep it just in case."

"Don't be silly. You're gonna pull out of this."

"Maybe. This time, perhaps. But the next time could be the last. Go ahead. Take that paper."

I went to his much-beloved linen jacket, hanging on a hook on the wall and took out a piece of paper from the left hand side pocket.

"Are you sure about this?" I asked.

"Yes, I'm sure. I want Freya to have the flat. I don't want it to go to my wife or son. I want Freya to have it so she'll always have a place to stay in Cyprus. She loves this place so much."

"Is this wise?" I said. "I'm just asking. This is your business."

"You don't understand," he said, between short, sharp breaths. "Something happened. To me, I mean. I felt something. I don't want to give this feeling a trite label. Love? Maybe. I know she can't cook and she never lifted a finger to clean the place. And men? Let's leave that aside for the moment. All those things are true. But they are trivial. She's a wonderful girl. That's what counts in the long run. What I want to tell you is that she made me feel something, gave me something that I did not have. That's all."

He fell silent and I could see that the effort of making this speech had exhausted him. His eyes were liquid with tears.

I remained silent, unwilling to argue or debate the point with him, deny him his wish even though, to me, it appeared to be rooted in sentimentality.

"You know, let me tell you something, something you will not believe or understand." Cardiff said. A little smile flickered around his lips. "She is so innocent, so innocent, that's what got me. You know what I mean?"

"I guess so," I said.

He sensed the doubt in my voice, because he went on.

"No, you don't. But I'm telling you, she is the new woman, totally without guile, sinless. She has no notion of what sin is, no concept at all. Right and wrong, yes. But not sin. That's what I mean when I say she is innocent. You and I are old-fashioned. We belong to another era. We were taught that promiscuity is wrong. Sex outside marriage is sinful. These notions were dinned into us. But Freya is free of all these dead moral concepts."

He stopped to catch his breath. He seemed very worked up now, much like his old self, speaking almost as though he were giving a lecture in class. He wanted to drive home his point, make sure that I understood what he had to say.

"Could you push this pillow up behind my back?" he asked.

I propped him up.

"Better?"

"Yes, yes, much better. Thanks," he said and then added: "You know what I liked about her?"

I winked at him.

"Let me guess. She's young, thin ... what else?"

He clicked his tongue in disapproval.

"Admirable qualities. Certainly. But what I really like, what really appeals to me is that she's an out and out pagan. A free spirit. Fearless."

"A pagan? In what sense?"

"The Greco-Roman sense. She hasn't been tainted by Christian dogma. She has no notion of sin and guilt."

"Okay. But shouldn't that worry you?"

Cardiff chuckled. "No. That doesn't worry me. But there is something that does."

I shot him a questioning look.

"She lives in the present – like a wild animal. She never thinks about the future."

"She's young," I said. "Did you think about the future when you were her age?"

"I did, actually. I thought about it all the time."

"Does she think about the past?"

Cardiff burst out laughing.

"Are you joking? The past means nothing to her. She never looks back."

"What about history – the story of England?"

"Irrelevant. Look. At first I didn't understand her. But now, now that I am here, in this hospital bed, I see things more clearly. Freya is a natural creature, like those women on the South Sea Islands used to be. They were innocent too until the missionaries infected them with the virus of Judeo-Christian morality."

"I see your point," I said. "The Missionaries looked upon them as lost sinners and then set about saving their souls."

"Right," he said. "But Freya, you see, is free of all those phobias and complexes that you and I inherited."

"Does she know this?" I asked.

"No, no," Cardiff said. "Of course not. She has no clue. But it doesn't matter. She is like a new species, that has to be protected and nurtured."

Cardiff was trying to understand Freya, explain her behavior to himself, to me. I wondered if this was even possible. I thought Cardiff had started drifting into complicated regions of psychology. But I did not challenge him. I would do that another time, when he was feeling better. There would be other opportunities to pick apart his ideas. When he had his health back and we were sitting in the *Pegasus* drinking, that would be the time to engage him in a lively debate.

"Fine," I said, "I'll keep this … this letter. You can have it back when you are on your feet."

"Thanks. I knew I could depend on you. You can go now, if you wish. It is getting quite late."

"Okay," I said. "I'll see you tomorrow."

"Oh, one other thing, switch the bloody telly off, will you?"

"I'll come tomorrow after classes," I said. "You behave yourself now. And leave the nurses alone."

He rolled his eyes in mock agony and grinned.

I patted his hand, switched off the TV and left.

I took the back road to Karmi, leaning sleepily on the steering wheel to enjoy the roll and sway of the lazy turns now brindled with shadows. Darkness came in close to the car as soon as I had left the built-up zone of Kyrenia behind but the cone of light made by the headlamps kept pushing it back as I moved forwards. The landscape of fields and orchards and hills on either side of the road became a negative of itself with blotches of inky black trees in clumps against a backdrop of gray lead.

I kept thinking about what Cardiff had said and couldn't quite understand his motive behind what he planned to do. Innocence is one thing and I quite accepted his theory that Freya had no sense of guilt. She could go from man to man as casually as a butterfly goes from flower to flower. My mind revolved around the issue of love and – well, I better spit it out, *loyalty*. Did she really love Cardiff? Did she *care* for him in any sense of the word? Did she feel any kind of loyalty towards him… any devotion? I realize that with these two words, loyalty and devotion, I am moving into the realm of Romance and Idiocy. To expect loyalty and devotion from Freya would be like expecting water on the moon. Perhaps she did love him in her own fashion. Perhaps by refusing to allow herself to conform to conventional notions of "love" she had transformed herself in Cardiff's eyes into a genuinely sincere and honest person, someone who embodied freedom and a new kind of selflessness.

Once Cardiff told me (we were deep into some whisky at his flat) that Freya didn't really like or enjoy sex that much. But she felt no qualms or reservations about "giving" herself. Freya regarded the sexual act as something totally normal and natural, something as normal and natural as breathing, not something to be ashamed of. He said he appreciated this sort of honesty and candor.

"For too long we've been burdened with notions of guilt and sin all tied up with sexuality," Cardiff said. "It's high time we freed ourselves."

"But, " I began.

"Wait. Let me finish. We don't have a right to litter the world with babies that just happen to get conceived during a moment of heedless passion. Don't misunderstand me. I firmly believe that children, whether legitimate or illegitimate, are miracles of Nature and must be cherished. But we are living on an over-burdened planet. No one has a right procreate in an irresponsible and heedless manner or spread disease. That is criminal behavior."

He laughed.

"We've pushed sexual freedom to an absurd extreme in my dear country. And here's the irony. When the English arrived in India equipped with straight-laced Victorian values, they were shocked and scandalized by child brides and child marriages. And when they became rulers, they did everything in their power to stamp out these practices. Now look what's happening in England, in America, in Brazil – babies having babies. What progress! Wonderful indeed!"

All very well, but in my system of values a wife (even an ex-wife) and son deserved precedence over a girlfriend. Cardiff had divorced his wife, yes, but his son had a claim. I reached into my jacket pocket to make sure that I still had the paper he had given me, wondering if I would be able to do what he had told me to do.

All of us in the Law Department – the faculty, the secretarial staff – we were all alarmed by Cardiff's sudden hospitalization and everyone feared the worst. The signs had been there of course – we all knew his lifestyle – but no one had said or done anything to make him change his ways. The chaps who orbited around Cardiff were a bunch of hard-drinking, crusty old codgers, an exceptionally headstrong lot with a fierce sense of independence. Not one of them would have tolerated being told what to do, what not to do or how to live. Nor would one of them even dream of interfering in someone else's business. As an American I had a certain license and fewer inhibitions about speaking my mind. I could have said something to Cardiff, but I had not been very close to him lately. Moreover, I felt I had no business advising him on the virtues of moderation when I shared and applauded his desire to live passionately, to squeeze the marrow out of life.

Furthermore, Anara and I stayed in Karmi much of the time while Cardiff circulated in Kyrenia. At times he had Freya with him and at other times he drank with other friends, older, academic types. Freya swooped hither and yon like a barely-tame bird of prey, heedless of the handler's commands. She flew away whenever the whim struck her and returned whenever she felt like returning.

Cardiff's illness got me roped into teaching courses that he had taught – Tort, Jurisprudence and Criminal Law, subjects I neither liked teaching nor had much background in and I found myself spending more hours at the university than I wanted to.

During this phase of our lives, Anara and I found ourselves in an odd situation: we hardly saw each other. Except for Mondays, her day off, we were only together when we were in bed between midnight and six a.m. She came home exhausted and showed little interest in any amorous activity. At times I would be awake, beer in hand, watching TV and we would talk briefly about something she had done or seen that evening. At other times, I'd be asleep. And though I never said this to her or admitted this in front of her, I preferred sleep to sex between midnight and six. And when we did have sex – any healthy man lying beside a lovely girl is bound to become aroused – these couplings tended to be brief. A dull, mechanical routine, reduced to the barest essentials.

But Anara never complained. Even if she did feel the lack of uninhibited intimacies that we had once shared so naturally and spontaneously and with such enthusiasm, she said nothing, thinking perhaps that her work and the visa business came before everything else. She seemed stoical but this may have been a mask of sorts, because she also had another side, a sentimental side. She did miss her child, though she never actually verbalized these feelings in front of me. One afternoon, (it must have been a Monday because she hadn't gone to work) she called Almaty. I did not understand what she said because she spoke in Russian but after the call she broke down and started to cry.

"What is it?" I asked, putting an arm around her shoulder, trying to comfort her. "What is it?"

She just shook her head and kept on sobbing, harshly, violently, drawing each breath like a choking gasp. I had never seen her crying like this, indeed, I had never seen her cry.

"Is Mama okay?" I asked, expecting some sort of bad news.

"She's fine," she said between hiccups.

"And your daughter? Is she okay?"

Anara nodded.

"I miss her," she said. "She is being such a brave little girl."

"She is," I said. "She is a brave child. Just like her mother."

I took her into my arms and held her close to my chest, stroking her head gently. I could feel her thin shoulders spasming and shaking as the last of her emotion drained out of her and she slowly grew quiet.

"Don't you miss your daughter?" she asked suddenly.

"Not really. I think of her at times and worry about her."

"You never call her," she said.

"True. Seems a bit meaningless. I'm not a part of her life anymore. My son and my daughter are both like strangers to me."

"No, no, they are a part of you. They will always be a part of you."

"I guess. But listen tell me, do you want to go back to Almaty?"

"Yes, of course," she said. "When you leave, I leave."

"You could stay on once you get the work visa, make money,"

"No. When you go, I go. This place means nothing to me without you."

"Maybe I'll return with you to Almaty. We could get an apartment. I could teach."

"Would you accept my girl?"

"Yes, yes, certainly," I said. "In my eyes, she is your child. The father played a role – a minimal role according to my way of thinking. He has certain rights. Granted. But the child is essentially yours. You carried her inside your body for nine months. You brought her into this world. You raised her. She is your creation."

"I have photo," she said. "I can show you."

"Really?"

I released her from my embrace and she went downstairs. She kept all her personal possessions, clothes and shoes in one of the bedrooms on the ground floor. When she came back up she had a thick book in her hand. It had a black, imitation leather cover.

"What is this?" I asked.

I had never seen this book before.

"A bible."

"Let me see," I said.

"Wait, one moment," she said and suddenly opened it and pulled out a large, color photograph and handed it to me.

"Here she is."

I took the photo from her hand and examined it. The picture, a studio photo, showed a pretty child of about six or seven years of age, dressed in a fancy party frock decorated with pink ribbons and lace and embroidery. The girl's facial features had much of Anara in them and yet they were somewhat different and she had brown hair and grayish-green eyes.

"She is lovely," I said. "Didn't I tell you? Except for the color of her hair and eyes, she is very much like you."

"She has the eyes of her father," Anara said. "He's Russian."

"That explains it," I said. "She is a beautiful girl. You are so lucky to have her."

"She is beautiful and she is a very sweet child," Anara said, in serious tones, looking down at the book in her hands.

"Let me see the bible," I said and took it from her.

I thumbed through it but could not read a word. It was all in Russian.

I saw now how much of Anara lay below the surface like the taproots of a tree, how much of herself, her inner self she kept hidden from the gaze of the world. She lived at two levels it seemed, the surface and the subsurface and only on rare occasions did I get to see her hidden side. Coupling brings two bodies together, but after the "act" is over, we find ourselves alone once again, and are forced to confront our imprisoned, separate selves. I knew she ached to be with her daughter, but being with me in Cyprus also meant a lot to her and she could not give up what she had with me.

In fact, neither one of us (I think) wanted to give up what we had, I mean what we had together. The thought that Anara could or would or might leave me for another man stung me like a scorpion. Nor could I tolerate the idea of sharing her with anyone. This attitude did not have anything to do with what Cardiff would have called traditional morality. I simply wanted to spend all my free time with her and expected her to spend her free time with me. We had a life together and I did not want anyone or anything interfering with this life or disturbing it in anyway. We were happy being with each other.

Karmi seemed like a corner of Eden to me, a protected refuge, a place of shelter. My house fulfilled my childhood fantasy of living in a Robinson Crusoe-style tree house – a secure, self-sufficient, self-contained world no one could enter once you pulled up the rope ladder. I did not want any intruders to disturb us. Karmi nourished us in mysterious ways, held us trapped in a kind of dream world. Surrounded by nasturtium-festooned walls, the irises in flouncy party gowns and the ivory trumpets of the Datura plant it was easy to pretend that we were in an Hieronymus Bosch "Garden of Earthly Delights."

"Come," I said, taking her by the arm, "let's go to the lily pond and feed the fish."

I knew this would cheer her up, pull her out of the pit of grief. She enjoyed the ritual and it would remind her why we were in Karmi and not somewhere else.

Indeed she did cheer up and dried her tears.

"Yes, let's go, before it get too dark. The shadows are already getting long," she said.

She got some slices of day-old bread and we walked hand in hand down the stone steps that led to the pool. "Poodie," her little ginger kitten, hopped and skipped ahead of us, very baby-cat awkward, tail held straight up, little pink anus exposed. I wished I had left him locked up in the house. He was running the risk of being given a good drubbing by Black Bart, the meanest cat in Karmi. Black Bart ruled the area around the pool and guarded his territory with a ferocious determination. Poodie mewed plaintively, letting us know that protecting him would be our job.

An apricot light stained wispy clouds that floated above Karmi and threw a warm blush the over the houses. Karmi was sinking into shadows. Feeding the fish had become a sort of ritual that both of us enjoyed, perhaps she more than I. As you broke the bread over the water, the surrounding silence seeped into you and the cares of the world seemed to drop away and you started to feel at peace. The fish didn't really care whether you were there or not. But feeding them nourished you, gave you something you could not get from a grocery store. Dare one call it spiritual food? Perhaps. Perhaps you are rewarded in some way when you look after the natural world. Anyway, it's a nice thought.

Anara climbed on top of the wall of the pool and stood there with her head bent as though she were thinking of something. She crumbled the bread into small pieces and dropped them into the dark water. As the particles sank, tiny fish raced to attack the rain of crumbs, gulping them greedily. Their dull brown backs made them invisible against the murky bottom of the pool. You only saw them when they made sudden, darting moves.

Water lilies floated on the surface of the pool, their white petals gesturing like the fingers of oriental dancers. A pair of green turtles sat on a tuft of papyrus roots, taking the last of the light on their slender necks. As the gloom of dusk spread, I could hear the rustling sound made by the water that overflowed out of the pool and trickled down a narrow stone channel.

Just as we were about to return to the house, I saw Fiona coming towards us swinging a plastic bag full of cat food in her left hand. I greeted her, without realizing that her presence had created a crisis. Poodie snaked himself around her ankles and mewed. Fiona bent down to caress him.

"Is this your new kitty?"

Just as she uttered those words, a blood-curdling MEOWWW arose from the leaf litter beneath the Carob tree. Black Bart had been waiting for his dinner. Seeing Fiona paying attention to Poodie, he objected loudly. Black Bart had fought and won many battles and he had the scars to prove this. His ears looked chewed up as though they had been edged with pinking scissors and there were many islands of bald skin on his back. Uttering a horrible scream he charged at Poodie. Poodie's hair bristled. He arched his back and held his tail straight up and started to hiss and spit.

Black Bart's ears were flat against his head and his yellow eyes were filled with hatred as he advanced swiftly to rip out Poodie's heart.

Anara jumped off the wall of the lily pond and tried to scoop Poodie into her arms but he panicked and ran from her. Black Bart gave chase, caught up with Poodie and whacked him with his right paw and sent him flying into a bed of geraniums. Poodie let out a yowl of pain. Anara ran as fast as she could and tried to catch him again. But Poodie was back on his feet and racing up the road towards our house as fast as he could with Black Bart hard on his tail. Eventually, the two went over a wall screeching like banshees. Anara ran after them, calling out, "Poodie, Poodie, come back."

Fiona stood there doubled over with laughter.

"Don't worry, they are just showing off," she said. "It's all a part of being a Karmi cat. You have to protect your territory."

"Poodie shouldn't have come down to the lily pond," I said. "He won't forget this lesson now."

"No, I don't think he will," Fiona said and placed a cupful of kitty kibble for Black Bart near the wall of the lily pond.

"I don't suppose these two will ever become fast friends," I said.

"I rather doubt that," Fiona replied. "Moreover, for this lot, fighting is more fun than being friends."

"I'd better go see if I can help Anara get Poodie back in the house," I said and started trudging up the road.

Cardiff spent just a little over a week in the hospital. The doctors somehow managed to control the symptoms and sent him home. He looked rather frail and I really wondered if the underlying maladies had been cured. One chilly night, I met him at *Pegasus*. In the circular fire-pit olive wood logs blazed, splashing flame shadows on the walls. There were several people there, regulars who lived nearby and treated *Pegasus* as an extension of their living rooms. We were sampling some Cypriot brandy to keep warm. An unusual flush stained Cardiff's usually pallid cheeks and he seemed to be in a talkative mood.

"How are you feeling now?" I asked him.

"Fine," he said, taking a meditative pull on his cigarette. "But the doctor says I should give up smoking."

"Well, give it up then."

"I have," he said. "I only smoke when I am drinking."

"Hard to break old habits, isn't it? How was it growing up in Britain?" I asked. "Tell me about your formative – or should I say de-formative – period, the years that really influenced you."

"Hah! The post-war period," he said with sudden animation. "That's my era, you know. I firmly believe that we are molded by the time period in which we grow up. You agree?"

He looked at me as if challenging me to disagree.

"Sure," I said, "Possibly."

"No, no – certainly! Consider this. It was a time of shortages, rationing, cleaning up the rubble, mourning the dead. What a magnificent mess! The Empire lost and gone with it all the pomp and power. All those comfortable Civil Service jobs, for god's sake! All the cheap raw materials and captive markets where we could sell our tin trays and chintz. I remember those years mainly as a series of gray, grainy photographs in newspapers. A gray world seen through curtains of smoke and fog. Black and white movies and newsreels, gray cities, gray landscapes, gray rivers, gray seas and gray skies. And the endless English rain. All the famous landmarks of London covered with a soot: St. Paul's, Westminster Abbey, the Houses of Parliament, the British

Museum, the National Gallery, St. Martin in the Fields. And the Thames – quite dead, toxic with pollution. Then the Sixties began and color seemed to come back into our lives. One started to feel twinges of hope. Austerity ended. Prosperity began."

"Were you happy?"

He thought for a moment.

"I don't think we even tried to be happy. We were too busy trying to make sense of our lives," he said shaking his head. "We were so confused!"

"That sounds odd," I said. "Nobody was confused in the United States during the Fifties. Everybody was very confident, very self-assured. Why were you chaps confused?"

"Well, you guys were largely untouched by the war," he said. "But in England the war destroyed more than buildings. Everything got wrecked: the old politics, the old morality and the old ideas we had believed in – everything lay in ruins. We were left with Freud and Marx. And they confused us even more."

"Well, we got a dose of that stuff too but in a much modified watered-down form."

"Right, all that stuff about sexual complexes and the workers' paradise. The ideas that D.H. Lawrence obsessed about."

"What did you do?"

"What could we do? We got into sex in big way in our socialist Welfare State."

"Was it fun?"

"I guess so, in a circular, repetitive kind of way."

I had to chuckle.

"Look," I said. "I've got to run. It is getting late. You better head home too."

"You go. I'll stay here awhile. Home is a cold apartment and a cold bed."

"Where's Freya?" I asked.

He shot me a look of surprise and then his face turned into an expressionless mask.

"How should I know?" he said. "I don't try to keep track of what she does or who she does it with."

"This is the post post-pill generation," I said. "Very independent."

"Very."

"No sense of belonging to anything or anyone, I suppose."

"Not really. All that is old hat."

"It's a new breed," I said. "They've changed Descarte's dictum," I said. "Instead of 'I think, therefore, I am' this generation says: I feel, therefore, I am."

"I would change 'feel' to another four-letter word beginning with an F."

"I feed, therefore, I am."

"No not that one," he said grinning.

"Oh, I get it," I said. "Do you think she'll come back?"

He shrugged.

"Okay," I said, hitting his shoulder gently with my fist. "See ya later, gator."

And I left.

∼

CHAPTER SEVEN

Section 1

Several nights running I heard odd noises coming from the terrace, the clicking of claws against stone and the sound of heavy breathing, strange snuffling and muffled growls. One night a loud crash made me jump out of bed and switch on the outside light. Some creature or creatures had knocked over our metal garbage can, scattering garbage everywhere. The sudden flood of light scared them and they scampered away. I barely got a glimpse of some blurred shapes and saw vague, furry forms melting swiftly into dark shadows beyond our wall. Were they dogs or wolves? I wasn't sure. Some days later I was woken up again by the sound of nails scraping against flagstones and hoarse gasps and a sort of slobbering. The dogs were back, looking for food, I suppose. But I had placed several heavy rocks on top of the cover of the garbage can to weigh it down. They would not be able to push it over no matter how hard they tried. Drowsily I rolled over and reached across the bed in the darkness to feel Anara, expecting her soft curves. But I found nothing. She wasn't there. That's odd, I thought and glanced at the digital clock on the desk where lit-up numerals announced 4:30 in the penumbral gloom. I sat straight up, jarred into full wakefulness.

What could have happened, I wondered? Usually, she was home by 1:30 or 2:00 a.m. at the latest. I reached for the my mobile phone and dialed the number of her mobile but I couldn't connect. It looked as though she had it off. This was unusual. Normally, I could always reach her while she was at work. My first instinct was to panic. Disjointed thoughts flooded my mind and it took an effort of will to focus, to think rationally. There could be several explanations, I reasoned, why she hadn't come home. Several plausible scenarios flashed through my mind rapidly, flickering across the brain like a montage of film clips. The Renault could have broken down, leaving her stranded and she had decided to stay at Regina's place. Or she might have been delayed by some crisis at work. Perhaps they needed her to help with some private party and had asked her to stay on after her shift ended. Or something else, something really terrible could have happened. She could have had an accident, wrecked the car. She could be lying in a hospital even now, badly injured, unconscious. Dead! I shuddered and tried not to imagine such horrible scenes. Perhaps I should call someone, I thought. But who the hell could I call at this ungodly hour? I made an effort to control my overactive imagination and decided to wait till the sun came up before I started calling people. She might show up yet. It was only 4:30. Sleep was impossible now. So I got out of bed and boiled some Turkish coffee. In the pre-dawn darkness, I paced the courtyard, coffee cup in hand and I waited for first light while I tried to figure out who to call, who to contact. Cardiff was the first one I wanted to reach but rousing him at this early hour seemed cruel. He never went to bed till the wee hours and slept late. Next I thought of calling Regina. But she also stayed up late. Moreover, I had a nagging feeling that if Anara had decided to stay at Regina's place, she would have called me. Contacting the police seemed a bad idea, or at least a premature one. I had a dread of involving the legal authorities of Cyprus in our affairs. There was no telling what they might say or do or demand or what awkward questions they might ask. Nor did I have any trust or faith in them. I decided to freshen up and get dressed.

Perhaps the new day as it dawned would bring some news, some sort of information that might throw light on the mystery.

Since Anara had taken the Renault to work, I rode the scooter to the university. I was in a kind of numb state of mind and found it hard to focus on the teaching. Somehow, I got through my classes even though my anxiety rose with every passing hour. I had made up my mind to have a talk with Cardiff before I did anything or said anything and I looked for him before and after every class. And I kept trying Anara's mobile too, every half hour but the phone appeared to be off. I ran into Cardiff around noon. He was standing near the ornamental pool, smoking and chatting with students. I pulled him aside.

"Something rather odd," I said. "Anara did not come home from work last night."

Cardiff gave me a puzzled look.

"Did she call? Did she say where she was?" he said.

"No, that's the odd part. I haven't heard from her. She has the mobile phone. She could have reached me on the landline."

"No word at all?"

"None."

"That is odd." Cardiff said, tapping his lips with a forefinger. "Have you tried her mobile?"

"It is switched off," I said. "I've been trying since dawn."

"Very strange," said Cardiff. "Why don't you just go over to the *Starlight* and see if you can talk to someone?"

"I will, as soon as I can get away from here."

"Okay," he said. "Let me know what you find out."

I nodded and we parted.

Cardiff did not express any serious concern and his calm manner calmed me down somewhat. I figured there had to be an explanation – a logical, rational explanation. There was no reason to torment myself by jumping to bizarre conclusions or imagining the most extreme and the most awful situations. The fact that she had not come home worried me, but what caused deeper concern was that she had not called. Even if her mobile was out of call units or had used up battery power, how hard was it to find another phone? There were many pay-phone stalls around Kyrenia. She could have even borrowed someone else's phone and called. This is why I couldn't help thinking that for some reason she couldn't use her own phone or get to one either. This was a scary thought. Cardiff was obviously not taking the time to think through the different possibilities that were poisoning my peace of mind.

In the afternoon, I rode the scooter to the *Starlight* and went into the parking lot behind the casino. I spotted the Renault right away, parked in a corner, along with a few beat-up, junky old cars that obviously belonged to the low-level employees. I walked around to the front of the building and found neither doorman nor any parking attendant to greet me, nor did the Casino appear to be busy at this hour. A few neon signs were still on but they looked faded in the light of day and did not convey the sense of fun and excitement they did at night. In the main salon, the cleaning crew was busy vacuuming and dusting. There was no one around the roulette machines, card tables or at the slot machines that flashed and blinked invitingly.

I stopped an elderly Turkish lady who was running a vacuum cleaner and asked her if Vitaly was in his office. She stared at me blankly and did not respond. Obviously she had not understood me. No English, probably. I cornered a maid finally. She didn't think Vitaly was around. And what about Anara? She had no knowledge of Anara either. Actually, the women who made up the cleaning crew did not mingle with the girls who worked in the gambling salon. The waitresses considered themselves princesses who were serving drinks only until they got jobs as fashion models and movie stars.

I asked several other people if Regina were around but no one had seen her either. It seemed futile to linger around the *Starlight*, so I decided to get back to *Pegasus* and have another talk with Cardiff. I left the Renault where it was just in case Anara needed it. If I had to, I could come down in a taxi later on to pick it up and drive it home. The *Pegasus* also looked deserted with only the normal quota of two or three mummified Brits watching the re-run of a soccer match on TV and drinking beer. Cardiff had not shown up. So I got myself a scotch and soda, used my mobile and called Regina. She was a bit surprised to hear my voice.

"Hello," I said. "How are you?"

"Fine," she said.

"Hey, have you seen Anara?"

"Anara? She in casino last night."

"She did not come home."

"Not come home?" Regina sounded confused.

"I'm getting worried," I said. "I don't know where she is."

"Did you ask someone?"

"I did. I asked a few people. No one knew where she was."

"I left casino around one or one thirty. I said goodnight to her. Then I walk to my apartment."

"Her car is still there behind the casino."

"She did not take car?"

"No, the car is still where she parked it. That's the odd part."

Regina went "Hmmm." She seemed genuinely nonplussed, confused.

"Could you do me a favor?" I said. "Could you call Vitaly and check with him? Then call me back."

She said she would and I made sure she had the number of my landline in Karmi.

There was still no sign of Cardiff so I threw back what remained of my drink and decided to head home. I wanted to be near the landline phone in case anyone called. Once back home, I made some food. I ate and left a portion for Anara, in case she came home late. I was anxious but not too worried. I got some brandy and it helped me keep the worry under control. She couldn't just vanish into thin air. There had to be an explanation. But if she really had disappeared, I wondered how my Karmi neighbors would react? If she never came back, I would have to create a believable story to explain her absence, a kind of narrative that satisfied their curiosity and kept gossip and wild conjectures to a minimum. Not saying anything would just fuel the rumor mill and was not a good approach.

The Bralestones said not a word even though they must have noticed Anara's absence. Even if they didn't see us, they heard the plaintive whine of the Renault as it climbed the last gradient into Karmi every night and the steady put-putting of the scooter. They associated those sounds with our comings and goings. But Brits are reluctant to pry into someone else's business. Barbara, who was more sociable and closer, kept quiet for a couple of days but then one afternoon she saw me in front of her house and started to quiz me.

"Haven't seen your lady love," she said.

"She went to Istanbul to see her mother for a few days." I told her.

"Ah, that's good," Barbara said and then dropped the subject.

People did leave Karmi, quite suddenly at times, but usually there was a simple reason that explained the departure. So-and-so left to see a doctor in England. Another person had to return Germany to take care of a sick parent. Mr. and Mrs. XYZ went back to London to sell some property. As long as you heard some sort of excuse, you were satisfied. A rational explanation took the oxygen out of speculation and outlandish theories. So whenever anyone asked about Anara, I said she had gone to Istanbul to see her mother and to embellish the story further I would add that it was a sort of family reunion. Most people were satisfied by this explanation and did not ask any more questions. But if someone asked: "When will she be back?" I just shrugged and threw up my hands in the air. I had answered their question and that was all they were going to get from me. People from north Cyprus often went to Turkey at a moment's notice to take care of family business or handle some private matter. They looked on Cyprus as an extension of Turkey. Having floated this piece of fiction, I was able to pretend that nothing was amiss. I maintained a cheerful calm in front of my neighbors but as more and more days went by and her absence started to become a permanent feature of my life, I started to sink into a swamp of depression. And the only way I could slow down this descent was with booze. It seemed to be the only medicine that helped me, enabled me to keep a grip on sanity. Without the liquor to numb my brain, I think I would have gone crazy – killed myself or killed someone else.

The people from who I expected help, information, some explanation, were all unhelpful, elusive and strangely reluctant to talk to me. Regina said she had met Vitaly, had spoken to him and he had no idea where Anara was. He seemed to be under the impression that she was sick or had taken some days off.

"Isn't he worried?" I asked. "Doesn't he care that something could have happened to her?"

"He is worried," Regina said. "He wants to see you. Please come to Casino."

"Okay," I said. "I will."

I had to have a face-to-face chat with Vitaly. It was not something I wanted but I felt I should meet him and discuss the situation before I took any other action. I also had to retrieve the Renault. I couldn't just let it sit there. Moreover, the intermittent rains of spring made the scooter a less than ideal form of transportation.

That very evening I called a taxi and went the casino. I was filled with an odd repressed anger and a feeling of frustration. But why Vitaly should have been a target of my hostility, I do not know. I had no proof that he knew where Anara was. It may have been his vast calmness that irritated me more than anything he said or did not say. He received me in the same office where we had met on my last visit. He looked the same and wore the same loose-fitting dark suit. The little room also looked exactly the same.

"Where is Anara?" he said blandly, pre-empting my query and extended a pudgy paw across the steel desk.

I did not want to shake hands with him. The thought of touching his cold, rubbery fingers made me nauseous. But what can you do when a man puts out a hand? You take it.

"I am here to ask you the same question. Where *is* she?" I said.

He shook his head sadly from side to side.

"This is bad," he said, "What will you have?"

"Nothing," I said, sitting down on the edge a chair and looking at him intently. "Look – I'm very worried. What should I do?"

"Did you have a fight … an argument of some kind?"

"No, we did not have a fight," I said rather heatedly. "We never fought."

"Girls run away often," he said scratching the surface of his desk meditatively with a forefinger. "Run from husband, boyfriend, family. These things happen. I know."

"She was happy with me. We were happy. She had no wish to leave me. Also, how could she run away? You have her passport."

"No, no," he said suddenly. "I gave it back to her. I don't have it. She asked for it and I gave it to her."

This came as a shock.

"What? You gave it back to her!"

"Yes. She has passaport."

"She never told me. This is very strange. Are you sure? Did she get her work visa?"

By now my hands were trembling.

"Yes, yes, I get work visa for her, for many girls. No problem."

"She never said a word to me about this. How can this be?"

He shrugged.

"I don't understand," I said.

And I truly didn't. My brain was filling up with loud, resounding noises. Things were crashing around in there. A tornado seemed to have touched down inside my head and all manner of debris was flying round and round.

I was having a hard time believing Vitaly.

"Should I go to the police?"

He looked at me levelly with his cold eyes.

"As you wish," he said. "I will also check, talk to the other girls. It is possible she may have said something to someone."

I wanted to bring up an unmentionable topic. Did he think she had been kidnapped? But I decided not to utter the word. That path of conjecture would lead us nowhere. Moreover, I did not want to spend any more time with him.

"Okay," I said, "You do that. Let me know if you hear anything."

He nodded. The interview was over. And later, as I drove home, brooding over what he had said, I was convinced he was lying to me. Anara would have told me she had gotten the work visa. It was something both of us had been waiting for. Why would she hide this momentous matter? What could she possibly gain by not telling me about it. Vitaly had to be lying. The bastard was not telling me everything he knew. He seemed too detached, too unconcerned. Sure, he had seen many employees come and go, certainly lots and lots of girls. Scores came with elaborate dreams dancing in their heads. They saw visions of money, of golden-haired boyfriends, of devoted husbands and rich sugar-daddies who lived on hundred foot yachts and would buy them designer clothes. But most of them left with little more than an album of memories, some painful, some of them X-rated and little else. I could never think that Anara was like one of those shallow, superficial, dim-witted girls. She was different. She was neither greedy nor silly, nor stupid. She had a solid core of decency. I could never accept the idea that she might willfully mislead or deceive me.

I had no really close friend or advisor to turn to except Cardiff. He was the only one I could trust. I called him and told him about my conversation with Vitaly.

"Wasn't very helpful, was he?" Cardiff said.

"No, not at all. But I can't help thinking he knows more than he is telling me."

"That is possible. Though I don't suspect the use of force or violence. They can use other tactics to make these girls heel: promises of money, glamorous jobs in glamorous places. They don't always have to break bones, you know, to make them cooperate. That's a Hollywood fantasy."

"Never!" I said vehemently, almost yelling at him. "Never! I know Anara. She would never let herself in for something like that. She was… is a good…"

"Calm down," Cardiff said. "I didn't say she wasn't. I'm just mentioning possibilities, outcomes, modalities. Many girls look for such opportunities. Poverty isn't pleasant. Moralists tend to gild it with pretty clichés but most people want to be rich and they will do whatever they can to make money."

I had to agree. Prisons were full of people who tried to take some sort of criminal short cut to wealth.

"Should I go to the police?" I asked him.

"No," he said. "Wait a bit longer. She may turn up yet."

Then he reverted to the usual questions: Did you chaps quarrel? Was she angry with you for some reason? Why do you think she might want to get away? Were you having problems? Trouble getting along? And so on.

"Good questions all," I said. "But no, no, no and no. We were getting along fine. We never quarreled. Nor did I hear her complain about anything."

"Well, then the only other explanation is that she's been kidnapped."

My heart missed several beats and I pressed the phone more tightly to my ear.

"You think so. But why? Who would kidnap her? And why?"

"That is the only logical explanation," Cardiff said. "If she didn't go willingly, she must have been taken against her will."

How to describe the days and weeks that followed Anara's disappearance? How to put into words what I felt, what I thought? All I could come up with would be a catalogue of complaints, angry tirades targeting invisible, unknown enemies. The sudden and unexpected disappearance of a person you love, a person you've shared bed and board and body and soul and mind with is an odd thing. You feel angry, frustrated, sad, upset, irritated, even delusional: all sorts of emotions and feelings wash over you like a tidal wave. You want to blame someone for the emptiness in your life, for the yawning void that exists where no void existed before, for causing you distress, anxiety, pain – but I found that I could accuse no one. Who could I blame? All I could do was seek relief in alcohol. Only brandy and beer and wine could insulate me from thoughts that stung like electric shocks, that I did not like but could not suppress. Booze brought anesthesia, oblivion. The rest of the time there was always an acute sense of loss that gnawed away at my insides, refusing to go away. And mixed in with this was also a vague fear. Was I safe? At odd moments, this question floated up to the surface of consciousness. Was I safe?

Perhaps the most difficult thing to accept was the feeling of helplessness I experienced, of utter impotence and powerlessness. It dawned on me that I was very much on my own. I needed help but there was no one I could turn to for help. I had no connections on the island, no influence, neither the kind that rich people have, nor the sort that high social status bestows on you. I did not have a group of helpers or supporters, nor any family members who might rally around me, offer sympathy, solace and assistance.

Furthermore, I kept thinking I was letting Anara down somehow. My inability to search for her and rescue her felt like an ultimate kind of rejection, a terrible betrayal. I wondered what she might be thinking, wherever she was. Nevertheless, all through this hellish period, never, not even for a fraction of a second did I entertain the idea that she might be dead. That thought never crossed my mind. I had a firm belief that she was alive. Somewhere.

And the foul weather added to my misery. By now we were well into the rains of spring. More rain fell that spring on the Beshparmak range than had ever fallen according to records that went back several centuries. The house was damp and cold and the walls were always wet and an aggressive black mold began to spread over them like a terrible skin cancer. I went running to Fiona.

The first thing she wanted to know was if I had heard from Anara.

"Yes," I said. "Her mother is better. She should be back soon."

When I told her about the mold, she clicked her tongue sympathetically.

"You've got to get rid of it," she said.

"But how? It's everywhere – on the walls, around window sills, in the corners. It is bad behind the china hutch and the dresser where the wall is always damp."

"Move the furniture away from the wall," she said. "Then dip a sponge in bleach and swab the infected areas."

"Will the bleach kill it?"

"Yes, it will. But you must do a thorough job. Even a single spore left in a crack can start multiplying and spread over the same area again. As long as the walls are damp, you will never get rid of it completely."

"What a mess!"

"There isn't much you can do about. Just try to kill as much of it as you can."

That was good advice. I did get rid of the black mold on the walls but getting rid of the dampness proved impossible. These old Greek houses were dampness generating machines. The thick stone walls soaked up the moisture in the air and then exhaled it into the rooms. On hot summer days the rooms were cool and comfortable but during the rainy season they became cold and damp. The old-fashioned windows leaked in cold air and the dampness seeped into my bones. Everything: tables, chairs, dinner plates felt wet to the touch. Even bed sheets and blankets were moist and clammy. No matter how much kerosene and gas I burned, I could never get the living room warmed up to where it felt comfortable.

Now my mind really went into overdrive. I started imagining all sorts of bizarre scenarios, plots and counter-plots as I tried to comprehend the totality of the situation. The single most important and significant question I confronted and tried to answer was basically this: why had Anara run away? I even sat down and wrote out the "options" or "possibilities" with a certain focused thoughtfulness. Was there something I had missed? Perhaps I had not been paying attention and had missed some signs or signals. I jotted down some ideas to try and see the situation more clearly.

Anara had gone away because she didn't want to live with me anymore. Even as I wrote this down, I could see this was a silly idea, regardless of what Vitaly had implied. I rejected it right away. It made no sense at all. We had been living happily, without quarrels and tensions of any kind. She "loved" me, at least she claimed to and had said so on several occasions. We had a good relationship in and out of bed. And we had the same goal in mind: getting her a visa. So why would she leave me?

She had been "abducted" and taken to the Greek side against her will. This sounded plausible. But if one accepted this premise, then an even more vexing question arose: by whom? Who could have abducted her and transported her across the border? I had no answer to this question. However, if you accepted this theory then the rest of the situation became more understandable. If she was being held against her will, she would not be able to contact me. Her kidnappers would make sure she had no access to a telephone. They would take away her passport. They would make sure she could not escape or contact anyone. I liked this explanation. In a limited way, it seemed rational, made perfect sense, fit in perfectly with what I knew of Anara's character and personality.

She had gone because someone had offered her a "better" deal. This was an interesting idea and it merited close analysis. Could it be that she had been promised a better job, more money – some grand and tempting castle-in-the-air where she could play the princess and live happily ever after? People can be tempted, even sincere, honest, earnest people. And in the casino environment, all kinds of men hovered around the girls, ready with all sorts of grandiose offers. As I pursued this train of thought, I came up with the most ugly scenarios. Could it be that beneath the seemingly sincere and devoted and faithful Anara, there was another person, an entirely different character, a schemer, a liar, a devious and clever manipulator? Had she been lying to me all this time while she used me? No. No way. I could not accept this idea. It was too awful, too painful. There was another way to consider this thing, look at it in a more charitable light. Perhaps she was so innocent, so gullible that some clever, silver-tongued scoundrel had managed to win her trust, seduce her with promises and turn her head completely.

Anara had planned this "vanishing act" with a "third party," a Kazakh boyfriend or the absentee husband about whom she had provided me scant information. This was definitely a diabolical idea. I was ashamed to even think it, much less write it down on paper. And yet it wouldn't go away. It stuck stubbornly in my brain like a burr. But did it make sense? Was it plausible? Perhaps she had been in contact with this individual all along. Perhaps this person had arrived in north Cyprus and met with Anara. Perhaps she had vanished into Turkey with this person. Perhaps this had been her long range plan all along. Once again my suspicions and conjectures began to flounder in a wilderness of forking paths. Here each possible outcome split and led in different directions. I could follow these trails endlessly and get myself lost in a self-tormenting nightmare of tangled plots and counter-plots. But that way lay madness and I retreated from this in horror.

Like a drowning man, I thrashed and clawed my way up to the surface of reality again and decided to call Yulie. To strengthen my nerves, I had a couple of beers and a shot of brandy. I did not quite know what I would say to her. But once I had her on the phone, a flood of words flowed out and I found it comforting and easy to confide in her. She was genuinely distressed but calm and rational.

"I'm so glad you called," she said. "I wanted to talk to you, but you know how it is?"

"I really must talk to you," I said. "Something, something bizarre has happened."

I valued Yulie's opinion, her point-of-view. As a woman, I figured, she would be able to look at the situation in a way that men could not. Both Vitaly and Cardiff were limited to an essentially masculine perspective, a purely male viewpoint.

"What do you mean? What happened?"

"Anara's gone."

"Gone? Gone where? Did she return to Almaty?"

"No, no. I don't know where she is. She just vanished."

"I don't understand. Didn't she say anything before she left?"

"That is the odd part," I said. "She never said a word. She went to work as usual and then she never came back."

"This is strange," she said. "What could have happened?"

"I don't know."

"When, when did this happen? Have you been to the police? You should file a report, don't you think?"

"This happened about two weeks ago. And no, I have not been to the police."

"But you should. You should. This is not right. She could be in danger, in some kind of trouble."

"I thought I better wait a bit. In fact, a friend – he is a lawyer – advised me to."

"But why?"

"I don't want her to get into any sort of trouble," I said. "And the few times that I did interact with the police did not fill me with confidence."

"I have heard of such disappearances but never gave them much thought. This is very strange. Was she upset? Angry with you?"

"No, no. Everyone seems to think that we had a falling out of some kind, but honestly we didn't. We were on the best of terms. She was happy. A little anxious about the visa, perhaps."

"She told me the casino people would get her the work visa," Yulie said.

"Right," I said. "That was the deal."

"Look, this could turn out to be nothing, just some whim. But let me think. Do I have your permission to mention this to my father? He may have some ideas. Okay. I will call you back."

"Okay," I said.

Days went by in a fret of worry and waiting. The nights passed in liquored-up stupor. I started to lose weight and kept on losing it. For a while I thought I had picked up a virus or something or had some sort of wasting disease and seriously considered consulting a doctor. But these were superficial concerns. Deep down, I knew that there was nothing wrong with me. The weight loss was the direct consequence of poor diet and constant tension. I avoided my colleagues and my neighbors as much as I could, not wishing to get into lengthy conversations with them that nearly always led to queries about Anara. I preferred being alone, in fact, craved solitude. Some people need the company of others in order to remain psychologically healthy. For me, being by myself was more desirable than being with company. I don't quite know why.

Since her disappearance, I had not been to the downstairs bedroom where she kept all her personal items. And, to be frank, nor did I want to. A kind of vague, undefined dread had turned that room into a forbidden zone. There was also a sense that I would be intruding upon her private space were I to go fumbling through her clothes and possessions. On the other hand, perhaps I was afraid of seeing something or finding something that might shatter the image of hers I still had in my mind.

I couldn't stand the thought of being near her clothes, breathing the odors that still lingered there. The feeling was similar to the unease I have felt about touching the personal things of a dead relative.

But Vitaly's statement that he had given her passport back to her had surprised me. Why hadn't she mentioned this? Was her passport still there among her things? Or had she taken it? I had to be sure. If I could have delegated this task to someone else, I would have gladly done that. But there was no one.

I went downstairs and switched on the light. The first item I noticed was her knapsack hanging on a peg, the same one that she had brought with her the day she arrived from Almaty. I had encouraged her to travel light, but I was still amazed when I realized that the knapsack was all the luggage she had brought.

She had taken over a closet and the few items of clothing she possessed were all there, folded neatly and arranged in orderly piles. There were three slacks, a pair of jeans, four or five blouses and T-shirts and a small pile of flimsy bras and underpants. On one side, hanging on coat hangers, I found two of her jackets: one made of fleece, the other a light, nylon windcheater. Her sensible walking shoes were on the bottom of the closet along with a pair of sandals and ankle-high winter boots. Her make-up stuff: mascara, eye-liner pencils, powder compacts, rouge pots and brushes were on the top-most shelf along with her small collection of earrings. My throat got tight when my glance fell on the bottle of perfume she had bought at Istanbul airport. An odor that could always lash my dormant nerves into wakefulness – orange blossoms, honey and lavender. Anara!

I managed to calm myself and began looking for the passport. I lifted up the folded items carefully to look underneath, even searched the pockets of the jackets but found nothing. What I did find were the pink corduroy bell-bottom slacks and the matching jacket she wore the day she came from Almaty and I saw her get off the plane from the observation room at Erjan airport. She looked so chic as she walked across the apron and entered the airport building. I could hardly believe my eyes, hardly trust my luck. The thought that she would soon be in my arms, made my knees go weak.

The clothes she wore were so much a part of her personality, expressed her simplicity and naturalness. She could be elegant and alluring in the plainest garments. In a pair of jeans and a cotton blouse she turned into a fashion model. Her stylishness expressed itself in the way she walked, the way she held her head, in the straightness of her spine.

"Anara," I whispered. "Anara."

Then it occurred to me to look inside the knapsack and I took it off the peg and unzipped it. When I put my hand inside, my fingers closed around a book of some kind. I pulled it out and saw that it was a bible, a Russian bible, the same one I had seen before. I riffled the pages and a photograph fluttered to the floor. It was the picture of her daughter, Sarah. The muscles of my throat choked off my breathing. I started to gasp, struggling to get air into my lungs. Hurriedly, I put the photo in the bible, placed the bible in the knapsack and hung it on the peg again.

I made an effort to turn my mind to happy memories. The time when she went crazy over irises. She wanted to pick them and put them in a vase. I tied to dissuade her, pointing out that Irises did not like being picked. But she cut some anyway, trimmed their stems and arranged them in a vase with great care.

"Don't they look wonderful," she said clapping her hand and doing a little dance around the room.

"They do," I said. "But they won't last long."

And sure enough, within hours they were drooping and dying and she was so disappointed. I consoled her, of course, and we comforted ourselves with the thought that next spring they would return in greater numbers and put on an even more glorious show.

It is amazing how a place that you have loved and adored, loses its charm, loses all its magic, all its allure when some great unhappiness or misery descends on you. You turn inward and focus on your own problems and stop noticing your surroundings. The mind is its own place, said Milton, and can make a hell of heaven or a heaven of hell. This proved so true in my case. Karmi was as lovely as ever, but now I barely noticed its beauties. Nor did the changes in weather, the comings and goings of pleasant days, mean anything to me. Around this time Yulie called me.

Section 2

"Look, I'm coming to Kyrenia on Saturday. Can we meet?" she said.

"Fine, I said. "Come up to Karmi. We can have lunch."

So on Saturday when she pulled up in front of the Greek church, I was sitting on the bench that overlooked the plaza waiting for her. It was nearing noon and the sky held a serene brightness and the air was steeped in the hot honey odor of alyssum.

I did not want to invite her into the emptiness of the house.

"Let's go to the *Crow's Nest*," I said to her. "It's just a short walk and they have a small terrace outside where we can sit. They make excellent sandwiches."

"Still no news of Anara?" she asked.

I shook my head.

"I was so shocked," she said. "I just couldn't believe my ears."

"Imagine my surprise," I said, as we walked down a flight of stone steps that led to the street behind the church.

"You don't think she went back to Almaty, do you?"

"She may have, " I said. "But why would she do this so abruptly and without saying a word?"

"Some family emergency? Perhaps something she couldn't tell you?"

"We had no secrets between us. Moreover, if she really had to go back for some reason, I would not have stopped her. I would have helped her."

We were the only ones on the terrace of the *Crow's Nest*. I went and got a glass of Chardonnay for Yulie and a beer for myself from the bar and we sat down under the shade of a mulberry.

"You still haven't gone to the police, right?"

I shook my head.

"And the conversation with Regina yielded nothing?"

"Regina and her boss, Vitaly, both of them say they know nothing," I said.

"I find this hard to believe," Yulie said. "Don't you?"

"That world of the Russian speakers – I couldn't enter it."

"It's a tight little community," Yulie said.

"If I only knew someone who worked at the *Starlight*, someone who was there every day and saw what went on," I said, "that would be a big help."

"My father had the same idea," Yulie said. "We need more information, insider information actually."

"I could go try and talk to Regina again or go back and have a fit in front of Vitaly," I said.

Yulie shook her head.

"Won't do much good," she said. "You'll get the same answers. And in front of the police, they will repeat the same words. They've got their line and they will stick to it."

"They will stonewall me. I know that." I said.

"But listen," Yulie said. "My father gave me the name and phone number of a boy who used to work at the *Starlight*. He may have some information."

"Really? What sort of work?"

"I'm not sure. Helping in the kitchen, I think."

"A cook?"

"Something like that?"

"You think he might be able to help us?"

"My father says that the kitchen crowd knows more about what happens in a hotel than the manager. They see what comes in the back door and leaves by the back door."

"I see what you mean. Can I meet him, talk to him?"

"I could call and find out if he'll meet us."

"Give it a try."

"But he lives in Famagusta now. We would have to drive there."

"Today? We could go. I'll drive us there."

Yulie dialed a number on her mobile and talked to someone. As she spoke I didn't pick up anything of what she said. The conversation went on for about ten or fifteen minutes. While she was on the phone, I went into the bar to see what we could order for lunch.

"So," I said, as I came back. "Will he see us?"

"Yes. His name is Ali. He will be free around 5:00 today."

"Great," I said. "That gives us just enough time to have lunch and then drive there."

I had never been to Famagusta before. It was another one of those excursions that I had planned which got pushed to the back of my mind after Anara's disappearance. With Yulie in the passenger seat up front and me at the wheel, we cut quickly through the eastern slopes of the Beshparmak where they crumble into sand and outcrops of liver-colored rocks. Then the road straightens out and shoots east in a hurry. It is the same highway that you take for Lefkosa and Erjan airport. Coming down the long decline, I started going very fast, keenly aware that the gearbox of the Renault could fall apart.

On either side of the road, the Mesaoria had greened up due to the spring rains and all kinds of wild flowers had burst into bloom.

As I drove, I could also see fields of wheat and barley as well as small kitchen gardens.

Yulie didn't say much as we drove, beyond some general comments about the landscape sweeping past us and neither did I, both preoccupied with our own thoughts.

"Where will he meet us?" I asked her as we got closer to our destination.

"Under the *Venetian* Lion," she said, "near Othello's Tower."

"The Othello's Tower business – that's a myth, isn't it? There is no historical Othello. The only Othello I know of is the character in a play by Shakespeare."

"That's true," Yulie said. "I think the Cypriots just appropriated him because his story fits nicely into the story of the Venetian era."

Coming into Famagusta from the west, you see the usual pastel villas and housing developments that remind you of American suburbia. Here and there apartment buildings, banks and Governmental installations obstruct the view to the east. I kept going east towards the harbor. Famagusta is not a big town and I managed to find my way to the old fort and Othello's Tower easily. I parked the Renault and we got out. The sun was setting and its oblique rays bathed the weathered stones of the castle in a bronze glow.

A strange, unfamiliar sadness came over me and I wondered if I should have come. I felt a bit uneasy about what Ali might reveal. Famagusta is famous for betrayals and treachery. Walking among the ruins, one became keenly aware of Time's destructive hand. Here entire civilizations got wrecked: The Crusaders, the Venetians, the Turks, the English. I thought of the famous siege of Famagusta when the Turks led by Lala Mustapha attacked the fort with a large force. The *Venetian* governor Bragadino, held off the attackers for several months. Eventually supplies ran out and Bragadino was captured and killed. According to Father Calepio, an eyewitness, Bragadino's nose and ears were cut off and he was flayed alive. Then Calepio writes, "His skin was taken, stuffed with straw, and carried around the city."

Yulie and I walked along the wharf where cargo ships with spidery cranes poking up out of them were loading and unloading goods. Then we turned and went looking for the winged lion of Venice.

As soon as we passed beneath the marble lintel that shows the lion carved in bas-relief, a thin, young man with a head of tousled, curly black hair detached himself from a wall, came up to us and said something to Yulie in Greek. Apparently, he had no difficulty spotting us, even though there were other tourists milling around in groups. Yulie must have given him a good description. The fact that Ali spoke Greek, surprised me. Not many Turks did. When I mentioned this to Yulie, she laughed and said yes, it was Greek but really bad Greek. "You must be Ali," I said.

The young man nodded and put out his hand. "Come," he said, "I know a place where we can talk." He spoke English with an accent that is common all around the Levant, sneezed several times and seemed to be struggling to breathe through his nose. "Allergy," he said. "I'm sorry ."

"It's all the pollens in the air, right?" I said. He nodded.

I was ready for a drink by now, and I thought it would be polite to invite Ali to join us for a meal. He would know of a quiet place, I figured, where we could talk. I wanted to get away from tourists and parties of noisy British soldiers on leave from their base in Dekhelia. "Should we take the car?" I asked.

"No, not necessary," Ali said. "We can walk. It's a short distance."

"Let's find a place where we can have a drink," I said to Ali.

"Follow me," he said cheerily.

I was glad to hear him speaking English. This would certainly make it easier to find out what he knew. He led and we followed, down Liman Yolu Sokak, away from the harbor and its acrid odors.

By now the evening had settled into a shadowless dusk and the shops and restaurants were all lit up. We walked past Mustapha mosque now exuding a warm peach-colored glow above the violet tops of flowering Jacarandas and ended up at the *Agora Kebab Restaurant*.

"It has the best kebabs in all of Cyprus," Ali said.

A traditional domed oven sat outside to emphasize the fact that the restaurant served true Turkish cuisine. The place was almost empty when we came in and the waiters grinned at us, genuinely happy to see us. We sat down and a waiter came around right away to take our orders.

I asked Yulie what she wanted to drink.

"A beer is fine," she said.

"I'll have the same," I said.

Ali said he wanted a cola. Drinking beer, he said, would make his allergy worse. "I suffer at this time of the year," he said, sneezing several times. "I think I am allergic to everything."

He grinned apologetically and pressed a handkerchief to his nose.

We chatted about local food for a bit, then he became quite curious and wanted to know why I had come to Cyprus, how I earned my money, and how I happened to know Anara and Yulie.

I gave him a brief background, not wishing to seem secretive or unwilling to trust him with fairly ordinary facts about life and work. He had agreed to meet me to try and help me and I wanted our meeting to serve as the starting point of a friendship. In general, people tend to be a bit tense when you meet them for the first time. In north Cyprus this tension is even more apparent. Even thirty years after the division of Cyprus Turks don't trust the Greeks. And when a Turk meets a stranger the stranger has to be assessed, he has to be quizzed to make sure that he understands, accepts and appreciates all things Turkish. Ali, too, was anxious to be re-assured that I loved north Cyprus.

"I love it," I told him. "It is very beautiful."

Ali grinned happily.

"I've been very happy here," I said to him, "until this thing happened. My world turned upside down."

He nodded, suddenly very serious.

"Did you know Anara?" I asked him.

He shook his head.

"No," he said. "But I saw her often. She stood out. She looked Chinese."

"She is a Kazak, from Almaty," I said.

The waiter brought our drinks and then stood there to write down our food order.

"You decide what we should have," I told Ali.

He shrugged and made a face.

"I am not hungry," he said.

Then he pointed at a menu item. Yulie and I decided to go with the specialty of the house, Adana kebab. Ali approved.

"You will like," he said.

"You know she just disappeared," I said, after the waiter had left with our order.

He gave me a look I knew well. I think he was dying to ask me if we had quarreled or if I had beaten her or if she had started to not like me anymore, but he restrained himself. His next question was more pertinent.

"Did you go to the police?" he asked.

I shook my head to indicate that I had not.

"You see, I want to find my friend," I said to him. "I don't want the police to find her."

"I understand," he said. "Police make big problem for you."

"Yulie said you worked at *Starlight*. Did you see anything, anything odd or strange?"

Ali looked around the dining room of the restaurant to see who else was there. Some boisterous Europeans had taken up two or three tables and were busy eating and drinking and talking in loud voices. They paid no attention to us. Ali sipped his cola, trying to assess me with beady black eyes. He had no reason to mistrust me or fear me since I had come with Yulie, but I still detected a certain hesitation. My being American was a minus but my being a college professor gave me extra points and put me on the plus side.

"I did not see anything," Ali said, moving his head from side to side. "Girls come and go. From Rumania, Roosya, Bulgaria. They come and they go. Why? Where? Ali does not know."

He shrugged wearily.

"Did you ever talk to her?" Yulie asked him.

"No," he said.

"Did you see her with someone, some person, somebody special?" I said.

"Yes. Many times. I would see her talking to two men – businessmen. They not gamble. She speak in Russian with them and I do not understand Russian."

"I've met those two," I said. "They are from Ukraine not Russia."

"Maybe she go with them," Ali murmured thoughtfully.

"But why would she go with them and where?" I said. "She was happy with me."

Before he could answer, the waiter brought our food. I ordered another glass of beer and more cola for Ali. He had ordered a plate full of French fries. He poured a lot ketchup on them and started eating them eagerly.

"Why did you quit your job at the *Starlight*?" I asked him, in an effort to make him open up a bit.

"I found better job here in Famagusta," he said.

"Good," I said. "I am happy for you."

"Thanks," he said. "I drive truck for my uncle. He has many trucks and he needs me."

"Good for you," I said. "You mentioned those Russian girls ... you have any idea where they go?"

"They want to make money," he said. "They go Greek side. Many more tourists in Greek side."

"Can they get visas?"

"They go secretly, no need visa."

"But how?"

"Vitaly set up everything. He arrange everything. Easy for him."

"Does he own businesses in the Greek area?"

"Yes. He has casino near Paphos," Ali said.

"Really?" I said.

I didn't know this.

"What is it called?" I asked.

Ali shrugged.

"Don't know," he said.

Suddenly, I found I had no appetite whatsoever. Yulie was also nibbling sparingly, absent-mindedly as if her thoughts were somewhere else. But Ali, on the other hand, seemed to be enjoying the French fries. He poured a liberal amount of ketchup on them and attacked them with the gusto of an American teenager. At first he had been uncomfortable, uneasy, unwilling to say much. But under the influence of cola and fries he started to warm up and became more talkative. I had noticed that, in general, Cypriot-Turks don't like being treated to meals by someone they don't know very well. There is always a worried cautiousness beneath the cordiality and politeness. Why is this person treating me? What will he want in return? But when they are playing the role of the host, they are serenely gracious and perfectly at ease and keep pressing you to eat and drink more and more. Fortunately, Ali was young and informal and visibly glad to have a plate full of fried potatoes in front of him.

Yulie didn't say much as we ate, beyond some murmured remarks that were intended to encourage Ali to keep on speaking his mind. She wanted Ali to be the center of attention just the way I did and was content to listen. As the meal wound to a finish, we chatted a bit more about tourists and gambling casinos, but it was obvious that Ali did not have much more information to impart to us. But what he had told me was significant and had given me several ideas, several avenues that I wanted to pursue further.

It had become quite dark by the time we came out of the restaurant.

"Thanks," Ali said, as we stood outside.

"Thank you for meeting me," I said. "You have been very helpful."

He shrugged and smiled briefly and put out his hand.

Then as I turned to leave, he looked at Yulie.

"One moment," he said.

Apparently, he wanted to say something to Yulie, but he didn't want to say it in front of me.

"You walk on to the car," Yulie said to me. "I'll catch up with you."

"Sure," I said and started slowly up a poorly-lit street, heading for the wharf area.

I had only gone half a block when Yulie caught up with me.

"Everything okay?" I asked her.

"Oh, yes," she said.

On the way back to Karmi, she was unusually quiet.

"You seem tired," I said to her.

"A little," she agreed.

"Do you mind if I ask you what Ali said to you? Does it concern me or Anara?"

"He just wanted to emphasize what he had said earlier: about the girls being taken to the Greek side."

"He felt pretty sure Anara was on the Greek side," I said.

Yulie nodded.

"Yes," she said. "But you must understand that the Turks are always ready to blame the Greeks for all sorts of problems."

"Did he say anything else?"

"No," she said and shook her head and kept her eyes fixed on the road. I got a strange feeling that she knew something she did not want to reveal. Ali had told her something that she was reluctant to share with me. I didn't think he'd told me anything really surprising or new. But what he had said confirmed and solidified the rather ill-defined thoughts and ideas that had been floating around in my head.

The tires hummed as we sped towards Karmi through the gloom of a moonless night.

"What are you thinking of?" I asked Yulie.

"About Anara," she said. "I'm wondering where she might be? In what kind of situation? How can we find where she is?"

"Do you think she is in the casino that Vitaly has near Paphos?"

"That is a possibility."

"Do you think you could you go there, sort of look around?" I asked. "It would be easy for you. If I go they might not let me back in. I've heard they really hassle Americans."

"I could if I knew the name," she said.

"I can get the name," I said. "Leave that to me."

"Then I'll go," she said. "I'm as eager to find her as you are."

I felt a surge of relief and optimism go through me. I knew then that moment that Yulie would do everything in her power to help me. I no longer felt alone and friendless.

∼

CHAPTER EIGHT

Section 1

Cardiff called. He said he wanted to see me. I made vague excuses.

I had stayed away from him since the start of spring semester. The urgencies and barely controlled chaos of counseling and classes kept me distracted. Someone mentioned that Freya was busy doing what she did best: shuttling hither and yon, always on her mobile phone, always on the move. She had spent some time in a drug rehab center or clinic. When they let her out, she took up her old routines with her old contacts once again. She and Cardiff were in a turbulent phase at about this time and I didn't want to play the role of referee as they sparred. Then I heard someone say that she'd gone back to England. Whether she did or did not, I cannot say. Cardiff and I were not in touch during this period. Without Anara around to push me into activities, I turned inward, seeking a quiet isolation and the serious brooding that it promotes. I treasured my solitude, guarded it jealously. I had no desire to meet anyone.

My duties at the university kept me busy: lectures, student conferences and all those long, dull committee meetings. I must admit I behaved badly during these sessions and my colleagues were angry with me. My chronic irritability and complete lack of interest in academic issues did a great deal of damage to my standing in the Law department. But I was past the point of caring.

Cardiff called in sick several times. And whenever he couldn't make it to school, other teachers had to be roped in to take up his load. Having to take on extra work did not please the teachers very much and their attitude toward Cardiff became a bit unfriendly. I took over two of his courses to keep the students busy till he returned. I didn't mind this. Frankly, the extra work kept me from brooding and fretting over my personal problems. When he did come back, I could see he wasn't well. He was much thinner and his complexion had taken on a yellowish cast. The skin on his face was stretched tight and the hollows below his cheekbones were deeper. His big, nicotine-stained teeth were now more prominent and pushed forward in a kind of permanent snarl. I was shocked to see the changes in his appearance.

As I hurried to class one morning, he stopped me on the front steps of the Admin building.

"Did you hear about Tony?" he said in a hoarse whisper.

"Who?" I said, unable to connect the name with anyone I knew.

"The disco owner – the Turkish chap you met in *Triton?*"

I remembered.

"They've hauled him in."

The news still did not mean much to me.

"I've got to run," I said, trying to break away.

"How about lunch? Saturday. My treat." he said.

I stood there, hesitating.

"Come," he said with a certain hissed intensity. "You must."

"Where?" I shouted, as I pulled away from him.

"*Balik Restaurant.* Harbor."

I gave him a thumbs-up without checking my stride and hurried on.

That evening I turned on the TV to see if I could find out anything about the Tony affair. I hardly ever watched the local television channels because nearly all the programs were in Turkish. But every evening they aired a short news show in English for the expat community and that is how I managed to get the details of Tony-the-Turk's rise and sudden fall. He'd been involved in multifarious crooked deals: bogus real estate transactions, drugs, political gangsterism, bribery, tax evasion. The Law finally snared him and I read news reports that prosecutors intended to throw the proverbial *book* at him. The *Cyprus Daily News* printed stories about Tony over several weeks and I remember seeing a fat headline one day: "DRUG KING HELD."

The arrest of a well-known businessman, a "pillar of the community" created a mighty tempest in the tiny tea cup cosmos of north Cyprus. But to my American ears the words and phrases used by the news readers on TV, in fact, the whole sorry saga of Tony's criminal enterprise all sounded boringly familiar. I had seen and heard such stories so often in the American press. Tony, apparently, had been at the center of some kind of drug sales and distribution network. The well-dressed TV announcers did their best to squeeze as much mileage and as many air-time minutes out of the story as they could. For days on end, they fed the public all sorts of sensational fodder about narco-terrorists, the mafia, cocaine cartels and heroin smugglers.

So on Saturday, as I headed to the harbor to meet Cardiff, I felt well prepped. The day dawned bright. A brisk wind had swept the sky clean overnight leaving only a few feathery white wisps way up in the heavens. Deserts to the south of us were heating up, pulling in air from the north, making the Mediterranean thrash and heave. By the time I got to the harbor gale force gusts were whipping the ocean, and pushing massive rollers towards the sea wall. The awnings of the restaurants that lined the harbor flapped like wet laundry and the sailing craft dipped and swayed amidst their fractured reflections.

Cardiff was already at a table when I approached *Balik*. He didn't look well at all but he smiled bravely. With him sat Freya, looking cool and calm, the very picture of a demure demoiselle in a flowered summer frock. This was a shock. I had not seen her for a long time. Now she looked like different person altogether.

"Well, what a surprise," I said. "Why didn't you tell me Freya was back from England?"

"Because she never went to England," Cardiff said.

"Oh?" I said, my mouth open.

"She's been in the Greek side," Cardiff said.

"Oh?" I said again, not knowing what else to say.

She looked like a completely different person. The frock, a fashion U-turn from the torn jeans and trademark T-shirts, gave her a prim, almost prissy, look as though she had just stepped out of a movie made in the Fifties. Her hair cut very short seemed to have more life, more bounce and more sheen as it got flipped up by wind. She had also put on weight, particularly around the hips.

"A charming dress," I said, sitting down.

She smiled in a way I had never seen her smile, openly, spontaneously. It transformed her face

"Thanks," she said. "Guess where I got it?"

"You stole it from Lucille Ball," I said.

"You're close," she said. "I got it from a boutique in Shepherd's Bush that sells antique clothing."

"It's very becoming," I said. "I like it. And so appropriate for a day in spring."

I was glad to see the two of them in a happy, friendly frame of mind. Apparently, the last grand fracas had been forgotten and they had made a new start. Cardiff looked frail and weak but in excellent spirits. The sun had covered everything with a high-gloss coat of varnish. Even the buff bastions of the old fort looked new and clean.

"What should we have?" I asked Cardiff, when a waiter came to take our order.

He lit a cigarette and thought for a moment.

"How about Retsina? It's a perfect morning for a chilled Retzinato is it not?"

"If they have it," I said and looked at the waiter who nodded vigorously and he went off to get the wine.

The esplanade was filling up with tourists as the lunch hour drew near. They came in pairs or in groups of three and four, wearing the standard uniform of tourists: T-shirts, shorts and sandals. Of course, nearly all of them sported sunglasses and hats.

"You look well," I said to Freya.

She did indeed look healthier, more relaxed. Her glass-gray eyes sparkled.

"I feel well," she said.

"The medical chaps did her a lot of good," said Cardiff.

Freya directed a questioning glance at Cardiff and then she skewered me with a look that signified keen curiosity.

"Any news of your friend?" she asked, angling her head towards me.

She was trying to be sociable and polite, I suppose, but I had a feeling she did not remember Anara's name.

"No," I said. "Not a word."

She looked at Cardiff again, as if she were seeking his permission to say something.

"Go, ahead, my dear," Cardiff said. "You must speak."

"I think I saw your friend … what was her name?"

"What?" I said sharply. "Anara?"

Everything seemed to drift away from me suddenly and a vein pulsed wildly along my throat.

"Yes," said Freya. "I am positive it was her."

"Where? When? Was she alone? With anyone?"

Questions spilled out of me.

Freya leaned towards me and lowered her voice.

"I was in the Greek side. In Paphos," she said.

Cardiff noticed the puzzled look on my face.

"She had to get out of here," he said, tapping the side of his nose with his right forefinger. "She was in the thick of the Tony debacle. The star witness against him, you see. They were able to arrest him on the strength of the evidence that Freya provided. Nasty business. To keep her safe, they sent her to the Greek side till things cooled off a bit."

I was starting to see the picture. I didn't need details nor did I want them.

"I went into this hair-styling salon to buy shampoo," Freya said. "And I think Anara was there, getting her hair done."

"Are you sure?" I said, hardly daring to believe her.

She nodded.

"Did you speak to her?" I asked. "Did she see you, recognize you? Did she say anything?"

"No, no, I don't think so," Freya said. "I was only there for a few minutes. She did not see me. She was looking into the mirror."

"This is strange," I said. "I wish you had approached her, talked to her."

"I was in a bit of a jam myself," said Freya. "I was with some people."

"What was the name of this salon?" I asked.

"Orchid," she said. "Yes, that's it: The Orchid."

All of a sudden I lost my appetite. I just wanted to get away. I wanted to call Yulie. But out of a sense of politeness I stayed stuck to my chair. I also had a feeling that Cardiff had asked me to come for lunch because he wanted me to see Freya, see how she had changed and also to hear about Anara from her own lips.

"They closed down the *Triton*," Cardiff said.

"Too bad," I said, glancing at Freya. "You lost a good job."

She shrugged her bare, creamy shoulders.

"It makes no difference to me," she said. "I'm done with that scene. I would not have gone back there anyway."

"Perhaps a new owner will come along and re-open it." Cardiff said.

"You have other plans, I suppose," I said.

She nodded.

"I may take some classes at the university," she said.

"I was so surprised when I heard about Tony," I said. "How did they find out that he was into all those illegal activities?"

"Actually, they knew," said Cardiff. "Had known for a while, in fact. North Cyprus is a small section of a small island. No secrets here. They knew a lot about what he was doing but they needed solid evidence, proof, a trustworthy informant. Freya … ah, look, here's the wine."

The return of the waiter and the wine interrupted our conversation. No one said a word as we watched him open the bottle and pour but I was able to complete the thought that Cardiff had begun. Without Freya's testimony, they would never have been able to put together a solid case against Tony. She had, without a doubt, helped bring him down.

"Good," said Cardiff taking a mouthful and puckering up his lips. "Excellent."

The Retsina, Greek and superb, had been thoroughly chilled and stung your palate and numbed your teeth when you took a mouthful. And when the bouquet of pungent pine resin exploded in your forebrain the world suddenly became a better place.

"What should we eat?" Cardiff wanted to know.

"All I want is a plain old hamburger," I said, "provided they don't overcook the damn thing."

"That's the problem," Cardiff said. "They nearly always cook it far too long and the meat dries out. Moreover, they just don't get good beef here, I mean, well-marbled, tender beef. The cattle that are brought to market in Turkey are lean, not at all like the sleek, fat ones you have in the States."

This was bad news. So I opted for a chicken sandwich instead. They couldn't ruin that, I figured.

Freya wanted a Tuna fish sandwich. Cardiff shook his head and grimaced.

"You know what they do here, don't you? They open a can of tuna, mix it with mayonnaise and put it between two slices of bread," he said.

"Oh stop it, will you?" Freya said. "I like it."

"What about you?" I asked Cardiff.

"The name of this place is *Balik*. It means fish. We are in a fish restaurant on the edge of the harbor," he said. "It seems criminal not to order fish. They must have some sort of sea-creature on the menu."

Eventually, our order got sorted out and the waiter trotted off to get the food ready.

But even as we ate, my mind revolved around what Freya had told me. I felt a strong urge to go to the Greek side right away and see if I could find Anara. I had no idea what I would actually do once I found her but for the moment that did not matter. I figured I would do *something*, probably just grab her and jump into the car and head back across the border at top speed. That she might not want to return, never even crossed my mind. And what might happen at the border, was also unclear to me.

"Will you be going to the Greek side again?" I asked Freya.

"No," she said. "They want me here now. They need me here."

"Do you think I should go?" I said. "Try and find her."

Cardiff shook his head and put a hand on my arm as if he were restraining me.

"Could turn into a costly mess," he said. "I had a Canadian friend who crossed over at Ledra Gate check-point. When he tried to get back to the north side, the Greeks stopped him, wouldn't let him back into the Turkish zone. They made him go to Cairo. Can you imagine that? From Cairo, the poor bastard, flew to Istanbul and from there back to Erjan. The cost in dollars, actually, is the least of your problems. What you can't afford is to miss classes. Instead of just being a misadventure the whole thing would turn into a bloody disaster. Moreover, you really don't know where she is. She might not be in Paphos anymore. They could have moved her somewhere else to a new location."

This anecdote about the Candadian had the desired effect. It cooled off my hyper-excited mind. Charging into the Greek side like some Knight-in-a-Dented Renault to the rescue of a damsel suddenly seemed like a foolhardy idea. After we had eaten, we took a turn around the esplanade.

Cardiff grabbed my elbow and pulled me over to one side, letting Freya walk on ahead of us.

"Perhaps you could enlist the help of someone who lives on the Greek side," he said. "That would be better."

"I'll try," I said.

And it wasn't long afterwards that I called Yulie and told her what Freya had said.

"Paphos is not a very big place," I said. "Do you think you could drive over and look around?"

Yulie said going to Paphos was not a problem for her but going there without a sound plan of action, going there and simply wandering about with the rather illogical hope of running into Anara made no sense at all. She also pointed out that one sighting, and a dubious one at that, did not prove anything. What we had to do was find out exactly where Anara was staying (or being kept), then and only then the next step – that of attempting to make contact with her – could be taken. In short, we needed more information. She said she would discuss the matter with her father. This made sense.

So when I got a call from Gus a few days later, I felt we were finally moving in the right direction. He wanted to see me. He said he had a friend with excellent contacts in and around Paphos. Could we meet? Sure, I said. How about tomorrow? The *Colony Hotel* at six. He said, fine.

I got to the *Colony Hotel* around sunset fighting rush-hour traffic all the way. Office workers were going home and tourists were heading into town to find restaurants. Kyrenia's narrow streets meant for donkey carts were clogged with cars, taxis, and mini-buses. In the noise and glare, the *Colony* seemed out of place with its dignified façade of an Italian palazzo. The grand portico and the tall French windows exuded an air of patrician elegance. Pushing past large glass doors, I entered a quiet, softly lit lobby enclosed by arches trimmed with honey-colored stone. I made my way to a mahogany bar where a dark-eyed Turkish girl stood ready to serve. For what I paid for my beer, I could have bought ten bottles at a grocery store. But the beer tasted better here for some reason and soon I began feeling rather patrician myself.

I hadn't been there very long when Gus showed up. He looked around, a bemused smile lurking behind his droopy mustache. The lines that radiated from the corners of his eyes seemed like roads leading to sights he had seen. And from how numerous those lines were, I got the feeling that he had seen a great many.

"Would you like a drink?" I said.

"No, not here," he said. "This place is too expensive. Come, I want you to meet a friend."

He grabbed my arm and almost dragged me off the stool in his haste to get away.

"Where are we going?" I asked, once we were outside.

"To Lapta," Gus said. "Or as I like to say: lovely Lapta. It is the greenest spot in north Cyprus. Spring water is abundant and flows all year round and everything grows easily. A blessed place, truly."

In the parking lot, Gus insisted on taking his car. I had no objection to this proposal since his was shiny and new and German. Gus crossed himself and plunged into the rapids of traffic on Ecevit street and soon we had left Kyrenia behind us and were roaring along the coastal road. The sun had started to slip behind the Beshparmak range and an orange light struck the littoral at a tangent, transmuting the dust that lay across the low hills into powdered bronze. The mountains on the left were a dark magenta mass rising into a lilac sky.

"He's a Cypriot-Turk," Gus said. "They moved north during the '74 troubles, leaving farms and houses. But he's done well because he works hard and he is an honest... a good man. We've been friends for a long time. He has a rational head on his shoulders. He could help us or, at a minimum, give us good advice. I trust his judgment."

"And I trust yours, Gus," I said. "I have no idea what I should do."

"I understand," he said gently. "Don't worry. All will be well."

Gus's powerful car lapped up the miles to Lapta speedily and soon we were gliding past Five Mile Point and had left Alsanjak behind. Occasionally, I caught a glimpse of a slate-colored sea curling and uncurling on my right. all the way to the Turkish coast. About 500 yards past *L A Hotel*, Gus started to slow down and the car's headlights picked out a sign on the right side of the road: "*Silver Stone Restaurant* – European and Turkish Food."

"This is the place," Gus said and pulled hard right onto a dirt track that cut through growths of oleanders on either side and led towards a cluster of lit up buildings. "His name is Hakan Demir. He owns this restaurant and that row of holiday villas you see over there on the left. He also has several donums of land near Guzelyurt where he raises crops and keeps bees. In fact, he got me involved in bee-keeping."

By now an indigo dusk had settled over the coast and to the south the lights of Lapta town could be seen flickering like fireflies on the distant hills. The restaurant sat on a flat platform of basalt that pushed its pitted head into the sea. To one side there was an oval swimming pool now glowing like a huge turquoise lit up from within and a bar shaded from the sun by a canvas awning with red and white stripes. In front, a spacious terrace covered over with an awning and strung with colored lights, faced the ocean. Quite a few customers were having their evening drinks and food. As soon as we came near the cabana, a man jumped up and came towards us, holding out both hands.

"Gustavo, how are you?" he shouted.

"Fine. Fine. Hakan Bey," Gus said. "And you?"

An explosive laugh boomed out of Hakan Bey's chest and he gathered up Gus into an embrace and kissed his cheeks. A big, boisterous man and tall for a Cypriot, Hakan Bey also displayed an ample girth. He moved his heavy limbs in an unhurried manner but he had a quick smile and keen, expressive brown eyes.

I got introduced and we shook hands.

Gus had called ahead and told Hakan Bey that we were coming. Wisely and without preamble, Hakan Bey steered us away from the terrace to a small room on one side of the restaurant. Lit by a naked bulb dangling from the ceiling, the chamber contained very little in the way of furniture except for a table, a few chairs, a trestle bed and some shelves attached to the walls. Most of the floor space was taken up by assorted fishing tackle, snorkeling gear and Scuba equipment. The room had the look of a cavern carved by the sea and reeked of dampness and mildew like a wet-locker. As we sat down, I could hear the inrush and outflow of the waves surging over the rocks below. A waiter, who had followed hard on our heels, stood ready to take our orders. Hakan Bey told him to bring beer and something to nibble on.

We had just sat down when the electricity went off.

"No problem," Hakan Bey said, cheerfully.

He struck a match and the sputtering flame flung back our enlarged shadows onto the walls. From a shelf he picked up a hurricane lantern, lit it and adjusted the wick till it burned steadily. He set it on the table where it sat in its own circular shadow and lit up the room with a mellow light. The odor of burning kerosene spread through the room, dominating the sea-smells.

"We have a small generator," Hakan Bey said, "It produces just enough electricity to light up the kitchen and the restaurant. The boys will start it up."

"I don't mind these outages," I said. "I've become quite used to them."

"Do you like Cyprus?" Hakan Bey asked me.

This question was an all-purpose icebreaker, and had been fired at me many times by curious Cypriots.

"Of course," I said. "Very much."

My response pleased him.

"Good, good," Hakan Bey said, happily. "You stay for long time. You are not tourist."

"I'm learning a lot," I said, "about the island."

"The good and the bad," said Gus.

We chatted like this for a bit, just making small talk, as if all of us were reluctant to get into the real topic that had brought us together. Presently a couple of waiters entered bearing trays of food and drink. Hakan Bey helped them transfer everything to the table, opened the bottles and poured beer for us into glasses. There were plates of golden-brown strips of fried Hellim, thin sausages and the flaky, cheese-filled pastry – bourek.

"Drink," he commanded in his loud, booming voice. "Eat."

The food and drinks provided a pleasant diversion and silenced us for a while.

"Have you had the fried Hellim?" Hakan Bey asked. "Try it. It is good."

"I like it," I said. "It goes well with beer."

Hakan Bey seemed reluctant to bring up the business we needed to discuss out of a certain delicacy, I imagine, so I decided to bring it up myself.

"Gus has told you about the problem, right?" I said. "About my friend."

Hakan Bey nodded.

"I did not go into any details," Gus said. "Just the basic facts."

Hakan Bey nodded, his face suddenly very serious. The twinkle seemed to go out of his eyes.

"This lady … your friend, she disappeared. Right? Yes. Yes. I know. Gus said she was from Kazakhstan." Hakan Bey said.

"I met her in Almaty," I said. "I invited her to come and stay with me."

"She had job?" Hakan Bey asked.

"At the *Starlight Casino*," Gus said.

Hakan Bey gave him a sharp glance, distaste visible on his face. Most Cypriot Turks were double-minded about gambling casinos. They didn't really want these establishments but they had decided to tolerate them in order to stimulate tourism and bring in much-needed revenue. Cypriot Turks were not allowed to patronize the casinos but if they wished to work there they could. Casino jobs paid well and everyone wanted to work there, particularly the young. For some of them, the freewheeling atmosphere of liquor and money and music proved very alluring, very seductive.

"Do you think she has gone back to her home country?" Hakan Bey said.

"To Kazakhstan? Without telling me?" I said. "I don't think she would do something like that. She is a very rational, responsible person. If she had wanted to return home, she would have told me."

This made him furrow his brow and he chewed on a piece of cheese thoughtfully.

Then he said, "I must ask you a personal question – in order to understand the situation – please forgive me. Was she angry with you for some reason? What do you think?"

"It's okay, you can ask any question," I said. "The answer is, no, everything seemed normal. We got along well – no fights, no arguments, nothing like that."

Hakan Bey's query did not upset me. He was simply probing. I suppose he wanted to eliminate the typical causes of such disappearances. He sat there looking at me intently in the lamplight, a deep furrow of thought between his eyebrows.

"Gus tells me you have not gone to the police," he said.

I nodded.

He sat back and folded his arms on his chest and made a face.

"They will not do anything," he said. "They will write up a report that's all."

"I did visit her boss at the Casino," I said. "He said he had no idea where she was. He seemed to think she had quit."

"Tell me about this man," Hakan Bey said. "Is he a Turk or English?"

"Vitaly? He is Russian," I said. "He owns the casino."

Hakan Bey banged his fist on the table making the lantern jump.

"Russian," he said, almost spitting out the word between clenched teeth.

His reaction surprised me. I wasn't aware that Turks and Russians did not like each other. In fact, I had heard stories about Russian women flocking to Turkey in droves to find hot, eager lovers.

"He seemed … well, how should I put it? Not dangerous," I said. "He gave her the job, got her a work visa. He's been very helpful."

Hakan Bey clamped down on my shoulder his huge hand.

"Work visa? Hmmmm. Did you see it?"

"No, but…"

"Did you see the passaport?" Hakan Bey squeezed my shoulder again to emphasize his point.

"No," I said. "I have not seen the passport. Vitaly said he had returned it to Anara."

"Where is her passaport?" Hakan Bey said with a sudden urgency. "Does she have it? Do you have it?"

"I really don't know." I said. "I looked for it but did not find it."

"Ach!" Hakan Bey said, slapping Gus on the back. "That is what I feared."

"Do you think she has it?" I said.

Hakan Bey shook his head from side to side.

"I doubt that very much," he said. "Usually these casino owners keep the passaports. It's a way of keeping these girls under their control – prevent them from leaving."

"We were so happy about the work visa," I said. "For us, that was the most important issue."

Hakan Bey wagged his head sadly.

"No, no," he said. "You see, he may not have been able to get a work visa for her."

A shiver went through my bones and my stomach went all hollow and fluttery. Just then the electricity came back and startled me so badly that I jumped up from the chair. Gus pulled me back down with his hand.

"Vitaly may have lied to her," Gus said, "just to keep her happy."

"This is unbelievable." I said.

"This is Cyprus," Hakan Bey said and turned the wick all the way down to extinguish the lantern.

"She is illegal by now," I said, trying to control the muscles that were twitching along my legs, afraid to think or imagine what would happen when she got caught.

Gus nodded gloomily.

As we were talking, the waiter who had served us again poked his head to see if we needed anything.

"Irfan, could you send Hamid," Hakan Bey said. "Tell him to come right away. We won't keep him long."

"This boy, Hamid, is from Pakistan," Hakan Bey said. "He cooks here and knows some fellows who work at the *Starlight Casino*. Let us see if he can get us some information."

"I think I should go to the police," I said. "I am getting worried."

"Wait a few more days," said Hakan Bey. "I have a thought, an idea but we need proof. I am almost sure they have smuggled her into South Cyprus – the Greek side."

"But why would they do that?" I said in an overly loud voice, betraying my agitated state.

Hakan Bey looked down at the table and again shook his head from side to side. Gus looked away. Neither one wanted to give voice to or acknowledge their worst fears. They were too courteous, too well mannered to say anything that would hurt or embarrass me. At some point the door opened and a short, wiry, fellow with a thatch of black hair came in, his eyes bright with undisguised curiosity.

"Sit, Hamid, sit," Hakan Bey said. "We need your help."

Hamid sat down without saying anything.

"You have a friend – that Raza you told me about. You said he works at the *Starlight Casino*. He's a card dealer, a croupier, right?"

Hamid nodded. Evidently he understood English quite well but didn't seem to eager to use it.

"Is he still there?" Hakan Bey asked.

Hamid nodded again.

"Good," said Hakan Bey. "I want you to talk to him. Ask him about this Kazakh lady who works there. Her name is Anara. Find out what he knows about her. Can you do that?"

Hamid nodded again.

"Good. Excellent," said Hakan Bey. "Hamid is a very nice boy, a very hardworking boy."

He slapped Hamid's back in a friendly manner. "That's all. You can go now."

Hamid grinned shyly and backed out of the room.

"We may get some useful information," Hakan Bey said. "These boys all talk to each other and they know a lot about what goes on."

"Teshekkur ederim, Hakan Bey," Gus said. "This will help, certainly."

"Leave your phone number with me," Hakan Bey said. "I will call you as soon as I have some news."

I recited my number and he entered it into his cell phone.

We shook hands and he guided us back to the parking lot.

One the way back, Gus came up with some interesting ideas.

"I will ask Yulie to go to Paphos," he said.

"That would be very helpful. I'll find out the name of the casino that Vitaly owns."

"Good. You do that. She can start there."

I was starting to feel hopeful for the first time.

Gus gazed at the passing landscape in silence as we raced back towards Kyrenia. Obviously he did not want to share his thoughts with me or express them in words. I felt no need to coax him into conversation. When we got back into town, we said hurried goodbyes near the K-Pet petrol pump in front of the *Colony Hotel* and then he drove away. I found my Renault and headed back to Karmi.

By now I had more or less convinced myself that Anara had been smuggled out of north Cyprus to the Greek side. Against her will, no doubt. I just couldn't bring myself to believe that she could have gone willingly. That Vitaly was involved in all this somehow seemed probable. I had no proof, of course. And without proof I couldn't possibly confront him and accuse him. My only contact on the Greek side was Yulie and her parents. Whatever I could do to help Yulie, would in turn help me find Anara. So I called Regina.

"Hi, Regina, Robert here. How are you?" I said, trying to keep my voice as calm and neutral as I could.

She must have been taken aback by my call but she did not show any nervousness.

"Fine," she murmured in a distant, uncertain voice. "And how are you?"

I had not spoken to her since our last conversation. I think she may have been afraid to talk to me, afraid of what I might do or say. But when I spoke calmly and acted in a normal manner, she became friendlier.

"You haven't heard from Anara?" she asked.

"No," I said. "She may have gone to Turkey."

"Is possible," Regina said. "But why she not tell me or Vitaly that she go?? Strange. No?"

I decided to humor her, play the little game she wanted to play.

"Strange? Yes, yes, certainly, but girls do a lot of strange things, don't they? She may have had some reason why she went so suddenly, without saying a word to anyone. Family emergency, maybe."

"Maybe." Regina echoed my words.

"Hey, Regina some friends are going to the Greek side and wanted to find out about some nice hotel. They also want to gamble. Doesn't Vitaly have a casino there? Could you tell me the name?"

The question took her by surprise and before she could stop herself she said, "Oh… The *Venetian*."

The name tripped off her tongue as though she had repeated it often.

"Where is it located?" I said. "Limassol?"

"No," she said, "it's near Paphos, just north of Paphos."

It is also possible that she thought that there was no point in withholding the information because I could have obtained it from some other source.

"Thanks," I said. "Is it nice?"

"Very nice," she said, "I stayed there once. Good place."

"Great!" I said. "And how is Vitaly?"

"The same," she said. "He always the same."

"That's good, Say hello to him from my side. Okay?"

"Okay," she said.

"Take care. I'll chat with you later."

"If you hear from Anara, tell her to call me," she said.

"I will," I said and hung up and dialed Yulie's number. "It's called the *Venetian*," I said to her. "It's near Paphos."

"Good," she said, I'll go and check it out."

"This is so good of you," I said. "But please be careful. I don't want you getting yourself into any bizarre situation."

"I'll be fine. Don't worry. If I see anything or smell anything suspicious, I'll call you."

The very next call I made was to Hakan Bey.

He started laughing.

"Oh, that is funny," he said.

"I don't understand," I said.

"I know *Venetian*," he said. "I know where it is. Near Paphos. Not far from my farm but on the other side of the border, very close to the Green Line. An old road goes through that area but we cannot cross the Green Line at that point. It is forbidden. Military zone, you see. Many landmines still there. Very dangerous. You step on one – BOOOM! – the end."

"I see," I said. Though I couldn't quite imagine what sort of terrain that was.

"You come with me," Hakan Bey said. "I show you."

"Do you plan on going to your farm in the near future?" I asked him.

"Yes. I must move my hives. Flower season here, you see. Now lots of wild flowers for my bees. I move the hives to the slopes. Would you like to see my farm? Maybe we will go, yes?"

"Certainly," I said.

"Good. Tomorrow is Friday. We go after prayers. It will be interesting for you to see that area."

"Fine," said.

I had never been to Guzelyurt, in fact, that whole side of Turkish Cyprus was an unknown world for me. This area was on the other side of the Beshparmak range, the side that faced south.

"Good, good. Meet me at my restaurant at 4:00. We will eat at my house."

"That sounds great," I said. "I'll be there."

We left *Silver Stones* late in the afternoon with Hakan Bey at the wheel of his weather-beaten Land Rover. He spun it deftly onto the coastal road, the tires spitting gravel and sand, and quickly gathered speed. He had an aggressive driving style as though he were accustomed to pushing the Land Rover boldly across rugged terrain. Fortunately, there was neither the traffic police nor any traffic to slow him down. The road skirted the scalloped coastline till we were well past Karsiyaka. Then some miles beyond, it swung south with a long curve, leaving the turn off to Kayalar behind.

"We will go past Guzelyurt and then turn left on the road that goes towards Lefkosa. My farm six or seven miles from Guzelyurt, between Sahinler and Sarhatkoy."

"Do you have a vineyard or an orange grove?"

"An orange grove," he said. "The government say pull out vines. Plant orange trees. Too much good wine from Francha, Italia, Espagne.

Our wine not so good. We cannot compete. Better produce oranges. We grow best oranges in the world."

"But the Commanderia is good wine," I said. "Don't you think?"

"Yes, it is. An excellent dessert wine and famous. Best after dinner. But it does not have big market outside Cyprus."

"Perhaps it needs more publicity."

"Perhaps."

We went past Guzelyurt in another thirty minutes at the most and were finally on the road that went to Lefkosa.

"Over there, is south Cyprus," Hakan Bey said, pointing to his right. "In fact, just a half a mile from this road is the Green Line. No one is allowed to cross here."

"Do people cross illegally?" I asked.

"Some do. But it is dangerous. Many mines everywhere left over from the '74 war. One or two people get blown up every year."

"I remember reading about a shepherd," I said. "He went after a stray sheep and got killed. The story was in a newspaper."

Hakan Bey nodded grimly.

"It happens" he said. "Unfortunate, but true."

We came very near Guzelyurt, but did not go into the town. Instead, Hakan Bey took a road that headed eastwards, curving up along a steep slope.

"If you keep going south you will enter Guzelyurt," Hakan Bey said. "The Greeks call it Morphou."

Now we were climbing a brown mountain dotted with sparse vegetation, mostly scrub pine and tamarisk, until we were overlooking a long valley with a small lake in the middle.

"That's Morphou dam," Hakan Bey said and slowed down so that I could get a good look. "The lake not very big now. But some seasons it fills up and gets very big." The road followed the contours of the slope going east but then made a broad sweeping curve near Mevlevi and we started heading south once again. We went for about two miles and then turned east again as we cut through a small cluster of houses.

"That's Sahinler," Hakan Bey said. "We are almost there."

And sure enough, just a few more minutes of driving brought us to the dirt turn off that led to his farm.

"We will stop for a while," Hakan Bey said. "You must meet my wife and have something to drink. We need not hurry. The sun is still high and it will stay bright like this till much later. We will have plenty of light. Then I will take you further up the road. I will take you to a perfect place. From this spot you will be able to see the *Venetian* very clearly."

Hakan Bey's wife came out of the house to greet us. She was an elderly lady with a serious countenance. She did not speak English beyond the usual "Hello," "Goodbye" and "Thank you." I was introduced and then she disappeared and came back with two beakers and a big, glass jug full of chilled orange juice on a wooden tray. At first I was a bit perplexed since I was really hoping for a beer, but then it dawned on me that alcholic drinks were seldom served in Muslim homes and certainly not by the womenfolk The juice turned out to be just great. I was thirsty by now and it went down very nicely.

"From our own orange tree," Hakan Bey said, smacking his lips with delight and then added, "Come, I will show you the bee-hives."

The bees were his pride and joy and lived in a fenced off yard behind the main house. He had over two hundred hives, he said. He had gotten into the bee-keeping business as a hobby but had grown to love it very much. Now it had become a financially rewarding venture. The hives were small white wooden boxes and they sat on the grassy slope in long rows, each hive about two feet away from the next one.

"But it takes a lot of work," he said. "Much, much time spent looking after them."

"Do they sting?" I asked, since by now we were close to the boxes in which the bees lived.

"Yes, but only if they get angry."

"Oh, good, I will try not to make them angry," I said.

After I had inspected the bee-hives and approved of the operation, we walked around a grove of orange trees and then it was time to get back in the Land Rover.

The sun was low by now but the light was still good. We drove less than a mile and then Hakan Bey turned onto what was little more than a goat-path. The Land Rover pushed past boughs of acacia raising a cloud of dust. Then we seemed to be going along the sandy bed of a dry stream that cut through a region of broken hillocks covered with thorn bushes and reed-like grasses.

"This becomes the Peristrona River further downstream," Hakan Bey said. "It gets bigger and during the spring rains it can get pretty wild."

Suddenly, rock and boulders blocked our path and Hakan Bey stopped the vehicle. "From here we go on foot," he said.

Then noticing the look of alarm on my face, he grinned broadly and added, "Not far. I promise."

"We may be in the Green Zone by now," he said in a hoarse whisper, as he led the way. "I can't be sure."

I didn't like hearing this.

"So we could be shot by border guards or blown up by a mine?" I said.

Hakan Bey gave non-committal grunt. "You see there is no wall or fence or sign-post to mark the border here."

I really wished he would stop and turn around but he kept going, leaping from rock to rock, stone to stone with amazing agility. I followed as best as I could grunting and panting.

Finally, he came to a rise and stopped. From this vantage point we could see the entire southern plain stretching to the horizon. Way in the distance I spotted an arrangement of red-tiled roofs.

"What is that?" I asked.

"That is Peristrona," Hakan Bey said. "And do you see that U shaped building, right there in front?"

"I don't see it," I said.

"You see that road coming towards us from Peristrona, coming straight north. Follow that."

"Yes, I see the road."

"Do you see where it stops among the trees and those buildings?"

"Yes, I see it now."

"That's the *Venetian*."

"That?" I asked, disbelief obvious in my tone of voice. The place looked like nothing, just a grouping of drab, barrack-like buildings surrounded by dusty-green eucalyptus and the dark cones of a few cypresses pointing skywards.

"It doesn't look like much," I said.

"There is a reason for that, my friend," he said. "They don't want to attract attention to the place. This isn't Monte Carlo."

I felt uneasy and rather upset looking at a structure where Anara may have been, possibly was being, detained against her will. I had a sudden desire to just keep walking towards the place no matter what the consequences but it passed.

"How far is it from here?" I asked Hakan Bey.

"About three or four kilometers," he said. "But because the ground is so broken up, it could take a person quite a while to get down there. It is not an easy walk. I did it many years ago, before the '74 war."

We spent a few more minutes gazing southwards. The country was rough, rugged and inhospitable, cut by dry stream beds, boulder-strewn and cluttered with tough weeds. Then we turned and headed back to the Land Rover.

Hakan Bey's wife had prepared a tasty meal for us, a real Turkish feast. The highlight being lamb, slow-baked in the out-of-doors oven.

There were just the three of us at dinner that evening and there wasn't much talk during the meal. When Turks eat, they eat with a serious concentration, mostly in silence. After we had eaten and finished having coffee, Hakan Bey suggested I spend the night at his house. I told him I really had to get back to Karmi, otherwise getting to the university on time in the morning would be difficult. I couldn't take the chance of being late. He understood my point and drove me back to *Silver Stones*, where I had left the Renault parked. We said good-bye and I headed back to Karmi.

~

Section 2

On Monday I woke up very early, before sunup, feeling the touch of a damp breeze flowing over my unshaved cheek. The room was still dark, but dawn seemed near from the milky light that stained the eastern horizon. The human residents of Karmi still slept but the birds were up. Sparrows twittered, not quite convinced that it was time to wake up and the magpies had begun to cackle in their hideous, mocking manner. If there ever was a species of bird I hated, it was those goddamned magpies. The house echoed with emptiness and loss, a feeling that became more intense as the sun came up. Although it was rather early, I decided to clean up and drive down to the university. It made no sense to sit around. Moreover, I was starting to feel a strong urge to take a swig of brandy and it was only the inborn sense of responsibility – towards myself, towards the university – that kept me from doing that. Perhaps it was an even more basic instinct: the desire for self-preservation. I knew for sure that if I started showing up at work with booze on my breath, I would be taking the initial steps towards ending my teaching career.

When I got to the office, I saw some of the secretaries flying through the corridors at top speed, their heels clicking alarmingly.

They all looked glum and preoccupied and harried. I got the feeling that something serious, something catastrophic had happened.

"What's going on Zeynip?" I asked the lady who supervised our office.

"It's Cardiff," she said. "He's been taken to hospital."

I checked my stride and waited for her to tell me more.

"It looks serious," she said. "I don't know much more than that. I've got to do something with his classes. Do you think you could take a couple till we find out more about his status, see what we have to do?"

"No problem. Just let me know when and where. I'll handle the rest."

She seemed relieved and hurried away. In the middle of a semester, the sudden absence of a teacher can create chaos. For a week or so, other teachers can fill in, teach the classes and meet with the students but by the second week everybody's nerves start twitching and stress fractures appear in Departmental discipline.

My main concern was not the problems of the Law department but Cardiff's condition and I wanted to get over to the hospital as soon as I could to find out what had happened. I didn't know if Freya knew about this latest turn. She had not been staying too close to Cardiff lately as far as I knew. I thought of calling her but then I changed my mind. I figured someone would surely inform her eventually. By the time I had wrapped up my classes and met with some students and other teachers who were also worried about Cardiff's latest crisis, the afternoon had waned into dusk.

When I presented myself at the nurses' station, I was told that he was in the same ward where they had taken him before but in another room, a room meant for patients who needed more attention, were "critical" in fact. She said I couldn't see him – doctor's orders – no visitors. His medical problems were more complicated this time around, his condition more precarious. The lungs were barely functioning, barely keeping him alive, and his heart had suffered major damage due to arterial blockages. They were giving him oxygen and keeping him under observation.

"I'll wait in the lobby," I said. "Let me know if he can see me later on."

From the hospital, I walked over to a small Mom 'n' Pop grocery store half a block away that sold cigarettes, bread, milk and soda. I bought some bananas and apples, a packet of English cookies, two bars of *Cadbury* chocolate and a liter box of orange juice.

Then I walked back and sat down in the lobby to wait. The lobby was drenched in a sickly fluorescence and dozens of other people were also sitting or standing around, all looking wan and worn, the strain of worry visible on their faces. The glare falling straight coming down from the ceiling gouged out dark hollows in their cheeks and around their eye-sockets.

I had been there about half an hour when Freya showed up. She saw me and hurried over. She seemed on edge, nervous.

"How is he?" she said. "Have you seen him?"

"No," I said. "The nurse wanted me to wait."

"Dammit," she said. "I hate hospitals. I don't want to wait."

She looked around to see if she could locate the head nurse.

"Have you talked to the doctor, the one who is treating him?" she asked.

"He's doing his rounds. I'll see him when he's free."

"I have to meet some people in a half an hour," she said. "I'll try to come back later."

I nodded, almost happy to be left alone. Her presence irritated me. Over the last few weeks, she had never once called me to ask about Anara or how I was faring. Sharp medicinal smells raked my sinuses, stinging odors of disinfectants. There seemed to be a pervasive tension in the air and my nerves felt as though they were stretched as taut as violin strings. I hated hospitals too but I also knew that I had to stay there. One cannot refuse the bitter cup at times. You just have to take it.

Eventually the doctor emerged. A slender man in a white coat with a trim, gray-streaked mustache, he wore his stethoscope draped around his neck. His manner was calm but distant, as though his mind were processing thoughts that had nothing to do with patients or diseases.

Several people rushed up to him, asking urgent questions in rapid Turkish and tugging at his sleeve. He stopped and spoke with them. I followed at a respectful distance, unwilling to intrude. The doctor kept moving forward, shaking off more and more questioners with each response. Finally, seeing my opportunity, I went up to him. The name-tag on his lapel said *Dr. Mettin Gozde*.

"Doctor Gozde," I began, a note of hesitation in my voice as if I feared hearing what he might have to say. "Cardiff – how is he?"

The doctor turned to me. Slowly the bland expression on his face changed and he permitted a brittle smile to make his lips twitch. He remembered my face from my visits during Cardiff's last hospitalization.

"One minute," he said, and having satisfied the last of the questioners he turned to me, grabbed me by the arm and said: "Come."

Linked like this, we walked down to his office at the end of a corridor. He sat down behind his desk and I took a chair facing him.

"Can I see him?" I said.

"Not this evening," he said, in perfect English. "He is resting right now."

"How is his condition? What is the problem?"

The doctor removed the stethoscope from around his neck and flung it on the desk.

"The problem? Everything is the problem. All the problems you can think of," he said. "The heart is damaged, his lungs are weak and his liver is not functioning properly."

I took a deep breath, but much of this did not surprise me.

"Can I see him?"

"No, I don't want him disturbed right now. He had a bad day, couldn't breathe. He is resting now. Can you come tomorrow?"

"Of course." I said. "Can you explain? His illness ... can it be cured?"

"We hope," the doctor said. "At the moment a pulmonary infection is my worry ... we are doing more tests. The problem could be more serious. Mr. Cardiff has been a smoker all his life."

"I understand."

"He is also very weak now. Very thin. He must rest and gain some strength."

"He never ate much," I said. "Lived on beer and cigarettes."

The doctor nodded. He understood, of course.

"Do you think he can return to teach fairly soon?" I said. "The students, the other teachers – we are all worried."

The doctor shook his head.

"We can hope," he said. "But I must tell you his condition is serious."

Having said this much, the doctor got up and put out his hand. This meant that the interview was over. He had other matters to attend to and I had to leave.

When I returned to the lobby, Freya was there talking to a nurse, basically pestering her to be allowed to see Cardiff. We were again told to wait. Finally, towards dinner time when the patients were getting their evening meal, a nurse took us to Cardiff's room.

He was sitting up in bed, but looked frail and sort of dazed. When he saw us, he flashed a weak smile. He tried to say something but I put my finger to my lips, to indicate that he should remain quiet. I placed the packet of food I had purchased on the table by his bedside. Freya held his hand and just looked at him. We were only allowed to spend a few minutes with him. The nurse waited for us and then ushered us out.

Over the next few days, Cardiff seemed to get better and we were hopeful that he might be back on his feet soon. When I visited him he complained about being in the hospital and wanted to leave.

"You are better off here," I told him. "Free meals, twenty-four hour service – what more do you want?"

"I want brandy and cigarettes," he said. "They won't let me smoke or drink."

"But booze and tobacco are both bad for you," I said. "In fact, it's the smoking that has affected your lungs."

"I know," he said. "The damage is done. A few more cigarettes are not going to make any difference."

"You have a point," I said. "But hospital rules are hospital rules."

"I wish I could get out of here," he said again. "Just for a little while. I don't mind dying. I mind being stuck here."

"I understand perfectly how you feel," I said. "I'll get you out of here as soon as you are a bit stronger."

I meant what I said.

I called Freya. I wanted to tell her about Cardiff's condition and his complaints. I didn't know what else to do.

"He's weaker, much weaker than before," I told her. "He can barely get out of bed and stand up on his own and needs help getting to the bathroom."

She did not respond for a second or two then she said, "I feel terrible, seeing him like that, so helpless."

"I understand," I said. "That's what bothers me the most."

"Did he say anything?" she asked.

"Yes," I said. "He said he wanted to go for a swim."

"Really? Where? In a pool? Does he have the strength?"

"No, no, not like that," I told her. "He wants to be on a beach, step into the ocean, feel the water around him. He's tired of lying in bed."

"Will they let him go?" Freya asked. "The hospital staff, I mean?"

"Probably not."

"That's what I thought," she said. "It's a crazy idea."

"I told him that," I said. "But he got rather worked up, said he didn't have much time, wanted me to help him."

"What should we do?" she wanted to know.

"We could ask the doctor," I said. "He might let him go for a couple of hours."

"Will he?" she said.

"I don't know," I said. "We could ask. Cardiff really wants to get out of the hospital. He's miserable."

"I know," she said in a low voice. "I can't bear to see him like that."

"I wish I could do something, something to help, to make him feel better."

At this point I was just talking to myself. I didn't really have any concrete ideas in my head. But my tone of voice must have started a train of thought in Freya's mind.

"Look," she said, "maybe we can take him for a swim, sort of steal him."

"Really? Could we carry it off, without getting stopped?"

"We could," she said. "I'm sure."

"But how?"

"During visiting hours the lobby is always crowded," Freya said. "People come and go. No one tries to stop them. Families, children, entire clans. The place turns into a bloody bazaar. We could easily walk out with him. I doubt if anyone would notice."

"What if someone stops us?"

"We'll just say we were taking him for a little walk around the parking lot."

I had my doubts about the whole idea but I thought we could give it a try.

"Fine," I said. "When do we do this?"

"Friday evening," she said. "Around seven. It is the busiest time."

"Okay," I said. "I'll meet you in the parking lot at a quarter to."

"Good," she said. "See you then."

I was elated. I would not have attempted this caper alone, but with Freya's help and complicity there was a possibility that we could carry it off. I wanted to please Cardiff. I knew how wretched he must be feeling, lying there in that stark hospital alone, wishing he were dead if only to end the endless waiting.

We – I mean, those of us who are in good health – we can never imagine how bad it can be for a person who finds himself trapped inside a body that is dying inch by inch, slowly and painfully. The mind wishes to escape from the decaying carcass, break free of it. The spirit rebels against the pain that diseases inflict, the tyranny and oppression of the body's prison house. But the tentacles of the flesh will not let go, will not surrender, because the body has a mind of its own. The tentacles keep flexing, the twitching continues even when the lines of communication to the brain have been cut. The male Praying Mantis comes to mind.

I had no idea where we would take Cardiff but in my imagination I had created the image of place that would be appropriate: a sheltered cove, a deserted sandy beach watered by moonlight where the waves got rocked to sleep as they came in shoreward, an isolated, remote place where we would not be observed or disturbed. Here I hoped to let him soak in the sea, feel the caresses of the currents and let fish nibble away at his nipples. I was certain the sea would revive him. Freya had left the selection of the beach in my hands.

Friday dawned warm and got hotter as the day wore on, devolving into a balmy evening. At the appointed hour, I drove the Renault to the hospital parking lot and waited for Freya. The flat she lived in happened to be directly behind the hospital.

I had brought a trench-coat and a fedora. I don't know why. I thought we might need some sort of outfit to serve as a disguise. I had only been there a few minutes when I saw Freya. I got out of the car and waved to her. She saw me, came over and we shook hands.

"All set?" she asked.

"Yes," I said. "Did you talk to Cardiff? Is he expecting us?"

"Yes," she said. "I spoke with him on his mobile. He's ready and waiting."

"Come on then," I said and we walked wordlessly into the lobby like a pair of conspirators.

The place was noisy and crowded. Dozens of men, women and children milling. Everyone seemed to be talking at the same time. The rush and hurry and panicked agitation of the crowd was much like the free-for-all you see at train stations. If the security guard was anywhere, I did not see him.

I moved with purposeful steps, with Freya at my side. We went down a dimly lit corridor that always held the chill of the morgue and past the Male ward. When we got to Cardiff's room, I saw that he was lying with the sheet pulled all the way to his chin. He grinned happily when he saw us. There was no one else in the room.

"Thank god, you are here," he said. "I'm glad to see you."

Freya leaned over him and gave him a quick peck on his left cheek.

"We are too," she said.

"Are you ready?" I asked him, holding out the trench coat and the fedora towards him.

Instead of answering me, he gave me sly look and threw off the bed sheet in one swift move.

"Holy Moses!" I said, breathing in sharply. He was lying there completely dressed in his favorite linen suit. He was wearing his shoes and had even gone to the trouble of putting on a necktie.

"I brought this trench-coat and this fedora for you," I said. "You want to look like Humphrey Bogart?"

"I don't think that will be necessary," he said. "Just help me up, will you. Once I'm on my feet, I can manage."

So I quickly threw on the trench coat over my shoulders and placed the hat on my own head to free up both hands.

Freya got on one side of him and I on the other and we helped him out of the bed. He had lost so much weight that I could have easily carried him in my arms. His limbs were thin as sticks and his head looked too large for his body.

Once he was standing on his own two feet, he pushed us away.

"It's okay. I'm okay now. I can walk. Slowly. Okay?"

I nodded to indicate agreement. I wasn't going to rush him out of there anyway. I aimed at pretending that we were just having a stroll, just letting him get some exercise.

When the three of us came out of his room, a nurse who just happened to be walking by saw us. All of us waved at her cheerily. She waved back and then hurried on to do whatever she intended to do. I don't think she suspected that we were actually doing anything unusual or against hospital regulations. We moved slowly but steadily towards the front lobby, the only way out of the hospital. I figured, once we melted into the crowd that filled that hall we would be invisible, we would blend into the herd, just another group of visitors. And that is precisely what happened. A few people stared at us out of idle curiosity since we were foreigners but even as foreigners we were ordinary and hardly worthy of attention. Most people paid us no attention whatsoever nor did any security guard try to stop us. We trooped solemnly out of the lobby to the parking lot. Cardiff was unable to deal with the four steps that descended to the flat concrete apron of the parking lot, but with Freya supporting him on the left and I on the right, we managed to get him down. I heard him moan a bit but he never complained. I helped Cardiff into the front seat of the Renault, Freya hopped in the back and I drove us out of there slowly and carefully. Cardiff was breathing very hard now, but he managed a chuckle and slapped his knee.

"Fantastic! Glad to be out of the bloody place," he said. "I feel like a new man. Let's get a drink somewhere."

"Where are we going?" Freya wanted to know.

"What do you say to Karpaz?" I asked Cardiff.

"Why not?" he said. "That would be lovely. I haven't been there in ages."

He spoke in a low, hoarse whisper and then leaned back in his seat and closed his eyes.

"Let's pick up some food," I said to Freya. "I've already taken care of the drinks."

"Won't we be able to find a restaurant in Karpaz?"

"There is a small restaurant at the spot where the road ends and all the tour buses stop. But it has very little apart from dried up bourek. I speak from experience. Moreover, I doubt very much that it will be open by the time we get there."

"I don't really care if we eat," Freya said.

"But I do," I said. "I think I'll get some roasted chicken from *Ezic*."

I had a cooler filled with ice-cubes in the trunk to chill a bottle of Californian Chardonnay and half a dozen bottles of beer. I had also wrapped a bottle of good Turkish red in a towel and placed it on the backseat. And as a special treat for Cardiff I had made up a thermos flask of Gin and Tonic. I figured he'd enjoy that.

When we got the food, Cardiff woke up and sniffed the air hungrily. "Do I smell roasted chicken?"

"Yes," I said. "That's for later. Now go back to sleep. I'll wake you up when we get to Karpaz."

I flung the Renault back onto the main road and soon we had left the lights of Kyrenia behind us and were cutting through the pass below St. Hilarion. Then just as we dropped onto the flat plain of the Mesaoria, I became aware of the moon, almost at the full and bright as a beacon, hovering in the eastern sky. Distant trees and bushes stood out as black silhouettes against the backdrop of a silver-gray landscape. On we banged into the night, past warehouses with corrugated tin roofs that shone like slabs of mica and distant farms where a few yellow bulbs glowed dimly. There was no traffic whatsoever and I made steady progress towards the horizon.

At one point Freya asked me some questions about Anara and I told her that Yulie was looking around Paphos. After that she dropped the topic and no one spoke for a while. I drove with my eyes focused on the gleaming strip of road in front of me that pointed straight at the heart of the peninsula. I knew and, I am certain, Freya also knew that Cardiff was sinking fast. It was important for him to conserve his breath. I wanted him to rest until we got to Karpaz. What we were doing also worried me. Our little escapade would not be considered a jolly prank by the hospital authorities. If we got caught we could face some serious repercussions.

Cardiff stirred in his sleep, groaning lightly as he struggled to breathe. His face was very pale, and his cheekbones stood out harshly above the black hollows of his eyes. I wanted him to see the chalk-white surface of the moon leaning over us, but I did not dare wake him. Freya must have dozed off also because I did not hear her say anything or make a sound. The steady hum of the Renault's motor had acted on them like a sleeping potion.

Finally, land's end seemed close. I could sense the presence of the ocean on my left and my right. The narrow wedge of land tapers to a point here like a javelin thrust into the body of the Mediterranean. All around I saw nothing, no trees or bushes nor any commercial structures but pale patches of sand and spiky tufts of grass that glittered like metal wires. I pulled into a paved parking area alongside a small building that was all dark and shuttered up. This could have been a restaurant but I sensed no activity of any kind either inside or outside and the parking lot was empty. I got the feeling that we were completely alone. I switched off the headlights and killed the motor. Silence engulfed us and in this vacuum of sound I could hear the slow shuffle and boom of the sea. By now the moon had gone down and in the dark clarity of the sky, stars sparkled hard and bright as diamonds. Slowly my eyes became accustomed to the available light and I was able to see fairly well.

"Hello," said Freya waking up suddenly.

Cardiff stirred sleepily, making an effort to rally his senses. The drugs they had been giving him to keep him alive also made him lethargic and listless.

Freya and I got out to stretch our legs and look about the place. The moon had slid lower in the sky by now so there wasn't much light but I could see that we were just a few feet from where the waves were licking at a beach of fine, white sand. A natural breakwater made of rocks and sand went out into the ocean and then curved around like an arm, forming a sheltered cove where the wind and waves were quite tame.

"This is great," Freya said.

She took off her sandals, put them inside the car and walked into the sea.

"It's warm," she said, "Tepid. Like bath water."

"Should we wake up Cardiff?" I asked her.

"No," she said. "Let him sleep. What's the hurry? He seems to be comfortable."

"Fine," I said. "I'll find a place to spread out blankets and set up the cooler."

The night was lucid with the light of a million stars and a warm breeze drifted over us. I found a low tussock of grass that formed a natural couch above roundels of sugary sand. It was a sheltered spot and faced the sea and seemed like a good place to pitch our camp. I got a rug out of the trunk and some towels and spread them out and then got the ice-chest and the wine. Freya helped bring out the food and arranged everything on the towels.

"What would you like?" I asked her.

"I think I will have a swim first," she said.

"Did you bring your bathing suit?" I asked.

She laughed.

"I don't need it. There is no one here to object."

"That's the spirit. I'll follow you but first I'm going to have a beer."

She unbuttoned her dress and let it drop. She wasn't wearing anything underneath, neither bra nor panties.

I averted my gaze and started rummaging about in the ice-chest. I took a long pull on the beer bottle and then decided to go check on Cardiff. When I looked back, I could see Freya's arms rising and falling as she swam and her pale body outlined against the fissures and fractures of the sea.

Cardiff had woken up and sat looking at the ocean.

"We have arrived," he said quietly.

"Would you like a drink?" I asked him. "I have a Napa valley Chardonnay, a Turkish red, beer and a thermos full of gin and tonic."

"I need something strong," he said. "How about a jigger of Gee 'n' Tee?"

"Would you like to come and sit on the sand? The spot is quite nice and sheltered."

"Will you help me?"

I took hold of his elbow and lifted him up and he put an arm around my neck and stood up shakily.

"I'm glad to be out of that bloody hospital," he said.

"How are you feeling?"

"A bit rocky," he whispered. "Where is Freya?"

"Swimming."

"Good, good," he murmured. "Thanks for doing this."

"Don't mention it," I said.

We walked slowly across dry, crumbly sand, our shoes sinking a few inches at every step.

"We should have taken off our shoes," he said.

"Doesn't matter now," I said. "Mine are full of sand."

"Mine too," he said.

I helped him to the blankets and helped him settle himself comfortably with his back propped up against the sandbank.

"Feel a bit wobbly just looking at the ocean," he said. "Like a boat, rocking and bobbing."

"Let me get you that drink," I said. "That should help."

I unscrewed the metal top of the thermos and poured a small amount of Gin and tonic into it and handed it to Cardiff.

"Go ahead," I said. "Enjoy it. I'm going to crack the Chardonnay."

We could see Freya swimming parallel to the shore, her arms coming up and going down, scattering foam and water drops as she threshed the sea.

"She's a good swimmer," I said "Right?"

"She should be." Cardiff murmured as if talking to himself. "A natural born sea-nymph. She's been coming to Cyprus since she was a child."

"Would you like to go in?" I asked him.

"Yes," he said, "but you chaps will have to help me."

"Okay," I said. "Let's wait till Freya comes out."

The night was calm and beautiful and it felt good to be drinking with the slow music of the waves in the background.

After a while Freya came out of the water and wrapped herself with a towel.

"So how's our patient?" she asked Cardiff.

"Right as rain," he said.

"How is the water?" I asked her.

"Warm as bathwater," she said, "especially close to the shore."

"Cardiff wants to go in."

"Great," she said. "Let's all go in."

The two of us helped Cardiff get his clothes off and then walked with him into the sea. The water was warm, having retained the heat it had soaked up during the day. We went in till the water was almost at our hips and Cardiff was secure on his feet. He stood there with me on one side and Freya on the other, breathing rapidly. A wan smile flickered across his lips.

"This feels good," he said, "but I would like to sit down."

I helped him sit down and now the sea encircled his chest, cradling his disease-wracked body in warm currents.

"Like mother's lap," he said, licking the salt spray off his lips.

There was hardly any meat on his concave chest and his rib-cage made a well-defined pattern of light and shade. Freya sat down beside him, propping him up with an arm.

"I'll go get some wine and join you chaps," I said.

The night was warm and calm. I wondered where Anara was and what she was doing.

"I know what you are thinking of," Cardiff said. "Don't worry. You will get her back."

"A nice thought," I said. "Thanks."

Cardiff got tired quickly so we brought him back out and helped him get dressed. He looked happy though exhausted. All in all, I suppose we spent nearly two hours on the beach, eating and swimming and drinking and when we started back towards Kyrenia it was close to midnight.

For the journey back, I prepared a comfortable bed for him in the back seat of the Renault with some blankets and a couple of pillows. He settled back with a happy sigh and closed his eyes. Freya rode in front with me. Neither Freya, nor I said much on the homeward trip.

I was glad I had helped Cardiff fulfil his last wish. As we were driving back, thoughts about my own mortality drifted through my mind. How would I react if I were in a similar situatiion? Would I moan and lament and run around seeking some medical miracle? Or would I accept the inevitable with good grace? When disease and pain rack one's body, it is best to call it quits. I loathed the idea of lying there strapped to a hospital bed, being kept alive by machines. That was no life. I knew Cardiff felt the same way. He had lived his life with appetite and gusto. He was not afraid of dying. Once when we were drinking and talking in *Pegasus*, he had said as much.

"I don't fear death or what lies beyond," he said. "What I fear is being paralyzed, or being in a coma – existing like a vegetable. I hope someone will do me the courtesy of finishing me off."

I think both of us – Freya and myself – knew that Cardiff would not be with us very long. Though how many days or hours he might have one could not say. When we got back to the hospital, the parking lot was empty and so was the lobby. We tried to rouse Cardiff but we couldn't. He seemed to have sunk into some sort of coma. We called the attendants and with their help got him onto a stretcher and into his room and placed him on his bed. When I left, that morning, Freya was sitting by his bedside, holding his hand. The nurse on duty asked us where we had taken him. Freya said we had just taken him to his favorite restaurant for a meal. She gave us a look of disbelief but did not make a fuss. I think she knew that hospital rules and regulations mattered little when the patient is determined to break free and move on.

Out of consideration for the state Cardiff was in, Freya was allowed to stay with him overnight. She was quite calm and told me to go home and get some rest.

"If you need anything," I told her, "call me."

Cardiff lay quite still with his eyes closed, his breathing very shallow. I grasped his left hand and squeezed it gently. His skin felt dry like paper and cold.

"Good-bye, dear friend," I said under my breath.

I looked at Freya and saw that her eyes were wet with tears.

I gave her a grim nod, fearing the worst and headed back home.

∼

CHAPTER NINE

Section 1

When Freya called me next day, I expected bad news. And the news was bad. He slipped away quietly in the wee hours, she told me, without waking up. She had been at his bedside.

"Are you still at the hospital?" I asked her.

Yes, she said, but arrangements were being made for the removal of the body.

"I'm on my way."

Cardiff's death was painful. But even as I write this sentence, I find it simplistic – totally inadequate. It says nothing, expresses nothing. It doesn't convey what I really felt. No, I didn't cry when I heard the news, nor later at his graveside when we were burying him. Tears seemed inappropriate, quite the wrong response. Cardiff loathed sentimentality and being mourned in this manner would have annoyed him. What I felt was something deeper than sorrow, a kind of hollowness in the pit of my belly – emptiness – as though I had lost something valuable, something I needed. But the sense of loss I experienced had a different texture from the sense of loss I experienced when Anara disappeared. Somehow, I never thought she was gone from me forever. I felt sure I'd see her again, be with her again. Her absence from my life seemed like a lunar eclipse, the passing of a shadow over a bright surface. But losing Cardiff was an irrevocable, final loss.

I missed the easy companionship, the drinking-buddy camaraderie. And even though I had known him for a short time, his personality and temperament suited my moods and attitudes. I knew little about his pre-Cyprus life – the childhood in Britain, the formative years in schools and universities. We never had the time or the opportunity to talk about that phase of his life; nor did he show any inclination to discuss his past. But when we did get together and talk, our conversations flowed frank and free. I valued his advice. Perhaps this was why his rapid decline and abrupt demise shook me; perhaps his death reminded me of my own mortality and the dwindling sum of years that lay in store for me. I felt his loss even more keenly than the loss of my father. I had been very close to my father, and I had a warm and affectionate relationship with him. He died after a long, degrading hospital stay. His last months in the hospital were a torment for him and for me. When he finally passed away I was filled with an acute sense of relief. At first I was ashamed of the way I felt. But then it occurred to me that he must also be happy to be free of pain and suffering. But a parent's death is something you expect and you prepare for it over the years. My mother's death, whenever it comes about, will not be a shock. I have been rehearsing the event in my mind, imagining it, playing it like a tape in my head over and over. I know it will happen at some point in the future, a natural ending in the scheme of Nature. Nor is the death of someone who is terminally ill so traumatic, even when the person is close to you. You expect it. In certain cases you even welcome it, hope it will happen soon. You don't want a loved one to go through a prolonged end, endure the humiliations and indignities of a long, drawn-out death.

This is why Cardiff's passing away filled my mind with contradictory emotions. I was glad he had died without waking up from the coma.

He did not experience the gradual breakdown of internal organs, loss of control over bodily functions, the loss of all faculties one by one: sight, hearing, taste. He died quickly, quietly, melting away into an endless sleep, drifting perhaps from one multi-colored dream to another. For who is to say that this life we experience as real, full of vivid experiences is not just a dream. Or could it be that we are all actors in someone else's dream, as Borges believed, and we fade away as soon as the dreamer wakes up.

A grave had been prepared for Cardiff in the small British cemetery that stretched for half a block along the coast road between an auto dealership and a bank. Half a century earlier this piece of land must have been a pleasant field on the edge of town. But now the coast road was a crowded thoroughfare and the small cemetery was in the wrong place. The people who had gathered for the funeral were an ill-matched group. Many did not know each other, were seeing faces they had never seen. Cardiff made friends easily with all sorts of people, and from every level of society, high and low. He knew intellectuals and civil servants and shopkeepers and waiters. Among those present there were colleagues, drinking companions, and even bartenders who had served him and liked him. His ex-wife was not there and I felt grateful for that. I would not have known what to say to her. Nor was his son present. People looked ill at ease as they shuffled about in the bright sunlight, on a day that seemed to be brimming with life. A priest had been located and at the right moment he uttered the familiar, formulaic words, (dust-to-dust … certain hope of resurrection …) that do nothing for the dead but provide solace to the living and are supposed to help you make sense of something outside of sense and reason: the end of a human life, the final disappearance of someone you knew so well, shook hands with, sat and chatted with, got drunk with.

Freya looked pale and a bit dazed in a navy blue dress, her rain-gray eyes rimmed with red. Her Mum and Dad were with her, thank god, propping her up on either side in case she stumbled or staggered. They had taken the first flight out of England upon hearing the news and had arrived just in time to be at the graveyard that day.

After the burial "ceremony" (if that is the right word), people shuffled about, awkward, unsure as if they didn't quite know what was expected of them. I said some meaningless words to Freya and her parents. People shook hands with each other and exchanged a few formal sentences, others gave each other those tentative, half-embraces that show a reluctance to touch another person or be touched, still others dabbed unwanted tears and murmured hurried goodbyes. Some decided to go to the *Windmill Hotel* to stiffen wilting nerves with drink. I turned towards *Pegasus* with Ben Britton, since it was on my way back to the university.

The days and weeks that followed Cardiff's funeral seemed one long blur of meaningless activities. I performed my duties, of course, but like a numb sleepwalker, not quite present in the real sense of the word. I also did my best to stay in touch with Freya, mostly by phone; I left several messages and offered what comfort I could, trying, in a way, to keep Cardiff's memory alive. She proved elusive, slow to return calls, her long silences and mysterious comings and goings enigmatic as ever. I had neither the time, neither the energy, nor the will to trace her movements or keep up with her. Finally, one day, she did slow down her locomotion just long enough for us to chat and I invited her up to Karmi.

"I have something for you," I said. "Cardiff left it with me – a letter, some kind of a document."

"Really?" she said.

I think she was genuinely surprised.

"Yes," I said. "He wanted me to give it you."

I offered to pick her up and bring her to Karmi but she told me that she had purchased a car and was now quite mobile. So we agreed to meet at the *Viewpoint,* Karmi's solitary upscale restaurant that had just opened up for high season. It was owned and operated by a friendly Turk and offered spectacular views of Hilarion and the swale that tumbled in green declensions to the coast. Sunset drinks on the *Viewpoint* terrace were a ritual and a rite held sacred by many devotees of Bacchus.

Freya arrived wearing a black strapless cocktail dress and high heels with a Kashmiri shawl wrapped around her bare shoulders to ward off the evening chill. She looked quite glamorous and also much older. In her left hand she held a small purse or reticule made of a silvery metallic mesh, just big enough to hold car-keys and, possibly, a money clip. As usual, she wore neither make-up nor any jewelry. I was on edge as I greeted her, nor did she appear to be at ease and shot nervous glances in all directions as if to make sure that there was no one around whom she did not wish to see or be seen by.

We took a table on the terrace. From here one could see all the way to Kyrenia in the valley below. The only other customers sharing the terrace with us were a pair of elderly Nordic-looking women with boy-cut white-blond hair and deeply tanned leathery faces. We ordered our drinks and sat in front of each other held fast in a silence that appeared to be pregnant but refused to give birth to conversation. I had swallowed a mouthful of brandy before leaving the house in the hope that it would make it easy for me to talk to Freya, but it had not done much. Without some more booze in me, I knew I would remain trapped in an awkward silence, unable to produce small talk that seemed a necessity just then. For a while we sat and watched the dying light on the stones of Hilarion. Presently our drinks arrived: orange juice for her and a scotch and soda for me and we sipped in silence.

"How have you been?" I asked her at length, a normal enough question, I thought.

"Not so good," she said.

"Are you planning to take classes in the fall?"

She shook her head.

"I don't know. Have to think about all that."

"How are your parents? Have they gone back to England?"

"Yes," she said.

Sitting there, I could feel Cardiff's invisible presence. He seemed to be hovering near us, inches away. But talking about him, even mentioning his name seemed wrong. As if obeying some unwritten rule of decorum, I didn't bring him up and neither did she.

"Nice view," she said, after a lengthy silence, trying to keep the conversation neutral and unemotional.

"Yes," I said. "Would you like to eat here?"

"No," she said. "I'm not hungry. I just wanted to see you and talk to you. Can we go for a walk? I'd like that."

"No problem. We can also go and sit on my rooftop. The view is the same but the drinks will cost less. What do you say?"

She flashed a quick, fugitive smile and nodded in agreement. I called for the bill, paid it and we walked out. As we were crossing the plaza, she noticed the bench that faced the church, the same one where Anara and I had often sat to watch the pigeons circle above the bell-tower.

"Can we sit here for a while?" she said. "Do you mind?"

"Not at all," I said. "I sit here often and smoke a cigar."

"Go, ahead," she said. "Have one. I love the smell of tobacco smoke honestly, I do."

"You seem to have given up cigarettes?" I said.

"I have," she said. "But if you want to smoke – no problem."

We sat down on the bench that faced the church and the flat, graveled expanse of the plaza. There was no one around as usual and only a few cars were parked carelessly around the perimeter. I pulled a cigar from my pocket, tore off the wrapper and got it going with a few long puffs. Soon clouds of fragrant blue smoke were drifting all around us in long, tenuous skeins.

"I must say the changes I have seen in you are remarkable," I told her. "I was certain you and Cardiff were through that night ... when you ... I mean, the crisis."

She shrugged and pulled her shawl more tightly around her shoulders.

"That wasn't really me," she said. "I was out of control. Or to put it differently, I was under the control of certain chemicals."

"That was clear enough," I said, and took out the document that Cardiff had given me. "Here, take it. This is for you."

"What is it?" she asked. "Do you know?"

"Yes, he told me. It's a codicil to his will. When he gave it to me, he explained what he wanted and why."

"When?" she wanted to know. "When did he give it to you?"

"Some months back ... last fall actually."

"I suppose I better see what it says," she said and took the paper from my hand and started to read.

The sun had dropped below the western escarpments and directly above us the sky had taken on a saffron tint. Occasionally, a car crunched across the gravel and stopped. People got out, doors slammed and the silence smoothed itself out and I could hear the rustle and lisp of the little stream that went down the stone channel nearby. Squadrons of swallows were diving into the clouds of gnats that rose like smoke above the tree tops.

"He says he wants me to have the apartment," she said in a toneless voice. She did not sound pleased.

"Yes," I said to her. "He told me that in very clear terms."

"But why?" she said, sounding a bit exasperated. "I never asked him for anything."

"Don't you want it?"

"Of course not," she said. "What will I do with it?"

"Live in it," I said. "If you don't want to live there, you could rent it out."

"But I don't want the responsibility, the bother."

"You could sell it," I said. "Put the money in the bank."

"I don't want his money," she said.

"Well, according to this codicil, you are the rightful owner."

"Oh, God!" she moaned, "what a mess!"

"Well, think about it for a bit," I told her.

"What if I tore this up?" she said suddenly. "What will happen?"

"Nothing. The property will go to his legal heirs," I said. "He divorced his wife many years ago, but I know he has a son ... lives in England."

"I don't know," she said. "I don't know what to do."

"Don't do anything hastily," I said. "Wait a bit. Talk to your parents."

"No," she said. "I don't want them to know about this. But ... maybe I should wait... perhaps his son will come."

"Yes. I'm sure he will come," I said. "In the meantime, stay there. Don't leave it vacant. Squatters could move in ... vandalize the place."

"I suppose you are right," she said. "Do I have to pay any rent? Make a mortgage payment?"

"No, that's all paid up," I told her. "Cardiff owned it free and clear. You just have to pay for the electricity and the gas. That's all."

"This is such an odd feeling for me," she said. "Owning a property. I'm so used to renting."

"You can get used to owning," I said. "You won't have to worry about coming up with the rent money every month."

"That's true," she said and then sat there quietly. We sat there for a while enveloped in silence as the light thickened and darkness spread across the plaza.

"I must be going," she said finally.

"Fine," I said. "I'll walk you to your car."

"Thanks," she said in a soft voice.

"No problem." I said. "You are free to do whatever you please. The choice is entirely yours. But if I were you, I'd wait a while, consider all your options."

We walked to her car. As we walked across the gravel, our shoes made a crunching sound as though we were walking on broken eggshells. This was no surface for high heels and Freya wobbled a bit. She put a hand on my arm to steady herself and then stopped and looked at me.

"What news of Anara?" she asked.

"None, really," I said.

"I have to tell you something," she said in a scared sort of tone. I looked at her, but in the dim jasmine-scented gloom I was unable to read the expression on her face.

"What is it?"

I thought she wanted to say something about Cardiff.

"That day, when we had lunch at the *Balik* ..." she began and then stopped mid-sentence and looked down at her feet.

"Is this about Cardiff?"

"No, no," she said. "About your friend."

"What about her?"

"You have not heard from her? She hasn't called?"

I shook my head.

"That day, at *Balik*, I didn't tell you everything," Freya said, suddenly.

"What do you mean? You told me you saw her in that ladies beauty salon in Paphos."

"Yes, I did see her there. But I should have also told you something else."

I frowned at her, narrowing my eyes to focus them more acutely.

"What?"

"I saw her at the *Venetian.*" Freya said. "It's a sort of casino-cum-resort."

"At the *Venetian!*"

"Yes," she said. "I was staying there."

My mouth opened in utter astonishment. I could hardly believe what she was saying.

"Are you sure?" I said.

"Yes," she said. "It's near Paphos."

"I know where it is, Freya. But Christ almighty, why for god's save didn't you tell me this before? I've been sick with worry. How was she? Was she okay? What did she say? How long were you with her? Did she ask about me?"

"She was fine, fine, fine," Freya said. "Really. We spoke for just a few minutes. Then she rushed off. I don't think she wanted to talk to me."

My brain was trying to process a million thoughts at once.

"What did you say to her? Did you ask her what she was doing there?"

"No. I didn't get a chance," Freya said. "She asked about you and I told her you had been trying to find out where she was."

"Did she tell you what happened? How in god's name did she end up in Greek Cyprus?"

"Not really. She just said, It was all a mistake. And please don't tell Robert you saw me."

"That's it?"

"You must understand, it all happened in seconds. Our paths crossed in a corridor. I was really taken aback, really surprised to see her. I think she also got a bit of jolt. She was stunned to see me there and I was even more shocked to see her."

"I don't know what to think," I said. I was starting to feel dizzy and the plaza seemed to swing around me in a slow, circular motion. I reached out and held on to the roof of Freya's car.

"Did you see her again? Tell me, tell me the truth, please."

"Believe me. I'm telling you the truth." Freya said.

"Why didn't you tell me this earlier?"

"She begged me not to," Freya said. "I promised her I wouldn't say a word. I couldn't betray a trust."

"And now, why did you break the trust now?"

"Well, a lot has changed. Cardiff..."

"Cardiff... did Cardiff know?"

"Yes, I told him."

"What did he say?"

"He said it would be better if I kept quiet, at least for a little while. He was sure Anara would contact you herself -- sooner or later."

I nodded.

"Now that he's gone and I may be returning to England, I felt I should speak out," she said.

"I wish you had told me this earlier," I said, in an exasperated way. "I've been going crazy with worry. Now, at least I know where she is and that she is okay."

"Yes, yes, she looked okay," Freya said, hurriedly. "I just didn't know what it all meant. The whole situation."

"And you never saw her again?" I asked.

"I told you – no. Never," Freya said. "I left very early the next day."

All kinds of thoughts were churning around inside my head: anger, fear, frustration and even a flicker of hope. I was glad Freya had actually seen Anara, actually laid eyes on her. That was good news, surely. But now a million other questions also demanded answers: Who was she with? Was she afraid? Was she in danger?

I clutched Freya's arm.

"You must go back," I said to her. "Please. You must. You must return and try and talk to her, see what you can do."

"I can't," she said in a flat, emotionless voice that carried a note of finality. "I wish I could. But the Turks have me on a list and so do the Greeks. I cannot leave the Turkish side and the Greeks won't let me enter Greek Cyprus."

"Could you try?"

"It won't work. I know. They will stop me at the check point."

"Is this connected with the Tony business?"

"In a way," she said. "Now that the Turks have got all they want out of me, they would be very happy if I just disappeared."

"I wish I could go," I said.

"No, don't do that," she said. "You are bound to get stuck or they'll put you on a plane to Cairo."

"I bet she has no papers, no passport."

Freya nodded, evading my probing gaze.

"She is surely illegal by now," Freya said. "You won't be able to help her. You need someone who speaks Greek."

She got into her car, shut the door and rolled down the window glass.

"You need someone who knows the area," she added, "and has contacts in the Greek sector."

I knew she was right. Freya possessed the keen, wide-awake instincts of a wild animal. She had learned much on the streets where neither predator nor prey could boast of a special advantage. And where survival depended not on winning fights but on how you dealt with defeats. As she backed her car out and drove away, I wondered why Cardiff had kept quiet. Was he trying to protect me? Did he think I might do something rash and stupid, something that might jeopardize my job, perhaps even endanger my life? I brooded over these questions for a long time but no sensible answers presented themselves.

$\backsim$

Section 2

I realized now, more clearly than ever, that I needed to contact Yulie. I needed her help. I also had to pull myself out of the pit of despairing lethargy I had been floundering in for quite some time. Apart from teaching and keeping up with some other duties at the university, I did little else. When I got home, I fed the fish, fed the cat, fed myself and got drunk. I preferred drinking above all other activities and on weekends I worked particularly hard to absent myself from thinking, feeling and imagining. As soon as I got home, I started drinking and in no time at all I got myself into such a sodden stupor that even stirring an inch from the couch seemed like a monumental task. The sun rose, the sun went down, day turned to night and then back to day but for me it was all one seamless, timeless black abyss. A lizard-like sloth held me in its grip. Finally, I made the phone call that I knew I had to make. I called Yulie and told her what Freya had said.

"Can you come to Karmi," I said. "I need to talk to you."

"Of course," she said. "Certainly. How about Saturday afternoon?"

The impending arrival of Yulie made me sober up.

On Saturday morning I drank several cups of Turkish coffee, shaved and showered and changed into a crisp shirt and a recently laundered pair of jeans. Then I drove down the mountain to a grocery store to buy real food, something I had not paid much attention to in quite a while.

The day dawned bright and clear. To the north, above the Turkish coast, I could see the purple silhouettes of the Taurus Mountains. And above them, white clouds rising up like bubbles, forming and bursting and re-forming continuously. Yulie arrived around noon, looking daisy-fresh in a flowered cotton skirt and a blue blouse. Her hair, a tousled mass of honey-gold curls bright with highlights, threw a warm glow over her cheeks. She came bounding up the stairs with an energetic briskness, carrying a sack of groceries in the crook of her right arm.

"I have a plan. I have a plan," she cried out.

"Good," I responded, "Glad you've got one because I don't."

"The pieces are all falling into place," she said as she floated into the living room. "The picture is getting clearer. Do not worry, my dear."

"I'm glad you think so," I said, unable to suppress the note of doubt in my voice.

"I'm certain," she said, placing a brown paper bag on the dining room table.

"What is all this?" I asked.

Without responding she started to empty the bags and lay out their contents on the table. An impish smile crinkled the corners of her eyes, as she pulled out a bottle of burgundy, wedges of hard cheese, tinned black olives and a couple of large eggplants.

"Looks like you raided a grocery store."

"We are eating at home, right?" she said. "I plan on making moussaka so I brought the ingredients. We can talk while I cook. We have much to discuss, much to talk about. We better hash out everything right here."

"I was going to take you out. I haven't been in a decent restaurant in ages," I said to her. "But this is fine. How can I help? What do you want me to do?"

"Open, the wine," she said. "I'll take care of the rest."

"I can do that," I said. "That's easy."

"You could also make us a nice salad. How about that?"

It was a relief being busy. The orderly ritual of preparing food, calmed the clamor in my brain and helped me think more clearly. Quiet, domestic rituals such as this one had helped Anara and I bond in a tight, happy union. I got a bottle of white wine out of the fridge.

"I found this *Vinho Verde* by chance," I said. "It's been chilling since yesterday. I think you will enjoy it since you like white wine."

"I don't know this one," she said, picking up the bottle and looking at the label. "Where do they make it?"

"Portugal. *Vinho Verde* means green wine but actually it's pale gold. Very refreshing."

"Pour it Roberto and then lend me your ears, because I have much to say."

I poured the wine into two glasses and raised mine in a toast.

"To what?" I asked.

"To success," she said.

"That sounds right to me," I said and took a big gulp.

Neither tart nor very sweet, the wine went down smoothly and easily.

Yulie took a sip.

"This is nice," she said and then set about making the moussaka. She did all the preparatory work skillfully, all the slicing and dicing that precedes the making of the dish. I took charge of making the salad. As she cooked she talked and as she talked her hands also spoke, carried on a monologue in their own language, fluttering, gesturing, inscribing patterns in the air.

"My father tells me that Hakan Bey is ready, willing to help," she said. "He knows people who go back and forth across the border, who know that area."

"It's a wild landscape," I said. "He took me there. From one spot we could even see the *Venetian* in the distance."

"There used to be a lot farms and orchards there," Yulie said. "But then the United Nations took a broad strip and made it the Buffer Zone between north and south Cyprus."

"It looks like a wilderness now – really rough terrain."

"That's why it is a good place – I mean to cross into the Greek side or back," Yulie said. "This is the best place for Anara to slip back into the Turkish zone."

"What about border guards? Turkish and Greek. Don't they patrol both sides?"

Yulie laughed.

"Not really," she said. "There are no real roads through there and it's not the sort of landscape the guards like walking through."

"Too rough?"

"Exactly."

"But how can I reach Anara, tell her what she must do?" I said.

"Leave that to me," Yulie said. "I will take care of that."

Yulie moved about the kitchen like a professional cook as we talked. She opened and sniffed the jars of herbs and spices that I had to make sure they were fresh. She inspected the pots and pans and touched edges of the knives to see if they were sharp. She seemed perfectly at home in the kitchen as though this were her natural domain.

As we talked, the aroma of frying meat and onions became an appetizing fog. Yulie loaded the casserole pan with all the layered ingredients of the moussaka and got it ready for the oven.

"I didn't think you would enjoy cooking," I said.

"I don't think about it," she said. "I just do it. It's like breathing for me."

"I learned it the hard way," I said, "from recipes. It's still a hit-or-miss process for me."

"I was lucky, I suppose," she said. "My father is an excellent cook. I learned a lot from him, mostly by watching what he did and how he did it."

"Yes, I remember. He mentioned that he cooked at the *Dorchester*. He must be good."

"Well, this is all set to go in," she said. "But we'll put it in later, when we are ready to eat. This last stage doesn't take very long to cook."

"Fine," I said. "The salad is ready."

"Good," she said. "Let's go for a walk. I'll tell you what I have in mind."

When we stepped out of the house, I was surprised to see that the day that had dawned clear was now clouding over.

"Looks like it might rain," Yulie said.

"This is odd," I said. "Where did this come from?"

Strong gusts were bending the cypresses back into black crescents. Yulie and I took the upper road that curved behind some large houses.

"I know where this goes," she said. "Come, I want to show you something."

We followed the road up the north-facing slope of the mountain where it became a natural shelf. From here one could see all the way down the slope to the foam-fringed coast.

Way down one could see the military monument that marked the spot of where the Turkish army had landed. Diminished by distance and barely visible through the haze, it did not look very grand or impressive. The monument marked the exact spot where the Turkish soldiers had first come ashore. This was where the first Greek defenders had tried to stop them.

"That's where Herakles died," Yulie said, pointing at the memorial. "In fact, some of the villagers came up here that day to watch the action, to watch their brave sons defend the fatherland."

"Sounds horrible," I said. "So needless too. Surely the politicians could have found another way to solve the crisis."

Yulie shook her head.

"My father tells me that both sides had locked themselves in the iron cages of their respective 'positions.' They could not get out. History had put them there and there they stayed."

"That's the iron law of tragedy, I suppose. Once people get stuck in a particular groove, the rest become inevitable."

"But there has to be a way out, don't you think?" Yulie said.

"I agree."

"Now take this situation Anara's stuck in," Yulie said. "We have to get her out of it."

Her plan was simple as it was logical. I will go and stay in the *Venetian*, she said to me. When I see Anara, I'll talk to her. Of course, I'll only approach her if she is alone and *if* wants to talk to me. If she is with people and I sense that she does not wish to see me or be seen by me, I'll keep my distance. I won't say or do anything that might frighten her or endanger her in any way. I certainly don't want to set off any alarms or make anyone suspicious. As carefully and cautiously as possible, I will try to find out what is happening. My goal will be to just let her know that I am ready to help her in any way that I can.

She stopped to catch her breath.

What Yulie had detailed was exactly what I wanted her to do. I had no need to add or take away even a single detail.

"I can't tell you how grateful I am," I said.

"Bir shey degil as the Turks say – it's nothing. Don't mention it."

"No. Seriously. I don't know what I'd have done if you weren't around to help."

"You would have found a way."

"Sure – probably rushed into the *Venetian* and… what would that have accomplished?"

"Not much, I dare say. It would have been rash."

"I did think about it. In fact, at times I even feel guilty that I didn't act, didn't go there myself."

"Good God! I am glad you didn't. You could be in some mess there now, or – and this is even worse – you could have made matters more difficult for her."

I had to agree. Yulie's certainly was the voice of Reason – the voice of pure Greek rationalism.

"Let's go home and eat," she said, "before we get wet."

As we started back the first few fat rain drops hit the ground with the velocity of bullets. The wind was quite strong by now and made the palm fronds swing straight out all in one direction.

"Let's run," I yelled and grabbed Yulie's hand. We raced down the sloping road as fast as we could and got home just moments before a steady, sluicing downpour began in earnest. We avoided getting drenched by mere milliseconds. I put a lit match to the oven and it gasped awake and Yulie placed the casserole inside to finish off the moussaka.

"This won't take very long," she said. "I hope you're hungry."

"Very," I said and proceeded to set the table. We had only been in the house a few minutes when the electricity flickered and then vanished plunging us into semi-darkness. The power failure came as no surprise. This was a regular feature of Cypriot life. We could lose power at any time, night or day, for a few minutes or a few hours. And whenever a storm rolled over the island the chances were high that we would have an outage. I was ready with packets of candles, several flashlights and my trusty hurricane lamp. I assigned to Yulie the task of lighting the candles and turned my attention to the hurricane lamp.

"I would like to ask you a question," I said, fiddling with the wick, raising and lowering it to get optimum brightness with the least amount of smoke. "If you don't mind?"

"What?" she said. "What would you like to know?"

"Why are you still single? Don't you want to get married?"

"Hah!" she said. The sound she made could be interpreted as self-mockery or laughter.

"Or is it that you never found the right person," I said, in an attempt to provide her with an answer. "Or are you still looking?"

"Well, let me see," she said, tapping her lips with the index finger of her right hand. She looked like someone thinking deep thoughts.

"Idle questions," I said. "You don't have to answer."

"No," she said. "I'd like to answer. It's just ... I'm trying to actually think of an answer."

"Is it hard to come up with reasons?"

She nodded.

"Perhaps the easiest answer would be: I never met Mr. right, someone I really loved."

"I can understand that," I said.

"But that is not the whole truth. The fact is: I did get married ... long ago. I was very young. The marriage ended in a divorce."

"Sorry to hear that."

"Don't be," she said. "I wasn't. I was glad to end it."

"Why? What happened?"

"We weren't compatible. Unfortunately, we didn't see this before we had tied the knot."

"These things happen," I said. "Don't you think people hide their true selves? Or to put it another way: it is hard to see all sides of a person. Most of the time, you are lucky if you get to see *one* side clearly."

She chuckled.

"You are so right," she said. "He was a very scientific man, very intelligent. I'm rather ... how shall I put it? ...not very scientific no, not at all scientific."

Then, as if to reciprocate, I told her about my two failed marriages, the two disastrous decades and the two lost children. Yulie wondered aloud why we just happen to choose the wrong persons.

"The funny part is that on the surface we looked compatible," she said. "We met in London. His parents were Greeks also and from Cyprus – Limassol, to be precise. Refugees just like us. We shared a common past, a common culture. But in spite of all the links, the shared experiences, we could not get along. In some ways, maybe we were too much alike. And yet, something essential was missing, some mystery ingredient, some vital common thread that would link us. I tried for two years to save the marriage but finally gave up and asked for a divorce. He agreed rather quickly. He had also realized that what we had was the shell of a marriage with nothing inside."

I knew what she was trying to say. She didn't have to say more. Nor did she. By now the smell of hot, melting cheese spilled out of the kitchen and she turned her attention to the food.

"The moussaka is ready," she announced.

"Great!" I said. "Let's eat."

She brought the baking pan to the table and I got the salad from the fridge. The room filled up with the rich odors. The musky smell of eggplant blending richly with the aroma of baked meat and cheese.

"This smells wonderful," I said. "Let's open the burgundy. We need a bold wine to do justice to this dish."

"By all means," Yulie said, a look of amusement on her face. "That's why I brought it."

We ate the food and drank the burgundy and talked as the rainy afternoon evolved into a rainy evening.

"It feels good to be in this house," Yulie said. "And if I close my eyes, I can almost resurrect the old days."

"Houses get under one's skin, don't they?" I said. "Especially places where you've spent your childhood – those early years."

While we ate, the rain continued in a steady downpour. We ironed out more details of her plan, looking at all the angles and possibilities.

"I may not be able to call you often," Yulie said. "And even sending emails might be hard. But I will try to stay in close touch."

"That's all I ask," I said.

"A lot will depend on how she reacts, on her situation and what she wants to do," Yulie said.

"I understand," I said. "She will have to agree to the game plan before anything can happen."

After we'd eaten, Yulie helped me get the dishes out of the way. I washed, she dried. I could hear it thrumming on the roof, tap-tapping against the windowpanes and gurgling in the gutters. Flashes of lightning were followed by cannonades of thunder. This was no ordinary storm, nor did it seem likely that it was going to quit very soon. Yulie unlatched a window to look outside and a sudden blast slammed it wide open. She fell back with a cry just avoiding getting struck in the face. Wind and water rushed into the room, hissing and spitting. "Oh, no," she moaned. "What have I done? Look – the floor – everything's wet."

I leapt up and wrestled the window shut.

"I'll get a towel," I said.

"I had no idea … this is crazy," she said.

"Back in the States we say: ain't a fit night out for man or beast," I said grinning and started to mop up the floor and the windowsill with a dish-towel.

"I should be going," she said. "I have a long drive and it's getting late."

"Wait, what do you mean – going?"

"I can't stay here."

"Sure you can. You're not going anywhere."

"But," she started to object.

"But nothing," I argued back. "I can't let you go on a night like this. You won't make it down the mountain in one piece."

"I'll be fine. I've driven in rain before."

"No, no," I said, getting a little worried. "This is a gulley-buster. There are places lower down where the road will be flooded. The car is bound to stall. You'll never get across. I don't want your blood on my hands, for god's sake. You better stay right here. Just call your parents and tell them you're in Karmi. It's just too rough, too wild outside."

She protested and argued for a while. But in the end I managed to convince her that staying put made sense.

"You can sleep on the couch," I told her. "It pulls out into a bed. I'll be downstairs."

"Thanks," she said. "You are right, I suppose."

"Of course, I'm right. I'll go get some bedding and something for you to wear."

Leaving her to make the phone call, I went downstairs and got sheets, pillows and blankets and a clean towel and brought everything up.

"You can watch TV if the power comes back on, " I said as we were making up the bed.

"No," she said, "I'd rather just go to sleep."

"Help yourself to anything you need from the fridge."

"I'll be fine," she said.

Just as I was about leave, she stopped me.

"I just wanted to say, I'll do my best to find Anara," she said. "I know how much you must miss her."

"I know you will. And believe me, I'm deeply, deeply grateful."

Then I said goodnight and picked up the bottle of brandy and a glass from the dining table.

"This should put me to sleep," I said and headed down the stairs.

Later, as I lay there in the darkness with my eyes closed, listening to the storm and sipping brandy I couldn't help thinking that the situation had its awkward aspects. I was certain that Yulie looked upon me as a friend and nothing more. But because she was young and attractive, there was always a kind of sexual tension between us. I could deny it and she did her best to ignore it but it never quite went away.

She knew the sort of mood I was in, the combination of frustration and despair that filled my nights and days. She also knew that I was a one-woman man, that there was no room in my life for anyone except Anara. I didn't think I had to verbalize these ideas in front of her. I was sure she understood all this instinctively the way only women can.

And yet there were times when I found myself very attracted to her. Her golden grace and the natural sexuality she exuded had aroused me the moment I saw her. But I did not desire her. No. I must re-phrase this: I did desire her, but I did not want to take any steps in the direction of fulfilling this desire. There were enough complications in my life.

The brandy dissolved my anxieties and gradually I started to sink into a sleep. My last thoughts were about the troubles between the Turks and the Greeks. I started thinking about Yulie's grandparents and how they had to leave the house in a hurry. The decisions they must have confronted: what to take, what to leave behind. Painful decisions. Furniture, personal possessions. The farm animals must have been transported to her uncle's farm over several days. But on that last day, the cats presented a real dilemma. They were so attached to the house. And the children – Yulie and her sister – were attached to the cats. They must have cried and hung on to them. In the end, the cats had to be left behind. Along with much else, all the paraphernalia that surrounds our lives: kitchen utensils, clothes, farm tools, books.

Refugees must evaluate each object carefully during an exodus, decide what must be taken and what must be left behind

As I drifted off I could almost hear the quarrels, the arguments, the threats and shouts: Hurry up. We don't have much. Just leave it. There is no room for these things. My brain became an echo chamber for shouted dialogue. And in my dream people came and went, people spoke in loud voices but could not understand each other. They spoke different languages. Nor could I understand what they were saying. A jumble of voices resounded and echoed inside my head. Then suddenly they all vanished and quietness settled around my ears. I began to breathe more easily. I felt as though I were back in Almaty, at the start of spring and a rain storm had come and gone and I lay on my bed, savoring the cool, fresh breeze that flowed into the room and made the translucent nylon curtains rise and sway as though they were in the arms of an invisible dancing partner. I thought Anara came and lay down beside me and put her arms around my neck.

"Where have you been?" I said.

But I am asleep, I thought. This is a dream. And I made an effort to open my eyes but I couldn't no matter how hard I tried and then I heard someone say: "Sssshhhh" and I felt soft breasts pressing against me and a mouth on my mouth and a tongue against my tongue, saying something simple and logical. I pulled her tight against my body and caressed her curves and said: "Anara, Anara."

Again I heard "Sssshhhh" and a hand began wandering all over me.

My eyes were closed tight. I think I was afraid of opening them, afraid that if I looked this apparition would vanish. I could sense nothing more than my nakedness confronting the nakedness of another body and the faint odor of gardenias. I could not tell where I was or who was with me. All I knew was that comforting warmth had enveloped me. Suddenly thunder exploded with a terrific violence directly above my head and my eyes flew open reflexively. Then came a flash of lightning that filled the room with a white light for a microsecond and I saw a bronze-gold halo of hair. I shut my eyes tight and buried my face in her neck. My breath came and went rapidly in the hollow behind her ear lobe and an uncontrollable spasm carried me away on a torrent of release. When I woke up next morning the storm had cleared, the sun stood high in the sky and I was alone.

I felt fortunate that Yulie had agreed to help me. And she was amazingly well suited for the task that she had taken on. She enjoyed an exceptional degree of freedom. She could go where she wanted and do as she pleased. She lived with her parents and just happened to be between jobs and had no concerns about missing work. And being Greek she could move about in the south with total confidence. In fact, at one point she said to me: "Cyprus is *my* island – all of Cyprus, not just the south side – this is where I was born; this is where I grew up. It is my homeland. I know every inch of this place the way I know my own backyard. In England I felt uncomfortable, unsettled, but not here."

Having Yulie helping me was one of those miraculous strokes of good luck. Fate had smiled on me, placed a hand over my head and said, "Bless you my son, go forth. Do what you must do. You will succeed." What was that line about "the kindness of strangers?" It was true. In the days that followed, Yulie stayed in touch with me through phone calls and emails. Here is the first one she sent when she got to Paphos: "I'm here, finally, staying with family friends. I'm in the old part, not very glamorous, – laundry drying between dull apartments buildings. But the parts along the coast are very chic. New hotels, resorts, condominiums and villas all facing the sea. Swimming pools in random shapes, fountains, terraces. There is money here. Lots of money. More later. Y."

Then one day she called me, all excited and breathless and we talked for a few minutes.

"I found that beauty shop," she said, whispering like a conspirator in my ear. "*Orchid*. Where Freya saw Anara."

"I don't believe you."

"In fact, I am standing right in front of it."

"I'm impressed," I said. "You're a regular Sherlock Holmes."

I really was amazed by the ease with which she had found the place. Knowing Greek, of course, came in very handy.

"Come on. It wasn't very difficult to find it. Paphos is a small town."

"How did you find it?"

"I checked the phonebook, found the number, called and got the directions."

"What's it like? Big? Small?"

"Very slick and smart – lots of mirrors and marble and chrome-plated furniture."

She chuckled and said, "I've even spoken with the manager."

"Man or woman?" I asked.

"Oh, he's a very good-looking Greek. Very young."

"Just your type," I said.

"No," she said. "He was rather like a girl, very girlish in fact."

She said she had also chatted with the girls who worked there. Just a friendly chat. Two of the girls were Greek Cypriots and the other two were Bulgarians who only spoke Russian. All four were very young.

"I see why Anara would come here," Yulie said. "There is a Russian connection. You see, don't you?"

"Yes," I said.

"It's a nice place, but expensive," she said. "Not the sort of place locals would patronize. It's strictly for the tourist trade."

"Did you ask about Anara?"

"No, no. I didn't want them to think I was looking for her," she said. "But I did have a brief talk with the Greek girls – idle chatter really, about tourists, fashions, hairstyles, etcetera. They were rather ordinary girls, like many others I see around Limassol and Nicosia. Not very educated. All they want to do is earn money and spend it."

The manager, she informed me, was very shy and quiet, very reluctant to say much as though afraid of saying the wrong thing.

"What's the next step," I asked her. "What are you going to do now?"

"I'm not sure," she said. "But staying on in Paphos for long doesn't make much sense. I really should get to the *Venetian*."

Then she hung up.

By now the cycles of rainstorms over north Cyprus were tapering off. We were seeing more sunny days. Summer seemed round the corner. There were many new faces around Karmi now. Homeowners were returning, cleaning their villas and settling in for long stays. I reacted to this influx with mixed feelings. On the one hand I was happy to see Karmi waking up from winter sleep. When I took a circuit around the village after dinner, I often ran into someone walking a dog or taking a turn with a companion. One was greeted by a cheery "Hullo" and one felt a certain obligation to be civil and say "Hi" in return. On occasion, I would display a tight polite smile. On the other hand, I had become rather accustomed to the emptiness – a Karmi all swaddled in its misty winter trance. I resented the sudden appearance of these new arrivals. I resented being woken up out of my trance.

The tension of waiting for news from Yulie did little to improve my mood. Night and day, I remained in a kind of suspenseful anticipation. So much now depended on what she might be able to do. I started biting my nails during this period, drawing blood at times. Somehow the action of gnawing on my own cartilage and the consequent pain calmed me down, got me through the day. Teaching had become even more of an agony. I had lost all interest in students. Nor was I interested in pleasing my superiors. At about this time, I also started getting urgent and angry calls from my mother. And every conversation I had with her, followed a familiar pattern. She started off by pleading and bringing up all kinds of reasons why I should return. When I refused to give in to her demands, she fell back on threats and accusations.

"Robbie, come back," she would shout into my ears. "I need you here."

"You know, I can't, Mom," I would say: "What is the problem now?"

"The roof is leaking in three places. What should I do?"

"Call a roofing company."

"They'll try to cheat me. They always try to cheat old people."

"No, they won't, Mom. Get three estimates. That's what most people do."

"What are you doing there, anyway? You can't possibly be making any money. You know what your Aunt Martha says? She says you are a total loss in every way – as a father, a husband, a lawyer and as a son."

"Well, tell her from my side to butt out of my life."

"I'm dying and you don't even care."

"I care, of course, I care. I'm also dying. We are all dying. How can you say I don't care?"

"I can barely move."

"I told you to go into an assisted care facility."

"And do what with the house? Lock it up? Set it on fire? Give it to strangers? Sometimes you talk like an imbecile. This is your inheritance. You should come and look after it."

"I will, Ma, I will. As soon as the semester ends. Okay?"

"You won't. I know you."

"Look, I have to go now. Bye."

So went these phone calls, several over several days, till I developed a dread of the phone's shrill ringing. Then, one day I got an email from Yulie. I don't remember everything she said, but what follows contains the gist and has something of the flavor of her breathless, disjointed prose:

"Robert, I am here at the *Venetian*. My second day. Haven't seen her. One of those "resorts." The main building has two floors and faces a swimming pool. Shaped like a heart! Can u believe it? On either side of the pool are more rooms, facing the pool area. Like your fancy motels in California. What was that popular song? *"Hotel California: such a luvly place."* I'm being silly. This is it. I've been sitting by the pool in the afternoons. Quite a few European girls: topless and young and blonde. A few elderly German women. Tourists. Wrinkled and very brown. Hah! Hah! This place is north of Peristrona. A strip of land between Peristrona and the Green Zone. It is a dry and dusty area. I wonder why they built this place out here? Perhaps they got the land cheaply. Perhaps they just wanted to be out here in no-man's land. Away from neighbors and prying eyes. I must say the compound has been landscaped with care. Lots of well-tended greenery: plants, flowers and trees, all brought in, of course. Roses, Bougainvillea etc. Haven't seen men around the pool. A group of Japanese businessmen came in a van and then disappeared into their rooms right away. Then the young girls got up and left. Very strange. Okay, must stop now. More Later."

What could I make of this missive? I didn't know what to think. Was the *Venetian* a brothel masquerading as a "resort" or a "resort" that also functioned as a casino-cum-brothel? Greek laws permitted prostitution and prostitution in Greek Cyprus was regulated and managed the way it was in Holland. Like the Dutch, the Greeks had decided to bring it out into the open and control it. Suppressing it had never worked and would never work.

And the management of the *Venetian*, I had no doubts, did all it could to satisfy the needs of the guests, particularly the male guests. As long as the girls co-operated and there were no complaints, it all went smoothly.

I read and re-read Yulie's emails and saved them for future reference as a kind of running diary of her activities. I found these written messages from her more satisfying than phone calls. Phone calls aroused a kind of dread. I was terrified of what she might tell me, what I might hear. But emails, for some reason, carried lesser immediacy, were less alarming. These messages I received from her in written form seemed to have greater authenticity, greater validity. It is human nature, I suppose, to tend to believe what you see in writing, assume it is the truth. Words spoken into your ear may have an instant emotional impact, but are forgotten quickly and easily. The breath of the speaker turns into sounds. But then these sounds and the freight of the meaning that they carry, sink together and drown in silence.

If Anara was at the *Venetian*, I wondered, why hadn't Yulie seen her? This was the question that tormented me. My biggest fear was that she was no longer there. This one, single thought, was a knifepoint pressing against my chest. It kept me awake half the night. Had she been taken to some other location? In that case, Yulie might never be able to track her down again.

Then, just as I was about to sink into total despair, I got another email from Yulie. Here is what she wrote:

"Saw A today, in the dining room. I was having breakfast and she came in with a couple of girls – both European. She saw me and raised a hand. Then she turned away and sat down at a table. She recognized me (I have no doubt) but did not approach me. And the look she gave me – eyebrows raised – meant only one thing: *stay away!*. I did not approach her but went on eating. Actually, her reaction did not surprise me. I expected something like this. I pretended I didn't know her. She looks well. Now I must find a way of catching her alone and talking to her. All well, in general. Don't worry. Will write more later. Yulie."

Don't worry. How could I not worry? Now I was really on the rack. All I could do was fret and wait. Then, just as I was about ready to crack, Yulie called.

"We spoke," she said, breathlessly.

"What did she say?"

"She's very frightened," Yulie said. "They have guards and the girls spy on each other. If they suspect that she is talking to an outsider, they might move her to some other place. That's why she has to be so cautious."

"Did you tell her you were there to help her?"

"I did. She understands. She promised to try and meet me again, so we can talk more freely. Keep an eye on your email. Okay?"

That was all she said. But it was enough. Her words sank into me like an infusion of hope and optimism.

I decided to go and see Hakan Bey and let him know what Yulie was trying to do. I wanted to keep him in the information loop. It was possible that Gus had told him that she was at the *Venetian* but even so I thought I should have a talk with him.

Section 3

As it turned out, Hakan Bey already knew a little about the developments.

"Yulie's at the *Venetian*," I said.

"Yes, yes," he said. "I know. Gus called me and told me."

"She met Anara, in fact, has talked with her."

"That is excellent. I have also spoken with an old friend who knows the area around the *Venetian*. We can move forward quickly when your friend is ready."

"This is the best news, Hakan Bey. Thank you."

"Don't mention it. Why don't you come over to the restaurant? Eat with me. We can talk."

"Fine," I said. "I'll see you tomorrow. At six?"

"Inshallah," he said and hung up.

Our brief spring had expired and the days were starting to feel sultry. The orange blossom shed their petals and baby green oranges were starting to form. The loquats were starting to turn a pale orange, a sure sign that they were ready to be eaten. The sky was once again that hot, molten cobalt blue typical of high summer and it hurt your eyes to stare into it. By the time I got to *Silver Stones*, a kind of bronzed mauve glow had spread over the western sky and the parking lot was full of cocktail hour cars. A group of European men in bathing trunks were sitting around the circular cabana bar drinking beer and smoking but many of the tables on the terrace were still free. Hakan Bey greeted me warmly and motioned me to a table overlooking the rocks where the sea heaved and thrashed. "I'm glad you called," he said in his bass drum voice. "I was expecting to hear from you."

"Well, the situation is reaching an important turning point," I said.

"Are you ready?" Hakan Bey asked me.

"Of course," I said. "I'm ready. I am just hoping that Yulie can set it all up with Anara."

"I spoke with my friend – the man whose orchard is near the *Venetian*."

"On the Greek side?"

"No, on our side," Hakan Bey said. "But right next to the Buffer zone. From his farm you can look across the Green Zone and see the *Venetian*. If you threw a stone, you would hit it. Well, maybe not that close. I am exaggerating. But the point is that he has agreed to help us. All she has to do is walk towards the rising sun at dawn. In ten minutes she will be through the Green Zone and in my friend's orchard."

"This sounds good," I said. "What about border guards – Greek and Turk – don't they patrol the border?"

"They do. Hakan Bey said. "But people – sheepherders, smugglers, those who have always lived along the border – they go back and forth all the time. They know the safe pathways. They know how to avoid the patrols and checkpoints."

As we were sitting, a waiter came over.

"What will you have?"

"A beer is fine, effendim."

He ordered lemonade for himself and then turned to me. His voice was a growl and his manner suddenly more serious. "If we do this just when the sun is rising, it will be easy for her to keep her direction. She must not go right. She must not go left. She must come straight towards the rising sun. That side has been cleared of mines."

I nodded.

"I will make sure Yulie explains all this to her."

"Still many land mines in that area," Hakan Bey said, a note of warning in his tone of voice.

"Yes, I am sure. I've heard people say that."

"Green Zone full of mines, he cautioned."

"I saw a news story – I think it was my first or second day here – a shepherd got killed trying to get back a goat or sheep that had strayed."

Hakan Bey nodded grimly.

"Very bad, very bad," he said.

"The war ended in 1974 but people are still dying because of the war. Shameful."

"Who placed them?" I asked. "The Turks? The Greeks?"

He shrugged.

"Who can say? Maybe both sides. They did not want people crossing the border."

"Why weren't they cleared after the war?"

"Nobody wanted to do that," Hakan Bey said. "It's a dangerous job. The mines are hard to find. Even some of the de-fusing teams sent by the United Nations were blown up. Then they said: just leave them where they are. Fence off the area."

The waiter came again and we ordered some food, mainly sheesh kebabs and rice, as I recall. I wanted to know more about the friend whose orchard abutted the Green Zone and overlooked the compound of the *Venetian*.

"Very good man," Hakan Bey, said. "Don't worry. He will help. His farm is very close to *Venetian*. And he knows that area like this." He displayed his right hand with the palm up.

"I know him for long time," Hakan Bey continued. He placed his forefingers together side by side and moved them as though he were rubbing two sticks, adding, "We are very close."

"Is he Cypriot Turk?" I asked, more out of idle curiosity than for any other reason. In a sense, I already knew the answer. But then what Hakan Bey said, took me by surprise.

"Let's say he is a Cypriot," Hakan Bey said, smiling mysteriously and looking over to the coast of Turkey. "His family background is Turkish but he also speaks Greek and is very Greek in his habits and customs."

Hakan Bey made a fist with his right hand and stuck out his thumb and pretended to suck it as though he were drinking from a bottle: the universal sign of boozing. Apparently, his friend was a drinker. This surprised me. Muslims, in general, did not use wine or other alcoholic spirits. Of course, there were exceptions and in Turkey the taboo against wine was more often broken than kept. We chatted some more as we ate and drank. I assured him I would contact him as soon as I heard from Yulie. By now the terrace had filled up with noisy diners and loud talk and raucous laughter rose up all around us. Many of the people there were regulars customers who knew Hakan Bey and made it a point to greet him. I realized it was time for me to leave. Other duties and cares beckoned Hakan Bey. He walked me to my car. We shook hands and I drove home in darkness – the lights of oncoming cars stabbing my eyes and in my ears the unrelenting whine of the Renault's weary engine.

Many more days went by and I didn't hear from Yulie. She was not the type to send unnecessary emails or text messages or use up air minutes to chatter. Nor did I feel any need to pester her with queries or instructions. I figured I'd keep myself busy and keep my anxiety in check. Sunny summer weather woke the students out of their state of winter hibernation. They organized picnics and music concerts and festive parades and cultural fairs. These festivities kept me distracted.

Then all of a sudden I got a call from Yulie.

"I'm in the car," she said breathlessly. "I'm coming to Kyrenia. Can I see you?"

"Of course," I said, a bit taken aback by the tone of urgency in her voice. "Were you able to meet Anara? Have you had a chance to talk to her?"

"Yes, and yes," said Yulie. "This is why I have to see you. I have a lot to tell you."

"Okay" I said. "How about the bar of the *Windmill*?"

"Okay."

"About what time do you think you'll get here?"

"Around eight. That's not too late, I hope?"

"Not at all. I'll be tied up all day at the university anyway. See you at the *Windmill*."

"Fine," she said. "I should be there by eight."

The bar room of the *Windmill Hotel* was a spacious, high-ceilinged room on the second floor with big glass windows that faced north and overlooked the swimming pool. All through the summer months tourists of various shapes, sizes and ages lay around it soaking up the sun. But when I got there, no one was around the pool. The water glowed eerily with a liquid blue fluorescence. Cardiff and I had sat here often drinking far into the night. After *Pegasus*, he liked this place the most and I understood why. It had been designed for quiet, intimate talks. There were comfortable, over-stuffed leather club chairs for you to sit on and low tables for your drinks and they never inflicted any music on you either canned or live. It was an old-fashioned bar in an old-fashioned hotel, lit by an amber light that bounced off the many-colored liquor bottles sitting on the shelves behind the counter.

Yulie arrived a few minutes after eight, looking a little road weary, her normally bright eyes a bit dim. I hurried up to greet her.

"This looks like a decent place," she said, as she sat down. "I just might spend the night here. I have no energy left to drive to Nicosia tonight."

"Good idea," I said. "I'm sure you're tired."

I asked her what she wanted to drink and she opted for orange juice. "That's all I want right now," she said in response to my look of surprise. Keen as I was to hear her report, to de-brief her – in a manner of speaking – I waited for her to settle down and catch her breath and relax. I could sense a certain tension in her demeanor and her gestures.

"Are you hungry?" I asked her. "I bet you haven't had dinner. We could eat here if you like. They have a pretty good chef."

"I am hungry," she said. "But let's wait a while. We can eat later."

"Fine," I said. "Whenever you are ready."

"It's a mess," she said finally, taking small tentative sips of orange juice. "There is no other way to put it."

"So she actually talked to you."

"Yes."

"Damn! I'm so relieved. This means she trusts you. This is a good sign."

"Well, it wasn't a real conversation," Yulie said. "And it all happened quite by chance. I was coming down a corridor and I ran into her. Suddenly we were face-to-face and for once she was alone. Our eyes met. I was speechless – didn't know how she would react. But before I could utter a sound, Anara grabbed my arm and pulled me into a kind of linen closet, shut the door and put a warning finger to her lips. We sort of embraced each other and she put her head on my shoulder and started to sob. When we did speak, we spoke in whispers. She asked me what I was doing in the *Venetian*. Looking for

you, I said. Then she asked about you, how you were. Worried, I told
her, very worried. Then I asked her what she was doing there."

As Yulie spoke, I squirmed and writhed as though I were being
prodded with knives. I had a peculiar deju vu sensation. I felt as
though what I was experiencing had happened before. I felt as though
I were reading a story I had already read or watching a movie for the
second time. Scenes, words, images – real and imagined – all blended,
all flowed into each other in a seamless and familiar narrative.

"So what was her response?" I asked Yulie. "Did she say anything
about Vitaly? How or why she was in the south side?"

"Yes," Yulie said. "But it was all disjointed and jumbled. She did
try to explain but we were together very briefly, just a few minutes.
She kept saying: I am stuck. I'm stuck. Apparently they had told her
she would make a lot of money in a few hours at this special function.
Some well-known gamblers, real free-spenders were coming and the
Venetian was short-handed. They needed some girls – ambitious ones
– to entertain the guests and serve food and drinks. She was told she
didn't have to worry about border formalities – all that would be taken
care off. She was smuggled in along with a few other girls. No papers.
No passports. Nothing. The border guards never even peeked into the
van they were in."

"So she doesn't have her passport?"

"I don't think Vitaly ever gave it back to her."

"That goddamned liar … that sonovabitch!"

"And, frankly, my guess is that he never got the work visa
for her."

"That is what I feared," I said.

"They lie and make promises," she said, "to keep control over the
girls. Happens all the time."

Anger boiled up inside me. Up till now I did not have a target to
aim my resentment at. All my feelings had remained trapped inside me

like some toxic gas. The pressure had been building without any outlet or release. But now these feelings began to harden into hatred. Now I had someone to hate, someone at whom I could direct the full force of my hatred – Vitaly. He was the villain of the piece. He was the source and fountainhead of all my problems. He was the motherless bastard who had misled Anara. That evil scumsucker had deceived me, had obviously deceived Anara, had got her into this illegal mess and had caused both of us untold amounts of pain. I swore under my breath and made a vow to shoot the pig or run him over with my car. But now other matters, more urgent issues demanded attention and I had to control my rage.

Yulie and I talked for a long time. I told her what Hakan Bey had told me. She promised to prepare Anara and iron out all the details of the escape plan with her. Yulie planned to return to the *Venetian* the very next day.

"Can you go back there?" I asked.

"Of course," she said. "It is a resort. Anyone can check in."

As I left her that night, I felt supremely confident. The plan we had made seemed clear and logical. I felt light-of-heart and confident that with Yulie's help, I would succeed in getting Anara back into Turkish Cyprus.

∾

CHAPTER TEN

Section 1

The days that followed went by in a state of mental blankness. Bright dawns ended in gloom-drenched dusks, sleepless white nights turned into days dark with dread. I existed in a kind of vacuum that could not be filled with rest or meaningful activity. Summer arrived. And with it came the breath of a scorching, withering wind. *Sirocco? Khamseen?* Whatever its name, I felt it on the back of my neck. And each day that went by brought reminders of the killing heat of June, July and August yet to come. The date when I was set to depart got closer and closer. I had no plans for staying on in Cyprus through the summer months.

The semester now wound down towards its scheduled climax. We started exam week and the tense boredom of keeping an eye on budding minds as they did their best to cheat. Then began the orgy of paper grading and posting of scores. This was always a time of hectic activity and high tension for students and teachers alike. Everyone felt the pressure. Students were cranky and irritable, the stress of last-minute cramming and sleepless nights visible in the dark circles under their eyes. Many lost weight. I could see them becoming thinner and thinner. Their anxiety also manifested itself in other, more obnoxious ways. They would tackle me in the echoing hallways, shouting questions:

"Effendim – what will be on the final examination?"

I would shrug and throw up my hands.

In the cafeteria they crowded around my table, jostling each other. I felt as though a flock of birds were attacking me, pecking away at my flesh.

Ozan – a square headed youth – wanted to know if he should read chapter 3. Jeyda, who sported a silver ring in her navel, wondered if the test would cover chapters 7 thru 9. Fatma – the one with black Byzantine eyes – asked if the final exam would be True/False statements or short answers. Their anxiety was infectious and I did my best to get myself out of their clutches as quickly as I could.

And all through this period, I waited to hear from Yulie. She did not call me with any degree of frequency or regularity, probably because she had little to report. And I limited the calls I made because I didn't want to become a nuisance. Here is one of the emails she sent me at about this time, not verbatim but as I recall it. I may have left out some irrelevant bits of information but I am sure I've the captured the main points she made.

"Hello Robert: Back at the *Venetian*. It's a funny sort of casino. Not like the others I've seen. Not all lit up with neon signs like those places in Vegas or Monte Carlo. I think they want to keep a low profile, make it look like an ordinary hotel. Yet – some strange comings and goings. People arrive in groups – mostly men. They come in white vans and are hustled off to their rooms quickly. There they stay, for the most part, seldom emerging. Occasionally, vans full of girls arrive. They too are rushed to some part of the hotel. Most are young, most European. 'Working girls,' I imagine. If this is a brothel, it is surely a very peculiar brothel! There are some families here, and children, tourists from Greece. No locals, though – too expensive for locals, I think." I got several more missives like the one above, with pretty much the same amusing, sarcastic commentary on what she saw and heard.

Here is another one:

"All day by the pool, reading and waiting. Watching the bikini brigade. Bleached looking girls. They don't tan. They just turn red as boiled lobsters and get big, blotchy blisters! Much laughter and chatter. Nothing else to report."

Then one day, she called, breathless, excited. "I met with Anara today," she said in a hurried whisper. "We were alone for quite a while in my room. We are starting to finalize the details of the plan bit by bit."

"Fantastic!" I said, trying to control my excitement.

"She wants to get away," Yulie said. "You were right: she has no documents, nothing and someone is with her all the time. There is no rough stuff, but she definitely is in a trap, a nice, comfortable mouse-trap with plenty of cheese inside. One evening I saw her with a fat fellow in a dark suit and a tall blonde."

"I know those two," I said. "That must have been Vitaly. Everyone works for him. The blonde was probably Regina. She is usually at the *Starlight*. I wonder what she's doing at the *Venetian*."

"They were in the dining room for a few minutes and then walked off down a corridor," Yulie said. "I did not see them afterwards."

"How did Anara look? Is she okay?"

"She is fine, in general, but very scared."

"Be very careful," I said to Yulie. "Don't do anything … I mean, they shouldn't suspect her, or lose trust in her. If they find out that she is thinking of getting away, shit! … you know. They'll move her to some other place. If they do, we are screwed. We may never find her again."

"I know," Yulie said.

"If you guys get a chance, I'd like to talk to her," I said. "I'm sure she has no mobile phone. They must have taken that away, but she could use yours."

"I'll try," Yulie said. "Okay, I better hang up now. Keep an eye on the email."

One morning, I was chatting with students between classes and smoking a cigarette near the ornamental pool when I got another call from Yulie. It made my heart stand still. "We had another talk," she said, in a small, whispery voice. "I can't stay long on the phone. Read the email I sent. Okay?"

"Okay," I said. "Thanks."

I don't know how I got through the remaining classes, but once I was free, I rushed to my office and opened my email account. This time, Yulie did not waste words on greetings or preambles but got straight to the point. I could sense an urgency in her curt, choppy sentences. What I have below is a kind of summary of what she wrote not her exact words.

"I met her this morning. Many people in the dining room, having breakfast. She was with a few other girls. Then she went into the ladies toilet and I followed. We were alone. We hugged and talked for a few minutes. She wants to call you and she will when we are in my room. She is under constant watch but in decent spirits. We worked out a few more details but we did not have much time. One of the girls came to check on her. She slipped into a stall and I pretended I was washing my hands. I'm sure I'll meet her again soon."

After I had read this, I was like a fish on a hook. I could not sit. I could not stand. I wanted to do something but I did not know what that might be. Somehow I got through the rest of the afternoon and hurried home. As the Renault labored up the mountain slope, I could feel a tired throbbing in my head. Kestrels circled above Hilarion, trying to catch updrafts of warm air. Karmi sat in a stupor of sunlight exhaling the hot honey breath of alyssum. It occurred to me to call Hakan Bey and let him know how things were going.

Hakan Bey said: "Hmmm, hmmm." Then he added: "This good, very good. We are making progress. I will let my friend know. He has been asking me how matters stand. We must alert him."

"Yes," I said. "We may need his help at a very short notice."

Hakan Bey agreed.

A couple of days later I got a very long, very comprehensive email from Yulie, the most detailed one that she had sent me so far. Even her style was a bit different, very sober and straightforward and it contained so much information – some new facts, some old ones --that I decided to save it. Here it is:

"Robert, sorry I haven't called or sent messages recently. I just wanted to wait until I had something important to report. Now I have. Okay. Let me say right away that Anara is FINE! So don't worry. She is in good health and in good spirits. She wants to … in fact, she is *eager* to get away, return to Karmi. We are going to make a plan. She CANNOT call you. She has no phone. I offered to get her one – she said it would create problems. She has been told (perhaps I should say "warned") not to make phone calls. These people are serious. They mean what they say. Here is the main point I want you to understand: SHE IS NOT HERE BECAUSE SHE WANTS TO BE. She was misled, tricked. Lies. False promises. So far she has given me just a rough outline of what happened. Some of it you already know, I mean the business of being smuggled into the Greek side and all that. When you two are together, I'm sure she will tell you the whole story. I only got the main points: a tempting offer, quick money, an evening of helping out and then she'd be back. Etc. Etc. No need to go into all this. I'm sure you understand. Oh, yes, one more thing: She DOES NOT have her passport. In fact, no identity papers of any kind. If she went to the police … arrest and deportation.

"I never know when or where I will be able to talk to her. All I can do is be here and be ready. She does not want them to think that she is unhappy or that she wants to leave. You were right about one thing: *If they get a whiff that she is planning an escape they WILL take her away from here.* We have to be very careful, very very careful. Trust me, as soon as I can I will let you know the exact day and date. This should happen soon. I am hopeful. Be patient. She is waiting for some people to leave. And don't worry. All will be well."

Soon after I had read this email, I called Hakan Bey again and told him all that Yulie had told me. He said he had spoken with his friend and now it was simply a matter of waiting.

The finals were finally behind us. I spent the last, hot and hectic days of May wading through exam papers, calculating the course grades and entering them into the university's computer system. Then followed some beer-sodden, mosquito-bitten nights and the depressing realization that I had managed to pour very few legal principles into the heads of my students over the last four months. But at least I was free now of all university-related responsibilities. And when I got that last call from Yulie (just before she left the *Venetian*) I was glad to hear from her.

This time we had a long conversation.

"It's all set," she said. "This Sunday at sunrise."

"This is it, then?" I said.

"Yes," she said tersely. "She is ready."

"Are you still at the *Venetian*?" I asked her.

"No," she said. "I checked out this morning. I'm in Peristrona."

"Peristrona?" I interrupted her. "Why?"

"Yes, yes, don't worry," she said. "It is very close to this place and I am with some family friends."

"But … but Yulie why did you leave the *Venetian*? Don't you think you should be there, until …"

"No, listen to me," Yulie cut in abruptly. "This is best. She agreed with me. Listen, it is all set. The time, the day. She knows what she has to do. I went over all the details with her."

"Okay," I said, "I'm glad to hear this."

"I met her in Paphos a couple of days ago, at the hair salon," Yulie said. "The girl who was supposed to keep an eye on her had her head under a dryer and we stepped outside for few minutes. She is worried that they may move her. She wants to act now, before it is too late. She wants to get away."

"We are ready," I told Yulie. "I spoke with Hakan Bey. I will meet her as soon as she enters the Buffer Zone. Hakan Bey's friend will be with me. We will lead her out of there."

"Okay," Yulie said. "Sunday morning then – sunrise."

"Sunrise," I said, my pulse throbbing at my throat.

Moments after my conversation with Yulie, I called Hakan Bey and relayed what Yulie had said.

"Fine, he said. "My friend is ready. Come to my farm on Saturday evening."

"Thanks," I said. "I'll be there."

Events were moving swiftly now. And I was more than ready to get all this behind me, get her back home safe and sound. The moment that I had been waiting for – that she must have been waiting for, had come.

Now all of a sudden everything took on an air of unreality. The mind is a fragile organ and when it is under stress it starts to short-circuit like an overloaded grid. It rejects, ejects, and cancels what it cannot process. It gets stuck in circular, obsessive thought patterns. It starts to behave like a defective software program, looping, following the same set of instructions over and over again.

When I looked back over the recent past, it all seemed like a dream: my arrival in Cyprus, my days and nights with Anara, the good times and the bad and her sudden disappearance. Even the way Yulie had been able to find her seemed unreal. And now we were going to rescue her. I had never doubted Anara's sincerity or what she felt for me and I understood completely how she could have been misled by goons and thugs.

Towards sundown on Saturday I began my preparations – carefully, deliberately – with a sort of intense focused attention. I didn't think I was going to be doing anything really dangerous. Even so, every ordinary action, each familiar gesture took on a certain objective importance. I was acutely aware of brushing my teeth, combing my hair, tightening my belt, and tying shoe laces as though I were looking at someone else performing these tasks.

Being alone, as much as I had been, had taught me how to focus on my mental life. I had learned how to reach into labyrinths of Memory and rescue precious moments. And even though I couldn't see Anara or hear her voice, I felt her presence in every room of the house. The aroma of the hair shampoo she had used lingered in memory as it did in the blankets – essence of lemons and lavender blending with her natural musk.

Attending to the necessary tasks helped me keep my nerves under control. This was not the time to take the eye off the target. And even though the urge to take a hit from the brandy bottle was strong, I vowed not to drink. I wanted my head clear. Much too much depended on a clear head and calm one. I couldn't afford to make blunders or forget something or get flustered. The business ahead required a cool, rational attitude.

For some reason, I decided to take along some sandwiches and treats for her. I don't know why. I guess I had a vague fear of being stranded without food or drink in *no man's land* or something. I made a couple of chicken sandwiches, exactly the way she liked them, with big dollops of mayonnaise and very little mustard. When she said "mayonnaise" it always sounded like "mynez" and always made me laugh. That may have been the way Russian-speakers pronounce the word. And the first time she said it, I couldn't figure out what she meant. I also filled up a thermos with strong, black coffee to keep myself awake. I figured I would need jolts of caffeine. As a special •

treat for Anara, I got an apple, a carton of cherry juice and a small container of peach yogurt, plus a packet of cookies and a bag of potato chips. I also took along a couple of one liter bottles of water. I placed the food and the thermos in a light, nylon backpack I normally used to take books and papers to school. In a sturdier canvas haversack, I placed binoculars, a flashlight, heavy-duty wire cutters, a pair of pliers and a small spade. Like a good little boy scout, I believed in being prepared for every eventuality. As I was about to haul everything out to the Renault, I wondered if I should also take the revolver. I got it out of the drawer and held it in my hands. It was still all wrapped up in the oil-soaked brown paper. I undid the wrapping and stared at it for the longest time. It felt heavy and cold in my hands. Did I need it? Would I use it? Would I have the nerve? It may be very satisfying to fantasize about blasting away at people, the way children do when they are playing Cops'n'Robbers. Bang! Bang! You're dead! But shooting at someone in real life is a different matter. Real life is not a cowboy movie or a gangster flick. It isn't a simple matter to kill someone and the consequences are damned serious. I thought and thought for the longest time and finally I decided to take it, if only to boost my personal sense of security and increase my self-confidence. I doubted very much that I would ever use it. But it felt good to know that if I needed it ... Moreover, in certain situations, just letting people know that you are armed is enough. I didn't think, I would have to shoot anyone. Nor did I expect to be shot at.

Too restless to watch TV, I turned it off and stepped out of the house and took a turn around the upper road. The nearly full moon spread a milky light over Karmi, making the houses glow as though they were made of marble. Many of the houses were now all lit up. The celebrants of summer were back. Patios and terraces and verandas were all lit up and the sounds of lively conversation and laughter floated in the warm air. These were summer people, tourists or vacationers, without a care in the world, or so it seemed to me. All they wanted to do was focus on their simple pleasures – drinking, talking, renewing old friendships and arranging temporary sexual liaisons. When I first arrived in Karmi, I had wanted to be like them. I didn't want any worries. I just wanted to enjoy life. I didn't want to become involved with the problems of the island and its inhabitants. But now I felt like someone from another planet, cut off, separated from them, an outsider. I would never be one of them. I would never belong to this carefree club.

For a long time I stood on the ledge one thousand feet above Kyrenia, smoking and thinking. I thought about the events that had brought me to this moment in time. A Scops owl called out once from a stand of cypresses below the church. Then it melted into the dark shadows of pines further up the slope. Its two-tone call began on a note of optimism, then died away in a despairing quaver. Was this an omen?

Just then I heard my mobile ring.

"Hello," I said. "Yes?"

"Honey," I heard a faint fluttery whispering. "Honey, it's me. Anara."

To say that I felt my knees buckle would not be an exaggeration.

"Anara? Is that you? Baby, can you talk?"

"I'm at a pay-phone," she in a faint voice. "Can't stay long."

"Can you speak a little louder?" I asked.

"No," she whispered. "I will see you tomorrow. Inshallah!"

"Inshallah!" I repeated. "God willing!"

I was silent for a few seconds. Then I heard her say: "Honey, I made a mistake. I'm sorry."

"Darling, don't worry. Listen. Everything will be fine."

"Are you angry with me?"

"No, not at all," I said. "I just want you with me."

"Yes," she said. "Tomorrow."

And then the line went dead.

I walked back to the house in a state of stunned shock. She had taken a big chance calling me on a pay-phone. I just hoped she hadn't been spotted. All kinds of disastrous scenes played themselves out in my head and an energized restlessness made my limbs twitch. I couldn't stand being in Karmi a moment longer. I locked the front door, jumped into the Renault and started down the mountain.

As I rumbled west along the coast road, I did not run into much traffic. The moon rode high and clear behind me. On the right, I could see the ocean. On the left lay the lap of the Beshparmak range where the lights of village houses glimmered between the orchards. The orange trees were like splotches of ink against silver-grey fields – the whole scene a black and white negative.

I swept past Alsanjak and Lapta and Karshiyaka with the tires singing a dirge. Beyond Kayalar, the road turned left, away from the sea. Here the Beshparmak dwindled down to low ridges and scrub-covered hills. Here the tall peaks had been rubbed down, abraded and degraded by time and weather. Amidst stretches of grasses with soft beige-colored tips like foxtails, patches of bleached sand showed up like lesions and hardy weeds that had been seared by salt-laced winds. In the pallid moonlight, the monochromatic landscape had the spare, lean look of a pen-and-ink sketch.

Clear of the usual speed traps, I pressed down harder on the accelerator to gain speed. All of a sudden, the dead zone came to an end and the countryside took on a different look. The low hills gave way to a region of fields and farms and in the distance I could see the lights of Guzelyurt. As I turned away from Guzelyurt south and east, on the road that led towards Sahinler and Serhatkoy, I entered a strange Martian landscape, eerily red in the car's headlamps, treeless, indeed plantless, just a crumbling expanse of rust-colored dust, and beyond that, strange leprous scars on the land that glimmered ghostly white. I had entered the zone of Bronze Age copper mines. Miners had dug, tunneled and gouged the earth with a vicious and efficient savagery and the tailings and slag they left behind now formed a dead, barren zone where nothing could grow.

After a few miles, the landscape changed again and I was in a zone of great fertility dotted with vineyards and orchards. Here and there I also saw lovingly tended vegetable gardens, trellises for tomato plants and a patchwork of fields where crops of bercim and clover were being raised for cattle and sheep. I slowed down, not wishing to miss the turn off that led towards Hakan Bey's farmhouse.

The jagged ramparts of the Beshparmak loomed over my left shoulder against a stainless-steel sky and on my right rows and rows of orange trees slipped past. Eventually, I saw the dirt road that led to Hakan Bey's house. My wheels spun as I turned onto soft sand and I punched the gas pedal to gain momentum. The car lurched forward and I heard the crunch of crisp gravel and crumbled stones. I drove down a sort of ultra wide goat-path with wild growths of Calamus reeds on either side and then suddenly I was in front of Hakan Bey's house with its barns and ancillary structures on one side and on the other a dark slope dotted with small white boxes that served as bee-hires hives. Hakan Bey came out to greet me, not in his jocular, hearty manner, but with a serious expression on his face.

Section 2

That evening we sat down to a quiet meal prepared by his wife and the table took on a gloomy, foreboding *"Last Supper"* sort of aura with me at one end of the table like the ghost of Banquo. There were only three of us present. Hakan Bey's son, Ismael, had gone to Kyrenia to spend the night with some of his friends. The three of us sat staring at the table like a congregation of mutes. Hakan Bey did not say much, and his wife, who spoke no English said even less as she moved back and forth with a quiet efficiency between the kitchen and the dining room. We were served a simple but exquisitely prepared meal – stewed lamb, steamed rice and pita bread – that we ate in a brooding, monastic, almost meditative silence. I had no wish to make small talk and, mercifully, the others did not seem to want to either. My mind was too busy mulling over past events and those to come.

After we had finished our coffee, Hakan Bey led me to a small, windowless room.

"Ismael sleeps here when he's home," he said. "I hope you will be comfortable."

It was definitely a boy's room, furnished simply like a monk's cell, with a narrow bed, a small desk, a rush chair and nothing else and had a funky, airless atmosphere that made me feel claustrophobic. On one wall there were six large hooks lined up in a row for hanging clothes and whatever else you wanted to keep off the floor.

"Try to sleep," Hakan Bey said as he stood at the door. "I will wake you up when it is time to go."

"I'll try," I said. "And please tell your wife the dinner was delicious." He nodded.

"I'll drive you to the edge of the Green Zone. It is only a matter of one or two miles."

"Thanks," I said. "Thank you for all that you are doing."

He raised a deprecatory hand, as if he were waving away the sound waves of the compliment before they reached him.

"You cannot drive into the Green Zone," Hakan Bey said. "No road, you see. And the ground is too broken up – big rocks, steep valleys and ridges. Also you will attract attention, even at night. Border guards on both sides patrol the area. Stay on path. Okay? Don't get off path. And don't make noise. Walk for about fifteen minutes and you will come to an old stone wall. Stop and wait. My friend will meet you there and take you the rest of the way."

"You won't come with me?"

He shook his head.

"The Greeks know me well and hate me. If they catch me they will shoot me. If they catch you, they will take you to the American embassy."

"And this man I will meet – can we trust him?"

"Yes, yes. He has good relations with the Greeks. He goes back and forth all the time. His farm is nearby and he knows this area like the back of his hand. Good man. She knows what she must do? Right?"

"Yes. Yulie spoke to her, explained everything. At first light she must come towards the rising sun. Eastwards."

"Eastwards is good. All clear."

Hakan Bey waved goodbye and closed the door softly.

I lay down on the bed fully dressed, without even bothering to take off my jogging shoes and pulled a blanket over myself. I tried to go to sleep, but I couldn't. Worrisome thoughts kept racing through my mind, churning it into a kind of whirlwind. But, at some point I think I did drift off. When I opened my eyes again, someone was shaking my shoulder roughly and I saw the blinding circle of a flashlight in front of my eyes.

"Robert Bey, wake up. It's time."

It was Hakan Bey. I got up at once, breathing in rapid gusts, suddenly very alert and got out of bed.

"Come," said Hakan Bey, in a hoarse, commanding whisper.

We emerged from the room and proceeded through the dark house single file on soft cat feet with Hakan Bey in the lead. He did not turn on any lights. The yellowish splash of light from the torch provided sufficient illumination. Outside, the night was calm and clear and eerily quiet. Once my eyes adjusted to the gloom, I was able to see everything quite clearly.

Millions of stars that looked like small chunks of ice shimmered and glimmered in a black sky. A dog barked somewhere far away in a tired, sleepy way and then went back to sleep. The air felt chill and damp and a dense dew had collected on the Land Rover making it look wet as though it had just been washed. I placed my kit bag in the back but kept my knapsack with me and climbed into the front seat. Hakan Bey clicked the engine awake and it began chug chugging in a rough idle that made the old Land Rover shudder and twitch. He scrunched it violently into gear and we were on our way.

"I won't turn on the headlights," he said. "Lights can be seen from miles away. We won't need them anyway."

We really didn't need the headlights. The road gleamed blue as an oiled gun barrel in front of us and the black silhouettes of orange trees on either side of the road were clearly visible as guide marks.

"What about the noise of the engine?" I asked.

"Sound doesn't carry far, especially with all these gulleys and gorges," he said. "It gets blocked, muffled by the folds of the land."

"How far do we have to go?" I asked.

"Not far. Only a mile or so," Hakan Bey said. "My friend will meet you when you get to the stone wall. If he isn't there, wait for him. He will take you the rest of the way. Do not step off the path. Most of the mines have been removed from this zone, but you never know. You understand?"

"Yes," I said. "I understand."

"I'm glad the night is clear," Hakan Bey said. "But we are near the coast and a fog does tend to creep in towards dawn."

He drove slowly and carefully, for a few minutes. We were in a region of rough terrain that made up the southern flank of the range, a harsher, more ravaged and inhospitable zone than the north-facing slope.

After we had gone a short distance, he pulled over to one side of the road. As soon as the engine stuttered still a profound silence crept close to my ears and muffled them in a cocoon of quietness. We waited for a few seconds to get adjusted to the quietness and then stepped out.

Hakan Bey got my bag from the rear and handed it to me.

"You have everything?" he asked.

I nodded wordlessly.

"Come," Hakan Bey said and walked down a goat path that I could barely see. Low hanging branches of the bushes whacked my face and eyes as I scrambled after him. Eventually, we came to a little plateau. In front of me lay a barren, much-eroded plain dotted here and there with vegetation. In the far distance, almost at the horizon I saw a cluster of lights.

"The lights of Peristrona," Hakan Bey said. "Keep them in front of you as you go."

"Okay," I said.

We shook hands.

"Alright my friend, you are in the Green Zone now. Good luck."

He turned and started back and I continued on the goat path, pushing back the vegetation that impeded my progress as best I could. I checked my watch and noted that it was almost four-thirty in the morning. I had approximately two hours before the sun rose. I started walking at a steady pace, as carefully and quietly as I could. When I looked around, I did not see a single dwelling or farmhouse or any sign of a settlement anywhere, only the low, scrubby vegetation that hemmed me in from all sides. Every few minutes, I stopped and rested and took a drink of water and then started up again. All the while I could see the lights of Peristrona glimmering like a cluster of fireflies in front of me and above me all I saw was a star-spangled sky. Nor did I hear any sound, either of man, bird or beast. And the only smells were those of wild thyme and fennel, the pungent aroma of eucalyptus leaves and the dry, dusty odor of stones still giving off heat collected during the day.

I moved forward in a bent-over posture at a steady pace, making as little sound as possible. After a while, I breasted a hill and came up against a barbed-wire fence. A weathered wooden signboard dangled from a wooden post. I knew what it said. "Military Zone. Stay away" it said in Turkish. From this vantage point, I could see a small valley laid out below me. And all around was a region of thorny bushes and weeds with huge rocks and boulders pushing up here and there: a forbidding, no-man's land that not even a goat would have been able to traverse.

I walked for another few minutes and suddenly found myself enveloped by a thick, damp fog. It had materialized mysteriously, as if it had oozed up out of the earth or had been exhaled by the sparse vegetation. I lost sight of the glimmering lamps of Peristrona and it became harder to see where I was going. I slowed down, putting one step in front of the other with great care vaguely aware that I was still following the narrow trail that I had been on. Then all of a sudden I ran right into a low, stone wall. It had been built out of the sorts of stones that tumble down a stream, rather rounded and rubbed smooth by the action of the water. The wall was about four feet high and appeared to veer diagonally down a slope. Perhaps it had been built to mark some sort of a boundary or to enclose a sheepfold. The fog lay thick around me limiting my field of vision. I felt as though I were in a windless, lightless dungeon. Not a breath of air stirred the leaves and branches of the trees. Hakan Bey had warned me of this peculiar atmospheric phenomenon but even so it took me by surprise and a prickling of anxiety started up the back of my neck.

Streamers of fog rolled and crawled all around me. I stood there in a state of dumb shock, wondering how Hakan Bey's friend would find me in this curdled cloud of nothingness. I thought of turning on my flashlight but decided not to for fear of betraying my presence to any border guards who might be in the area. I checked the time: it was nearly 5:30. I had almost given up hope of meeting up with my contact, when I saw a dim, frail speck of blurry brightness way off in the distance, bobbing and swaying side to side. The light, weak as a candle flame, appeared and vanished in a random pattern – now visible, now gone, now visible again – as the person who carried it side-stepped obstacles, sank into hollows and reappeared, following a twisting, turning path as he came towards me. I stood there almost paralyzed trying to control my breathing. Then the light vanished altogether and my eyes could see nothing except shape-changing monsters of gray mist that seemed to be everywhere. I waited, counting the hammer-strokes of my pulse to calm myself. After what seemed an age, I heard ragged breathing and the scrape and shuffle of footsteps and out of the roiling plumes of fog a grotesque gnome reared up right in front of me and thrust a lantern in my face. Suddenly I was staring at Erkan Bey and his gap-toothed grin. "Robert Bey," he said, sticking out his right hand, "how are you?"

It took a while for me to find my voice.

"Erkan Bey," I stuttered. "Didn't expect … I'm fine. And you … how are you?"

I did not know what else to say.

"I am fine," he said in guttural, growly tones.

"Hakan Bey did not tell me I would meet you here," I said. "I wonder why?"

Erkan Bey chuckled and chortled in a breathless, asthmatic expression of amusement.

"I did not expect you," he said.

"Didn't you ask him?" I said.

"No."

"You had no idea who you would meet here either?"

Erkan Bey shook his head from side to side vigorously and started to laugh in a wheezy, soundless way.

Now I also started to giggle uncontrollably. All the tension that had been accumulating in my muscles, building up all day in my body and brain now found a sudden release like a spring clicked free from its wound up state. It was partly hysteria I suppose and partly relief, a real and profound relief that flooded through me. I started laughing and couldn't stop. I laughed till tears were streaming down my face and I fell over Erkan Bey and hugged him and then the laughter turned into heaving, ragged sobs. I was just so relieved to see him. He supported me with his gigantic arms and let me lean over him until I was able to calm myself and straighten up.

"We don't ask too many questions," he said. "When a friend asks for help, we just say 'okay' that's all."

"Well, I am glad and I know Anara will be overjoyed to see you."

"Come," he said. "The sun will be up soon. We don't have much time. And we need to be at the flat rock when it comes up. Follow me."

He uttered these words in a low growl as though he were grinding English vowels and consonants between his teeth and made a sign for me to follow him. Then he swung around and went loping and swinging forward like a gorilla. His bowed legs made an ogival arch through which I could see a pebble-strewn path illumined by the weak glow of the lantern. We walked silently, the fog around us still thick and impenetrable. Occasionally, Erkan Bey would stop and raise his head and listen intently to see if he could detect any sounds in the damp gloom. I heard nothing and we would move on. We must have walked for ten or fifteen minutes, but I cannot be certain. The fog seemed to be lifting and Erkan Bey stopped and extinguished the lantern. In the eastern sky a deep lilac glow infused with a soft rosiness seemed to be spreading. To the north the Beshparmak range was a dark massive rampart behind which the sun would soon begin its climb. But even when it was above the horizon the valley where we were would remain dark for quite a bit longer. Then just as the sky became brighter and brighter, the fog melted back into the earth as mysteriously as it had materialized and we found ourselves in a clearing, overlooking a valley that extended southwards. In the distance I saw a cluster of houses and lights.

Erkan Bey pointed.

"Peristrona," he whispered and then hunkered down on a flat, stone platform that seemed man-made but was a natural formation. I lay down flat on my belly next to him and took out my binoculars.

"When the light gets stronger, you will see the *Venetian* over there in front of you. They have a big swimming pool shaped like a heart."

"I see it already, they have it lit up," I said.

"Your friend knows what to do?" he asked me.

I nodded.

"Yulie gave her instructions," I said. "She knows. I just hope no one tries to stop her."

"I hope so too," Erkan Bey said.

"When the sun clears the peaks of the Beshparmak, she should come out of the hotel," I said.

Erkan Bey did not say anything more, but his silence told me what was on his mind.

Now the silent, stomach-twisting wait began. I felt no desire to talk and, mercifully, neither did Erkan Bey. We just lay there on our bellies, absorbed in private thoughts, unwilling to give them voice, or share them. The sky above us looked like an inverted bowl and it slowly began to fill up with a pale persimmon light and the stars winked out one by one. In front of us the valley also emerged from shadows and began to reveal its colors. The bare stretches of ground were mostly beige, buff or brown with livid streaks of rust red soil where the tailings from the now-defunct copper mines had been dumped and allowed to wash out towards the sea by annual rainstorms. The entire area was seamed and riven with dry streambeds and rocky canyons. Dusty green lines of bushes and reeds and grasses growing along the banks marked the meandering tracks of these water courses. The terrain had an eerie, Martian look in the pale dawn light.

The sun still had not appeared above the peaks of the Beshparmak to the east but by now night had fled and a shadowless glow fell on the land and brought into focus distant farmhouses, storage sheds with silver roofs, the clean, sharp cuts in the earth made by roads and here and there dark green patches where crops of Alfalfa was being grown for the animals. The land seemed fertile, needing only water and careful husbandry to produce all kinds of crops all year round.

"You see that compound with the white building in the middle?" Erkan Bey said, pointing downwards.

I nodded.

"The hotel," he said. "*Venetian*."

From where we were positioned, on a flat hill, overlooking the swale of land that declined directly south and away from us, I could see the *Venetian* clearly. It hovered like a white-walled mirage above tops of the tamarisk bushes and calamus reeds. Through the binoculars it seemed even closer and I felt as though I could almost reach out and touch the decorative flowering shrubs that lined the driveway.

It was a U-shaped, two-story structure with a red-tile roof and a veranda that ran all the way around on both sides and it sat in the midst of well-tended grounds. Pink oleanders and crimson bougainvilleas grew in wild profusion, climbing up the white walls and around the windows. A large, rectangular lawn bordered by thin, young cypresses took up the central area of the U and in the middle of the rectangle of grass there was an azure swimming pool shaped like a large heart. To one side, there were other buildings, large sheds, warehouses and garages and another set of simple apartments that may have served as flats for the staff.

As the light became stronger and stronger, I began to see more features of the hotel. Several cars were parked to one side along with some vans and a couple of white panel trucks, the kind used for deliveries of food and laundry. From a wrought iron gate, a paved driveway led to one wing of the U where the offices must have been located and where guests checked in and registered. A low wall made of tan cinderblocks and about a foot high ran all the way round the compound.

In the pearl gray, early morning light the entire scene looked normal and unremarkable, just like an ordinary motel you might find along any superhighway in the States. There were no garish flashing neon signs or billboards picked out with blinking bulbs to call attention to the place nor did I notice any other feature that might have given a hint that this was a gambling den or a brothel.

At first, I did not notice any activity inside or around the place. Nothing stirred. No one came out. No one went in. On one side of the gate I noticed a low kiosk with wide glassed areas on all four sides and inside, a guard, his chin resting on his chest, fast asleep.

Just then in the sky to the east thin clouds that were stretched like scarves turned a startling salmon pink and the brazen disk of the sun peaked slowly above the jagged horizon made by the Beshparmak mountains. Quickly amber beams of light set afire the wisps of mist and fog that still lingered in the draws and hollows and lit up the eastern façade of the "*Venetian*" as though it were a movie set. Through my binoculars I saw Anara emerge from a side door and slowly go towards the pool area. She wore blue jeans, brown jogging shoes and a plain white polo shirt and moved with cautious confidence, heading straight towards us. The cool, lucid, early morning rays caught her face and lit it up with a clean and tender brilliance.

"*There she is,*" *I said to Erkan Bey.* "Do you see her?"

"Yes," he said, hoarsely. "She should run. Why isn't she running?"

"She wants to look normal. If she ran, someone would run after her."

Anara walked slowly, very slowly around the curved edge of the pool as though she didn't have a care in the world, nonchalance in her every step, till she arrived at the bottom end of the heart that pointed straight towards us. From here, she could start curving back up towards the hotel buildings or she could keep moving in our direction and reach the wall. She had reached the crucial synapse of her history and mine, a cusp where her kismet converged and collided with those of many others. It was a decisive and dangerous moment. The distance between where she stood hesitant and thoughtful and the wall was only five feet at most but it could have been five hundred feet or a thousand miles. It was the distance between Never and Now. She looked back for a brief second and then she started running, almost casually, it seemed to me, her elbows and her heels moving out sideways in the typical way that girls run. Just then a couple of lanky, very fair, youngish-looking men dressed in white shirts and dark slacks, the standard uniform of waiters in Cyprus, emerged from the building. They looked at her and then at each other. One of them said something. Then, almost hesitantly, they started after her. They looked European but could have been fair-complexioned Turks. I could see their lips moving as they got going in a brisk trot but I could not hear what they were saying. They were obviously calling for help, trying to wake up the guard at the gate. But the guard, enclosed on all sides, probably couldn't hear them. Suddenly he did wake up and stepped out of his kiosk and looked around trying to comprehend the situation. Presently three more men emerged rapidly. They wore blue jeans and black T-shirts. They were a different type altogether; with sturdy, stocky bodies and black hair cut very short. They carried rifles with stubby barrels and wooden butts and magazines that curved down just in front of the trigger. Kalashnikovs?

My heart sank and my breath came and went in short gasps. Will they shoot? I wondered.

I saw Anara jump over the wall easily and head straight in our direction at a rapid trot. Run, run, run, I hissed.

The light came in tangential rays, pale yellow as straw but strong and I could see everything in front of me quite clearly. Now she was in a region of low trees and had to bend low to get past them. Just then a wide figure came waddling out of the left wing of the building. I recognized him right away. It was Vitaly, dressed as always in a baggy, brown suit, his round bald head glistening in the sunlight. I felt my pulse stumble, tripping backwards. But I wasn't surprised. I expected to see him. It was the sense of confirmation that pushed up my blood pressure. He lumbered towards the pool as fast as his heavy-hippo legs could carry him, waving his arms and shouting directions. From where I was, I could see his mouth working but he was too far for me to hear the sound of his voice. The two waiters ran up to the wall and then stood there not quite certain what they were supposed to do next. The three guys with guns who were behind them, jogged up and crouched down behind the wall and got ready to open fire. Vitaly lurched up clumsily, gesturing with his hands, stamping his feet and pointing.

Was he ordering them to open fire? I wasn't sure.

One of the men crouched behind the wall who was nearest to Vitaly either did not hear him or did not understand him. I heard his gun go off – rat-a-tat-tat-tat – three times and saw small puff of smoke at the mouth of the gun barrel. Vitaly turned on the fellow angrily and tore the gun out of the guy's hands and flung it away.

The noise of the gunfire echoed and spread all around us, much like the sound of a car engine backfiring somewhere nearby. The man had fired carelessly, in the general direction of Anara, not aiming to hit her but to frighten her into stopping and turning back.

But Anara did not check her stride or slow down. Instead, she started moving faster, bent over double, dodging low hanging branches of thorny acacias and mastic trees. The sound of the gun going off did scare her because I saw her hunch up like a football player running towards the goal posts through a cluster of defenders determined to stop him.

Vitaly and his goons just stood there, not quite sure what to do. They made no attempt to jump over the wall. Now Erkan Bey and I stood up and started waving our arms. I don't think she saw us but it seemed the right thing to do at that moment. Another few seconds and she would be within hailing range. But then to my complete surprise I saw her veer sideways and start heading northwards.

"Nooooo" I screamed, unable to restrain myself.

Erkan Bey clutched my arm and squeezed hard.

"Why did she turn? Where is she going?" he cried out. "This bad, very bad."

I don't really know what made her turn left. From where we stood, we could not determine what she saw, what obstruction made her turn. Perhaps there was some sort of rocky formation. Perhaps there was a canyon with steep sides, a feature we could not see. Perhaps she found her path blocked by a dense stand of cactus and thorny bushes. But something did make her turn away from her eastward run.

I saw her moving at a diagonal from us along an ash gray slope where only a few stunted bushes impeded her progress. By now I think she had lost her bearings and was simply running, madly, blindly, like a panicked wild animal, just running for her life.

Through the binoculars she looked very close.

"Anara!" I screamed, unable to stay silent anymore. "Here! We are here. Anara!"

She may have heard me but I cannot be sure. She kept veering more and more to the north and then all of a sudden the entire universe crashed around my ears. I heard a loud explosion, like a clap of thunder that kept on echoing and rumbling and a cloud of dust below her feet began lifting her up, up, up as if in slow motion. I could see her entire body arch back and her bare arms windmilling as though she were trying to regain her balance. She opened her mouth but I did not hear a sound. For me the world came to an end at that moment.

Section 3

All that happened afterwards is a confused collage of sounds and fractured images. Nightmare scenes. Horrific. Monstrous.

"Allah! Allah! Allaaaaaaaah!" I heard Erkan Bey shout, each successive cry louder than the one that came before, the last breaking from his steel-hooped barrel chest like the ragged roar of a wounded lion. The sound turned my bones to jelly and flowed down into the gulleys and canyons, reverberating, multiplying among the rocks and then rising towards us like echoes coming back up, treading on each other.

I flung aside the binoculars and shouted – probably her name – "Anaraaaaaaa!" – one long, loud, endless anguished howl that tore open my lungs. Then both of us were running, slipping, skidding down the slope over broken shale that made it difficult to keep one's footing. Erkan Bey led and I followed, sliding and stumbling after him. At one point I crashed into some thorny bushes but felt nothing at all. I picked myself up and hurried forward. I could see Erkan Bey just ahead of me. He seemed to be standing still for some reason, looking down at something. I caught up with him and then I saw what had made Anara turn. In front of us was a kind of trench or gulley, too wide for us to jump over and the sides were quite steep.

"Come," Erkan Bey, shouted and started a barely-controlled slide down the crumbling slope. I was right behind him and in a second we were at the bottom, where a thin trickle of water flowed over pebbles. We jumped over the stream and scrambled up the other side, grabbing roots and low-hanging limbs to pull ourselves up.

Then, as I raised my head out of the gulley, I saw her directly in front of me, no more than a yard away. She lay perfectly still in the strong sunlight, her body twisted in an unnatural pose. We had not taken more than a minute or two to reach her. Dust and debris was all over her clothes and in her hair and smoke still whirled and swirled above her in a cloud. I got a whiff of a peculiar odor, perhaps some type of explosive – TNT? Dynamite? But now a deafening and implacable silence had assembled all around us. Not a sound could be heard, not the rustle of a leaf, nor the chirping of a bird nor any chatter of human voices.

Anara did not utter a sound. No cries for help broke from her lips, no screams, no moans. Her breath came and went in short, shallow gasps and her eyelids were fluttering rapidly over blank, unseeing eyes. Her feet, now shoeless, were a mangled and bleeding but the upper part of her body and her face appeared unmarked. Perhaps shrapnel had missed her vital organs, I thought and a wave of relief swept over me. Erkan Bey, said not a word, nor did he tarry. He grabbed her knees and lifted her up. Following his example, I put my arms around her shoulders and together we picked her up skidded and slid back into the gulley. We followed the streambed for about ten yards. Apparently, Erkan Bey knew of an easier and quicker way back to his farm. How we completed that journey, or how long it took, I do not remember. Nor do I remember the thoughts and emotions that churned in my brain. Perhaps I muttered some prayers. To which deity? I cannot say. I'm sure I asked all of them to have mercy, to spare her life.

We made it somehow to Erkan Bey's farmhouse and laid her on a plain wooden trestle table under the feathery leaves of a Jacaranda that was covered with violet blossoms. If she could have seen it, she would have oooh'd and aaaah'd over it no end. Nothing pleased her more than flowers and trees in bloom. But she had gone into shock and now her eyes were closed. Erkan Bey called an ambulance. It came. I sat in the back with her as they drove as fast as they could over bumpy roads to the nearest hospital, the one in Guzelyurt no doubt. Attendants rushed her into some remote recesses of the hospital, leaving me sitting in a sterile waiting room where an angry Attaturk frowned down on me from a wall. How long I sat there and what I thought about is all beside the point. But when they brought me the bad news, everything went black around me, nothing made any sense and nothing mattered anymore. I felt as though my life had also come to an abrupt end. The doctors, I was told, discovered that a piece of metal about the size and shape of a quarter had somehow slipped in between her ribs and pierced her heart. They couldn't stop the internal bleeding. The brave little pump simply stopped.

I cannot remember much of what I did or was done to me after that day. Memory is a traitor. Memory betrays you, lets you down when you need her most. Trusting memory is like skating on thin ice in spring. But logic asserts that I must have gone through all the normal and expected legalistic ceremonies and funerary rituals, now a blur of faces and places like a passing montage viewed from the window of a fast-moving train, sweeping swiftly by, relentlessly pouring away into the past, beyond your control. The few people I knew in Karmi and at the University rallied around and helped or tried to help. Yulie was around and so was her father. There were long interrogations at the police station and even longer sessions at *Pegasus* and other bars around Kyrenia where I went to bludgeon my brain with booze.

Revenge, they say, is a dish best served cold. And from experience I can vouch for the veracity of these words. I also began to appreciate and understand the true meaning of the word "revenge." In the days and weeks immediately after her burial, my mind simply went blank. I sank into a numb, dumb state of paralyzing melancholia. I didn't want to see anyone, talk to anyone, be with anyone or do anything. I hid myself from everyone and let this inertia take me over completely. But then Yulie's visits and the courteous intrusions of my neighbors pulled me out of these mental doldrums.

Now a cold, savage anger began to grow inside me. I wanted to lash out, hurt someone, kill someone, not really caring who that might be. But after a while this generalized, formless rage hardened, matured and ripened into a pure, detached hatred that focused itself on one person and one person only: Vitaly.

I became obsessed with an intense need to "get," Vitaly, to destroy him. I blamed him for everything that had happened. He was the root of all evil, the source of all that I had endured. He had misled Anara. He had made her a virtual prisoner. He was responsible for her death. His minions had shot at her, tried to kill her. All this was clear enough. And even though there were many monsters and villains in this saga, I felt that Vitaly was the biggest monster of them all. I wanted him dead. I wanted him to suffer. I wanted to rub him out, wipe him away from the face of the earth.

Slowly, slowly, I felt my hatred for Vitaly change into pure and absolute loathing. My brain became a ticking time bomb of revenge: tick, tick, tick.

I began to make plans.

At this point I didn't care how or where I killed Vitaly as long as I did it *Now! Right Away! This Instant!* I didn't care who saw me or if I got caught and was tried and hanged for the crime. I had lost the will to live. I didn't care what happened once I had done the deed. I even thought of shooting Vitaly and then shooting myself. That way I wouldn't have to sit through a lengthy, meaningless trial that would be a worse fate than the peaceful oblivion of death.

But then I thought: why should I hang for shooting a mad dog, a filthy pig, a venomous snake? I was the hand of justice! I was judge and jury. I was a vigilante rooting evil out of society, saving future victims like my innocent Anara. Why should I kill myself? I had done nothing wrong. I should be meting out the sentence. I should be the executioner.

This realization came to me like an epiphany, a revelation from on high. I gradually climbed out of my insanity and became coldly rational once again. I would kill him, yes, but I would do it stealthily, secretly, cleverly. Not stupidly and carelessly. Not in a manner that would put me behind bars or put my neck in a hangman's noose. Revenge is best when served cold. I would be patient, clever, imaginative. I would wait, bide my time. I would prepare the dish slowly, pay close attention to the recipe and then let it bake for a long, long time. Then I would let it cool off for a long, long time. Only then, when everything was ready, only then would I serve it to our "sweet" Mr. V and watch with relish as he ate every goddamned loving spoonful!

I now realized I would need more time. I could not leave Karmi at the end of May as I had planned. I would have to extend my stay through summer. I contacted the Dean of the Law department and told him that I would teach Summer School classes if he needed me. Being shorthanded, he was only too glad to take me up on my offer and gave me a couple of courses. This was a stroke of luck. The teaching would bring in a small income and give me an excuse to stay on the island.

Right away I informed Fiona that I wanted to extend my rental contract through the summer months. She was a bit surprised by my sudden change of plans but saw no problem with letting me stay on. I don't think anyone else was clamoring to rent my house. Fiona was courteous and polite and there was a subdued gentleness in the way she talked to me. Like everyone else in Karmi who had known Anara, Fiona had been shocked by the tragedy. But I noticed a kind of stoic resignation in all the residents of Karmi that we knew: the Bralestones, Barbara Preston, Karen and Derek. They expressed their sympathy in a tight-lipped and reserved manner. When they spoke to me, it was in a restrained way, respectful of my loss but not overly emotional. I was grateful for the polite distance that they maintained. And I stayed away from them as much as I could, as though afraid that they might actually get a peek inside my brain where murderous plans were being devised. Some ideas had made an appearance on the stage of my mind, but they were dimly illuminated and had vague outlines and I had trouble seeing them. But then, slowly, over the course of several drunken evenings, something started to come into sharp focus in my mind like an image developing on photographic paper – watery and wavy at first, then as clear as an image reflected in a mirror – the revolver Gus had given me floated up from the depths of forgetfulness and began haunting every waking minute. I took it out of the desk drawer and stared at it. The oily, blue steel glistened and fractured the sunlight into rainbows. I opened the packet of bullets and counted them. The box plainly stated that there were "twelve cartridges" but I wanted to be sure. Then it occurred to me that I had better test the gun also, to make sure it was in working order. So one afternoon, I huffed and puffed up the escarpment that loomed behind my house, went down the other side until I had found a narrow gulch where the sound would be muffled. Here I fired off a couple of shots at some bushes. The pistol had a vicious kick, I found out, but other than that it functioned exactly as it was meant to function.

Now I became a night-stalker. There is no other way to describe my activities. In the morning hours, I taught my classes, met with students and generally conducted myself like a normal member of the faculty. During the long, hot afternoons I mostly slept. But once darkness settled on the island in earnest, I would head down the mountain and park the Renault behind the *Starlight casino*. The pistol, loaded and ready, lay on the passenger seat with an oil-stained handkerchief draped over it. When I felt hungry, I bought kebabs from street-vendors and when I needed a bathroom, I used the public toilet near the harbor. I had only one goal now – sending Vitaly to Hell. If I could manage that, I didn't really care what came next or what happened to me. I didn't think very far into the future. My mind had locked onto Vitaly like some sort of guided missile. That we were going to collide, of this I had no doubt. It was only a matter of time. This outcome seemed pre-ordained, more or less pre-configured. The co-ordinates had been programmed into my brainware. All the parameters had been encoded. My trajectory was destined to intersect with Vitaly's at a moment not too far in the future. I wasn't angry anymore. I wasn't bitter. I was quite calm, in fact. This was just something I knew I had to do. I suppose I could have stormed into his office in broad daylight and shot him dead, but I was afraid of being stopped by someone. I could be tackled even before I got off a single shot. This was a chance I was unwilling to take. I wanted to bring down my prey when there was no one else around. I wanted to swoop down on him unexpectedly like the angel of death.

Yulie called me many times. Often I did not pick up and she left messages. When we talked, she offered to come over but I made excuses. I was afraid she would find out what I intended to do and try to dissuade me. I did not want to be dissuaded. Moreover, I considered myself a walking corpse and I didn't think she should be getting too close to me. I also kept my distance from my Karmi neighbors. They had all come by the house one by one – Barbara, the Bralestones, Fiona and Stewart, and Derek and Karen – and had silently shaken my hand

and pressed my shoulder. Words, they knew, were no consolation. What was there to say? I was glad when they left me alone. There is one thing quite remarkable about the British in particular and Europeans in general: they know when not to intrude.

It proved harder to keep Yulie at a distance. She called me often and I would have to come up with plausible reasons why we couldn't meet. One evening, I ran into her outside Astra market. I heard a rapping on the glass of the Renault and saw Yulie moving her fist in a winding motion, urging me to roll down the window. I got out of the car and hugged her.

"How are you?" she asked. "Why haven't you called me?"

"Really sorry," I said, hanging my head. "Just busy with school work – exams and stuff."

"Are you well?"?" she asked, looking straight into my eyes.

I didn't quite know how to answer this question.

"Well enough," I said.

"Can we sit down and have coffee somewhere?" she asked.

"Not right now," I said. "How about lunch on Saturday? High noon. *Balik*. My treat. What do you say?"

"I'm worried about you, Robert," she said. "You don't look well."
"I'm fine."

"When are you going back to the States?"

"Soon, very soon."

"Please take care of yourself," she added, "The living must keep on living. This may sound trite but it is the truth."

I didn't want to alarm her or argue with her.

"Very true," I mumbled, "very true."

I said goodbye and started back to Karmi along the winding country road, meandering through fields of lucerne. It wasn't until I had slowed down to negotiate the sharp S-bends of that cut through Zeytinlik that it occurred to me that I should have asked her what she was doing in Kyrenia? Why was she in front of the Astra? It seemed rather odd that she should suddenly materialize right where I had parked my car.

But these thoughts vanished as soon as they appeared. I was too intent on my own campaign. The business of tracking Vitaly, finding and confronting him absorbed all my attention, soaked up all my energy. In my mind, my imagination, there was no room for anything else, except that one last, final scene in which I took care of Vitaly.

So many sleep-starved, red-eyed nights I waited in the Renault in the rank, smelly parking lot behind the *Starlight*, the pistol resting heavily in my lap. No, I did not think of it as a "Phallic" object. For me it was just a convenient a tool I could use to kill Vitaly and do it with a minimum amount of effort. Because I possessed this small but efficient gadget, I did not have to be a giant in strength, nor an athlete, nor a muscled gladiator. A thin, scrawny, weakling like I was could end the fat bastard's life by pulling back the trigger with my forefinger. Q.E.D. Quite Easily Done. Had all this transpired before pistols had been invented, I would have had to do the deed with a sword or a knife, a messy business that also requires nerves of steel and considerable physical strength. Under those circumstances I might not have had the stomach for the job. The thought of pushing a blade into his bloated body repulsed me. I didn't want his greasy, sticky blood on my hands nor did I want to smell the contents of his bowels. But the pistol made it all easy and my life became the routine of a hunter. Often I took some coffee in a thermos to keep myself awake and settled in for the long, tedious hours of watching and waiting. The employee parking lot behind the *Starlight* was a neglected rectangle of cracked and crumbling concrete lit by a single sodium lamp that created a small puddle of piss-yellow light. Four or five large metal garbage bins stood against the wall along with several beat-up old Fiats and Renaults that belonged to the waiters and cooks and the cleaning crew. The lot enclosed on three sides by towering windowless rear walls of apartment buildings reeked of urine, a powerful ammoniac odor that burned my sinuses. But here I sat for hours watching a gritty wind move bits of trash and torn candy wrappers hither and yon. Mangy cats wailed and skulked in the shadows. Occasionally a stray dog wandered in, sniffed around, lifted a leg on the lamppost, pissed and trotted off.

How many nights I kept my vigil, I do not recall. One blended into the other till I simply lost count. Finally, one night, around about ten, as I sat there dozing, eyes half closed, struggling to stay awake, the black steel double door that took up most of the rear wall of the casino creaked open and in the murky mustard-colored gloom, I saw a large silhouette materialize. This was the chance I had been waiting for. I felt as though my life had simply been a long period of preparation for this moment. I was quite calm, rather sleepy, as a matter of fact. I grabbed the Webley, took the safety off and eased open the door. The large man stood there, a black silhouette framed by the doorway with a bright swathe of light behind him. He lit a cigarette and quickly surrounded himself with a ghostly gold halo of luminous smoke. I gazed at him transfixed. The revolver felt strangely heavy in my hand. I looked at it with amazement as though I had never seen it before. I thought I should step out of the car but I couldn't move my legs or flex my knees. I felt as though I were paralyzed below the waist. My legs refused to obey the orders that my brain was sending. This was odd and I remember wondering why this was the case.

Some minutes went by, leaden minutes weighed down with lead wings, and then I felt my mobile vibrating against my thigh. The sensation snapped me out of the trance I was in. I pulled out the phone to see who was calling. Yulie.

"Hello," she said, "hello. Where are you?"

The question startled me and I wondered why she wanted to know where I was.

"Home," I said in a choked voice. "Karmi."

"Really?" she said and I thought I detected a mild note of sarcasm in her voice.

"Where are you?" I said. "Nicosia?"

"No," she said. "I'm in Karmi."

"Karmi?"

"Yes. In fact, I am standing at the front door of your house. It is all dark. Are you inside? Can you open the door?"

"Well … well," I was starting to stammer and stutter.

"Tell me the truth Robert. You are not in the house. Correct?"

"Well, no."

"Where are you? Just tell me. I want to see you."

I hesitated for a few fleeting seconds. Then I said, "I am near the harbor, by the sea wall."

"Stay there," she said in a commanding voice. "Don't move. I'll be there in a few minutes."

I sat there breathing heavily, rather dazed and disoriented with the pistol inert and metallic in my lap. The large man took a few steps forward and looked at the night sky. His fat, round face was as pale white as that of a bloodless corpse. I could see the red glow of his cigarette dangling from his lips. Then he took one final puff, exhaled the smoke, flung away the stub, stepped back inside the building and closed the door.

Like a dazed, mindless robot, I started up the Renault and drove slowly towards the harbor and parked across from the Dome. It was a mild, warm night, sensuous and silky and quite a few people were walking along the sea wall, enjoying the cool breeze that came off the water. Presently, I saw Yulie walking up to me, her eyes wide with worry.

"Are you okay?" was the first thing she said to me.

"I'm fine," I said. "Just fine."

"God, you had me worried."

"I'm glad you are here," I said, "to help with a ceremony."

"What? What are you talking about?"

"Burial," I said, pulling the pistol out of the pocket of my slacks and showing it to her.

A gasp of surprise and shock broke from Yulie's throat.

"What is this?" she asked.

"Don't you remember? It's the pistol we found in your sister's hope chest."

But before she could say anything more, I assumed a pitcher's stance, my right arm stretched behind my head, my left flung forward for balance and with a little skipping jump to gain momentum I flung it over the dark and restless sea as far as I could with as much strength as I could muster.

The glittering object traced a parabolic trajectory as it cut through the night sky, lost altitude and finally struck the water and sank below the waves.

∾

EPILOGUE

There isn't much more of relevance that I can add to what I have said. With the sea-burial of the pistol I reached an end-point, a kind of closure. I left Cyprus soon afterwards and have never returned. I don't think I could see the streets of Karmi again or walk along the beaches without risking a total mental breakdown.

I did not dwell on the details of Anara's interment or on the legal and logistical consequences of the explosion that killed her because I simply couldn't. The wound was too raw, the pain too unbearable and going over all that would have been akin to probing a wound with red hot needles. Everyone connected with the matter – police officials, border guards, the tourist bureau – wished to forget the incident and consign it to history as quickly as possible. As the grieving friend of the deceased, I was given special consideration and treated with great courtesy. Her burial was conducted in haste, because the climate did not permit delay and I as a foreigner had no role to play in the necessary Islamic rites. The only thing I can remember clearly is standing in a dusty graveyard on a hot day throwing fistfuls of dry, crumbly soil into an open grave.

There was one more painful duty that I had to shoulder. I had to tell Anara's mother what had happened. I did not relish this responsibility nor could I avoid it. Instead of making a phone call, I decided to write to her. In the letter I chose my words with care and it took half a dozen drafts and nearly as many days to compose. I left out the business connected with the gambling casino and our visa problems. Instead, I told her how happy Anara and I had been and what a wonderful time we had been having in Cyprus. Unfortunately, while we were enjoying a picnic near the border between the Greek side and the Turkish enclave, Anara stepped on a landmine and died. The landmine had been there since the Greco-Turkish conflict of 1974. It was all a needless, meaningless mishap, an accidental tragedy. I concluded by saying that I had filled up a carton with Anara's belongings and would be shipping them to Almaty. That was all.

Yulie and I have stayed in touch through emails, letters and the occasional phone call but as the years flicker by these are getting fewer and fewer. Our only link, it seems, is a painful memory that grows dimmer as the gulfs of time and space between us widen. She moves on with her life and I stumble ahead with mine. Someday, perhaps, the arcs of our individual destinies may intersect.

Here ends "Well Met in Cyprus."